Masquerade

Series:

Louisiana Secrets – Book Four

Patti Corbello Archer

Copyright

Masquerade Romantic Suspense Series: Louisiana Secrets: Book 4

This book is a work of fiction that includes a real historical French pirate and privateer, Jean Lafitte (1780-1823), who frequented Lake Charles and other coastal areas in the Gulf of Mexico. For the purposes of my book, he became a make-believe ancestor driving the story line for the main character in book 1 - Bloodline. He is referenced in book 2 - Obsession. In book 3 – Killer Dance. And again, in this book.

All other characters, the story, and the plot are fictitious. Any similarity to real people (other than Jean Lafitte) living or dead, is coincidental and not intended by the author.

-Published through Kindle Direct Publishing with Amazon.

-Cover design by the author through Canva.com.

Welcome

Welcome to Masquerade – book four in my Louisiana Secrets series.

You will find extraordinary characters and incredible relationships. Attraction and passion. Mystery and suspense. Depth. Intrigue. Action and thrills.

But most importantly, you will be immersed in another wild love story. A place where love's powerful beauty always reigns. Always thrills. And is always flaming hot.

Come… The story begins in New Orleans…

Patti Corbello Archer

Amazon.com/author/patticorbelloarcher.cajunlady

PattiArcher.com

Masquerade

Chapter 1

New Orleans

It was almost midnight when the elevator slid to a smooth stop on the third floor of the Omni Royal Orleans Hotel. FBI Special Agent Piper Pierce shifted her backpack and watched the doors slide open. The bellhop pushed the luggage cart forward, then stopped, as a man in a black tuxedo stepped in front of the door. Blood dripped from his lip onto his white shirt.

Eyes riveted on the bloody man, Piper halted the bellhop with one hand and unsnapped the gun at her side with the other. She met the man's dark gaze with a clearly implied warning. He froze. And then she caught the flash of humor in his eyes. The twitch of a grin. Realizing the theatrical danger of the moment, Piper took a step closer. Game on.

The bloody, but handsome man, took a step into the elevator. His eyes roamed the gorgeous brunette, intrigued at her willingness to play. Except…her hand was still on the gun.

Meeting her gaze, he said in a husky Italian accent, "I've been waiting for you all my life."

Piper touched the fake blood on his shirt and said, "No, handsome, you haven't."

Three more interestingly dressed characters stopped at the elevator doors, curious at the unfolding drama. Cleopatra in bright gold. Cat Woman in black leather. And a man wearing a large jester costume. His headpiece was decorated with glitter, sequins, and feathers of purple, gold, and green. Mardi Gras colors.

Piper smiled. She had learned at the airport forty minutes ago that although Mardi Gras day was over, the season of celebration continued.

Her bloody opponent smiled in return, revealing a fabulous set of vampire fangs, and said, "I bet you taste as delicious as you look."

The bellhop stifled a laugh. Piper said, "Count Dracula…fancy meeting you here."

He winked. "All I need is one bite." And lifted a hand to her neck.

She caught his wrist and smiled. "It looks like you've already eaten."

His laugh echoed as she walked away. Piper grinned. She should have known Dracula would be in New Orleans.

A few minutes later, she was in her room and the bellhop was gone. She bolted the door and leaned back against it. She barely noticed the décor as she looked across the room - a million thoughts running through her mind. She was finally in New Orleans. At the French Quarter no less. She needed what it offered. Desperately. The commotion. The noise. The distraction. And time to think about how to make the phone call she had put off for way too long.

Her secrets fought to be free. But not tonight. Maybe not even tomorrow. She had to prepare herself for the right time. She dropped her backpack and jacket on the bed. Her gun. Badge. And phone. Then kicked off her boots.

Barefoot, she followed the sound of jazz to the balcony. Pushing open the glass doors she stepped into the cool night air. She breathed it in. A new state. A new city. A new home. A new job. And a new…well, everything.

Looking over the rail at the people, she smiled. It was after midnight and the French Quarter was still awake. Musicians played on the street corner with instruments that were soulfully beautiful. The sax. Horns. And drums. Conversations drifted up from balconies below. There was laughter in the air. Dancing. And more costumes. It was thrilling to be right in the middle of intrigue.

Wait. She was lying to herself. It was a whole lot more than that. It was thrilling because Maverick was here.

Angry voices shattered the magic of the night. An argument between a man and woman pealed sharply from next door where curtains fluttered from a partially open balcony door. Grimacing, she headed back inside to shower. Hopefully the couple would calm down by the time she was ready for bed. The last thing she wanted to listen to tonight was fighting on the other side of the wall. Or worse, having to arrest someone on her first night here.

Her phone started ringing as she shut the door. She glanced at the phone. It was her cousin Dakota. Special Agent Dakota Nash.

She answered, "Why are you up so late? Hasn't your new daughter changed your schedule?"

Dakota said, "Not sleeping is my new schedule. Skye doesn't care about the sun and the moon. She lives in a world of pink luxury without time."

"And you love it."

"Every bit of it."

"How's Gabrielle? Is she getting any rest?"

"She's wonderful. But quit asking questions. I called to check on you. How's your room? I can't believe you booked a hotel in the French Quarter. That is literally one of the busiest tourist attractions in the world. Why would you want to fight crowds as you get ready for your new job? Unless…you're seeking a distraction."

Ignoring the truth, she said, "It can't take long to find a place to sleep, shower, and change. It's not like I spend much time at home. Besides, it's Friday. The moving truck won't get here till Monday."

"Have you called Maverick yet?"

"Really? I just got here. That is none of your business."

"Which means you haven't."

"Dakota, stop it. Maverick—"

"Is like a caged lion where you are concerned. You know that. When you disappeared undercover in Atlanta, I dealt with him. For almost two months. He doesn't even know your case is over. If he finds you there without you calling him—"

"I'm going to hang up. I was accosted by Dracula in the elevator. I have screaming people in the room next door. And now you."

He laughed. "You've already met Dracula. I told you Mardi Gras was crazy."

"Mardi Gras was last week."

"No one cares about time there. Just like Skye."

Piper laughed. "Go hug Gabrielle for me. I'm ready to shower."

"Wait—"

She hung up.

The bathroom was filling with steam as Piper listened to the water jets. She stepped out of her jeans, the FBI pullover, and a soft spaghetti strap undershirt. Black with lace. Her weakness. She loved lace. Working in a masculine world of suits and guns, lace gave her feminine power. Along with perfume and attitude.

A door slammed on the other side of the wall, but it didn't stop the raging argument.

Piper sighed. Although she was unable to understand the words, their tones were clear. Anger. Big time. The man was louder, but the woman was sharp and raging. No doubt she would have to call 911 after her shower.

Piling her long brown hair in a messy bun, she wiped off her makeup. Then leaving bra and panties on the floor, she walked into the shower. Three massive shower heads found her, and she groaned in pleasure.

A scream pierced the night as she reached for the soap.

Then a gunshot.

A bullet tore through the wall, shattering the glass. Piper ducked for the floor. A second bullet hit her arm on the way down. Blood joined the water swirling down the drain.

In a second, Piper was out of the shower reaching for her jeans. She pulled them on wet. A glance in the mirror confirmed her arm wound was shallow. Bloody, but not life threatening. Pulling on the black lace top she ran for her gun, phone, and badge.

Screaming was going on everywhere. Gun in hand, she opened the door to the hall. More screams. Running. Doors slamming. A third gunshot went off.

Piper yelled down the hall. "I'm FBI! Stay in your room. Lock your door and stay on the floor."

Heading toward her balcony, she called 911. "I'm FBI Agent Piper Pierce. I'm at the scene of gunfire in the Omni Royal Orleans Hotel in the French Quarter. Third floor balcony room 5316 – right next to mine. Possible domestic fight. Three shots. Sounds like a man and woman. Their hall door is shut. I'm in plain clothes and have been wounded in the arm. I'm going to attempt balcony access. Do not shoot me."

She stepped onto the balcony and heard moans in the night air. A man pleaded as a woman raged in fury. Piper saw the curtains flutter. Their balcony door was still open.

Against the wall, she edged to where the balconies connected. The sound of jazz had stopped. And now the street was quiet except for occasional running footsteps and frantic conversations. Piper heard sirens in the distance. Which meant the couple would too. She looked over the rail at the street below. She was three floors up with a wounded arm. Barefoot. And ignored the fact she was terrified of falling. She texted her new boss a 911 code and hotel info. She knew with cops all over the French Quarter, she would have help soon.

Tucking the gun in her jeans, she climbed over the rail and dropped silently onto the next balcony. She took cover in the corner and peered through a gap in the dark drapes.

A blonde woman in a red dress stood straddling a man in the bed. Blood stained his white shirt. A lot of it. He was moaning.

The woman sneered, "You brought this on yourself, Jackson. You should have remembered what I said in my online profile. I don't play games, and I don't take betrayal well. At all. And yet, you spent a few hot weeks diving between my legs…while lying to me about leaving your wife. Why in the world did you think tonight's breakup would go well?"

Jackson gasped, "Sara, please—"

"Don't whine to me!" She yelled, jumping off the bed, waving the gun around. "You hear the cops? The sirens? Well, they're going to be too late!"

Silently, Piper stepped into the curtain folds at the door. Hidden. Motion on the balcony caught her eye. Two policemen. She flashed her badge and motioned them to cover her. They split up.

She slipped through the curtains. Piper said, "FBI. Drop the gun, Sara."

The woman swung the gun toward the balcony. Piper shot her in the middle of the chest. Blood sprayed as Sara flew onto a table and chair before sliding to the floor. A red puddle grew beneath her…a deeper red than the dress.

Piper yelled as she ran to the bed, "Shooter is down! Need a bus!"

The man was pale when Piper reached him. She touched his neck. There was a faint pulse. "Jackson, can you hear me?"

His eyelids fluttered open. "Tell…my wife—"

"Stay with me Jackson and you can tell her yourself. Hang in there."

In minutes, paramedics surrounded the bed, pushing everyone out of the way.

Piper stepped into the hall as police officers filled the room. Then FBI agents arrived, including her new boss, Special Agent in Charge Brock Donovan.

He motioned to her bloody arm and called another paramedic over. She sat on the stretcher and said, "It's just a graze. No big deal. I've had worse."

Agent Donovan said, "So I've read. Welcome to New Orleans, Agent Pierce. You weren't supposed to start work for another week though." Glancing at the still breathing man being loaded on a stretcher, he continued, "I know he's glad you were next door."

She nodded as his stretcher was pushed out the door. Then winced as the paramedic cleaned the one-inch gash on her upper arm.

The female paramedic said, "Your arm will be just fine – and you won't need stitches. If you have any fever or unusual tenderness, just see a doctor. But I doubt you'll have much more than a small scar in a week or two."

A police officer interrupted. "I need to get your statement, Agent Pierce."

Piper turned to the officer, but above his head, locked eyes with a tall blonde man in a black leather jacket moving swiftly down the hall. Hair, windblown. A detective badge hanging down his chest. He looked fierce. Sexy. And covered in tattoos. The look in his turquoise eyes said a million things that she alone understood.

He stopped in front of her. "Fancy seeing you in New Orleans, Piper." He took in her bloody arm. Bare feet. Wet hair and clothes. Then met her gaze. "How bad is your arm?"

She kept her voice casual, but her stomach was a mess. "Hey, Maverick. It's nothing. The bullet just grazed me."

Her phone rang. She ended the call without looking. She had enough to deal with. The confrontation boiling in Maverick's eyes made sure of that. Her phone rang again. As Maverick took the paperwork from the officer, she pulled her phone out. It was Dakota again. Could this night get any more complicated?

She flashed her phone to Maverick so he could see the caller. He took her phone and answered while watching her, "I'm with Piper, Dakota. We'll get back in touch. She's ok."

And he hung up.

Agent Donovan was surprised at the tension sparking between the two of them. He nodded at the well-known NOPD Detective and said, "Hey, Maverick. It's been a while. I forgot you and Agent Pierce knew each other. You worked together on the Montana fugitive case last fall in Lake Charles, didn't you?"

Maverick nodded and answered, "Hey, Donovan. I did. And I've been busy on a biker case that just ended. I heard the radio call on the way back to the station." He glanced at Piper and said, "I wasn't aware Piper was in town."

Hiding his amusement, Donovan said, "Well, then you'll be even more surprised to know she's now part of the New Orleans FBI Field Office. We are thrilled she chose New Orleans when she decided to leave Atlanta."

A trifle irritated as they talked over her, Piper said, "Well, great. I'm glad everyone is surprised. I was surprised to get shot less than an hour after arriving. So, let's finish up. I'm wet and it's been a long day."

Donovan said, "Make it ten days before you start work, Agent Pierce. No argument. Start work March 1st and not a day sooner. Call if you need anything at all. What about a vehicle?"

She glanced at Maverick and caught the clench of his jaw. He was storing all this new information. She replied to her boss, "The moving truck is towing my Jeep. It will arrive on Monday. I'll be fine. Thank you, Sir."

"I'm out of here then. It looks like Maverick can take it from here."

After he was gone, Piper glanced at Maverick as she slid off the stretcher.

Bluntly, he said, "Where's your room?"

She expected it and pointed. "Next door."

At a quick glance around her room, Maverick saw luggage on the bed and open balcony doors. He heard water running as he tossed his jacket on a chair.

Piper said, "I forgot the water," and pulled on her boots.

She hurried into the bathroom. Water and blood covered the floor as she crunched over broken glass to turn off the shower. Maverick followed and saw the blood. Busted glass. And two bullets in the wall. His jaw went tight at how close to death she had been. He'd almost lost her before he had her.

Walking back to the bedroom, they faced each other.

Maverick said, "Piper—"

She said, "Wait. I know it doesn't seem like it, Maverick. But I planned to tell you I was here."

"What about telling me where you've been for two months?"

Someone called from the hall. "Detective?"

Sighing at the interruption, Maverick said, "Come on in."

Crime scene investigators entered. Piper showed them the shower. They had to account for every bullet.

Leaving them to their work, Maverick said, "Let's go ahead and get your statement. Talk me through it."

Piper recounted specifics of the shooting as Maverick took notes, then drew the layout of the balcony. He glanced over the rail. It was quite a drop to the sidewalk below. Piper pointed out the path she had taken climbing across. And they headed next door to the crime scene.

The Medical Examiner's office was wheeling the body bag out as they arrived. Neither Piper nor Maverick commented. The woman had set off a deadly chain of events that cost her this trip to the morgue. Hopefully, her victim survived.

Inside the room, Piper showed Maverick where she had hidden in the curtains. Where the officers had covered her. And how the fatal shot played out. Afterwards, she signed the statement and handed over her gun for testing. It was over.

Piper met Maverick's gaze in the hall as they waited for the hotel to move her to another room. Used to being the tough one, vulnerability ripped and roared in her stomach because they both knew he wasn't going anywhere.

Before long, Piper led the way into the new room. She heard the door close. The bolt lock. She turned, knowing that delay was dust in the wind.

Maverick walked toward her. Slowly. His eyes, checking her out. With an alpha edge to his voice, he said, "You ghosted me for months, Piper. Months. Even with this…wild thing…going on between us. Even after the texts. The calls. The chats. And videos. And then poof.

"One day I can't find you anywhere. And your family won't tell me a single thing. No warning. No explanation. Until tonight." He paused. "I had to overhear your name on a dispatch here in New Orleans. The town where I live. And where I've waited."

He stopped in front of her. "Why is that, Piper?"

She let him release the frustration. The pain. She had made this hard for them and had to deal with it. Only she barely knew where to start. She said, "Maverick—"

He tilted her face. Brushed his thumb over her lips - opening them. He said, "I haven't kissed you since December, Piper. It's almost March."

His heart was all over her and she was a mess on the inside. She said, "It's not as simple as you might think. I had every intention of calling you…in a day or two. I just needed a little more time…to face you."

Frowning, Maverick slid his hands behind her neck, drawing her closer. Wanting to kiss her. Wanting to believe her.

Piper whispered, "Come on, Detective. Think about it. What does my being here really tell you."

His nostrils flared. His stomach and thighs clenched, and he wanted her more than anything else in the world. Lifting her off her feet, he caressed her. Smelled her. Ran his lips across her cheek – close to her lips, but not tasting them. Not yet.

His gaze met hers. He said, "You're here for me."

Chapter 2

Piper touched his face. "Yes—"

His mouth closed on hers. Desire exploded. Groaning, he pressed her against the wall. Drinking her in. Finally. Then, he stopped.

With his breath brushing her face, he said, "What exactly does that mean, Agent Pierce?"

And Piper went with it. This was why she came. "You're distracting me. You always have. We've rocked what - a half dozen hot embraces before I left for Georgia. And then we turned into this. I dream about you. Imagine. Wonder. And I'm doing things I would never do – like moving to New Orleans without even telling you. But I need things from you, Maverick. I need—"

He captured her lips again. He had his answer. And nothing else mattered. She'd figure it out. He already had.

Her phone rang. He pulled it out of her back pocket and threw it in the pile of luggage on the bed. His kiss covered her laugh. His phone rang next.

Breathless, she said, "You know it's Dakota."

He growled and ended the call. She giggled and his phone started ringing again. Letting her slide down, Maverick kissed her one more time and grabbed his phone.

He answered sharply on speaker, "What, Dakota?"

Dakota laughed. "Well, I recognize that tone. Just answer a few questions and I'll leave you alone. Or…" And his voice sharpened as he said, "If you prefer, I'll drive over there now. You choose."

Maverick said, "Ok. Easy does it. We've had a lot going on. She just finished her statement and got moved into a new room."

Dakota said, "I figured. Is your arm ok, Piper?"

"Yes. The shock was getting shot in the shower."

"No doubt. Leave it to New Orleans. Listen, I know you haven't had a female target before – any issues with that?"

"No, but mainly because the man was bleeding out on the bed."

Maverick drawled, "You get one more question Dakota."

"Will she be with you?"
"I'm working on it."
"Over and out."

❖

After the call ended, Maverick turned back to Piper.

She put her hands on her hips and said, "Ok. We've got to get this behind us, and I'm going to say it as nicely as I can. Just because you and I have this thing, don't think you are free to make decisions for me. You're not. We both wear guns and have badges, so scratch that off any macho list you have."

He held up his hands. "Ok. I get that. And I promise I won't go into the man/woman discourse about me being stronger and instinctively created to protect you. Instead, I respect and appreciate that you are a brilliant agent, and that we are fully capable equals. Especially since you are bad to the bone and smoking hot."

She wasn't amused. "You still went into the discourse. You said it. Though you tried to disarm me with the smoking hot comment."

He touched her cheek. "It may take a while to calm the instinct in me."

She saw the truth of that, and said, "Make sure you try. And don't bother with flattery. I'm confident. And I don't need a boss. I need a man. And if I need a hero, you will be my pick every time. But let me need a hero first."

"You are right. We are both alphas. But that means we'll have to learn yielding for the sweet stuff – or we'll miss it. And I already know you trust me, or you wouldn't be here. So, tonight let's move on to the most pressing decision. Come home with me, Piper. I can't leave you here. I just can't."

She slipped her hand in his. A yield without words.

He smiled. "I stay at a friend's loft here in town whenever I'm working. They are out of the country for a year. It's close to the Mississippi River. I also have a sailboat at a marina on Lake Pontchartrain. And I have a camp south of New Orleans. So, you choose. Where would you like to go?"

"It's late. You pick."

"We'll go to the loft."

***

It was almost three in the morning by the time Piper checked out. The bellhop loaded her luggage into Maverick's Ram truck. Big. Gunmetal gray and totally masculine from the massive front grill to the custom taillights. The floor of the truck was thigh high on her.

She said, "Where is the suave detective in suits that I met in Lake Charles that drove a fancy car? And where is the ladder to get in this thing?"

Maverick laughed as he opened the passenger door for her. The footstep rail automatically lowered. She climbed in.

He said, "I need the truck for my boat and camp. And I'm not usually quite as rugged as I am tonight. The tattoos wash off…in time. It's the thrill of undercover work."

Buckling her seatbelt, she said, "You are the hottest biker I've ever seen."

She expected a macho comeback or a laugh at least. He didn't do or say anything. She glanced at him.

His eyes held hers. "You haven't seen anything yet, Piper. And to be clear, we would have had more than a half dozen hot embraces in Lake Charles if I'd had my way. But it's late. We'll leave that discussion for another time."

"That's big of you, considering I'm in your truck going home with you."

He laughed. She was so full of attitude.

Piper had no idea where they were headed. She only knew that she had just opened herself up to Maverick. Not around family. Not on a case. Not on the phone. Not texting. But, in your face attraction. Where their past encounters became their present - though there were limitations. But he didn't know that yet. There was a lot he didn't know. But she trusted him. She was here, wasn't she?

She settled back and watched the busyness of the French Quarter fade as they drove down Royal Street. After that she lost track of all the street names he turned on. All she knew was that they were headed to a place by the Mississippi River. A loft with only her and him – and a bed. She refused to let her mind play out any upcoming scenarios. If, he was the man she believed him to be…"

Maverick said, "Is there anything you need before we get there? We'll be there in about five minutes if you think of anything. Have you eaten?"

"I haven't, but I think I'll pass on food tonight. I would love something cold to drink if you have anything."

"I have plenty to choose from." Then he pointed ahead as the area turned into more of an industrial setting. He said, "You'll be able to see the river soon, a lot of trains, and the National Rice Mill Lofts building. It has five floors and 69 lofts, townhouses, and studios. It's a creative area and classified as a bohemian Bywater neighborhood. Very cool."

"I like the sound of that. I love bohemian anything." Then she saw the river and said, "New Orleans is nearly surrounded by water and swamp. How many bridges are here?"

"Too many to count. But there are five large ones, including the 24-mile-long Lake Pontchartrain Causeway. And you'll be able to see the Crescent City Connection bridge from the loft. It's 170 feet high and quite a sight at night."

Minutes later, he turned into a parking lot near a pristine well-lit brick building with huge windows. Clean. Old industrial. But modern.

Maverick unlocked the door and wheeled the luggage in. As the bolt locked, their gazes met. He kept it simple. She'd had enough for one night. "I have two showers. If we hurry, we can be asleep before the sun comes up."

"I would love to shower. That didn't work out so well for me earlier tonight."

He touched her face. "That was so close Piper."

She held his hand there. "Yeah. But the good guys won tonight."

While Piper showered in the master suite, Maverick checked the fridge. He had soft drinks, tea, juice, water, cold coffee drinks and even red wine. Perfect. And there was also plenty of food for an omelet or sandwich in the morning.

Sitting by the window, he checked his mail, then phone messages. His boss confirmed he was off till Wednesday. He made a mental note that Piper's moving truck would arrive Monday. And as far as he was concerned, she already had a place to live. Looking out the window he watched a riverboat go by.

Then he headed to the guest shower.

Later, he heard Piper blow drying her hair. He fixed her a wine and Sprite punch with ice and strawberries, then left it on the snack bar. And with only moonlight, he settled cross-legged on the large sectional sofa overlooking the river. A few minutes later he heard her footsteps.

His eyes drank in the sight of her in low waist shorts and a workout top. Sparkly blue. And perfect.

He said softly, "Hey."

Piper smiled at Maverick on the sofa in filtered moonlight. Bare chest and gorgeous. She said, "Hey there. The shower was wonderful. I found the soap this time. And no bullets."

He chuckled. "Funny. And I fixed you something cold to drink. It's on the snack bar."

Ice clinked as she drank. "Hmmm you remembered. Thank you. I love strawberries."

"You'll find that I remember a lot of things."

She walked toward him and took another sip before setting the glass down by the window table. She looked outside trying not to be nervous. It was easier to fight criminals than approach intimacy.

Maverick held out his hand. "Stop thinking, Piper. Come here and let's enjoy the view. We'll drift off to sleep. I know you're exhausted."

She let him draw her down with him as he laid back. Her hand slid across his chest as her head found his shoulder. He wrapped his arms around her. Kissed her forehead…then her lips.

He said, "Just sleep, baby."

Baby was the last thing she remembered.

***

Four stories below in the parking lot, a shadow watched Piper move away from the window. A man dressed in black lowered his binoculars. He headed toward the truck of the big blonde man. He quickly reached over the bed rail and attached a tracker, then faded into the darkness. Down the road he climbed into his truck. He texted the man who'd hired him: Tracker in place. She's all yours.

***

Maverick woke the next morning to the feel of their bodies entwined. Warm with body heat and a tease of more to come. He groaned and snuggled, arms pulling her closer.

Piper said without opening her eyes, "Morning, Detective."

He kissed her neck. "Morning, beautiful."

Opening her eyes, she said, "You haven't seen me dressed up and beautiful since December."

Meeting her gaze, he said, "You're always beautiful…and I've missed you."

"I missed you too. It was so hard. More than you know."

"But I do want to know. All of it. Don't make me wait."

Their gazes lingered on each other. She said, "I'll tell you part one, if you fix me a cup of the famous New Orleans coffee you always brag about."

"I can do you one better. I'll throw in breakfast. And just how many parts of your secret stories are there?"

"More than three. Less than five."

"That's a complicated way to say four."

"Why make it easy?"

He laughed and drug her off the sofa with him.

They finished their first cup of coffee and Maverick began making an omelet and toast. Piper asked questions as she cut up fruit and an avocado.

She said, "Tell me about your life. All I know is your job and that you grew up in New Orleans. What about your parents? Do they live here?"

He flipped the omelet and said, "Well, it's kind of a mystery. I was adopted and raised in Louisiana, but I wasn't born here."

"Where were you born?"

"My birth mother arrived alone in New York City from Norway. She died in childbirth not long afterwards. She was only twenty."

Piper joined him by the stove and waited for the rest of the story.

He continued, "So, I'm American by six hours."

"That's unreal. Six hours and your nationality changed. But now that you mention it, I totally recognize the Scandinavian traits. You know, big hot blonde man with blue eyes."

Maverick laughed. "I love the way you put it. And before you ask, I don't know anything about my biological father. My birth certificate said unknown. Maybe she didn't live long enough to tell them. My birth mother's name was Liv Patterson."

"How do you have the same last name if you were adopted?"

"My mom had a note on her with the contact information for a distant relative in America. The foster system contacted them. Jonas and Grace Patterson. Grace was from New Orleans. They were older - and both gone now. But they were amazing parents. I was one of the lucky ones. But I didn't have siblings and have no idea about any Norwegian relatives. My dad wouldn't talk about it. I quit asking."

"Have you tried DNA tests or research?"

"No. I have enough mysteries to solve as a detective. Now, tell me about your family."

She followed his none too subtle hint to stop asking questions, and said, "I'm an only child. Go figure."

Maverick laughed. She clearly had only-child attributes.

She continued, "My dad is Dekker Pierce. Handsome, brilliant, and he works for the government. I think he's CIA, but he can't tell us anything or he'd have to kill us."

Maverick shook his head. She was on a roll.

She grinned and said, "And my mom is Captain Nicole Pierce. Beautiful, Intelligent, witty, and a pilot."

"You came from an impressive gene pool, Piper."

"They're great. But my parents divorced when I turned sixteen. I guess it was hard to love when one of them was full of secrets and the other was 40,000 feet in the air."

"Understood."

As they ate by the window, Maverick said, "What do you want to do today?"

"Play with you."

"In that case, I insist on defining play."

"You wished. I have a gun."

"I have your gun."

She stole his last strawberry. "Do you really think I only have one?"

"Right. I don't know what I was thinking."

His phone rang.

Maverick walked away as he answered, "Hey, Dante. You and Jinx still want to climb today?"

"Hey, Maverick! I hoped you'd finished the biker gig."

"I wasn't singing."

"Oh, that's right. You were acting."

Maverick laughed. "I have someone I want y'all to meet."

"I didn't expect that. What about the ghost?"

Maverick looked at Piper and said, "It is the ghost."

Piper laughed as she hauled dishes to the kitchen.

Dante said, "You're lying."

"I don't lie."

"You lied to the bikers."

"Then I only lie when I'm undercover. Now stop it. I don't want to get tangled in one of your question traps. What time are y'all heading to the gym?"

"Noon."

"Perfect. If…Piper wants to meet you."

Piper yelled, "I do!"

Dante said, "I don't blame her. I'm great. And I've never met a ghost."

Maverick laughed and said, "Don't forget she's tough. Do not underestimate her."

"I ain't scared of no ghost."

Maverick hung up laughing. Dante never stopped.

Piper said, "I can tell I like him already and I only heard one side of the conversation."

Maverick said, "You will. We've been friends since high school. He's a helicopter pilot for the offshore rigs and has a strong creole accent from growing up in the swamp. Be careful, he'll cook anything and try to make you eat it."

"Like swamp animals?"

"Yep."

"That's disgusting. Has he heard of the grocery store?"

He laughed. "I can't wait to watch y'all spar."

She said, "So, who's Jinx? I like the name."

"And it fits her. She's unique. Kind of like a gothic model turned self-defense expert. She's several inches shorter than you. Petite, but very athletic, with straight black hair to her chin and shocking green eyes. She teaches self-defense and has a podcast. But she's intense and not always the social dynamo that Dante is."

"I can't wait to meet her. Who is she to Dante?"

"He loves her."

"I see why. Is she interested in him?"

"Yes. But she's hiding it. She acts like a cat trying to make up its mind whether it'll let you pet it or not."

"She's got secrets."

"You ought to know."

She shrugged.

He asked, "So, is it time to tell me?"

Piper nodded. "Great segue. Almost like you planned it."

"I have skills."

"You definitely do." She walked to the window. After a few moments, she said, "This isn't a long story. It's just that I've never told it before."

Maverick said softly, "Take your time."

And he watched her let the memories come.

Chapter 3

Piper said, "I was sixteen. A junior in high school. My parents had just divorced, and I was overcompensating for it by being extra social to avoid the pain. Group dating with friends at school functions. Sleepovers. Going to the movies. Sports. Hanging out. Just normal teen stuff.

"I also spent a great deal of time with extended family since it wasn't unusual for both of my parents to be out of town at the same time. Just for short periods though. Overnight or something like that. And I was never left alone all night.

"Dakota had been teaching me karate for about six months off and on - usually when he was in town. I was feeling extra confident with the new skills. And cocky. But that was easy since my world was a safe one and I usually followed the rules."

She paused. "And then a new boy moved to our school. His name was Ty. A senior. He had that bad boy look. Tough. And I was intrigued. Especially, since all the guys I knew were terrified of my dad. Which did not impress me at all."

Maverick understood that. And he also knew the story wasn't going to end well.

Continuing, she said, "I liked the rebel feeling Ty brought up in me. It was exciting finding ways to talk at school. The hidden phone calls. The quick kisses. You know, young romance. And then one day he asked me to the prom at his old school. I was so pumped. A real date with a real guy. Not someone I'd known since I was born. But…I wasn't sure if I could work it out since I couldn't ask permission to go. My dad would have locked him in a dungeon. Or my mom would have dropped him out of an airplane."

Maverick didn't laugh. It wasn't meant to be funny. It had been her reality.

Piper said, "And then it miraculously fell into place. My parents were going to be gone overnight. So, I promptly lied and told them I would be spending the night with a friend. Then I borrowed one of my mom's party dresses.

Short, and black with spaghetti straps and matching heels. I felt beautiful. Exotic. And excitingly deceitful.

"To keep it a secret, I drove to the mall and met Ty. He was wearing a tux and driving a black sports car. It was thrilling. And for the next twenty minutes it was a real date." She stopped for a second. Tension evident.

"And then he took a detour. He said that he had forgotten my corsage at his house. Now, I didn't like the idea, but I hid it thinking, surely it wouldn't take long. But when he pulled into a house at the end of a road, it was dark. No one was home. That's when it occurred to me that no one knew where I was. Even me."

Maverick could see it play out in his head. His hands clenched.

"Ty knew I was getting uneasy, so he played the scene like it was real. Chatting about the prom, he walked to the kitchen and opened the fridge like he was getting the corsage. I heard the fridge close softly. Then he came back to the den and leaned against the wall. He smiled. But he didn't have a corsage.

"He caught me before I made it to the door. And that's when I learned that fear changes everything. I didn't even remember that I knew karate moves. I panicked. But he easily pinned me down. Gagged me. And probably didn't beat me because I froze. He tore my dress off in the frenzy of it all. Then…the rape was over.

"Surprisingly, he put me back together. I don't remember saying anything. He drove me back to my car at the mall and I drove straight home. I crawled in bed, heels and all. I wondered what I was supposed to do now. In the wee hours of the morning, I fell asleep still dressed.

"The next morning a friend called to tell me that Ty had been killed in a car accident. He hit a tree leaving a party. And honestly, I felt a rush of satisfaction - and didn't care that I did. To me, God understood.

"And that's when I made the decision not to tell anyone. I threw everything away. Even the bloody sheets. And then I showered, washing it all away. Mom got home about an hour later."

Piper turned to face Maverick and was swallowed in the first hug she'd ever gotten for the trauma. His muscles were rigid. His voice tight, trying to hide the fury as he said, "Piper…I'm so sorry."

She touched his face. "It was a lifetime ago, Maverick. But thank you for looking like you'd kill him if he was still alive."

They headed to the sofa. He said, "I can't believe how powerful you were even at sixteen. You took that blow all alone."

"I survived. Learned from it. There was no way I was wasting the lesson. But…it helped that I never had to see him again."

"Tell me how you turned all that into who you are. Your parents—"

"Will never know. It serves no purpose. It wasn't their fault."

"What did you do next?"

"I was devastated that I ignored my inner warning. Because I froze. And because I hid instead of calling 911. So, I began to dive into karate and self-defense. I worked on my fight or flight reflexes. I worked out in the gym. And I certainly paid attention to who was around me. And then I learned how to shoot."

"Surely your family asked about the changes you were making."

"Dakota and Dad quizzed me the most, but I wouldn't tell them. I didn't want everyone hung up on the trauma and be labeled as a victim. I wanted to use all my time and energy to get past it and help others."

Maverick got it. "The FBI."

"Yes."

"I get that." He hesitated. Rape left scars. He had to know. "What about personal relationships? You are a beautiful passionate woman. There's no way that didn't leave residue behind."

Now Piper hesitated. She wasn't ready to go there yet. "I used what I'd learned and set boundaries. Safety became critical. I never took the character of a man – or anyone - at face value. And I was never alone with a man when I dated. College men were more of a challenge. But the real challenge came at the FBI Academy - and professionally. Let's face it, I work almost exclusively in a man's world and around criminals that love to rip boundaries to shreds. I'm not a man hater by any means, but…I am crazy careful and tough on purpose."

He watched her for a minute. There was no way around it. He laid it out there. "Have you slept with a man since that night, Piper?"

Her stomach flipped. His instinct was dead on. "I'm going to leave that for the next story, Detective. I'm ready to spend some fun time with you. Let's play."

He nodded…giving her the out for now. "Ok…let's play. So, when is the next story, Agent Pierce?"

"In a few hours. Let's go meet Dante and Jinx."

Maverick pulled a shirt from the dresser. He smelled Piper's perfume wafting out of the bathroom. The door was ajar. He watched her brush her hair. Beautiful. Long, shiny and silky. It reminded him of liquid chocolate.

He thought of when they'd met in Lake Charles on the task force. He'd been a goner back then, immediately hooked on the tall, powerful agent. Sexy with attitude in a suit and heels. Gun at her hip. A force to be reckoned with. He smiled. And their chemistry had been a lab explosion. One she handled carefully. He was quickly learning why.

Piper walked out in designer workout clothes and a bare midriff. Ponytail swinging. Alluring blue eyes met his. Red lips turned up at his appreciation.

Maverick said, "You are going to need to touch up that lipstick before we get there."

"We'll see, won't we."

He looked her over. "You're in a hot mood I see."

"You mean this stretch material that hugs my body parts? And makes me smooth…and tight."

"Yeah. That."

Her eyes roamed his body and said, "Look in the mirror, handsome. You have the same thing on."

"My body parts don't look or feel like yours."

"Lucky me. I like you hard." She winced at his smile, and said, "That's not exactly what I meant."

"I know what you meant. But let's discuss what you said."

She cocked her head and teased, "Nope." And ran out of the room.

She screamed and laughed as he caught her.

***

Piper refreshed her lipstick in the truck.

Maverick said, "I told you."

"You have some on your cheek."

He glanced in the mirror. "It's evidence you're into me."

"My being in New Orleans confirms that."

"You being in New Orleans confirms a whole lot more than that. Which reminds me, are you going to call Dakota?"

"I'll text him. How long will it take us to get to the climbing gym?"

"Ten minutes, depending on traffic."

"What the name of it?"

"New Orleans Boulder Lounge."

"It sounds like a bar."

Chuckling, he said, "It does but it's just climbing – bouldering specifically. Which is climbing at shorter heights without the use of ropes. It's fun. A good workout too. I thought you'd get a kick out of it. And there is a lot of freedom without all the extra climbing gear."

"Does that mean you free fall if you slip?"

"Yeah. But there is a 14-inch pad that covers the floor like a trampoline gym. But there are multiple walls and overhangs to choose from. Just climb the height you like."

His phone rang.

Piper pulled out her phone, while Maverick talked with his boss. She texted Dakota.

Piper: That was quite a welcome back to Louisiana last night.
Dakota: Hey. That's New Orleans for you. Your arm?
Piper: A little sore. But we are going climbing, so I'll loosen it up.
Dakota: Climbing where?
Piper: A boulder lounge.
Dakota: Never heard of one.
Piper: It's not like Louisiana has mountains.
Dakota: True. But we do have gators.
Piper: Mountains don't have teeth.
Dakota laughed: That confirms you're back to your bad self. We'll see you soon. And one more thing. You and Maverick…he is the one for you.
Piper looked at Maverick and typed: I'm here, aren't I?

Seventeen miles away, a private plane landed at the Louis Armstong New Orleans International Airport. As it rolled to a stop, the stairs lowered. A man with brown hair and a beard appeared in jeans and a jacket, with a backpack over his shoulder. A duffel bag in his hand. After a quick glance around, he was gone in the waiting taxi.

He told the driver, "French Quarter RV Resort on Claiborne."

Twenty-five minutes later, the taxi drove through an iron gate at the resort. The driver stopped in front of the office and turned to the man in the backseat. "That'll be $36. Do you need me to wait for a ride anywhere else, Sir?"

The man handed him a hundred-dollar bill and said, "Keep the change. And no. I appreciate the offer, but it won't be necessary."

After checking in and gathering keys and paperwork, the brown-haired man headed to the 36-foot fifth wheel camper that was delivered for him yesterday.

Unlocking the door, he smiled. Who would think of looking for former Special Agent Cruze Taylor here?

Ignoring the extra rental touches of flowers, groceries, linen, and supplies, he pulled out a stolen laptop and sat at the table. Opening the GPS app for the tracker placed on the gray truck last night, he saw the location of his target. The green light was stationary. He tapped the target. An address box popped up: New Orleans Boulder Lounge, 2360 St. Claude Avenue. He checked the mileage distance from him. Seven miles. He laughed.

***

Dante and Jinx warmed up as they watched the newbies while they waited on Maverick and his ghost. Watching the newbies on the climbing wall was entertainment for the regulars. Newbies spent more time landing on the mat than climbing the wall. Especially their first few tries.

Jinx sat in a straddle, leaning forward with her arms reaching as far as possible. She laughed as two men slipped and fell, humiliated in front of their friends who took great pleasure in shaming them.

Dante didn't see the fall but heard Jinx laugh as he worked on his lunges. He said, "Jinx, what's your take on Piper the ghost?"

"Maverick can handle any ghost or woman, Dante. You know she must be extraordinary if he's hooked on her. I'm just glad she's finally here. I'm not sure what happened in Lake Charles when they met, but it rooted."

"She'd better be the real thing or I'll—"

The main entrance chimed when the door opened.

Dante turned toward the door, and said, "No way…"

Jinx giggled at Dante's shock. She waved at Maverick and a stunning woman. No wonder Maverick couldn't forget her.

As the four met up, Maverick said, "Piper, meet Jinx and Dante. I am positive you'll hit it off. And I have no doubt that sparks will fly with Dante. It won't be boring."

Ignoring Maverick, Dante dove right in and said, "I've never met a ghost."

Piper shrugged. She caught the innuendo. "We're even. I've never met a comedian."

Dante smiled as the others laughed. He said, "Are you as tough as Maverick says?"

"Don't let a little spandex and lipstick fool you."

Jinx said, "You go, girl. Tell it like it is."

Dante pointed to the bandage on Piper's arm and said, "Is that a war wound?"

Maverick and Piper's eyes met. Piper touched her arm and said, "I was shot last night. It's just a graze."

All humor fled as surprise registered on their faces.

Maverick said, "Did you catch the news this morning about the shooting at the Omni hotel in the Quarter?"

They nodded yes. Jinx looked at Piper and said, "It was you. You're the agent that took the shooter down."

"I was in the room next door. The shooter's shot went through the wall and grazed me in the shower. It went from there."

Horrified, Jinx said, "How in the world do you prepare for getting shot in the shower?"

Dante said, "You can't. That's crazy."

Piper said, "Arriving in New Orleans was supposed to be a surprise, but the shooting took care of that. Maverick showed up at the crime scene."

Maverick said, "Ok. Enough. We're all up to date. Let's climb. We have a newbie to introduce to the wall."

After they warmed up and changed into climbing shoes, Maverick led Piper to a beginner wall. He explained the various attachments on the wall and how they served different purposes specific to each climber. Footholds. Handholds like crimps, jugs, slopers, pinches, pockets, gastons, and underclings. Some are for fingers to grip. Or palms. The edge of a foot. Some for going up. Down. And some for resting.

Jinx joined them. "Piper, the men have a much longer reach and more strength. Watch me climb. Even though I'm shorter than you, it'll show you the strategy of your choices."

Piper said, "That works. I'm ready when you are."

Jinx wore a workout top with an open back that crisscrossed with matching leggings. Piper whistled at Jinx's back muscles as she pulled herself up, balanced and climbed.

Piper said, "With the muscles in your back, you could weld a sword. I'm impressed and I don't impress easily."

Jinx laughed. "Well, I'm impressed that you're impressed. Come on. You try it. Follow my lead and climb to my right. And Maverick, go climb with Dante. I've got her. If she can shoot, she can climb."

Maverick watched Piper maneuver slowly up the wall.

Piper called over her shoulder, "Go climb, Detective. Quit watching me."

"How's your arm?"

"It's fine."

Dante hollered, "Come on, Maverick. You're pitiful."

Piper fell twice. Everyone laughed and she took it in stride. It was fun and she enjoyed the challenge much more than she thought she would. Climbing wasn't bad…if the ground wasn't far away.

Taking a break to rest her quivering muscles, she was amazed at the speed in which Maverick, Dante, and Jinx climbed. The men were faster – not really a surprise. But they also fell faster and landed harder. Jinx was like a beautiful spider. A gothic one. Very cool.

Before long, Piper was following their lead on the wall again.

An hour later they'd had enough and headed outside. It was a beautiful day. Nice and cool – with sunshine. They stood on the sidewalk making plans for dinner.

Maverick said, "Piper, you pick the place. We can do dinner and jazz on the Steamboat Natchez Riverboat. Or go to an upscale restaurant. Or to a place locals hang out."

Piper said, "I know it's a tourist thing, but I would love to ride the riverboat at night."

"Then the riverboat it is." Checking Google, he said, "They cast off at seven. Why don't we all meet at the dock at six-thirty?"

Dante glanced at Jinx. She nodded. Dante said, "Dinner and dancing it is! See you then!"

***

Down the road, Cruze zoomed in on Piper. Beautiful deceitful Piper. He growled as a fresh rush of fury raged through him for all she had cost him. But following the fury was a rush of desire as he remembered yanking her pants down. The burn of both sensations confirmed he'd made the right decision.

He watched the blonde man's hand linger on Piper's hip as they walked toward a gray truck. He kissed her as she climbed in. A possessive one. Well…she sure wasn't fighting him off. Who was he? She hadn't mentioned anyone when they were working in Atlanta.

He snapped a picture of the truck's license plate as they drove away. He'd know soon enough who lover boy was.

***

On the way back to the loft, Piper considered the hours before they left for the riverboat. The thought of a long steamy afternoon with the man that she...

No. She couldn't say it. Not yet. She had to know first. Or did she? She debated. Could she bypass what she thought she had to do, and trust that her fear and doubt were unfounded? No woman wanted to do what she had planned. She looked out the window, her brow furrowed.

No. There was no avoiding it. She had to know. Which meant Maverick had to find out.

Maverick said, "Would you like to bring home a late lunch or fix something I already have?"

Piper tried to ease her tension and said, "Whatever you have at home sounds great. Honestly, I'm not even hungry yet. I might nibble later."

Maverick wasn't fooled. Part two of her story was ahead. Secret two. And since secret number one had been horrible, he figured secret two was on the nightmare scale as well. He glanced at her. He loved her no matter what she told him. He'd loved her since the moment he met her.

Ten minutes later, they pulled into the parking lot. Trains were passing. Boats busy on the river. Residents were in and out of the building. A typical New Orleans Saturday. Maverick made Piper laugh with stories about him and Dante as they headed upstairs.

As he unlocked the door, Piper said, "I really enjoyed our time with Dante and Jinx today. I like the fact that they are protective of you."

Maverick dropped his keys on the snack bar and glanced at her. Butterflies swarmed in her stomach. He was waiting. Time's up.

She said, "I'm going to freshen up and change. I won't be long."

Maverick did the same thing.

Before long Piper was back. She sat on the sofa facing him…knowing everything was about to spill out.

Maverick entwined his fingers with hers. "Secrets won't change a thing. You're just bringing me to where you are."

She squeezed his hand and said, "If only it was that simple. But…go ahead and ask me that question again."

Holding her gaze, he asked, "Have you slept with a man since that night?"

The words were soft but to Piper it was like a gong echoing through the room. A door thrust open to more horrible memories of the most intimate kind. But she had no choice if she wanted Maverick.

She got up and walked as she talked. "Your instinct is right on. I was unprepared for a crash and burn. Everything in my life had been successful except for the rape. And I had locked that away. Gone like it had never been. I was a strong, skilled, powerful woman. And I enjoyed the company of men. Affection and passion were fun and intriguing. I enjoyed the game. But sex…wasn't on my radar because…bluntly…what was between my legs was just my gender. It didn't really affect me at all. Although it affected the men around me."

She laughed without humor. "Sex. The major force that drives the world. People die for it. Commit crimes for it. Scream in passion. And jump in bed with complete strangers. While others crave a lifetime with one partner to share something magical."

Glancing at Maverick, she said, "My head knew sex. It was overflowing with knowledge. But it never connected with my heart and body. I learned that the hard way."

She sighed. "A little over two years ago, I dated an agent on our team in Denver. And while our relationship was passionate, there was no sex. But I knew he loved me and wanted more. I struggled though. Not because he wasn't a good man. He was. And one I deeply respected. And I thought I loved him. I just didn't feel the need for intimate contact. At all. He was confused at my stalling…my mixed messages. And no wonder.

"A few weeks after a heated confrontation about it, he surprised me with an engagement ring." She paused. "By then I realized something was wrong with me. So, to fix it, I accepted his proposal, and we celebrated in bed.

"To make a long story short, I never reached any measure of arousal. Which meant I couldn't have an orgasm. No matter what. And then I got tired of trying. But he insisted on trying all over again. But I felt broken. Exhausted. And I finally just faked it so he would stop. And he believed I had."

She let silence fall, then said, "But I was devastated. There was no way I could live a lifetime of lying to both of us. He needed a wife that could respond to him, and obviously it wasn't me. He didn't know I had a past. And I didn't know what to do with the one I had hidden. The next day I returned his ring and hurt him."

Maverick walked up behind her and held her. He wasn't surprised. That was why he asked the question. He kissed her head and said, "Piper, I know you. You are a fighter when faced with an enemy. What did you do next?"

She turned and met his gaze. He said, "Tell me."

"You'll be surprised."

"I doubt it."

"I called a sex therapist anonymously on a burner phone. I didn't want the FBI to know." She touched his chest. "She gave me two instructions."

Absolutely floored at the wisdom of her strategy, he said, "That was brilliant. What did she say?"

She stepped back and said, "It's time for secret three. Why don't you have a seat. I'll be back."

Chapter 4

In the bedroom, Piper stripped and removed a very special bag from her suitcase. Smiling at the reaction she expected from Maverick, she slipped on a black patent leather bikini. Shiny. And it couldn't be sexier. Her heels were next - matching stilettos. She posed in the mirror then added the makeup to go with it. The last piece was perfume. A dab on her neck. Wrists. Overflowing cleavage. And on her inner thigh.

She had worked hard on the woman in the mirror.

Maverick heard high heels click on the floor. Piper called down the hall, "Do you remember the conversation you overheard in Lake Charles about my workouts?"

He thought about Quest Search & Rescue's grand opening…and a conversation about…pole dancing.

Piper stepped into the room.

She lit him up and he didn't know what to look at first. Sultry eyes met his as she sensually strolled across the room in tiny pieces of black leather. She stopped near one of the support poles in front of him and turned, giving him a hot and slow 360-degree view.

His pants got way too tight. He stood. "Piper—"

She held up a hand to stop him. "Lesson one was to discover my sexuality. The beauty of it. How my body was created to work. And finding the instinctive nature of turning from thinking to feeling. I chose pole dancing workouts to help me."

She winked. "Why don't you put on a song, and I'll show you what I've learned."

In seconds, Maverick hit play on his phone. *I Put a Spell on You* filled the room.

Piper danced on the pole. Long hair sliding all over her. Maverick watched. Hungry. No. Starving. Not missing one steaming hot move she made. She used her body and hands to talk to him with sexy rhythmic bending and arching. Straddles. Slow kicks and squats. And promises with every look.

He tossed his shirt. Dropped his pants. And stepped closer. They stood inches apart. She paused, breathing hard. Drinking him in. He was gorgeous. A six-foot-four hot naked Viking. Hers. Firm ripped body. Blonde hair. Tattoos. And fiery blue eyes.

She whispered, "Are you ready for lesson two?"

"I don't need lesson two. I want everything, Piper. Marry me. I love you and you know it."

She trailed fingers down his stomach and said, "Not yet…lesson two is required to proceed."

"I'm dying. What is…lesson two?"

"It was for me to explore my body and find out…what…it…wants…"

He groaned as she ran her hands over her breasts...down her stomach…and slid into her bikini bottoms.

Maverick pulled her against him. "Piper…"

Breathless, she said, "It seems that I'm not broken after all, Maverick. But…I need you…to prove to me…that I won't be broken with you."

His lips covered hers and chemistry exploded. He slid his hand into her tiny bottoms. Her knees gave and he caught her. She arched, wild, while he finished what she'd started.

He carried her to the bedroom. She clung…lost in him. "Maverick…I love you…I need…"

"I know, baby, I know what you need."

She said in between kisses, "And…yes…I will…"

It took him a second to realize what she answered. And then they didn't make it to the bedroom. He pressed her against the wall.

She was going to marry him.

***

A long while later, Piper lay winded, snuggled in Maverick's arms. His hands caressed everything he could reach. She kissed his chest.

He said, "The courthouse opens at eight-thirty Monday morning. Let's be first in line."

Smiling, she said, "You really, really want to marry me I see."

He kissed her. "I've loved you since the first time I saw you at the airport."

"How? I was nothing but attitude in heels with a gun."

He laughed. "Hot and fabulous attitude in heels. I was hooked and burning. You knew."

"You weren't shy."

"Shy is not in my wheelhouse."

She giggled. "True." Then she paused and said softly, "I knew I loved you after the home invasion at Raven's. You took off your shirt and covered my chest in front of all the people swarming the house. The look in your eyes was shockingly loving amid all the ugly. You rocked me."

"I love rocking you. And plan to keep doing so, which takes us back to getting married. I can check with my preacher to see if he is available for a private wedding. Unless…you prefer something big—"

"No. Private sounds perfect. Where do you go to church?"

"A non-denominational church. I grew up there. Got saved. Baptized. And I try my best to go to church more Sundays than I miss. I won't be perfect when He calls me home. But then again, no one else will be either. What about you?"

"Mine was similar, except I was raised Baptist. But after the rape, it was hard to go to church and act like life was gentle and sweet. So, I made excuses. Then college and the FBI made it easier to make excuses. But…I have my private time with Him. And He never minds my secrets. It's not like God doesn't know them anyway."

"Beautifully put."

His stomach growled. Then hers. He glanced at the clock. Three in the afternoon. He said, "We won't leave till six to meet Dante and Jinx. How about a snack?"

They put together a tray with small sandwiches of ham and cheese with chips, nuts, strawberries, and olives.

Wearing one of Maverick's shirts, Piper licked her finger and said, "I wanted to ask. I thought you said most of your tattoos were fake, but they aren't rubbing off. And…well, we've done a lot of rubbing."

Maverick laughed. "That we have, beautiful. But these are different. They peel and stick. A blow dryer makes it look real. I have got to shower a week or so before they're gone. I like the rugged look sometimes."

"Rugged looks great on you. You sure shocked me at the hotel last night."

"I know the feeling. Shock was ricocheting all over the place."

She nodded as silence fell, then said, "Showing up like I did was hard for me. But I knew you were about to come looking for me. I forced myself to jump into the fire. I was going to have to wing it."

"How did you know I was upset?"

"Dakota had been after me to call you."

Their gazes met. It was time for another accounting.

Maverick pushed his plate back. "Well, that opens that door. When did your undercover case end?"

"A little over three weeks ago."

His brow creased. Two alphas faced off. He got up. "That's a long time to leave me hanging. Why didn't you call me?"

She stood. "I was injured."

Maverick felt the blow to his gut. Shock and fear first. Confusion and anger next. "Then why the hell didn't you—"

"Because I knew if I called, you would come. But I couldn't handle my injuries, all my secrets, and being in love with you. I needed time. It was complicated. And I had to move. And I still wasn't ready when I got here. But I had to come. I didn't ghost you on purpose, Maverick. I didn't."

Drawing her close, he said, "I get it, Piper. I believe you. So, what injuries?"

She said, "Let me start with the story. I had been in Atlanta about three weeks when an undercover case came up for a male and female. They needed a couple on a drug sting. An agent from South Carolina was coming on board for the case. Cruze Taylor. A well-respected agent in the bureau in his mid-40s. Married with teenagers. Intelligent. Professional. And excellent at his job."

She paused. "I knew him and had even worked under his lead a few times. But I didn't like him personally. He took advantage of his reputation and hit on the women agents. Young ones. But as far as I knew, he was all talk. I personally shut him down several times.

"But anyway, they gave the team a short break while we waited for him to arrive from the airport. I went to the restroom. One of the newer female agents was in there in serious distress. Pacing. Panicking. I tried to connect with her. Eventually she broke down and told me Agent Taylor sexually assaulted her a few months before. She had never told anyone and was terrified to see him. She wanted to quit."

And then Maverick knew. "You didn't."

She shrugged. "Someone had to. I called the Deputy Director, and in short order, the drug sting became a covert double sting with Agent Taylor and me as the couple. No one in our office knew but me. They told Sean and Dakota."

"When did you go undercover?"

"Everything was put into place, and we went in the first week of January. We were both wired. GPS trackers. Video. Drones. The whole bit. But I had a second hidden wire that he didn't know about.

"And Cruze was amazing on the drug sting. Skilled. Confident. He played it like the pro he was. You couldn't help but be impressed and learn from him. And for about three weeks we worked great together. But as it got closer to the end, he started the sexual game. The innuendos. Looks. Intentional touches played off as accidents. And then came suggestions that quickly became threats. It was hard to focus on the drug case with the sexual threat looming. But I made it through unscathed...until the very end."

Maverick's jaw tightened.

Piper said, "After the drug sting ended, we had a two-hour drive back to Atlanta. We were no longer wired or monitored for the drug deal, but on the covert sting, our team knew what might come next. My wire was in place, and we were ready for him.

"And on a deserted stretch of wooded highway, he took a turn down a dirt road. We argued about it. I insisted he turn around. He tried to intimidate me and ripped my shirt. And I knew he was going to go for the rape. I tried to get out of the car, but he braked, blocking my door with a tree. A tree. Who thinks of that?

"And then, I was locked inside. We fought in the cramped seats of the SUV. I hit him with a fist in the neck, then reached for my gun. He backhanded me in the eye – almost knocked me out. Then while he was undoing his pants, I kicked him in the mouth. He spit out two teeth and a lot of blood. He was furious and ripped my zipper open. That's when he saw the wire."

She paused and watched rage fill Maverick's eyes.

"I could hear the sirens coming as he choked me with one hand and yanked down my pants. I reached for my backup gun and was able to get off a shot in his shoulder. Then his door flew open." She paused. "And for a minute I thought the agents were going to kill him on the spot."

Maverick touched her cheek. Tender. But with a voice of steel, he said, "Did they?"

"No. But he paid."

"I don't care what he paid. He didn't pay enough. Where is he?"

"The Office of Professional Responsibility – basically the internal affairs for the FBI - performed their own investigation. No women had reported him. It was his word against the female agent that told me. But no proof. Just lots of whispered stories, except for me and the sting.

"But to publicly charge him for what he did to me would seriously affect my work as an undercover agent. I refused. So, he was stripped of his field rank and banished to a research bunker in the Catskill mountains. A place for skilled agents that cross an unfixable line. He's required to check in weekly and then take a mandatory retirement next year. I was told his wife is divorcing him."

"He deserves it. Have you seen him again?"

"Once, when they read the ruling against him."

"I don't see him letting the opportunity pass to say something to you."

"He didn't."

"And…"

"He said I'd pay. No surprise there. But for now, he's in the mountains required to wear a tracker and stay put - or lose his pension. He also reports in by video every week."

Maverick said, "You know he'll retaliate. There is no way he will let that go. Not him. He won't lose to a woman."

"I know. And that's a year away. But for now…"

She shrugged and walked toward the kitchen, dropping her shirt on the floor as she glanced back at him. Maverick darted after her. She screamed and rounded the snack bar. He slid into the cabinet. She laughed and jumped over the sofa – he followed and caught the end of her ponytail. She spun and kicked. He jumped back. Surprised and thrilled. He laughed.

She dropped into a karate stance. "Work for it."

He unsnapped his jeans. "I've got something for you."

"I see that."

A short scream later he threw her over his shoulder…captured.

***

Later, they dressed for the dinner cruise.

Piper glanced at Maverick's reflection in the mirror as he stepped into jeans, then reached for a white shirt. He caught her watching and winked. She smiled and put on the last swipe of red velvet lipstick before heading to the closet. Was it only yesterday she'd left Atlanta?

Maverick watched Piper, clad only in lace panties and a bra, decide on which dress to wear. He would never get enough of her. She was fabulous and smart. Her body, delicious. She fought like a warrior and made love like a wildcat. He'd had no clue when he got off work yesterday, that she'd turn his world upside down. She'd be his wife in two days.

Piper looked at a couple of dresses. One was a calf length leopard print with a deep V-neckline and a thigh high slit. The other was a sexy floral number with spaghetti straps and a jean jacket. She ran her hand down the leopard material. It was sultry. Bold. She glanced at the floral one. Feminine. Romantic. She slipped on the leopard one.

Maverick looked her over. "Why don't we stay home instead?"

Giving him a sexy smile, she pulled on knee-high boots. "Oops, too late. I'm dressed. Besides, we have guests waiting for us."

They met at the dresser.

She picked up a necklace. He said, "Here, let me help you."

She smiled. "Your fingers will be too big for the clasp."

Sliding his hands down her hips he said, "You didn't seem to mind the size of them earlier."

Tingles raced at his words. She whispered, "Maverick…"

He turned her around, "That's the look, Piper. It's when you give me that look."

She slid his hand down her stomach. "What about children?"

He kissed her. "I'm working on it. Are you on birth control?"

"I started a few weeks ago."

"Throw them in the trash."

The doorbell rang.

Maverick said, "Ignore it. They'll go away."

Piper said, "What if—"

It rang again.

Irritated, he headed to the door and looked through the peephole. It was a smooth-shaven serious guy in a navy suit. Maybe in his fifties. Brown hair. With the bulge of a weapon at his side. FBI?

Maverick heard Piper coming down the hall as he opened the door. "May I help you?"

The man looked beyond him. "Hello Piper. You look beautiful as always."

Piper stopped and stared. "Dad? What… How did you know I was here?"

Agent Dekker Pierce smiled and glanced at the blonde man. At their stunned silence, he said, "Are you going to leave me in the hall?"

Maverick hid his amusement once surprise faded. Piper's father showing up at his door had never occurred to him. Not a single time. He was long past high school. He said, "Please, come in. Shall I call you Dekker, or is Agent Pierce more appropriate?"

Dekker ignored the reference to his occupation. "Evening, Detective Patterson. Dekker will do. Your friends have a nice place."

Piper was floored as she looked at her father. She said, "What is happening here? When did you get to New Orleans? And how is it you already know about Maverick?"

"I arrived a short time ago. And why, is because you moved without telling me. I wanted to find out in person. Now I know." He touched her injured arm.

She said, "It's a graze. Nothing to it. And I haven't had time to call anyone. I've only been in the city for about eighteen hours."

"And yet you've already been shot, and you're staying with a man you neglected to mention."

"Really? Says, the man who lives a life filled with secrets. Besides, I never mention men to you."

He nodded. "My point exactly. You don't move for them either. But you did for this one. Now give me a hug."

Maverick watched Piper disappear into a bear hug. He liked what he saw. A dad who loved and worried about his daughter. And Piper was right, CIA was written all over Dekker. He had that deadly but silent intelligent presence about him. No wonder he found out who he was and where he lived. Although…Dakota or Sean might have told him. He owed them if they did that without warning him.

Maverick walked toward the kitchen and said, "Would you like something to drink? I have a little of everything."

Dekker said, "No, thank you. I won't keep you long. It looks like you are headed out this evening."

"Why don't you join us," Maverick said. "We're having dinner with some friends of mine on the riverboat to show Piper around. You'll enjoy them – and the food and music."

Piper said, "Come with us. How long are you in town for?"

"Just a few hours. I leave about three a.m. And yes, I would love to join you."

"Do you need to freshen up?" Piper asked.

"I did that just before we landed. I'm ready when you are."

Maverick said, "Give us a second," and after a fast hike down the hall, Maverick came out with a jacket and holstered his weapon. Piper followed a minute later slipping her backup gun in her purse.

Maverick met Dekker's gaze. It was a silent male exchange. A universal language well understood.

***

It was a beautiful night in New Orleans. The Steamboat Natchez was all lit up on the Mississippi River. Maverick dropped Piper and her dad at the dock and left for the parking lot.

Piper glanced at the river, then all the people waiting to board under a large striped canopy by the loading dock. She said, "I'm looking forward to this, Dad. It seems like all I have done for way too long is work."

"I know the feeling. But it looks like you found time in there somewhere to find Maverick."

She glanced to where Maverick's truck disappeared and said, "What do you want to know? And don't make me repeat what you know already."

He laughed. Bantering with her was always feisty. "Do you love him?"

"You could have worked up to that question instead of starting with it."

"But that's what I want to know. The rest is just details."

"You already know the answer."

"Say it anyway."

"Yes. I love him. Within days after meeting him."

"Then why did you take the position in Atlanta? Why the delay?"

She would never tell him why, and said, "It was the best decision at the time is all I will say. So, do you like what you've learned about him?"

He considered the wall around her that had been there since the divorce. They both knew it was there. Huge. Hard. Impregnable. And he wanted to know what caused it more than anything. But she wouldn't budge. He let it go and said, "He's clean as a whistle, but the most important thing is, he loves you."

She smiled. "I know."

"Your mother will love him. Does he know how much both of you look alike?"

"Not yet. Surprises are good for him."

He laughed. "Then he has a lot of good coming his way."

***

A taxi turned into a parking garage across the street. Cruze got out smiling at the invention of trackers. He leaned against a shadowed column and zoomed in on the gray truck belonging to Detective Maverick Patterson. He smiled…sort of. It was more a predator's snarl as he watched Piper's new man. It hadn't been hard to find out who he was or where he was likely to find him. People were such creatures of habit. Even detectives and agents when they weren't on the job. They were just as vulnerable as anyone else. Though their responses were deadlier.

Maverick smiled and waved at someone. Cruze followed the direction of his gaze and caught Piper's returning wave in the crowd by the riverboat. Cruze googled the riverboat office. They would be on a two-hour cruise based on the times listed.

Scanning the area, he made his way to Café Maspero to wait and finalize his plan. It was past time. Each day he delayed, made it one day closer to someone discovering he wasn't at work in the mountains. Urgency was a terrific motivator. Revenge too.

***

Maverick smiled as he joined Piper and her dad. Then Dante and Jinx met up with them. Piper made introductions.

Not surprising anyone, Dante jumped in with an inquisition, and said, "Dekker, Piper doesn't look like you at all. And you sure look like a Fed to me."

Dekker smiled at Dante's rigorous banter, and said, "Piper looks more like her mother. And are you aware that there are almost three million federal employees in the United States? Do we all look alike?"

Everyone laughed.

Jinx offered her hand and said, "Ignore him, Dekker. He's a debate kind of guy. It's a pleasure to meet you. I love Piper already."

Dekker held her hand. "He's already forgotten. And you are a beautiful woman, Jinx. Your coloring is striking. How is it you are unattached?"

"How do you know I'm unattached?"

"Because I am still holding your hand."

Dante rolled his eyes and made a face – then laughed with the others. Even Piper, though she was surprised at her dad's flirting. She'd never seen it before.

And the next half hour was busy getting tickets, boarding, and touring the decks until their dinner reservations were ready. They settled in by the rail of the top deck where a large group gathered by the band.

***

Maverick pulled Piper close. "You are gorgeous. I like seeing you have fun."

She said, "You are hot yourself. And I love this. The sound of the water, the music, the aroma of the food - and I bet there are dozens of nationalities on this boat. I've lost count of the accents I've heard."

Kissing her softly, he said, "Seeing it through your eyes makes me appreciate New Orleans all over again."

"Then dance with me! That jazz is calling. Unless of course you are remembering my pole dance."

His kiss was hot. He spun and dipped her. "You will dance for me many times, Piper. Many, many times."

***

Dante and Jinx leaned on the rail looking across the river. He turned her face to his. Her green eyes met his dark ones. She knew what he wanted.

He said, "Dance with me."

"You don't want to dance."

"Stop teasing, Jinx. You smell so good I could eat you alive. And you do it on purpose. Why?"

"Because you like my perfume."

"I like you, and you know it."

Her eyes lowered to his lips. He leaned close. "I have been your spar/workout partner/kissing buddy for well over a year. I know a great deal about you, and your body."

"Dante—"

"It's time for more, Jinx."

"That's a bold presumption."

"I'm serious, Jinx. Touch me. Talk to me. Bring your trust to an intimate level."

"You're talking friends with benefits."

He said, "Don't insult me."

Emotions flickered across her face. She touched his cheek and met his gaze…expecting him to kiss her.

"No, Jinx. It's your move. Show me what you want."

Jinx brushed her mouth over his. Breath mingling. He groaned. "Kiss me."

As her arms encircled his neck, her mouth opened over his.

***

Dekker walked along the rail, giving couples room to dance. He breathed in the night air. It was a romantic night. And it had been a long time since he'd had a sweet one like this. Someone tapped his shoulder.

He turned to face an attractive blonde woman in her 30s. Not his type but she seemed excited about something. He smiled. "Hello."

She said, "Sorry for the interruption but I'm Cindi. I'm with a group of nurses from the hospital." She pointed to a small cluster of women under the canopy and said, "See the lady with the black ponytail? That's Luna. It's her 38th birthday."

He saw the very embarrassed Luna turn away and look across the river. He knew where this was going.

Cindi said, "She's so shy – and totally beautiful. I just wanted someone to dance with her for her birthday. I know she's upset with me, but I caught her watching you and couldn't help myself."

"You're a good friend, Cindi. I'll take it from here."

Across the dance area, Luna was flushed. Embarrassed. And wanted to hide - if she didn't throw up first. She knew her friend loved her and meant well. But to ask a man…that man…

He joined her at the rail. She startled but stayed in place. He said, "Hi, Luna. I'm Dekker."

Her heart thudded. His voice was as sexy as he was. Dark and handsome with hazel eyes. She flushed as he smiled. And Dekker knew her friend had been wrong. Luna was much more than beautiful. She was enchanting, with eyes so light a blue they almost matched her silver shirt. Her lips, full. And all that beautiful black hair. She was a gorgeous woman.

She tried to explain, "They meant well, Dekker. They really did. You don't have to—"

He interrupted, "Please, Luna…I would love to dance with you." He offered his hand. And with eyes locked on his, she laid her hand in his. He found them a spot with a little bit of privacy and drew her into his arms.

He whispered, "Happy Birthday."

***

About twenty minutes later, Maverick and Piper paused at the rail to cool off and catch their breath. Maverick pointed at Dante and Jinx dancing a rowdy jitterbug. Then Piper looked for her dad and…wow. He had a slow groove going. A hot smile and a woman in his arms. Piper had never seen that look on his face…or those moves. And then he kissed the woman. A hot one.

Piper looked at Maverick, mouth open in surprise. Maverick shrugged. And she watched her dad, realizing how little romance she had seen with her parents. She was thrilled for him.

Dante and Jinx joined them. Maverick caught their looks. The touches between them. Well, it was about time.

Piper whispered, "Something's in the air tonight."

Maverick winked and glanced at his watch. "We need to head downstairs for our reservations."

Piper waved and caught her dad's attention. He motioned for them to go and flashed his hand twice. He would join them in ten minutes.

***

Maverick led the way into the formal dining room. It was set aside for a more private and elegant dining experience. Large paned windows lined the huge room giving spectacular views from every angle of the river and the city.

There were linen draped tables with place settings. The walls were white. Even the decorative paneled ceiling was white with hanging lights. Large wooden columns supported the ceiling while providing attractive spacing. It was a lovely elegance reminiscent of a time gone by.

By the time they were settled in their seats, drink orders were taken, and buffet menus provided. Dekker arrived just in time to join them in ordering. He sat between Piper and Jinx.

Dekker smiled and said, "Aren't I the lucky one between two beautiful women. I'm sorry I am late. I hope that I didn't hold you up."

Piper said, "Not at all. Perfect timing."

Jinx teased, "And speaking of beautiful women. That was a stunner I saw you dancing with."

Smiling, he agreed. "Absolutely." He didn't elaborate.

Piper asked, "Is she a tourist?"

"No. She's a local. A nurse at one of the hospitals. And no more questions. There is enough romance at this table to keep your interest off me."

Maverick and Dante toasted. "Hear, hear!"

Piper whispered, "Dad—"

He leaned close. "Let it go, Piper."

"You kissed her."

"And you are in Maverick's apartment."

Her cheeks went pink, but she pressed. "I'm fumbling this. What I wanted to say is that I've never seen you like that. You're a handsome man—"

And he knew she wasn't going to let it go. Women in love rarely did. He said, "Piper, tonight was a chance meeting. A flicker of time. A dance with destiny. Whatever you want to call it. I embraced the moment. Now, enough. Let's order. The waitress is waiting."

The women decided to split the Bayou Seafood Pasta. Luscious crawfish tails and shrimp in a white wine and garlic parmesan cream sauce over penne pasta. Along with Natchez salad and sugar cane vinaigrette. The men ordered Chicken and Sausage Gumbo. Rich. Flavorful. Traditional and delicious served over fluffy white rice. For dessert, they all chose Bananas Foster, a New Orleans original. Sliced bananas, seasoned sweet, then sautéed in butter and rum, topped with ice cream.

After ordering, they settled back to visit. A few late arrivals caused a momentary flurry of activity. Piper glanced up, and across the room met the gaze of Count Dracula. He smiled and got up.

Piper touched Maverick's arm and said, "It looks like I need to introduce you to someone."

"Who?"

"An Italian Dracula."

"Well, that's a first. Is he here?"

Piper stood without answering. Maverick followed suit just as a man joined them.

The man nodded respectfully at Maverick but focused on Piper. "Forgive me for intruding. We heard about the shooting of course. And then you were gone. Rumors flew, but we didn't know much until the news. It is quite a relief to see you safe."

Maverick touched Piper's waist. Code for - who is he.

Piper turned to Maverick and the others and explained, "We sort of met in the elevator at the hotel last night. I know him as Count Dracula – though he is missing the fangs and bloody shirt tonight. Cleopatra was part of his entourage. Along with Cat Woman and a Court Jester."

Everyone smiled. Of course. Mardi Gras remnants.

The Count shook Maverick's hand and said, "Unfortunately, I'd had entirely too much to drink. But she was a good sport with my theatrical drama." He sighed. "But to my sorrow, she wouldn't let me even have a taste of her blood."

Maverick chuckled. "You have no idea how lightly you got off."

"So, I learned. I can still hear the gunshots." He motioned back to his table where the other three waved at Piper.

Piper waved back. "Are you tourists?"

He laughed. "Actually, no. Students at Tulane." He bowed. "Future Dr. Georgio Bianchi at your service. And if I may have your name?"

"I am FBI Special Agent Piper Pierce." She indicated Maverick and said, "Detective Maverick Patterson. Others here are my father and friends."

"It is nice to meet all of you. And since I've monopolized enough of your evening, I'll take my leave. Again, Agent Pierce, I am grateful that you are well. I would hate to find you in my emergency room." And with a smile, off he went.

Maverick looked at Piper. "You played with him in the elevator?"

"He was such a cute flirty Dracula. Totally harmless. Now my shower was a different story…"

Laughter followed.

***

Following dinner, Piper said, "Jinx, I'd love to know how you got into podcasting. Especially self-defense. What's the name of it?"

"Prepared for Danger. It's on air six days a week from eight-thirty to nine p.m. And it's more a live forum inviting the public to call in with questions. I also bring in skilled guests to contribute their input."

"In what way?"

"We cover the need for safety in living alone. Dating. Bullies. Abuse. Strangers. Random theft attacks. And the danger of not paying attention to what's happening around you. I use questions and scenarios to shock them into an awareness of how they should assist in their own safety."

Jinx smiled. "And I know I'm talking to the choir here when I say calling 911 shouldn't be the only self-defense mechanism people depend upon. Making them aware of their own responsibility is my first goal. Then offering them a beginner's self-defense training class is next. Followed by, referring them to advanced training based on the needs they have."

Piper said, "That's a well thought out plan. You must be quick on your feet to respond to random questions on air."

"Pretty much. And I try to keep it appropriate for all callers. I also have a private follow-up list for callers needing professional help like counselors, law enforcement, and that kind of thing. I don't claim to have all the answers."

She pointed at Dante. "He's my security during the podcast and my spar partner. This isn't just for women. Males and females participate. No one wants to be a victim."

Dekker said, "What is your training background?"

"I am a Physical Education major with a minor in journalism. And a couple of certifications in self-defense. I was a cheerleader too if that counts."

He smiled. "Everything counts. Especially cheerleading for a podcast. You need high energy."

Piper said, "Why did you steer from Phys Ed to this?"

Jinx swirled the tea in her glass. They wanted the real reason her life had changed. "My best friend was kidnapped and murdered after leaving our favorite night club." She paused. "I had a flat tire and called her to come get me. She never made it."

Respectful silence followed. Piper knew Jinx didn't want or need opinions, encouragement, or nuggets of wisdom on how it wasn't her fault. Nothing they said would change the burden she carried. Only time. And saving one life at a time like she was doing.

Piper said, "I'm sorry. What was her name?"

"Demi. She was gorgeous, gentle, and smart - torn between being a nurse or a veterinarian. She would never have hurt a soul and was totally unaware of the evil in the world around her."

"But you were."

"I had suffered a few close calls which made me more careful. But nothing like I am now."

"Would you like another guest speaker on your podcast?"

"If you mean you, yes!"

"Not as an agent. I would offer my skills as a brown belt in karate. I study Krav Maga and mixed martial arts like many agencies, law enforcement, and military do."

"You bet I would. How about tomorrow night? Sunday is usually a busy night with calls."

Piper smiled. "I'm in."

The whistle sounded on the boat. It was time to dock. They gathered their belongings and slowly headed to the deck.

***

Next to one of the columns behind Piper, a man stood and dropped his phone in a pocket. He followed them out with the crowd. His appearance wouldn't have alerted anyone to trouble or drawn attention. Unless maybe to a movie fan who thought he looked a good bit like Indiana Jones. Old khaki pants. Weathered brown leather jacket. Boots. Plain brown hair and glasses. Nondescript. Made to blend in - except for his eyes. They were gold and locked on Piper.

He jiggled the keys in his pocket. Thoughts began to fall into place as he watched the detective's kiss linger on the beauty in the leopard dress.

He was wrong. He thought his hunt had ended with number three. But it looked like Special Agent Piper Pierce would be number four.

Chapter 5

As they exited the riverboat, Dante and Jinx said their goodbyes.

Maverick said, "Dekker, why don't you and Piper wait here. I'll get the truck."

Piper said, "We can go with you. It's not that far."

At the same time, Dekker saw Luna exit the boat. Their eyes met. He lifted a finger. She nodded. He turned to Maverick and Piper, who noted the exchange.

Maverick said, "Take your time, Dekker. We'll be back to pick you up."

***

Gold Eyes watched the couple as the crowd headed to the parking lot. He sized up the detective. Tall. Athletic. Tough. And he knew he would be dangerous based on the passion he smelt in the air.

Passing his own vehicle to follow them, eventually they climbed into a Dodge Ram. Slowing his pace as they drove away, he caught movement in the shadows. A man in a dark jacket and baseball cap stepped out and watched the truck drive off. His body language screamed fury. He flicked a cigarette and walked toward the French Quarter.

Getting in his SUV, Gold Eyes continued to watch the angry guy growing smaller in the distance. He was intrigued. Maverick and Piper had someone else watching them. What was that about? Taking off the leather jacket and glasses, he grabbed a hoodie and backpack from the floorboard and followed him.

This mystery was too good to pass up.

***

Back at the riverboat, Dekker smiled at Luna and said, "My job makes things complicated, but if you would like to keep in touch, I can make that happen. Say yes. Please."

She smiled. "Yes."

"Is it too late for us to meet somewhere for coffee? I'm flying out at three a.m."

"My friends will be dropping me at home." She debated with herself, then offered, "I can make coffee…but…coffee only."

"Understood. Coffee is perfect."

"Dekker…"

"I get it, Luna. It's conversation and time." He offered her a private card that simply had his name and phone number on it.

Maverick and Piper pulled up.

Dekker said, "Text me your address. I'll call before I get there. And Luna, if you change your mind, we can do it another time."

"Thank you. But tonight, would be nice."

Luna smiled as she headed toward a carload of rowdy friends dying for details. They wouldn't get any. Dekker was the best birthday present ever…and it wasn't even over.

***

Cruze ignored the crowds in the French Quarter as he made his way back to the RV park. It wasn't far. Only a mile and a half from the riverboat. And he needed the walk to work off the rage and desire Piper always stirred up in him. She had been sexy and hot for her detective tonight. That he'd never seen. Now he really wanted what was between those thighs.

On the job she'd always downplayed her sexuality and never welcomed anyone's interest. Especially his…which stung. But in the end, she played him. Deliberately. And set him up to lose it all. Publicly.

He reached the park gate and keyed in the security code. Then headed toward the back of the park. The metal gate clanged shut behind him.

With barely a pause, Gold Eyes unzipped his backpack and withdrew a drone. He set it on the ground. In no time, the drone was up and over the wall.

Cruze unlocked and entered the black and gold camper in the back corner. Throwing his jacket and cap on the sofa, he grabbed a beer from the refrigerator. He took a swig and turned on his laptop. Before long he was scrolling through pictures and data on Maverick and Piper.

Outside, the drone found a gap in the curtains. The man was on a laptop. Gold Eyes zoomed in on the screen. And in a relatively short amount of time, he learned more than he ever expected about renegade Agent Cruze Taylor, Piper, and Maverick.

Making a calculated decision on an already complicated scenario, he flew the drone underneath the RV and turned it off. And thoughtfully walked back to his vehicle at the riverboat. He had to go for it.

***

Arriving at the loft, Piper and Maverick walked Dekker to his SUV.

Piper hugged him. "I love you, Dad."

"I love you. And I'll give you a little warning next time I come to New Orleans."

"That was a shock. You've never done that."

"That's not necessarily true."

Piper frowned. "You've done it before? I can't believe it."

"Sure, you can."

"That's creepy."

He laughed. "Says an FBI agent skilled in surveillance."

"But why?"

"You rarely tell me what I want to know. You always give me the same offhand answer. So, sometimes I need to see for myself that you really are ok. I can watch you for a few minutes and know how you are."

"But I get the same offhand answer from you."

"And you're right. We need to work on that. But…another time. I need to go."

Dekker shook hands with Maverick and squeezed hard. "She's the best thing that will ever happen to you."

Maverick returned the pressure. "That's why I'm going to marry her as quick as possible."

Piper said, "Will someone tell me why I am not included in this conversation?"

Her dad climbed in the car. "Because you are the conversation."

***

Before long, Dekker turned onto Chestnut Street, a neighborhood in the historic Garden District. He texted Luna: I'm almost there.

He pulled behind a silver Honda.

Inside the house, Luna wasn't sure if she should greet Dekker on the porch or wait until he knocked. She was nervous. And then it was too late. He knocked softly.

Their eyes met as she opened the door. He'd taken off his suit jacket and stood there in slacks and a dress shirt with a gun on his hip. Was sexy intense a word? It must be, because the look in his eyes made her feel more woman than she'd ever felt.

Aware of the sparked connection, he smiled. "Hello again."

"Hi, Dekker. Please…come in."

He glanced around the den and kitchen. He saw cozy. Warm. Romantic. A touch of whimsical...and beautiful, like her. "I like it. It looks like you."

"Thank you. I like things that are interesting. Inviting to touch."

He touched her dark hair. It was loose now, thick and wavy. Soft. She had changed into a short shirt with a 60s vintage rock and roll poster design. Black lounge pants were tied around her hips, leaving her waist exposed. Her toenails were painted sunshine yellow.

He said, "You are innocent and sexy all at the same time. I couldn't wait to get here."

She admitted, "I am…thrilled you are here."

He smiled. "I like thrilled…but…you are nervous. So, why don't we go ahead and get past this…"

Their lips met. Open and eager. He drew her against him and her arms encircled his neck, her fingers sliding into his hair. He groaned and deepened the kiss. Their chemistry was crazy. But before long, Dekker paused. It would be so easy…too easy…

Breathless, Luna said, "Help me, Dekker. We need coffee."

After a soft kiss, he turned her toward the kitchen. "Break time. Coffee it is. Space activated."

Walking across the room, she sighed. "Honestly, I really would rather throw the coffee pot in the yard."

He laughed as he followed her, then leaned against the counter. "You are delightful."

She said, "What happened to sexy?"

"Be careful…or I'll throw the coffee pot in the yard."

She smiled and prepared coffee.

He watched her and said, "You know, I can imagine us together."

She closed her eyes. "Don't say that."

"Do you have any idea how arousing your response is?"

She blushed. "And obviously you know how arousing it is to talk about it."

"Guilty." He sat at the snack bar to give her some space. "I'm a lot older than you."

She shrugged without looking at him. "Not so much. Does it look like I care about that?"

"My daughter is maybe ten years younger than you."

"It still doesn't matter. And she's gorgeous. What's her name?"

"FBI Special Agent Piper Pierce."

She hit the red button on the coffee pot and turned to face him. "Wow. What an amazing profession. You must be proud."

"Since the day she was born."

Luna asked, "And her mother?"

"A pilot. Impressive herself. We've been divorced since Piper was sixteen."

Relieved he offered that information, she said, "You are still friends."

"We make better friends than spouses. What about you? Divorced or widowed?"

"Widowed. He was killed in an offshore accident."

"That's awful, Luna. I'm sorry. When?"

She paused. "Five years ago." And turned to get the coffee cups.

So many things about her gave it away. He asked softly, "Have you dated?"

She looked at the wall in front of her. She didn't want to tell him. He would know how significant tonight was to her. She ignored him and said, "What do you take in your coffee?"

He didn't answer. She knew he was still waiting. She turned to face him. "I haven't dated."

Sliding off his chair, he walked into the kitchen.

Backing away, she said, "No. Don't you dare feel sorry for me. I could have dated. I just didn't want to. No one gets that it was my choice."

He kept coming and finally pinned her in. Then picked her up and sat her on the counter. He said, "Now I know where your innocence comes from. Why me, Luna?"

She said softly, "I watched you on the boat. So sexy. So handsome. Strong. I loved the way you moved. The way you enjoyed the music. I could tell you liked the breeze. And…I was just drawn to you...a perfect stranger. And…then my friends caught me staring, and here we are."

He brushed his lips against hers. "We were supposed to meet."

"Maybe. What do you think would have happened if you had seen me first?"

"I'd still be kissing you on your kitchen counter."

She kissed him, believing him.

After that, they sat with coffee at the table. Close. Touching. Kissing. Laughing. Talking about all sorts of things. And it got late. And later. They both knew he would have to leave soon.

Dekker ran his finger across her bottom lip, and said, "Would you dance with me before I go?"

Music filled the room. A steamy oldie. Dekker wanted to dance with her. He stood and drew her into his arms and their mouths met. And for this song they both knew it was more than coffee. His hands slid down her hips and pulled her into him. Tight. The intimacy direct through their clothes. Their kiss breathless and hot. Chemistry on fire. And the lyrics of the slow groove fed the fire.

Dekker let Luna taste more of his hunger as he picked her up. Both groaning as her legs wrapped his hips. Voice tight with passion, he said, "Tonight is a glimpse of what we will be. We were never meant to be a one-night hookup. You were not meant to wake up in the morning wondering if you'd ever see me again. I will be back. Now, kiss me goodbye while I can still leave."

***

In the wee hours of the morning, an SUV drove slowly around the tall wooden fence of the RV park. Gold Eyes parked close to where he remembered Cruze's RV to be. Sitting in his car, he activated the drone hidden underneath the RV. He flew it back to the same window he watched through earlier. Images of Piper played like a video on the computer as Cruze cleaned his gun.

There was no doubt this man planned to take Piper. No doubt at all. And he had no problem imagining what the guy planned to do to her before he killed her. Gold Eyes wasn't shocked. He'd killed too. The problem was, Piper was his. Cruze was in his way.

Tapping his finger on the controller, Gold Eyes knew one predator had to die. And it wasn't him.

In minutes he climbed the wall behind the RV and flew the drone looking for security cameras or witnesses. The coast was clear. He grabbed a small rock off the ground and tossed it at the window where Cruze sat. It was loud in the late darkness. The sound of footsteps moved toward the door. He heard it open and Cruze came down the steps.

Gold Eyes headed in the opposite direction and waited in the shadow of the slide out.

It didn't take long. As soon as Cruze was satisfied that all was safe, he turned back toward the door. Gold Eyes hit him with a blackjack, and he dropped. Unconscious. But for good measure, he drugged him.

He'd be out for a long time.

Then he headed inside the camper and took the computer, gun, and locked the door. Then bound the unconscious Cruze, hooked him to a pulley, and winched him over the wall. What was a few more bumps and bruises?

By four a.m. Gold Eyes arrived at his ranch with the first game piece. Tomorrow, it begins.

Chapter 6

The next morning, Piper ran as fast as she could. Breathing in through her nose, out threw her mouth. But she could hear the pounding of his footsteps. He was almost on her. She growled as Maverick blew by her. He laughed, crossing the finish line and did the Rocky dance as he waited for her.

He teased, "You're pretty fast for a girl."

She jabbed him in the stomach.

He grunted at the blow, but still laughed. "No one can accuse you of good sportsmanship."

"I told you I like to win."

"But you knew you couldn't outrun me. I even gave you a head start. It was a sure lose."

She tossed her ponytail. "I still don't have to like it."

He swung her around and kissed her. "Piper, life with you will never be boring."

Teenagers riding skateboards gave wolf whistles as they passed by.

Maverick said, "Tell you what, beautiful. I'll race you back to the loft. The winner gets to have their way with the other."

She dropped to her feet and smiled. "I bet you let me win now."

He winked. He most certainly would.

***

Late that afternoon, they packed to head to Jinx's place for a workout before the podcast.

Piper said, "It looked like Dante and Jinx had a real date last night. Do you know what happened?"

"No," Maverick said. "But it's about time."

"Is Jinx from New Orleans?"

"Close. She grew up in Mandeville - across Lake Pontchartrain. She moved here for college and stayed. But they met at UpTown Climbing in Baton Rouge. I'll have to take you there sometime. It is a lot more fun than boulder climbing. The high wall is ninety feet."

Piper said, "Only ninety?" Then zipped her bag and put on tennis shoes.

Maverick watched her. She'd been a lot more cautious than he expected at the Boulder Lounge yesterday. She caught his gaze and smiled. He was digging. Let him dig. She wasn't going anywhere near that wall. Who wants to fall ninety feet.

She headed to the mirror with her makeup bag, and said, "Have you ordered the pizza yet?"

"We were talking about climbing."

"You were talking about climbing. Help yourself."

"Would you rappel down this building in a harness? It's about sixty feet."

"Would you do a bikini wax?"

He laughed. "I doubt it. That never occurred to me."

"My point exactly."

***

At the podcast studio, Jinx said, "Maverick and Piper will be here in less than an hour. Can you give me a good stretch before I work out?"

Dante said, "Sure."

She sat on the mat and spread her legs wide. He knelt in front, and she leaned forward, arms outstretched, stomach on the mat.

He grabbed her wrists. "Ready?"

"Go."

He pulled a little. Held. A little more. Held. Slowly putting pressure on her adductors and hamstrings. Her legs gave easily. By the fourth pull, she grunted. And on the fifth, she said, "Time!"

He sat back as she shook her legs. He said, "Let me rub it out."

She said, "I was tighter than I thought."

Moving between her legs, Dante slowly kneaded the muscles. He said, "You need the stretches more often if you're this tight."

She nodded; eyes closed as he worked. Then things changed. Awareness rose as his hands moved up her thighs. Other thoughts slid in. Breathless, she opened her eyes.

Dante's dark eyes watched her. He said softly, "It feels good, doesn't it."

She was too shocked to answer.

The front door chimed as it opened.

Maverick walked in with pizza and stopped, eyes on the couple. Piper ran into him. Looking at Dante and Jinx's position, Maverick said, "Sorry. I guess coming early wasn't such a good idea."

Getting off the floor, Dante said, "I can think of better."

Piper stepped around Maverick and said, "Don't you just hate that? When my dad showed up unannounced at Maverick's place last night, talk about embarrassing. Though at least he did knock. Our bad. We owe you."

Jinx gave Piper a tour of the two-story building. The gym and office were downstairs. The gym was about 3,000 square feet with mirrors and mats. Not many windows. And it had two metal doors. The concrete floor was painted turquoise. Large lighted fans were overhead, and the ceiling was painted black. Exercise equipment was across the back wall. A few tables and chairs were set up by a drink machine.

The office was in the back corner, soundproofed, and doubled as the podcast studio. It was neat, clean, and colorful with posters of the mysterious side of New Orleans.

Piper said, "This is a great setup."

"Thanks. It took a while to get it to come to pass with permits, certifications, and sponsors. But it's fully functional now. And I like to think that Demi would approve." She pointed to a picture on her desk of her with a blonde. Smiles across both of their faces.

Piper picked up the picture. Two beautiful women…and evil took one. She put it back and said, "I have no doubt she approves, Jinx. What about her family?"

"They approve but moved away. Too many memories and they had younger children to raise. But they keep in touch. And speaking of family, you've got a fine dad, Piper."

She smiled. "Right. But he's super private. Last night was the first time I'd seen him with anyone."

"You probably won't until he's serious about someone. What about your mom?"

"She's vocal about her dating life. I don't know why she hasn't remarried yet."

"What does she look like?"

"Me." She pulled out her phone and scrolled to a picture of them together.

Jinx gasped. "Has Maverick seen this?"

"No. I thought I'd surprise him."

"Girl, surprise him is not the word. Twins is the appropriate word. I hope I'm there when he finds out."

Piper laughed. "She's a pilot. A captain on commercial jets."

Jinx said, "I don't even know any female pilots. Dante might, even though he flies helicopters. What does your dad do? I saw the gun. He sure looks like he can use it."

"He works for the government. Mr. Confidential." She shrugged. "So, there's that."

"Your family could be a mini-series."

"Wait till you meet my Nash cousins. They have Native American heritage and ooze sex appeal."

"Like long hair Native American warriors?"

Piper laughed, "You pretty much nailed it. What about your family?"

Jinx said. "It was small. My mother raised me. She was an intelligent, traditional southern lady. A high school principal. But my gothic bent on appearance stressed her sensibilities. But she loved me."

"Was?"

"She passed a couple of years ago. So, it's just me."

"I'm sorry. You've been through a lot. But you have Dante. And it looks like you've decided to let him pet you."

Jinx laughed. "What does that mean?"

"Maverick said you were like a cat waiting to see if you were going to let Dante pet you."

Jinx laughed as they headed upstairs. What an appropriate comparison.

Jinx's apartment was not what Piper expected at all. It looked like one of the New Orleans posters downstairs. Except veranda style. Wrought iron table and chairs. Brick. Plants. Lamps. Colorful posters. Rugs. And a large black velvet sectional.

Piper laid out on the sectional. "This is like vacation. You need to be an interior decorator. When I finally buy a home, I'm calling you."

Jinx said, "Bring it on."

Dante called upstairs, "The pizza is getting cold!"

***

It was getting close to podcast time. Jinx and Piper discussed cues for live calls or problems. Maverick and Dante sat outside the closed office but could see them through a window that overlooked the gym. Too many things interfered with podcast sound to stay inside. Every sound, like breathing loud, coughing, dropping something, scooting a chair, etc., could affect the listening experience for the audience.

A few minutes later, Jinx held up three fingers, two, then one.

Jinx winked at Piper and said with high energy, "Hello, New Orleans! And everyone listening from around the world. Welcome to a live podcast on

Prepared for Danger – a forum where the critical importance of self-defense is addressed.

"And tonight, I have a special treat for you. Piper is here to join the conversation. She is a professional in every sense of the word. Experienced and skilled in dealing with criminals and investigations, she is also trained in Krav Maga and MMA. Both - truly great self-defense martial art styles.

"So, now I'll introduce you to Piper and then we'll open the call center." Smiling at Piper, she said, "Thank you for being on the show tonight, Piper."

"My pleasure, Jinx! Anytime I can connect with the public on the training side to prevent crime is a treat for me. I look forward to sharing any knowledge that I can. Come on callers, bring it on!"

Jinx laughed and said, "You heard her! The call center is open. If you have questions about self-defense…call 504-defense!"

Several lines began to blink.

Jinx answered line one, "You are on the air!"

A young woman said, "I'm not very athletic. Am I still able to do effective self-defense moves? Because…for three days I've heard scratching on the wall outside my bedroom at night. And I live alone."

Jinx said, "I'm glad you called. And yes. There are many levels of self-defense. I advise one-on-one training and a lot of practice. I've written your number down and will contact you tomorrow. But I wondered, have you called 911 for an officer to check?"

"Yes, I did. He drove by and called back saying he didn't see anyone. But I checked the wall the next day and there were scratch marks. Someone was there."

Jinx glanced at Piper. Trouble. Piper stepped in and said, "Contact the police department, explain like you did to us, and ask for a regular drive by for a while. But if you feel like you are in danger now, go stay with someone else. But wait for an escort to your car.

"Also, it doesn't hurt to let your neighbors know your concerns and think about getting a camera if you don't have security. Get a dog. And keep your key fob by your bed. The panic button makes a loud alarm. And be sure to get training. Living alone requires extra security measures. And just so you know, you did the right thing calling tonight. Your instincts are talking to you. Listen."

"Thank you…thank you so much! I will."

Caller two.

Jinx said, "You are on the air."

A young man said, "What about men and self-defense? Not everyone is the size of a linebacker."

Jinx said, "Anyone can be a target. Male or female. Young or old. Frail or tough. Everyone should have a self-defense awareness plan in place."

"I heard on the news in the French Quarter about a woman attacking a man. Online dating has real challenges. I would be too embarrassed to tell anyone."

Piper raised her finger. Jinx nodded with a smile. That had been Piper's case. Piper said, "Stranger dating has a huge set of complications even for men. If you don't meet publicly, you take a chance. If you give them all your information, you take a chance. If you trust too soon, you take a chance. Because if people have violent tendencies, they aren't always exposed early. Take your time and find out who they are. And if you see anything alarming or suspicious, shut it down. And if necessary, be embarrassed and get help."

"Right. I got it. Thanks."

Caller three.

Jinx said, "You are on the air."

An older woman said, "Have you ever been attacked?"

Jinx said, "Almost. I was watching and avoided the situation. But unfortunately, my best friend was killed later that year."

The woman gasped. "Is that why you do this?"

"Yes. Her life mattered. Your life does. All of you. We want you to be prepared in case danger comes calling."

The woman said, "Even for old women?"

"Especially for the elderly. In fact, why don't I call you tomorrow and we'll talk."

"Thank you!"

Caller four.

Jinx said, "You are on the air."

A man's voice said, "Hello, Jinx. This call is for Piper. Special Agent Piper Pierce. Talk to me, Piper."

Jinx was shocked. Maverick and Dante jumped to their feet. Piper motioned for Maverick. He slipped into the room. She passed him a note: Get Agent Donovan.

Smoothly, Piper answered, "Why do I want to talk to you, caller four?"

"Because you and I are going to play a game."

"I don't play games with strange men. Why don't you come by and introduce yourself. We'll take it from there."

"Not yet. We'll meet soon enough. But this is my game, and we'll play my way. You really don't have a choice."

"What makes you think that?"

"Because three brunette tourists are missing in New Orleans. It's been in the news. Very exciting. Have you heard about them?"

Piper hadn't been here long enough to know. She looked at Maverick. Grimly, he nodded, yes. She said, "I've heard of them. Why?"

"I took them."

The blow landed. A serial kidnapper…or worse. Piper said, "Then work with me so I can bring them home. Isn't that why you called?"

"It's a little more complicated than that. Look in the mirror."

Piper glanced at Maverick with a frown. He wrote: You look like the victims. She said, "Ok, caller. So, you like brunettes - I see your game. How about giving me your name?"

Twenty-two miles south of Jinx's place, Gold Eyes smiled. "Call me King. And the goal of the game is simple. You've got to find all three women…before you become number four."

The call ended.

Chapter 7

Jinx glanced at the number of people tuning in to the podcast as Piper headed out of the room with Maverick. Her eyes widened. Half a million and climbing. Were the listeners scared, curious, or entertained?

She chose to address the situation. "Listeners, we all know the last caller spoke from a predator point of view. But his threat and his purpose are why we do what we do on Prepared for Danger. Use tonight as a lesson to confirm that you need to learn self-defense. And I assure you, Agent Pierce, the FBI, and local law enforcement will find this man who calls himself King. And we pray the women he took as well. So, let's continue our mission tonight. Next caller…"

She punched the button for caller five. "You are on the air."

***

Piper shut the door behind her, and several things happened at once. Maverick's phone rang. Her phone rang. And several units from the New Orleans Police Department slid to a stop outside, lights flashing and sirens blaring.

Piper answered the call from her boss, "Agent Donovan."

He said, "I'm on my way. I want answers and a copy of that podcast."

"Yes, Sir." She glanced at the time. "It will be over in twelve minutes – unless he calls back."

"I would imagine he's done the damage he intended tonight. This is unbelievable. You haven't been here two full days and you're on your second case. And it looks like we'll be working with the NOPD again. Anything you need to tell me about you and Maverick?"

"That's probably a good idea."

"Then don't put it off. I'll be there in a few minutes. Stay with Maverick."

❖

Maverick glanced at the caller. Piper's dad. He answered, "Dekker—"

"I was listening to the podcast. Where is Piper?"

"We're still here at the studio. She's on the phone with her boss."

"Don't let her out of your sight, Maverick. This guy's the real deal. I've got a flight to catch. Be there by morning."

Piper met Maverick's gaze across the room. They met in the middle.

She said, "King had to watch me on the riverboat last night. That's the only tourist place I've visited since I arrived. And I admit, I was not watching the crowd."

He said, "None of us were. But if it was on the boat, everyone had a camera. We'll find him."

"The missing women, Maverick - how long has it been going on?"

"Three months. And Piper, you know this is going to get crazy. The podcast is worldwide. There will be no privacy, no personal life, no normalcy, until this is all over. But listen to me…we are still getting married tomorrow. I don't care what anyone says. You are going to be my wife."

She smiled in the middle of the firestorm. "I love it when you want me."

"When don't I?"

In minutes, two men stepped through the door and called their names. Agent Donovan and Sergeant Driscoll had arrived.

***

Jinx finished the last podcast caller and closed out the show. Very imposing men watched her through the window. She began to make copies of the podcast as Dante opened the door. Piper, Maverick, Agent Donovan, and Sargeant Driscoll stopped in front of her desk.

Jinx said, "How many copies do you need?"

Agent Donovan said, "Five."

"It won't take long."

Piper said, "You did great, Jinx."

Jinx shook her head no. "You did. That guy would have ripped me to shreds on air." She paused. "Now what happens?"

Agent Donovan said, "We investigate and find him. But since your podcast is his communication tool, are you agreeable for us to set up a temporary worksite here?"

"Absolutely. Whatever you need."

Both bosses stepped out and gave orders. In minutes, the FBI scrambled to set up an on-site investigation office.

***

Several states away, FBI Special Agent Sean Nash stomped snow off his boots and shut the door to his condo in Denver, Colorado. His phone rang.

His wife of less than a year, Special Agent Samantha Nash, poured coffee in an insulated mug. She said, "At this time of night, that call won't be good news."

Glancing at caller ID, he said, "You're right. It won't be."

Sean hit speaker, "Hey Jackson. What's up with Cruze?"

"He's missing. An agent assigned by the Office of Professional Responsibility gave him a surprise call. No answer. He contacted security at the Catskill location and was told Cruze called in sick a few days ago. They sent a couple of agents to check his apartment and found his tracker sitting on the bed. And that's all they found. So, we're days behind him. I hope he won't be stupid enough to go after—"

"He will be. No doubt he's headed for Piper. If only her bullet had been a little more to the left, we wouldn't be having this conversation."

"You've got that right. Tell Piper I'm sorry."

Sean headed for his suitcase. He always kept one ready to go.

Samantha followed. "I can't believe Cruze is in the wind. It's a no-win situation for him."

"He doesn't think he has anything else to lose," Sean said. "That's the worst kind. Listen, I'll call Piper on the way to the airport. Would you call Dakota with the update for me? Tell him I'll meet them in New Orleans. Now we have double trouble."

She said, "Piper didn't need this. And Maverick—"

"Won't leave her side. Cruze and King will be more than sorry they messed with her." He holstered his gun and hung his backpack on his shoulder. "I would take you with me if I could. If you finish the bank investigation and I'm still there, come meet me in New Orleans. I know Piper wants to work with you."

"There is nothing exciting about a bank investigation. I'll be out of here as quick as I can. I want action."

He pulled her close and kissed her. "Everything about you is action."

"And don't you forget it."

***

Back in New Orleans, Maverick tacked pictures of the three missing brunettes on victim boards. Piper read their personal statistics from the case files:

- The first woman was reported missing in mid-November. The second in late December. And the third in late January. All lived around Lake Pontchartrain.
- All three women had various shades of long dark hair. One had straight hair. One's hair was wavy. And the third woman had a mass of curls.
- Ages nineteen to thirty.
- Two white. One Hispanic.
- Two were single. One divorced with children.
- They were last spoken to as they visited tourist sites in New Orleans.

Piper's phone rang. "I'll be right back, Maverick. It's Sean."

Piper answered, "Hey Sean. I guess you heard about the podcast caller."

"Yes, in fact, I'm about to board a plane headed to New Orleans. Dakota, Adam, and Hawk are on their way from Lake Charles too. Unfortunately, you're going to need all the extra agents you can get. That's why I'm calling."

"What happened?"

"Cruze is gone. He's been missing two or three days."

Piper thought back to the last time she saw Cruze. She remembered the hate in his eyes. And even more, the lust. She rubbed the tiny eyebrow scar from his fist, and said, "I don't have time for Cruze right now."

"Don't ignore him, Piper. They are trying to track him but haven't found a thing yet. We both know Cruze has revenge on the brain. Where's Donovan? I know he's got to be there."

"Hang on…"

She raised her hand and caught Donovan's attention. She showed him the phone and he headed her way.

She put her phone on speaker, and told Donovan, "Sean is on the line. Cruze vanished from the Catskill location a few days ago."

Sean said, "Agent Donovan, I don't have to tell you this is a bad complication for Piper, or anyone who might get in Cruze's path."

Donovan said, "We'll he's not going to get anywhere near Piper with all the security now. I presume you and Dakota are headed here?"

"We are. Adam, and our cousin, Hawk, too. And no doubt Piper's dad."

"Good." Donovan said. "As for Cruze, we know his skills and what to watch for. What we don't know is anything about King. But we're working on it. Keep me updated on Cruze."

As Donovan walked away cussing up a storm, Maverick joined Piper.

Maverick said, "What's going on?"

She laid it out there knowing it wouldn't go well. "Cruze has been in the wind two or three days. The FBI figures—"

He interrupted with restrained fury, "I knew it. He's coming for you."

"It looks like it."

Maverick leaned down. Eye level. "I'm going to kill him, Piper."

"He'll never get close to me, Maverick. Look at the people here. And Sean's flying in. Dakota, Adam, and Hawk are driving in. And you know Dad will show up." She paused with a bit of irritation. "And don't forget, I do have a gun."

"Easy, Piper. That's not the point. Who's Hawk?"

"Their cousin. He's a great guy. A retired Navy Seal. Quite a hunk too."

Maverick said, "I'm not surprised considering the family. But I'm glad he's coming. He brings a whole new set of skills to the party." He touched her face. "Cruze and King can't have you, Piper. You're mine."

She smiled and said, "While my…I Am Woman vibes are offended, my heart kind of likes that kind of talk, Detective. Other parts of me too."

He didn't care who was in the room - he kissed her. Wolf whistles echoed.

Sergeant yelled, "Patterson! Get over here."

Maverick watched Dante laugh like a hyena in the podcast office as they crossed the room.

The Sergeant noticed Agent Donovan's chuckle, and said, "What? You knew about them?"

"I had a little warning. Not much, mind you. And give him a break. They just got some bad news. I expected him to lose it a bit."

"What bad news?"

Maverick and Piper stopped in front of them.

The Sergeant said, "Give me the bad news."

Maverick wasn't sure how much he could reveal about a private FBI case and looked at Agent Donovan for clearance.

Donovan said, "Look Sergeant, we've got a renegade FBI agent in the wind. It's presumed he is on his way to New Orleans."

The Sergeant looked at Piper. "For you."

"I'm afraid so."

"Why?"

"I was undercover on a sting targeting him. We fought. I shot him and kicked out a couple of his teeth. I'm pretty sure this is a revenge trip."

"How skilled is he?"

"An excellent experienced agent."

"This day gets better and better. Please, give me good news."

Maverick said, "Piper and I are getting married tomorrow."

"You're serious."

"I don't need permission, Sir. I'm not even on the clock."

Piper struggled not to smile. Agent Donovan didn't care. He laughed, liking Maverick even more than he already did.

The Sergeant took a deep breath and looked at Agent Donovan. "I've never had a detective married to an agent."

Donovan shrugged. "Not much I can do. She's not really on the clock either."

***

After the bosses brought the agents and the NOPD up to speed on the new threat to Piper, security settled in for the night. The bosses headed out.

Maverick, Piper, and three other agents from the FBI field office gathered around the victim boards. They reviewed and discussed the statistics on all three women. They found two linking factors:

One) The color and length of their hair

Two) They vanished after visiting a tourist site

Maverick said, "We don't have much to go on. It looks like he targeted a brunette sightseer each month for three months. And they simply never returned to their rooms. Let's go ahead and listen to the podcast conversation again."

And it didn't take long. The short conversation left them with more questions than answers.

Piper said, "The point of contact for me had to be the riverboat. We talked about the podcast in detail at dinner. I even introduced us to Count Dracula with our full names. King had the information he needed to set up tonight's call."

Maverick pointed to a large poster. I think we need to map out the riverboat dining room. And based on what the five of us recall, piece together the people around us, and go from there."

Piper said, "Agreed. When will the riverboat security footage arrive? Hopefully we'll have a suspect by tomorrow afternoon."

Maverick looked at the wall clock. "Mid-morning, hopefully. Your dad should be in before that. What about Dakota and the others?"

Piper said, "They'll arrive late tonight."

***

Somewhere in the dark, a door slammed.

Cruze woke to pain. He moved and heard chains. Felt them. And smelled hay. He struggled to get his bearings, unable to remember anything but walking behind his camper.

A bright light blinded him. He closed his eyes to the extra pain it caused.

A man chuckled, then said, "I bet your head is killing you."

Cruze ignored him, squinting. Raising a hand to block the light.

The man said, "You don't appreciate my attempt at humor?"

Cruze grunted, sitting up. His mouth was dry. He coughed. "Who are you?"

"Wrong question. Try again."

Cruze realized he was here for a reason. "Why am I here?"

"Now you are on the right track. Continue. Show me how smart you are Special Agent Cruze Taylor."

Cruze's mind worked through the puzzle he sat in. No one knew he was in New Orleans. Not yet. He was sure of it. Had he stumbled onto something in this city of over a million people? He had hardly spoken to anyone. All he had done was watch Piper a few times. He cussed viciously.

The man smiled. "Go ahead, spit it out."

"Piper."

"You are smart. I respect that. Too bad you got in my way."

"Then let me get out of the way."

"You already are. Nice and tidy, chained in my barn. Now, ask your first question."

Cruze knew he was a dead man. Absolutely knew it, but obediently asked to buy time, "Who are you?"

"You can call me King. Though in your profession, I'm a serial killer, perpetrator, criminal, offender, or psycho. But in my description, I'm a hunter. An excellent one. And Piper is mine."

"I can help you."

"Too late. After what I found on your computer, you're already being hunted. Though you do make it more interesting."

The blinding light went out. "Sleep well, Cruze."

Sitting in the dark, Cruze tried to lick his lips. He was dying of thirst. In New Orleans no less. A place surrounded by water. How was that for irony.

***

Back in New Orleans, a black pickup pulled up in front of the podcast studio at two in the morning. Patrol officers watched as three men got out of the truck.

The driver flashed a badge and said, "FBI Special Agent Dakota Nash. They're expecting us."

"Copy that. Go on in."

Piper looked up as the door opened. Dakota, Adam, and Hawk walked in with duffel bags. Three fine men with obvious Native American heritage. Sex appeal in abundance. And Sean hadn't even arrived yet.

Piper jogged over and disappeared into Dakota's hug. Then Adam's. She got a side hug and a smile from Hawk. Maverick joined them and met Hawk.

Dakota said, "What's up with all the tattoos, Maverick?"

"Undercover tats. I'm kind of enjoying the wild look. But I didn't expect to get married in them."

Adam shook hands with Maverick. "Congratulations on taming her. Need a preacher?"

"Yes, actually. Though I don't know if taming is the right word."

They laughed. It wasn't.

"I knew the wedding would be fast," Dakota said. "I made a bet with Gabrielle."

Piper said, "How much did you bet?"

"A new horse that you'd be married in a week. So, I won. But enough on that. Let's talk about Cruze and King."

Maverick said, "Come meet everyone and we'll show you what we've got."

***

As the sun rose, Dekker landed in New Orleans after traveling all night. Ten minutes later he was on his way to the podcast studio. Sean landed fifteen minutes later from his Colorado flight. He headed in the same direction.

Dante and Jinx were already up making breakfast burritos and coffee for the crew.

Three new agents swapped shifts with co-workers that hadn't slept much.

Dakota was on the phone because of news vans already lining up outside.

And Hawk and Adam took a walk outside to scope the area.

***

Maverick finished his first cup of coffee and went upstairs. He slipped into Piper's room and locked the door. He had fought to get her in the bed just three hours ago. Now, he looked forward to getting her out of it. The courthouse opened at eight-thirty, and he had a plan.

Kicking off his shoes, he slid under the covers and scooped her in his arms. Desire hit him hard at the smell of her. The heat. The softness.

Piper felt the evidence. Her eyes opened…sleepy, but aware. "Hey, baby."

His lips closed over hers as he rolled on top of her. "We've got to go. How long will it take you to get ready?"

"An hour once we get to the loft. What time is it?"

"Almost seven. You ready to marry me?"

Her smile hit him in the gut. He kissed her, loving her so much it hurt.

***

On the street, Adam and Hawk split up and walked the perimeter of the neighborhood. Other than a few vehicles on the road, three joggers, and an old man walking his dog, Adam didn't see anything out of place and returned to the studio.

Hawk startled two guys doing an early morning drug deal. They quickly scattered. And just before he got back to the studio, an old dog took a liking to him and followed. Tail wagging, snout nudging his hand for a rub every few steps.

Hawk joined Adam by Maverick's truck and watched the officers keep the reporters back.

Adam asked, "See anything?"

"Nothing related to all this. The drug deal I messed up was another thing. They're probably still running."

Adam chuckled. Hawk said, "How about we sweep Maverick's truck for a tracker. Does Dakota have an inspection mirror in his truck?"

"Not that I know of. I bet the police do. Hang on."

He returned with a long-handled mirror, and Hawk started on the bottom of the vehicle. Adam climbed into the bed of the truck to check.

A black SUV pulled up. Dekker walked over.

Adam smiled, running his hand under the side rail, and said, "Hey, Uncle Dekker. I heard you were on your way. Looking good for an old man."

Dekker laughed. "Morning, Adam. Hey, Hawk. It's been a while."

Hawk saluted him. "Hey, Dekker. I like that suit."

"Yeah. Me too." Dekker looked in the back of the truck and said, "It looks like you boys think Maverick got tagged."

Adam popped off a black magnetic case from under the rail. He held it up and said, "You were right, Hawk."

Dekker frowned. Not good. Not good at all.

Hawk nodded. "Let's make sure there are no more hidden toys."

Dakota came outside to join them. "Good to see you, Dekker."

"Uncle Dekker to you, boy." Dakota laughed and Dekker said, "How's Piper?"

"Doing good. Maverick just went upstairs to wake her."

"I'll just bet he did."

The men laughed. Respectfully, in front of Piper's CIA father.

Dakota glanced at Adam. "Did you tell Dekker?"

"Not yet. Hawk had an urge to check for bugs. I found this tracker."

Dakota said, "That's a Cruze toy."

Adam handed it to him. "I don't think he'll put another unless he wants a bullet."

Dekker interrupted, "Wait a minute. Back up. Tell me what?"

"You made it just in time," Dakota said. "We're security for a wedding this morning."

Dekker smiled and headed inside as he texted Nicole: Piper's getting married this morning.

Another black SUV pulled up. Sean was here.

Chapter 8

Piper and Maverick jogged downstairs as Dekker came through the front door.

In a second, Piper was in his arms. "I'm glad you're here for the wedding, Daddy."

"Me too. I just texted your mom to let her know."

Maverick urged Piper out the door, and said, "Let's talk in the truck, we have to go."

Piper called over her shoulder, "Hurry up, Dante and Jinx!"

Outside, Sean played catch up with Dakota, Adam, and Hawk.

As the others joined them, Sean gave Piper a bearhug. "Hey, cuz. How's your arm?"

She grinned. "Like the arm matters anymore with two cases fighting for first place."

Dante noticed Dakota slip a black box in another agent's pocket. What was that? He looked at Jinx to see if she noticed. She shrugged and whispered, "Agent stuff."

Maverick unlocked his truck.

Sean said, "Hey, wait up, Maverick. Let's go in my SUV. It's warmed up and ready to go. I've got room for eight and it looks like Jinx hardly counts. She's itty bitty."

Jinx said, "Really? We haven't even met yet."

"We have now. Hop in. I'm Sean."

Jinx asked Piper, "Are your cousins always bossy?"

"Where do you think I got it from?"

Dakota tossed his truck keys to Adam. "Why don't you and Hawk follow us? Leave Maverick's truck here - and keep an eye out for a tail."

***

South of New Orleans, King took a sip of coffee and opened the back door to let the cat in. A beautiful leopard Bengal with green eyes. She rubbed against his legs and gave a unique purr. Soft. Distinct. Almost a musical whisper. He'd know her sound anywhere.

He sat at the table and opened Cruze's laptop to check the tracker. Cruze had been helpful in so many ways. He'd been in the way, true – but still helpful in the long run. The pictures he'd found on his phone had been a bonus. As well as all the notes on Maverick and Piper. Now he knew there was a loft. A boat. And where the tracker was.

He tapped the app on the monitor. It opened. And the green light at the podcast studio still hadn't moved since he'd been on the air last night. He smiled, imagining the commotion as the broadcast ended. And then his smile faded as the green light vanished. Just like that. The tracker was dead.

His jaw clenched. He was annoyed. And someone usually paid when he was annoyed. Obviously, the tracker had been discovered. Which meant, Cruze put it in a lousy place. He glanced at the barn while tapping his finger on the table.

After a long thoughtful moment, he took another drink of coffee and stood. The door closed behind him.

***

Cruze had slept off and on as he sat chained to the wall all night. His head pounded like a never-ending sledgehammer and flies buzzed around the dried blood on his head. His tongue felt like a glue dot and was beginning to stick to the inside of his cheek. He'd unstuck it once during the night and tore the skin. His own blood had been the only liquid he'd swallowed since he'd been taken.

He wondered, had it been one day, or two?

The barn door opened.

Cruze watched the man draw closer. The metal cage door grated open, loud in the stillness.

King squatted in front of Cruze and fondled a plastic bottle of water. He knew the crackling sound teased the man dying for a drink. He said, "Tell me about Maverick's loft."

Grimacing, Cruze couldn't moisten his mouth. He looked at the water bottle. Unscrewing the cap, King handed it to him. He had come prepared for what he wanted. And until the bottle was empty, the only sounds were of water being gulped, crinkling plastic, and breathing.

The bottle dropped to the ground and Cruze coughed. Clearing his throat, he said hoarsely, "Maverick's loft is on the fourth floor. Tons of windows. But heavy security. Cameras. Lights. Lots of traffic."

"You didn't plan to take her there."

"No. Not inside. The parking lot, possibly. Or somewhere she was alone."

King nodded. Made sense. Maverick was big and would fight to kill. He said, "They found your tracker on the truck. You didn't hide it very well."

Cruze laughed. "And I presume you did nothing to make them look."

King appreciated his adept reasoning skills. Without responding to the remark, he said, "Tell me about the sailboat."

"Medium sized. Not much room to hide. Easier to ambush than the loft – at night anyway. But there is still uncontrollable traffic at the wharf. And no room for mistakes unless you plan to swim."

King stood and put his hands in his pockets. He admitted, "They know about me. Give me some insight into who will be protecting her."

With a laugh that made him cough, Cruze caught his breath, and said, "Her dad is CIA. Her boyfriend is a detective. A big man. Two cousins are agents and another one a search and rescue specialist. That's not counting the FBI, the NOPD, friends, and family. Who won't be protecting her is the appropriate question. Ambush is the way to go."

"I just want to know the players. My plan brings her to me."

"There's no way they'll expose her to you."

King laughed, "You have no idea how wrong you are. I have bait they can't refuse. And the whole world is watching."

***

In the SUV's middle bench seat, Maverick moaned. "Piper, please tell me you have your birth certificate with you and that it's not in the moving truck."

"I have it. I kept my important papers with me. They're at the loft. But that reminds me. The moving truck will arrive today. I need to send them directions to unload."

From the back bench seat, Jinx said, "Sorry I'm listening, but I've got room in the gym. It's not like I can have classes right now."

Piper said, "Jinx. I owe you. That would be perfect."

"You don't owe me. In fact, as horrible as it sounds, do you know how many people tuned into the podcast listening to King last night?"

"It never occurred to me."

"Half a million."

"Good grief. What's normal?"

"I usually run around 200,000 on Sunday nights."

Maverick said, "You're up there with the big dogs now, Jinx."

As chuckles faded, Dante said, "If you give the moving company my name and number, Piper. I'll tend to them for you. Obviously, I took off work for a few days."

"You rock, Dante. I appreciate it. I'm sorry you missed work."

"Look, I'm headed to a wedding with a security detail. A crazy man is calling the podcast. And I get to help a hotshot agent. I'll have stories around the coffee pot for days. I'll be THE man."

Everyone laughed.

Dakota asked from the front passenger seat, "What do you do, Dante?"

"Fly helicopters to oilfield rigs in the Gulf of Mexico. It's not boring. Maybe not secret agent category, but it's still not boring."

Smiling, Dakota said, "You are entertaining, Dante."

"And curious. What was the little black box you gave the agent before we left?"

Sean looked in the rearview mirror and drawled, "You're not entertaining anymore."

Maverick and Piper said at the same time, "What black box?"

Next to Piper, Dekker spoke up, "Adam and Hawk found a tracker on your truck. They'll run it for prints, but we figure Cruze put it there."

Maverick and Piper looked at each other. Thoughts in tandem. Cruze had been within striking distance. Why had he waited?

Maverick said, "Piper, that's it. We're not thinking about anything but the wedding right now. This several hours is ours."

A thought hit her, and she gasped. "Maverick, I don't have a ring for you."

He squeezed her hand. "We're good. I have my grandparents' matching gold bands. An heirloom. They're beautiful and engraved, even though I can't read them."

Smiling, she said, "It sounds perfect."

After a pause, Dekker said, "Why can't you read them?"

Maverick said, "I was adopted. My mother was from Norway based on my birth certificate."

Piper explained, "It's an intriguing, but sad story. His mother gave birth to him a few hours after they arrived in New York. He's American by the space of a few hours."

Dekker said, "I can't imagine. That had to leave you with a million questions, Maverick. But it does explain a few things."

"Like his size," Dakota said.

Maverick pointed at the driveway and said, "Enough about Norway. Sean, please just park this car."

Sean said, "Sure, Viking. I remember Samantha and I rushing to get married...every minute seemed like an hour."

"That would be accurate. So, hurry."

As they piled out of the car and headed to the building, Piper's phone rang with a video call.

Piper answered, "Mom! I'm so glad you called. Where are you?"

"Hi, sweetie. My plane just landed in Switzerland. Your dad texted me about the wedding. I'm so happy for you. I've heard about Maverick, but shouldn't I at least meet him before I'm his mother-in-law?"

Piper turned the phone to Maverick. "Meet my mom."

Maverick stopped. His smile froze as he stared at the spitting image of Piper. Everyone laughed. Maverick held the phone by Piper's head and looked at them side by side. He said, "Ms. Pierce—"

Laugh fading, she said, "Nicole. Please."

He started walking again. "Nicole then. And the resemblance is shocking. Obviously, Dekker got left out of Piper's looks entirely."

Nicole said, "True! But she is him in every other way. But speaking of looks, I see why she is taken with you. And…based on the speed you are walking; you are eager to marry her."

"And I am not shy about it. Though, I am sorry for the circumstances and the rush. I do look forward to meeting you in person, Nicole. Rest assured that I love your daughter."

They stopped at the elevator.

Piper said, "I love you, Mom. We'll take a few pictures, I promise. We've got to go…see you soon."

Only Dekker, Jinx, and Dante followed Maverick and Piper inside the loft. Dekker kept watch by the window and Jinx and Dante headed to the kitchen.

Maverick and Piper gathered their birth certificates and rings. Then packed a few summer clothes in a small bag. It was a warm late February day, so Maverick wanted to take her on the sailboat. Away from everyone. So, while Piper went to the master bedroom to shower and dress, Maverick headed to the guest bathroom.

***

In the kitchen, Dante and Jinx worked quickly. Dante pulled the cooler out of the utility room and put it on the snack bar. Along with champagne and a bucket. He put ice in it and wrapped glasses in a thick rag to keep them from breaking.

Jinx pulled deli items from the refrigerator – shocked at the abundant choices. After slicing everything for finger food and sandwiches, she sealed it in containers. In the freezer, she found bakery rolls - toasted and sliced them - and put them in a zipper bag. She went back to the freezer for something they could use for a wedding cake. She found a small round almond and cherry cheesecake. Smiling, she carried it to the cooler.

She picked up a squirt can of whip cream out of the cooler. She looked at Dante and whispered, "Really?"

"Maverick put it in his fridge. I just found it. Nothing wrong with slipping and sliding in whip cream on a sailboat. There's plenty of water to wash it off. Or eat—"

Jinx said, "Dante! Too much information."

Across the room, Dekker said, "I can hear you."

Dante said, "See. Dekker gets it."

Jinx glanced mischievously at Dekker's back. "Hey, Dekker. Have you talked to Luna?"

Dekker turned from the window and looked at Jinx over the top of his sunglasses. And that look said so many things.

Jinx instigated, "She was into you."

Dante took the can from her and warned, "You are poking the bear, Jinx. Don't get me killed trying to protect you over whip cream."

Dekker smiled and turned back to the window. Luna was definitely into him.

Dante squirted whip cream on the end of his finger and looked at Jinx. "Lick it off."

She shook her head no. He smiled and took a step. She backed up. Dante followed. She ended up in the hall against the wall.

He licked her lips and whispered, "Have you ever had whip cream on skin?"
She didn't answer. She couldn't.
He said softly, "Open your mouth."
"Dante—"
"Just…open your mouth."
She did, and he slid his finger in. His eyes closed at the hot sensation that made him want to be anywhere with Jinx but here. His lips replaced his finger.

***

Pulling on jeans in the spare bedroom after the fastest shower in history, Maverick thought about Piper. She was his forever…pure fire. As lovers. Friends. Including professional adventures. And one day soon, parents. He couldn't wait to watch her belly grow with his babies. Second generation American Norwegians. He'd have a real family with the love of his life.
He slipped on a white shirt and buttoned it, seeing tattoos through it. He zipped his jeans, then stepped into boots he wouldn't need once they were on the boat. He clipped on his gun, grabbed his jacket and checked the time. Piper wouldn't be ready for at least another thirty minutes. He headed to the kitchen.

And as luck would have it, Maverick had a front row seat to what happened with the whip cream. Startling Dante and Jinx, he said, "Maybe we should pick up another marriage license today. Or at least an extra can of whip cream."
Dante looked at Jinx. She licked the whip cream off her lip.

Across the room, Dekker just laughed.

Dante kissed Jinx. "We will pick up this conversation later."
"This was not a conversation."
"It absolutely was a conversation, and I heard all of it."
Pushing him back, she said, "You forget I know self-defense."
"And I'm your spar partner. I know all your moves."

Maverick laughed, "Sorry, Jinx. That was a good comeback. Now, y'all come show me what's in the cooler. Besides whip cream."

***

In the bedroom, Piper stood at the vanity in heels putting the last touches on her light makeup. Nothing exotic for a morning wedding, but still sexy. Just enough eyeliner and mascara to give her eyes a sultry pop, then pink lipstick. And after putting on pearls, she dabbed perfume in all the important places.

She picked up the white dress lying on the bed. She'd bought it the day before she moved to New Orleans…four days ago. Holding it in front of her, she swayed, feeling it brush against her skin.

Made of silk and white cotton, it was a deep V wraparound that stopped mid-thigh. Long sleeves. Ruffles around the edges. Light and fluttery. Fabulously feminine. And only one tie at the waist held it up.

She slipped it on. Tied the belt. And standing still, she smiled. This was the only time the dress appeared demure. And then she spun. Wide slits from her shoulder to wrist flared open on each arm. At the same time the front flapped open all the way to her waist – revealing tiny panties.

White ones. A whisper of lace for a husband.

She glanced at Maverick's side of the bed. He was everything she'd been scared to dream of. And now, hers for a lifetime. Her husband. She touched her stomach. And the father of her children. Love was so much more than sexual. And age wouldn't stop it. Nothing could. What stopped magic?

She headed toward the door. It was past time.

***

Maverick heard Piper's high heels and was in the hall as she opened the bedroom door. They looked at each other. Love palpable as the moment swept over them. Maverick said over his shoulder, "Please…give us the room."

After quick footsteps, the door opened and closed.

Maverick picked her up. High. His face against her heart. Her head fell back, fingers in his hair. Knowing love like this was extraordinary.

Maverick kissed her. "You're gorgeous, Piper. So, very beautiful. I'm just so sorry to rush you – barely giving you time to say our vows, before we rush to the boat."

She said softly, "I said vows when I walked out of your bedroom in a black leather bikini and danced for you. Gave myself to you. And I look forward to the hours on the boat today. Our life will always be fast. We need to take the time we get."

And then he said it. The thing he worried about. "You're rich, Piper. I can't compete with that."

Grateful he finally addressed it, she said, "Listen to me, Maverick. I was born into money. I didn't earn it. It sits in a bank account. I'm like you, I live on what I earn. Sure, there are times I access it. Like everyone with a savings account. But it's not who I am. And your bank account is not who you are.

Our children will never have to worry about finances. And we won't. Can't we be blessed knowing that?"

"As long as you tell me when you want to use it. That way, it gives me the opportunity to see if I can find another way."

She smiled. "I can do that."

***

Twenty minutes later, Sean pulled into the Ceasars Superdome parking garage and followed the signs to Benson Tower parking. Vital Records was in office 407 in the tower.

Dante glanced at the Superdome and said, "I wonder how many people get drunk at an event and run across the street and get married?"

Laughter filled the SUV. Only Dante would think of that.

A couple of minutes later, Adam and Hawk parked next to them, and all nine headed inside.

***

The click of high heels and the large number of heavy footsteps made the two women at the Vital Records counter glance up. Maverick and Piper entered the office as the others watched from the hall. Guns visible.

One woman left without a word to get the manager. The older woman at the counter glanced from Maverick to Piper and said, "May I help you?"

Maverick smiled. "We need a marriage license for a wedding today." They slid their identification and badges across the counter.

The woman said. "You do realize Louisiana has a 24-hour waiting period? Although it can be waived—"

Maverick said, "May I speak with the judge?"

The manager had just walked in, heard the question, and turned around to get the judge. It wasn't long, and with a bit of a grin, the judge entered with a cup of coffee.

He glanced at the badges on the counter and raised his cup to them. "I'm Judge Williams. I understand you are in a hurry for a wedding."

Maverick said, "Yes, Your Honor." He put his arm around Piper and said, "This is FBI Special Agent Piper Pierce, and I am Detective Maverick Patterson of the NOPD. We need a waiver to get married immediately. She was forced to take the lead role in a case which now requires a great deal of time and security. So, today is the day."

"Not tomorrow."

"No."

The Judge said, "I see. Will you need me to perform the ceremony?"

"No, Your Honor. Reverend Adam Nash is with us."

Maverick motioned Adam in. Adam slid his identification across the counter with a smile that had the women in the office whispering.

The judge leaned on the counter and looked at Piper. He said, "You know, this man is intent on marrying you today."

Everyone in the office chuckled.

Piper smiled. "I do. He's not shy about it."

The Judge laughed and said, "If you're an agent and he's a detective, who's going to be boss in your house?"

Maverick laughed. "Two alphas. Believe me, both."

The judge chuckled. "You're smart, and lucky." He flashed his wedding ring and winked. "My wife's an attorney. Best arguments ever."

They laughed as he reached for the form. After signing off on the waiver, he said, "Congratulations."

In minutes, they left with the license and found the first available nook with a semblance of privacy. And after a five-minute wedding, Maverick dipped and kissed his bride.

***

Back in the vehicle, they left for the sixteen-mile drive to South Shore Harbor Marina on Lake Pontchartrain. Everyone in the car felt the intimacy of the moment for the couple.

Maverick rubbed the engraved gold band he'd just placed on Piper's finger. "You deserve a limo ride, diamonds, flowers, and a million other things today. It never occurred to me that we'd get married on the run and have security deliver us to our honeymoon rendezvous."

Piper smiled. "Rendezvous works for me every time, Detective."

He kissed her.

Chapter 9

Maverick carried Piper down the wharf. Dakota and Sean led the way to check the boat. Dekker and Adam followed with their bags and the cooler.

Once the boat was cleared, they discussed security.

Dakota opened the recorder app on his phone and said, "We need the coordinates if you know where you're headed."

Maverick pulled up Google maps. "Here you go… Latitude: 30.03805910. Longitude: -90.01557590. Or, within that general vicinity."

"Got it."

Sean handed a very small clear patch to Piper. Plastic. With a black dot in the center.

She said, "Is this what I think it is?"

"It's a tracker—"

"You've lost your mind. I am not wearing a tracker on my honeymoon. Stick it somewhere else."

After the laughter, Maverick dropped it in his pocket and said, "Thank all of you for today. But as of this moment, no contact. Give us four hours. We're off grid until two this afternoon. I mean it. I don't care what happens anywhere but on this boat."

With a salute, the guys headed back down the wharf.

Maverick wrapped an arm around Piper and said, "Hang on."

Piper gasped as swung across to the boat. He touched her lips, "You've been captured by a Viking. You're mine for a lifetime."

He kissed her. Then tossed his jacket. His shirt. And his boots in the cabin. Barefoot in jeans and tattoos, blonde hair blowing in the wind, he led her to the helm and wrapped her hands around the wheel.

Behind her, he said, "Stay here and get the feel of her. I'll get us untied and then we are headed across the water. How does that sound, my lady?"

She whispered, "Hurry…"

He pressed against her back, running his hands down her stomach to linger possessively at the place he intended to go. And with a neck kiss, he was gone. Piper watched as he climbed around the boat and prepared to sail. Nimble.

Muscles flexing as he worked. Totally at home in this environment. He untied the boat and pushed away from the dock.

Smiling, he jumped down. "Do you need to go below before we take off?"

"I need to braid my hair. It won't take me long."

Downstairs in the tiny bathroom, Piper braided her hair thinking only about this new side of Maverick. Just how many sides did he have? She hurried back to the deck.

Maverick looked down in the cabin at the same time she jogged up the steps. The wind caught her dress and opened it, revealing that she was naked…except for panties. She smiled at the look on his face and posed. Maverick seared that image forever. White ruffles and beauty. His wife.

Pulling her lips to his, he kissed her. Hungry. Breathing deep as he inhaled her. "You are magnificent."

She kissed his chest. "I thought the dress would please you."

"You please me."

Drawing her in front of him, he started the engine. And before long they skimmed the waves to his private place.

Passion raged as they caressed on their journey. Eager. Breathless. And impatient until boat traffic faded.

Then under fluttering ruffles Maverick slid Piper's panties down and tossed them behind him. The small strip of lace danced in the wind, then rode the next gust off the back of the boat. Kissing Piper's neck, he unzipped his pants. And bracing himself on the rolling deck, he lifted her.

***

Maverick maneuvered the boat into a mini cove on the north edge of the lake. Uninhabited and marshy with a few large trees that helped hide the boat.

In her bikini now, Piper said, "I can't find my panties. I bet they blew out of the boat."

Chuckling, he said, "No doubt. Just think how excited a fisherman will be one day when he reels them in instead of a fish. I can imagine the stories he will tell."

"That's disgusting. Only a man would think dirty panties are erotic."

"Because a man knows how that hot tiny piece of lace got in the water in the first place."

"Regardless. I wouldn't touch strange men's underwear without gloves on if you paid me."

Maverick laughed as he took off his jeans and put on shorts…without underwear.

Piper said, "Where are yours?"

"In the way."

They settled on top of the cabin for a long while. Piper snuggled between his legs. Talking. Flirting. Just being together. The breeze was light, the sun warm, and the sound of water and slow rocking of the boat was perfect.

Maverick kissed her shoulder. Piper smiled and touched his wedding ring. He said, "I'm sorry my lineage is such a mystery. Hopefully the engraving on the rings is something worthy of you. I should find out."

She kissed him and said, "They are wedding rings. Surely, the engraving is a vow or commitment befitting the time they were made." Holding hers up, she said. "I claim they represent a great love from across the ocean. I refuse to think they're anything else considering we have them."

He kissed her. "I love you, Piper."

"I love you. And…I have a present for you."

"Give me a hint."

She stood and unclasped her top, tossing it in his lap. Then slowly. Very slowly, lowered her bottoms. And with her toe, tossed them in his lap too. She walked toward the mast and Maverick knew exactly what she was going to do.

She danced naked. For a minute. Almost two. Until he dropped his shorts. Laughing, she jumped the rail, landing on the deck. He swung over and blocked her path. And she wasn't near fast enough to get away. Not fast enough at all.

***

Back at the marina, Dekker looked at the news vans in a distant parking lot. "That's annoying."

Sean said, "But not surprising."

"What's your plan while they're off on the boat?"

"Adam and Hawk will stay here and keep an eye on the marina. Dakota and I are heading back to the podcast studio with Dante and Jinx. The public request for pictures on the riverboat has hit the news. Lots of messages are coming in. Why don't you take a break, Dekker. You probably haven't slept after flying all night."

"I slept some on the flight. I'm good. I think I'll grab a cab and run an errand. I'll be back here before they return at two o'clock. Call me if anything changes. I won't be far."

The SUV left.

Adam and Hawk split up for surveillance.

And Dekker called a cab.

***

South of New Orleans, King threw a glass against the wall. It shattered. The news had eagerly shared a video of Maverick carrying Piper down a wharf in a white dress. They had gotten married.

He growled. Piper hadn't taken him seriously. Now he was moving the game up. The first game piece would be in place tonight. How was that for a wedding present?

***

At the LSU Healthcare Network medical center not far from her house, Luna clocked out. She headed down the hall to the main entrance. Her phone chimed with a text. She checked while walking out to the sidewalk. It was Dekker.

Dekker: Hey there. You busy?

Luna: No. Perfect timing. Just leaving work. I took a few days off. How are you?

Dekker: I've been thinking about you.

Luna: Glad to know I'm not the only one.

Dekker smiled: You are charming. And beautiful.

Luna teased: I bet you've forgotten what I look like already.

Dekker: Hardly. And do me a favor.

Luna: Sure.

Dekker: Turn around.

She stopped but didn't turn. He stepped behind her and slid his hands down her arms. "I'd never forget what you look like."

She turned gracefully. Her blue eyes mixed with shock and something else. "Dekker."

He smiled. She was gorgeous in pink scrubs and a ponytail. "Hey."

"I never dreamed I'd see you today."

"Things changed. I'll be in New Orleans a while longer it seems." He paused. "I have a few hours free."

She thought of the dance and felt the rush. She looked at his lips, then his eyes. He read the answer and kissed her. A hot one. He was starving and couldn't imagine a time when he wouldn't be.

He said, "I know you don't live far from here; did you walk?"

"I did. Do you have a vehicle?"

"A taxi dropped me off." He removed his jacket and said, "A walk sounds good." He slipped an arm around her.

They walked the short distance. Their glances telling. Dekker's hand slid to her hip and pulled her closer. She leaned into him, wrapping an arm around his waist. Dipping her fingers under his waistband just enough to be intimate. He kissed her, hooked like a fish on a treble hook.

She said, "I…I do need to shower when I get home. It's the nature of working around sick people. It won't take—"

"Do what you need to do, Luna. I'm not going anywhere."

About ten houses later, she pointed up ahead to her Honda. Only one more house to go.

Dekker said, "Say the words, Luna. I know what they are, but I still want to hear them. Are you good with this?"

"No," she whispered. "I'm dying for this."

He groaned and pulled her with him as he increased the pace. To the driveway. The steps. The porch. She pulled out her keys, but he took them and unlocked the door - kissing her while he carried her in.

Breathless, Luna backed toward the bathroom and said, "I promise. I'll hurry. Five minutes."

He dropped his jacket and gun on a chair. Unsnapped his pants. And unbuttoning his shirt, followed her. She couldn't stop watching him. She dropped her purse. Kicked off her shoes.

Dekker's pants hit the floor. He scooped her up. "Tell me you didn't expect to shower alone…"

***

A few hours later, Hawk heard a sound he'd been expecting at the marina. He looked up, his long-layered hair flying in the wind. A yellow news drone buzzed over, and he knew they were waiting for the boat to return. He texted Adam: It's almost two o'clock. We've got a drone prowling.

He headed to the wharf.

Adam got the message and walked to the marina. He stationed himself at a wharf adjacent to the one Hawk was on. He saw the yellow drone. Then another flew in from his left. A small silver one. He texted Sean, Dakota, Dekker, and Hawk with a heads up.

A taxi stopped, and Dekker got out looking in the sky at the yellow drone. Then, across the lake. No sailboat yet. Dakota and Sean pulled up. They fanned the area.

Another news van sent up a drone. A blue one. Now there were three. But Adam was watching the tiny silver one that was trying to be inconspicuous. It hid among the boat masts as it drew closer to where Hawk sat on the wharf with a fishing pole.

Adam whistled and pointed, not wanting to attract the drone. Hawk nodded and cranked his line in to cast again. The sneaky drone settled on top a post about twenty or so feet away. It was shaped like a dragonfly, or a hornet set for takeoff. Sneaky.

Dekker texted the group: Three sails on the horizon. I'm guessing twenty minutes out.

Adam responded: Hawk's watching a small drone sitting on a post by Maverick's berth.

Sean instructed: When Maverick's boat is in sight, get rid of the drone. Quietly.

Hawk confirmed: I've got quiet ammo. Just watching for boat colors.

Five minutes later, Hawk texted: I see Maverick's boat. Ammo hot.

And with a quick throw, Hawk hummed a two-inch rock that hit the silver drone broadside. It scattered into a cloud of sparkly pieces that disappeared in the water.

Adam texted: Mission accomplished. Hawk, I forgot you were killer at skipping stones.

❖

On the sailboat, Piper had control of the helm. Her instructions had been to keep them headed due south with the engine as Maverick furled the sails. Finished, he jumped to the deck.

Capturing her for another kiss, he said, "If we weren't so close to the marina…"

She batted her eyelashes. "Your loss. You should have been faster rolling the sails."

"Furling."

"Same thing."

Hugging her, he said, "I loved this time with you. But we were too rough. I see marks. You'll have bruises."

She touched his face. "I'm fine, baby. We're both wild and you're a big man. Besides, I'm tough."

Blue eyes met blue eyes. "But your soft place is—"

"Easy, Detective…I see our security detail over your shoulder. And a couple of drones."

He turned to look. "Thanks to the news vans. We need to put on more clothes."

***

In a parking lot across from the marina, King cussed as he lost visual with his silver drone. He looked up. The sailboat would dock before long. He rebooted the drone. Once. Twice. Nothing happened.

He reached in the back for binoculars and watched as the boat drew closer, the engine churning water to slow the boat. And then the engine stopped. Maverick tossed a line to one of the feds he'd seen drive up, only then realizing it was Piper's dad from the riverboat.

Then several other men arrived. Ignoring them, he zoomed in on Piper wearing a short pink sundress. The wind blew it up revealing long beautiful legs, and unfortunately shorts, instead of panties. But she made up for it when she squatted into one of his favorite positions. His pants bulged in appreciation.

And while Piper walked down the wharf with her new husband and security team, he unzipped his pants.

***

Late afternoon, a blonde woman walked into the 8th District of the New Orleans Police Department on Royal Street. Beautiful and tall, with long wavy hair and blue eyes, she was dressed professionally in slacks and heels.

Sasha looked around. It was busy. But she had expected the French Quarter and Central Business District station to be busy. Someone bumped into her. Maybe swamped was a better description than busy.

She had never seen this many wild and colorful people in a police station since…well, ever. Costumes too. And all ages were there. Men. Women. Teenagers. Some waited calmly while scrolling on their phones. Some cried on the shoulder of others. Some in handcuffs kicked and screamed. And others yelled on their phones. No telling how many nationalities were represented. It was truly impressive.

Darting through a break in the wave of people, she got into a long line for the front desk. A young woman held the hand of a little boy in front of her. They weren't concerned at all about the commotion. But then again, neither was she.

Fifteen long, loud minutes later, the front desk officer said with a sharp edge to his voice, "Can I help you?"

Sasha slid her card across the counter and said, "I need to speak with Detective Patterson. Is he in?"

"Nope. He's out for a few days. Do you want to talk to someone else or leave a message?"

"If you would get your sergeant for me, I'll wait."

He looked at the card: Detective Sasha Tate, Tampa, Florida. He said, "Give me a second."

Walking into an office in the back, he talked to a black woman in uniform. She followed him out and walked to the end of the long counter. She motioned for her. Sasha maneuvered through the crowd and followed her into an empty room.

Sasha said, "Thank you for seeing me."

The Sergeant said, "Not that it's going to do you any good. Detective Patterson is in the middle of a case. You'll have to leave him a message. I'll send it myself."

Sasha said, "Understood. Just tell him that his sister is here. My cell number is on the card."

"I know Maverick. He doesn't have a sister."

"He does now."

***

At the podcast studio, the investigation team had divided into two groups. Maverick, Piper, Dekker, Dante, and Jinx made a map of the dining room and worked on who they remembered from Saturday night. The other group sorted messages and pictures sent in based on the news broadcast.

Piper marked on the dining room map:

- Two older couples at a table directly behind Maverick.
- A group of young couples were behind Dante and Jinx.
- Several men were at a table behind her dad. Three maybe.
- And to her front right there had been a group of middle-aged women.
- To her back, there had been lone men at two tables. One on each side of the support column. The one closest to her wore brown. Older. He stared into his phone the couple of times her glance passed his way. And the other man was black. Maybe thirty. She only remembered him making a few calls.

She made notes: Check two men by column and group of three men behind Dad. Then she scrolled pictures on her phone for anything from that night. There were a few pictures from the top deck. And two from the dining room, but no one caught her eye as suspicious.

Her dad sat beside her. She slid her notes to him. He passed her his. They were silent as they studied.

Piper said, "So the three men behind you talked work the whole time."

Dekker said, "Yes. They were at a salesman convention. Everything I heard was tourist oriented. Sights. Food. Costumes. Typical conversations for the riverboat."

"But the two guys by the column—"

"The black man was busy on his phone. Totally social, but not with anyone on the boat. And the man in brown just stared into his phone like he was watching a movie. He didn't engage with anyone at all. Seemed rugged. And his boots were unique too. I couldn't place the leather though. Some type of reptile or animal."

"So, you like the guy in brown to investigate? Any pictures?"

He passed her his phone. "Check the first three pictures."

Piper scrolled. The first picture was a selfie of her and her dad. The edge of a man's face could be seen in the background. He was looking over the top of his phone, part of one gold eye visible behind glasses.

The second picture caught one of his boots. They were western with side stripes – like a tiger or zebra – with a dark strip down the middle. And some type of teardrop or white spot on the top of the foot. Very unusual. That should be easy enough to research.

And the last picture caught the man's side as he stood behind her. A knife stuck out under a brown leather jacket. It had an ivory handle. Carved. She couldn't make out the image.

Piper said, "The boots and knife are interesting. Can you tell what color his eyes are? They look gold to me. That's rare."

"I think so. We'll have to blow up the images. And hopefully Maverick, Dante and Jinx have more info for us. We need to get on this yesterday."

***

Maverick was making notes about the map when his phone rang. It was the desk sergeant.

He answered, "Hey, Sarge. What's up?"

"Hey, Patterson. Detective Sasha Tate from Tampa is here to see you. She insists."

"Why does she want to see me? I'm not working on anything with Tampa."

"She said she's your sister."

Maverick's mind locked on the word sister. That was impossible.

Sarge interrupted his shock and said, "Come on, Patterson. Work with me here. What do I do with her?"

"Sorry, Sarge. That was unexpected. Just for the heck of it, do you mind telling me if we look alike?"

"Tall, blonde, blue eyes, beautiful, bossy. Yeah. Pretty much. Well, a lot now that I'm looking."

"I'll be there in twenty."

"I'll tell her."

Maverick was still grappling with his thoughts when he caught the look on Piper's face.

She said, "Who looks like you?"

"It's crazy. A woman at the station claims to be my sister. A detective from Tampa."

Piper's mouth dropped open. That would never have occurred to her. Now everyone was looking at Maverick.

She said, "But what if she is your sister? You're adopted. It's not impossible. I'll go with you."

"You can't. If it's a ruse…"

Hawk stood, glancing at Adam who followed suit. Hawk said, "Let us bring you and then you won't have to drive or park. We'll keep an eye out, so no one tails us."

Maverick nodded. "That works."

Piper said, "Let me know."

"I will. Stay here. I won't be long."

Maverick tossed his keys to Hawk on the way out the door.

A few minutes later, Piper's phone chimed with a text. Who would be messaging her from an unknown number?

Unknown: Hey, Piper.
Piper responded: Who's this?
Unknown: You know who this is. Are you ready to play with me?

Piper knew who it was. "Heads up, guys…King is texting me. I'm not sure how he got this number." Chairs scraped, then footsteps came behind her. Dakota, Dekker, and Sean read along.

Piper continued with the text: What do you want to play?
Unknown: Be on the podcast tonight. And no other callers till you and I are done.
Piper: Done doing what?
King: Setting up the game. I have a present for you.
Piper: Why wait for the podcast? Tell me now.
King changed the subject: I liked your pink dress on the boat today.
Piper grimaced: You didn't have anything better to do?
King: I want what Maverick obviously got.
Piper: You're not getting anything.
King smiled: You are. A taxi will arrive in a few minutes with a box for you. We'll talk about it on the podcast. Don't be late. The game begins in a few hours.
Piper: Where at?

Piper waited. No more texts.

❖

Dakota went outside to see if a taxi would show up.

Piper sighed, and said, "King's going to start all this tonight. I should have known. Prime time for predators – the middle of the night."

Sean pulled out his drone case, preparing for surveillance. "He needs the darkness to stay hidden. Did you find any pictures of suspicious men on the riverboat?"

Dakota interrupted as he came inside with a beautifully wrapped gift box. The cops brought the terrified taxi driver in for questions.

Sean scanned the gift box. It was clothing. Piper opened it wearing gloves while everyone watched and took pictures.

Piper studied the leopard bodysuit lying in the tissue. Tawny, with black markings. Stretchy. Shiny. Very expensive. There were matching boots with heels higher than she usually wore. And a stunning jeweled cat mask for the upper face. It was gorgeous. Except for the bodysuit crotch zipper that screamed sex toy."

Piper met Sean's gaze and said, "He's got a cat fetish."

"Absolutely…big cats."

"That's alarming."

He said, "Everything about him is alarming. I think he's a hunter. We need to tell Maverick about this."

"Not yet. The podcast isn't for a few hours, and I don't want to interfere with Maverick right now. I want this time with his sister to be real…and special. He'll be busy enough when he returns."

***

Hawk pulled to a stop in front of the police station.

Maverick said, "Just ride around the block. With this traffic it could take you a while. And I should find out quick enough if this is a hoax or not. Just make sure no one follows you. And if anything looks suspicious, call me."

Adam said, "We've got you. Go meet her, Maverick. We're all dying to know."

Maverick walked through the doors of NOPD District 8 and scanned the area. He met the gaze of a beautiful blonde propped against the wall. She smiled and Maverick knew it wasn't a hoax. He saw the smile in the mirror every day. And that was all he knew as he led her to his work area.

As the door shut behind them, Maverick said, "Please, have a seat. Obviously, we're related. But I'm going to need information. What's your name?"

"Sasha. Detective Sasha Tate."

And whether they looked alike or not, he had to play it safe for Piper. "I need to run your driver's license and badge."

"Of course." She laid them on the table.

Maverick took pictures and texted Dakota: Run these for me. He copied Piper.

Keeping it direct, he asked, "What proof do you have that we're siblings?"

She removed a couple of forms from an envelope and laid them on the table. "Our birth certificates. The dates will tell you that we are twins."

Maverick hid the emotion as he took pictures of the forms, then texted Dakota, copying Piper again.

And then he turned to the window and waited on Dakota. Silent. He had to have clearance to proceed any further. He couldn't watch her. Or talk to her. There was no way he could open himself up to more than what he had already been hit with. Not yet.

Sasha waited, giving Maverick time to adjust. She'd had years. He'd known for half an hour.

They waited eight minutes. Dakota texted Maverick: She's legit, man. So are the birth certificates. You have a legal sister.

Maverick turned with the first hint of a smile. "The FBI cleared you, Sasha. But we can't talk here. I've got to get back. Have you checked into a hotel?"

"The FBI? Why? And no to a room. I came straight from the airport."

"You dropped into the middle of a case. That's why the FBI. Well, part of the reason. But for now, do you feel comfortable coming with me? We need time, and I don't have it yet."

"Of course. I knew this would be an unexpected complication for you. I'm good. Whatever you need. Have I mentioned that I'm the oldest?"

He laughed at the unexpected sibling comment.

And Sasha choked on emotion. This was finally happening. She said, "Maverick, you're an amazing man. I feel like I know you because of the research. But I look forward to us getting to know each other. It's taken..." She swallowed the lump in her throat. "So long to find you."

Touching hair so much like his own, he said, "Thank you for looking."

"That's what sisters do."

And he grabbed her in a hug.

On the way out, Maverick messaged Adam and Hawk: Come get us.

As they waited for the truck, he said, "I can't wait for you to meet my wife, Piper."

"Your wife? I didn't see any documents that said you were married."

"I got married this morning."

She moaned. "My timing is lousy. My apologies to your wife."

"Don't apologize. It's a long story. And just so you know, you're about to meet a lot of people." He pointed at the truck pulling to a stop. "Starting with these two guys."

When the door shut, Hawk and Adam turned to look at Maverick and Sasha side by side in the back.

Adam whistled. "There is no doubt you are related."

Hawk said, "And she's beautiful. Her, way more than you, Maverick."

Maverick chuckled, and said, "Sasha, the passenger is Adam, Piper's cousin. And the driver is Hawk, his cousin. Guys, meet Detective Sasha Tate from Tampa. My twin sister."

Sasha smiled at the two gorgeous men. "I'm the oldest. Nice to meet you."

Maverick said, "I've been thinking about that, Sasha. We need to investigate the time. There's no way I would have been last."

***

Sasha frowned as Hawk pulled the truck through news vans along the street. He parked near a large two-story brick building with heavy police protection. She glanced at Maverick.

He said, “Now you know why I needed to get back. Come on in. I know everyone is waiting to meet you.”

Maverick opened the door and ushered Sasha in first. The clapping came next. Cheering. And Sasha watched a stunningly beautiful brunette with a pistol and badge at her hip head straight for them.

Sasha said, “You didn’t mention Piper was FBI.”

Maverick laughed. “Nope.”

Sasha thought…wow.

They met in the middle.

Maverick pulled Piper’s smiling lips to his for a kiss. She touched his cheek knowing what this meant to him. He said, “Piper, meet Sasha. My twin sister.”

Piper hugged Sasha and said, “I’m so impressed you found him. And you are as beautiful as he is handsome. I can’t wait to hear the whole story. I’m sorry all this is going on.”

Sasha said, “And I’m sorry about dropping in on your wedding day. You are a beautiful couple.”

Piper waved her arm toward the investigation bulletin boards, giant video screens, tables, and the team. “Thank you. But you didn’t interfere. You just joined the party.”

Sean, Dakota, and Dekker waved. Sean said bluntly, “Tell him, Piper.”

Maverick recognized Sean’s tone. And noticed the intensity in the room. His eyes met Pipers. “Tell me now. And you can tell me later why you didn’t call me.”

She handed him her phone. “King texted after you left. We don’t know how he got my FBI number.”

He read the text. “Out with it. What did he send you?”

She pointed at the gift box on one of the tables. With long angry strides, he crossed the room as everyone waited for the explosion.

Chapter 10

Maverick looked at the sexy catsuit with a crotch zipper. He barely glanced at the boots and mask as he turned to Piper. Struggling to keep his fury contained, he gritted out, "Forget it."

Though she understood, her temper flared at the order. "That's not your call. Besides, do you think I want to wear it? Of course not."

Face to face in a public argument, Maverick said, "He's setting you up. You know what that costume is. How do you know he didn't require this for the three victims?"

"I don't know. But if I don't wear it and play his game, we may never find them. That, I do know."

"He's going to set up a meet with you on live podcast tonight."

"I know."

"He's going to make you go in alone. It's not happening."

"I'll be wired. I can hide a weapon somewhere in that bodysuit. And you know we can watch him. He's not the government. He doesn't have what we have."

"We don't know who he is, or what he has."

She snapped, "Detective! I need you to make the best plan possible. He is not smarter than we are. And I am not weak. I need you to help me do my job."

They stared at each other as the seconds ticked by. No one made a sound.

Maverick leaned close, his face inches from hers. "I will follow you if I've got to crawl on my belly and no one can stop me. Is that understood, Agent Pierce?"

Piper smiled…and he kissed her.

***

Hawk led Sasha toward a break area with tables, chairs, a drink machine, and a stack of cots with blankets and pillows.

Sasha said, "That was an incredible argument."

Hawk smiled. "Now you know why they got married this morning."

"So, what's in the box that set Maverick off?"

"A podcast caller who calls himself King, sent Piper a sex toy catsuit. A fine one, complete with boots and a jeweled mask."

"A podcast caller? How did he connect with an FBI agent?"

"It's complicated. Have a seat and I'll fill you in as we get to know each other."

She raised her eyebrows. "We met, what? Thirty minutes ago? And you decided to just jump right in there."

He faced her. "And I'll never believe you prefer a man that didn't."

Sasha knew this game well…and he was right. She liked his directness and looked him over. The well used, but fitting description, tall, dark, and handsome, danced through her mind. She loved long hair on a man. She met his gaze again.

Dante and Jinx walked up. Sasha smiled at the couple. But Hawk's gaze lingered on Sasha a little longer. He knew what her look meant. Maybe. He trailed his finger down her arm...message received.

***

South of New Orleans, shadows transformed the barn into darkness as the sun set. In the last of the light, Cruze watched a large wolf spider climb over the chain on his wrist. Then it crawled on top of his hand and paused, front legs raised. King of the mountain. Cruze grinned and his lip split from dryness. He winced but still watched the spider.

He used to hate them, had killed dozens in his life without a thought. But not today. Now he didn't care about anything but that he was going to die chained in a barn. Him, with all his skills and accolades as an FBI agent. It was unbelievable. And even though he'd turned rogue, he didn't deserve this.

Hate twisted his gut. It was Piper's fault.

The barn door creaked open, interrupting his life musings. The overhead lights came on. Cruze squinted and watched the safari dude unlock the cage door.

King looked at the once impressive agent sitting on the ground. He was filthy. Bloody. With deadly eyes and cracked lips. He tossed him a water bottle. It was empty in seconds.

Cruze coughed and wiped his mouth, noticing the guy was armed with more than the usual pistol and knife. A Winchester rifle hung over his shoulder. Cruze met King's gaze. That's when he realized death had come for him.

King smiled, appreciating that the agent knew it was time. He said, "I've got something to show you. A treat. My pet, you might say. She doesn't get out often." He pushed a button on the wall.

Cruze stood at the ominous scraping of a metal door somewhere down the hall. Who keeps a pet behind a metal wall? A deep growl answered that question, and a shiver ran up his spine. He stepped back, hitting the wall. There was nowhere to go.

The thing rounded the corner, and Cruze's mind raced to grasp what he saw. Metal. Fur. Claws. Teeth. Even a tail. And it was huge.

King said with affection, "Vicious…come." And he smiled as his pet rubbed its head on his hip and purred while watching the man in the cage.

Cruze stared. Terrified at what that thing was here for.

King tossed a set of keys to Cruze. "Unlock yourself and follow me."

Cruze didn't move.

"Or" King said, "I'll get her to bring you to me. Which would you prefer?"

In seconds, Cruze's chains clattered to the floor.

King pointed to the barn door, and said, "Go. We'll follow you outside."

Cruze flinched at the spotlights that lit the yard. He squinted, looking around, not surprised to see they were in the country. A pond was between him and the trees in the distance. An old, but impressive white farmhouse with a back porch was across the yard. A small cat lounged on the steps, tail flipping. Several vehicles were in a garage. A gray SUV. A black truck. And a silver BMW.

The startling sound of the bolt action rifle cocking filled the silence. Cruze wanted to throw up, but fear choked him. He wasn't ready for this.

King said, "Run."

Shock kept Cruze in place. Was King going to hunt him? A terrifying roar behind him worked. He ran. Zig zagging until he rounded the right edge of the pond. Jumped a ditch. Climbed a fence and raced for the trees.

He never heard the shot as he landed face first at the edge of the forest.

Dead.

King went for the four-wheeler already fitted with the cart.

***

At eight twenty-seven in the podcast office, Jinx and Piper glanced at the clock. Three minutes till airtime. Maverick, Dakota, and Sean filed in and shut the door. Everyone in the gym had their phones to their ear listening and watching through the window.

Jinx held up three fingers, two, then one.

With high energy, Jinx said, "Hello, New Orleans! And everyone listening from around the world. Welcome to a live podcast on Prepared for Danger – a forum where the critical importance of self-defense is addressed.

"But before we begin, I need to bring up the shocking call during last night's show. Many of you will remember the caller, named King, that claimed responsibility for three missing brunettes in the local area. He also challenged Agent Pierce with the FBI to find him or become the next victim.

"And as it turns out, his calls on air are not over. Therefore, as a podcast community, we will support Agent Pierce and the authorities because he plans to call tonight. Right now. Which means, I ask everyone with self-defense questions to please hold your calls until after his call is over.

"So now, Agent Pierce, I turn the show over to you. And King…the lines are open. Call 504-defense."

A single line began to blink.

Piper answered line one. "This is Agent Pierce. You are on the air."

King said, "You're using your maiden name, Piper. As a new bride, you and I would be having a serious talk if you were mine."

"Then it's a good thing I'm not. In fact, I don't even know you. Why don't you tell me something about yourself. Fill the listeners in."

"I have no problem sharing with the world that I'm looking forward to seeing you in the catsuit I sent you today. It's a hot little number, isn't it?"

"What's another costume? Mardi Gras is barely over. I'd rather find out when I'm supposed to wear it."

"In a few hours. Tell me…did you find the hidden zipper?"

"Don't be crude, King. Surely you can do better than that. If you want the conversation to continue, make it worth my while."

"My game. My rules. If you want the women."

"That's what I'm here for – but you could have just called me instead of texting or using the podcast. You found my phone number."

"Surprised you, didn't it? But a worldwide audience makes things more entertaining. And forces you to comply."

"I'm here. You're the one wasting time. I need to get dressed for our meeting, so why don't you tell me where the party is."

"If I did that, we'd have way too many people for what I have in mind. Check your phone, Piper. I texted you the address."

Piper watched everyone scramble for her phone in the gym.

He continued, "And Piper, I'll see you at midnight. Bring your phone."

The call ended.

Jinx got on air and said, "Thank you self-defense callers! The line is yours now. Call 504-defense. Let's go…

Piper saluted Jinx as she shut the studio door. Then stopped and stared at the huge map of a graveyard on the screen. The name on the iron archway entrance said St. Roch. She sighed. That's just great. She should have known he'd pick a graveyard at night.

Maverick motioned her to join them and showed her the text:

Go to 1725 St. Roch Avenue and wait at the gate for my call.
Midnight sharp. Be in the catsuit and alone.
Follow my instructions if you want to know about Jessica.
And I better not see Maverick or a cop.
If someone interferes, someone dies.

Piper looked at the time. Eight-forty. She said, "How long does it take to get to the cemetery?"

Maverick said, "It's less than a mile from here so we won't lose much time driving. But we've got less than three hours to get you ready."

Dakota said, "We'll get back to the graveyard strategy in a minute. First, we need to talk about all we've learned so far on this guy. Put the pictures on the screen that include even a glimpse of him from the riverboat."

Three pictures popped up. Three pieces of a man. Part of the right corner of a face. A hand and arm. A sliver of hip, leg, and foot.

"Ok, Piper. You go first." Dakota said, "Profile him."

She said, "He's in his late thirties or forties. Confident. Dominant. Intelligent. A hunter – possibly even does illegal hunts. He could be a regular on safaris as well. And that type of hunting means he's got money.

"He was monochromatic at the riverboat…brown hair, khaki pants, and wearing a brown leather jacket. Even brown boots. The only thing memorable about his looks is that he appears to have gold eyes and wear glasses. He meant to blend in.

"The unusual thing about him is that he stared at his phone the whole time while facing our table. Obviously, he listened. Possibly videoed us too. By now, there's not much he doesn't know about us.

"Last is his thing with cats. Beyond the sexual fetish, what if he's into big cats? My dress on the riverboat was leopard print. The catsuit is leopard material too. What if somehow the cat thing is personal? Could he have one? Something tells me, if he does, he treats it very well. He loves them."

Sean walked in front of the tables, talking to himself as much as the others as he said, "Ok. So, he's a hunter turned predator, drawing on his obsession with big cats. Is he looking for a mate? Maybe the three women he took failed, and then he saw Piper."

Dekker interjected, "So, the affection you pick up on, Piper, is the mate hunger that Sean sees. If that's the case, King wants to get close to you. Test you. He doesn't want to hurt you. Not yet anyway. He probably would kill anyone that did. In fact, if you did engage with him tonight, getting physical or asserting yourself would reinforce his perception of you - making you more valuable. Which in the long run, gives you more power."

Maverick said, "I hate her engaging with him, but her value to him makes me feel a little better about tonight. But there will be more nights. He only mentioned Jessica. There are two more women in play."

Piper said, "A lion keeps a large pride. It's possible the women may still be alive."

Dakota said, "Not necessarily. Most big cats are solitary for the most part, except for reproducing. If the victims didn't meet his need, he may have killed them out of frustration. We know most predators don't care why they do what they do. They just have a compulsion to meet a craving that demands it."

Sean said, "We're getting a good read on him. Dekker, tell us about the boots and knife he had on."

"The boots are Stingray Western boots made by Dragon Leather. Eight hundred bucks a pair. The company is in Phoenix, Arizona. The bad news is they are sold by dozens of retailers. The good news is they are numbered on the heel and receive a certificate. If we get a name..."

Piper said, "What about the image on the knife?"

Dekker said, "It's a black tiger. Which is beyond rare. There's been maybe ten of them documented. So, it's got to be a custom knife since I'm not finding duplicate knives anywhere."

Sean said, "Maverick, give us an estimate on his size."

"Six foot one. Muscular. And not pumping iron muscular - but strong." He pointed to his hand in the pictures. "He's a hands-on kind of guy."

***

After a brief break, two graveyards with wrought iron archway gates were on the video screen. St. Roch Cemetery No.1 was at the address texted to Piper: 1725 St. Roch Avenue. A historic landmark almost 150 years old with a gothic-style chapel, stone walkways, and above ground tombs. Hauntingly beautiful was a poetic way to say scary.

But across the street at 1725 Music Street was St. Roch Cemetery No. 2. Which complicated their already complicated mission.

Maverick explained the perimeters. "Both cemeteries are surrounded by the St. Roch neighborhoods. Homes. Sidewalks. Cars parked along the street. Kids and pets. And Music Street runs right through the middle of them.

"No. 1 has a stone wall around most of it. Iron fencing in some places. A second iron gate is directly across from No. 2 on the other side of the street. No. 2 has partial iron fencing, mausoleums, and multiple gates that encase it.

"So, while fencing and walls provide a little determent from trespassers or trouble, it is not a secure location. Either of them. Access could be made everywhere. Although there should be less activity at midnight when it's closed. However, it's—"

Maverick paused and looked at Piper.

She frowned. "It's what?"

"It's haunted."

She laughed. "Right. Because at midnight in a graveyard, we need ghosts. I get it."

He said, "I'm not being melodramatic. Two ghosts are documented. A black ghost dog. And a hooded figure. Though I've not seen them personally. But since you're going in alone, I'm just throwing it out there."

She looked at Dante and Jinx for confirmation. They nodded. Dante said, "It's true. I know people who have seen them."

Ignoring the chuckles around her, Piper said, "Great. Is there anything else I need to know?"

Maverick pointed to the tombs in No. 1, and said, "Enlarge the picture for me."

As the picture expanded, the size of the tombs and layout inside the cemetery was easier to see.

Maverick said, "The cemetery has a large field of tall tombs built of masonry brick, stone, or cement. Most are taller than me. Some have statues.

And almost all of them are individual, meaning you can walk around them like buildings with tiny alleys – row after row.

"And if you are getting my point, there is no way to know who could be hiding around each one. So, in my opinion, to follow Piper, we need drone, radio, and decoys."

He sat next to Piper and waited for the strategy to begin.

Piper looked at row after row of tombs, and said, "He'll be hidden when I get to the gate. And it's clear that the only way we'll see him is if he wants us to. I won't know where he wants me to go in that maze until I get there. He said bring my phone - so he'll call or text.

"As for bringing a weapon, the catsuit makes that difficult. But I could try to hide a blackjack, knife, or small taser in the boots. He's going to expect me to have something. Just like I expect him to have plenty in mind."

Dakota said, "Before you arrive, we'll create a commotion and get a few disguised agents and officers into the graveyard with you. Not enough to be suspicious, but a few drunk thrill seekers and a couple wanting to make out would seem normal."

Sean said, "When you arrive, Piper, I'll have a drone on you. An earpiece so we can talk. And be tapped into your phone to get the messages with you. We will follow you as you follow instructions."

Looking at Maverick, Dakota said, "While King will be expecting you, Maverick, you've got a target on your head."

"Not in a wheelchair, I don't. Two old people visiting a graveyard wouldn't seem out of place at all."

Dekker said, "Good call. I'll push. We'll tail her."

Sasha raised her hand, and said, "I have a carry permit for my Glock. I'll be a thrill seeker."

"Make that both of us," Hawk said.

Dakota said, "Then you two will be the couple. That works." Sasha glanced at Hawk. He winked.

In the end, Dakota, Adam, and two detectives were set in place as thrill seekers. And Piper would arrive by taxi.

Dakota asked Sean. "What's your surveillance plan?"

"The FBI van will be stationed at St. Roch Park out of sight. NOPD units will be stationed several blocks away from the cemeteries. Drones will be stationed at all four corners of each graveyard to give us at least a visual inside and outside. Thermal body imaging won't be a great tool tonight. Too many areas to hide. But I'll have eyes on Piper. and give instructions based on how it plays out."

Dakota said, "In a nutshell, this guy's got a better poker hand. Number one, he made the plan and has the ambush advantage. Number two, he has the victims as leverage. And he's playing them one at a time knowing we dare not snatch him and lose the others. And number three, he's risking it all for Piper.

"Which means, Piper has the best opportunity to get his DNA. If you get close to him, cut him. Scratch him. Pull his hair. Even kiss him. Just get that DNA and hope he's in the system. We're flying blind on this case, but three women out there want to be found.

"Now, get dressed everyone. Sean and the surveillance team leave for setup in thirty minutes. The rest of us need to arrive at St. Roch No. 1 at eleven fifty-five. We're a go for midnight."

***

Upstairs, Maverick zipped the leopard catsuit all the way up. Piper popped the tiny radio earbud in place. Then squatted, testing the material, and touched the zipper that ran from front to back between her legs. She grimaced and stood, facing Maverick.

His furious blue eyes met hers. "He'll pay for this, baby. He chose to do all of this because it's our wedding night. He wants you."

She touched his chest. "The zipper is just an intimidation tactic. You know that."

"Don't think he wouldn't take the chance if he could."

"Come on, Maverick. The zipper distracts him. That helps us."

"Not in that spot, it doesn't."

She pulled his lips to hers. Tonight was supposed to be their time. She whispered, "When we come back—"

He finished, "You're mine…and we'll sleep another night."

Jinx knocked on the door and said, "They told me to tell you - fifteen minutes. Please don't shoot the messenger."

Her footsteps quickly faded away.

Finishing his old man disguise, Maverick tugged on his gray wig, mustache, and glasses. Then watched as Piper pulled on leopard designer boots. He said, "Those are going to be too tight to hide a taser."

She frowned in agreement and slipped a narrow double edge dagger down the right boot. Sharp. Deadly. And glistening black. It was hidden by the zipper. Next, she chose a long thin extendable blackjack and slid it in the other boot. She stood to look in the mirror and said, "That will work in the shadows."

And in a minute, she had her hair in a ponytail and put on the jeweled cat mask. She was ready. Maverick looked at her body outlined in tight leopard material. Nothing was left to the imagination as it literally hugged every luscious inch of her. Play toy extraordinaire. He growled in frustration. She was being paraded for the psycho's pleasure.

Piper knew this took a will of steel for him to press through. She said, "He'll get his in the long run, Maverick. Tonight is about his DNA and Jessica."

"No, it's not. It's about you. The rest is just a plan to get you there."

"Don't get distracted, Maverick. We need this to play out for me to get evidence. His touch is a means to an end. He'll get his payback in prison, and we'll never think of him again."

***

In a few minutes, two old men with a wheelchair left the podcast studio in an old car.

A carload of drunk thrill seekers followed.

Next, a blonde woman and a dark-haired man tailed the others in a black truck.

And last, a seductive cat woman climbed into a taxi.

Chapter 11

Tucked in the shadows of the tombs, King waited, pumped about his location for the first move of his game. Dark. Creepy. An ancient burial ground with an unusual history. A place full of hidden nooks and crannies for things that go bump in the night. Whispers. Breezes without wind. Tales of ghosts.

He glanced at his watch. Eleven-fifty. He smiled, remembering he'd walked right in with the last group of tourists at eleven, and simply disappeared. His command center and gear were underneath an ultra-light camouflage netting. A very special black and gray material that blocked body heat from thermal imaging by drones or glasses. Even his clothes had a layer. He wasn't going to make it easy for the FBI or Maverick. And he knew they would show up.

A vehicle parked somewhere toward the front gate, and he heard a rowdy bunch of men get out, slamming doors. Drunks from the sound of it. He checked his iPad. The tracker in Piper's boots was moving. His wildcat would be here in minutes.

***

Dekker pushed Maverick in the wheelchair down the street. They could see the taxi in the distance. Dakota's drunks were cutting up on the sidewalk. And Hawk parked half a block away. In seconds he walked toward the gate with Sasha tucked close. His hand slid down her hip - and she pulled it back up.

The taxi rounded the corner.

The drunk men headed inside, guzzling beer and screeching like ghosts as they scattered to the left. The couple ran in. Laughing, and ducked behind a tomb up the center aisle, kissing. The two old men reached the gate as the taxi stopped.

Piper got out.

An undercover cop on a porch a few houses down dropped an empty whiskey bottle. It clattered loudly as he staggered down the steps. He whistled and called out, "Hey kitty, kitty…"

Piper ignored him and stopped at the gate.

The graveyard was much creepier in person. It had deep pockets of shadows from the handful of flickering lampposts. And the statues by the tombs no longer looked like angels…more like gargoyles. She sighed as moonlight faded in and out. She met Maverick's gaze as the two old men entered and stopped a few tombs down.

Sean radioed, "Head's up everyone. We're a go. It's midnight. I don't see a sign of anyone else in the graveyard. But it doesn't mean he isn't here. Speak up if you see anything. I've got drone eyes on Piper."

***

King laid on top a tomb and watched the new graveyard traffic. No one was anywhere near him. He turned binoculars on Piper and groaned…hot in an instant. She was ready for him. Her body, perfect. Her pose, seductive. He smiled. He'd known she would rock the game.

But he made her wait while he watched. Thirty seconds passed. Her long ponytail swung as she turned her head, looking into the shadows. She slid her hand down her thigh and shifted hips. Impatient, and hungry for the hunt. His tongue touched his lip. This hot game would be over in five minutes.

Piper's phone pinged with a text. A different unknown number. She read: Walk up the center path. Slow.

She started forward one slow step at a time as Sean relayed the message to everyone. Maverick and her dad disappeared in the tombs to her right. She heard drunken sounds to her left. And she heard Sasha's laugh somewhere ahead.

She was almost halfway down the long path when her phone pinged. Another text: Stop. Do not move.

She stopped. And after a few moments, up ahead, a large shadow crawled out of the tombs. It walked toward her on four feet. But awkward somehow.

She remembered the ghost dog and whispered, "Sean, what is that coming toward me?"

"There's no heat source in front of you, Piper."

Stunned, she whispered, "You mean it's dead?"

"No. Don't panic. I'm flying low to check."

The drone dropped low and flew silently through the dark toward the moving shadow. Just as it got close, massive jaws caught it. And the terrifying roar of a big cat filled the night.

Piper screamed and ran into the field of tombs to her right. Tripping. Slamming into tombs. Heading further into the nightmare. In no time she was lost and disoriented. The moonlight faded and the cat's growls came closer. She looked behind her and slammed into another wall. Then strong arms caught her - one hand covering her mouth. She had one thought…please be Maverick.

That thought died as King whispered, "Shh. Easy wildcat. I've been waiting."

And pressing her against a tomb he kissed her. Hot and sensual like they were lovers. She bit his tongue and fought…until he slid his finger along zipper between her legs. She froze.

Instantly clear-headed, Piper said, "You'll have to kill me to get that zipper open. And then what fun will that be for you?"

He inhaled the smell of her and said, "Tonight's foreplay. You'll be ready for me when I take you."

The clouds passed and moonlight revealed him. Masked and dressed all in black. Gold eyes and a few sprigs of brown hair visible. His mouth was bleeding. It had to be the man from the riverboat.

She said, "Tell me about Jessica. Isn't that why I'm here?"

"Later. We're doing what you're here for…and you're too smart not to know that." He slid her palm over his mouth, licking it. She grabbed at his mask, scratching him, but it didn't budge. It was stuck.

He tightened his hold on her wrist and said, "Now, now. Don't be impatient. It's too soon for you to see me. But…I'll let you feel me."

And he slid her hand below his waist. It didn't take a genius to know where he was headed. She kneed him in the groin, hitting a hard cup. She winced in pain. He grunted from the blow and yanked her close as the big cat snarled behind them. Piper screamed, reaching for her dagger. She spun low, her blade glinting in the moonlight. And she simply stared.

King leaned over her and snatched the dagger like candy from a baby. "Vicious wouldn't hurt you."

Piper doubted that as her brain quickly put the puzzle of Vicious together. The big cat was a leopard. A huge robotic leopard the size of a tiger. It had a fur head with huge teeth. And a leopard painted metal body with a long fur tail. Sharp claws. And she certainly looked like she wanted to eat her alive. Or was Vicious jealous? Was that even possible for a robot?

King heard the yells of people running toward them. Grabbing Piper by the waist, he ran silently through the maze of the dead. Piper watched the big cat follow, still shocked.

Stopping next to a giant tomb with two large statues, King gave Piper a hard kiss and whispered, "Enjoy your wedding present."

And he slung her high in the air. Screaming for Maverick as she went airborne, Piper landed on top of the tomb - face down on something that smelled. And she heard flies. She pushed up and was face to face with a very dead Agent Cruze Taylor. She jumped up screaming at the huge gaping hole in the middle of his chest and fell backwards off the tomb.

Running, Maverick caught her.

***

As chaos tore loose behind him, King slipped on a hoodie, hid the robot, and disappeared into the crowd. The neighborhood had shown up in droves. He had planned the perfect getaway.

***

Piper pointed to the roof of the tomb. "Maverick! It's Cruze…he's dead! We've got to get back up there!"

Adam boosted Dakota to the top of the tomb. Maverick boosted Piper. Hawk boosted Maverick. And drone lights hit the body. Stunned silence fell. One, because Cruze really was dead. Two, because King had put him here. And three, at the size of the hole in his chest…with no blood anywhere. And in the FBI van, Sean wondered how in the world those two men had connected.

Dakota called the deputy director.

On his way to Piper, Sean called for the crime lab and a medical examiner.

And Adam called an ambulance.

Listening to the sirens as first responders arrived, Piper pointed to Cruze's shirt pocket. There was a touch of bright red. "Maverick, I think there is something in his pocket."

Maverick leaned close, not touching anything. "There is."

The Medical Examiner climbing up the ladder said, "Don't touch it. I'll bag it for you. And all of you need to scoot. There's not enough room for my assistant to get up here."

Maneuvering around the body, Piper said, "I'm sorry to say, I fell on him."

The Examiner looked at the bloodless gaping hole in the man's chest and said, "Well, you didn't mess up the original crime scene. He was dead long before he got here."

***

After the paramedics checked her for injuries, Piper was whisked off to the police station. She was swabbed for DNA, and they took her clothes. And after finding something to put on, the FBI and the NOPD took her statement. No one from her investigation team was allowed in the room. A dead FBI agent was a serious matter, meaning all i's dotted and t's crossed.

Agent Donovan began, "Agent Pierce. Excellent work during a shocking turn of events. We are enroute now to locate Jessica's remains based on the map included with the red lace."

She sighed. "I didn't expect two dead victims tonight. And I had held out hope that Jessica might be alive. As for Cruze…" She shrugged. "I'm clueless. I feel for both families. I guess this doesn't leave much hope for the other two women, does it."

"No. Or anyone else that catches King's eye. He's a serial killer. But for now, let's talk about Cruze since he became an unexpected piece of this case. It complicates everything. You had history with Cruze. Bad history."

"Yes, Sir. I did."

"After he vanished from his assignment in upstate New York, were you called?"

"Agent Sean Nash notified us late last night after the Sunday podcast."

"It was expected that he would target you. Did you suspect that he was in New Orleans when you arrived on Friday?"

"Not until a tracker was found on Maverick's truck this morning." She glanced at the clock. It was now three a.m. She said, "Technically, yesterday morning."

"So, you've been in New Orleans three days and a little."

"Correct."

"And two men targeted you in that short time."

"It appears so."

"Do you have any idea how Cruze connected with King?"

"No, Sir."

"Agent Pierce, have you been alone at all since arriving in New Orleans?"

"Yes, Sir. For about thirty minutes in my hotel room after checking in late Friday."

"And since then, who can confirm your whereabouts the entire time?"

"Detective Maverick Patterson."

"Your husband."

"Since this morning. Oh. Yesterday morning."

"Congratulations. It's been quite a day. So, tell us, when did you first hear about a wedding present from King?"

"On a text."

"And the next time you heard about a present?"

"When he threw me on top of the tomb."

With an abrupt change he said, "Did you hate Cruze?"

"Despise sounds more professional."

"Did he deserve what he got?"

"No FBI agent, or any human, deserves to be murdered."

"Go home, Agent Pierce. Enjoy your honeymoon. Forensics is trying to find out who this guy is."

"Thank you, Sir. Goodnight."

"Oh. One last thing, Agent Pierce. Do you expect to hear from King again?"

"Yes, Sir. He still has two more women. He's just getting started. And then he wants me."

***

Maverick, Dakota, and Sean grabbed a cup of coffee and waited for Piper. They could see her through the interrogation window not far from Maverick's desk. Adam, Hawk, and Sasha had taken a taxi back to the podcast studio. Dekker sat on the edge of a desk close to the room where Piper was.

Dekker texted Luna: Hey, beautiful.

Startled from sleep, Luna knocked her phone off the nightstand, then answered: Hey, Dekker. I wish you were here.

Dekker: You wouldn't be sleeping.

Luna's body tingled: I felt that.

Dekker: Me too. Have you seen a news bulletin?

Luna's heartbeat quickened: No. Why?

Dekker: A case Piper's involved in is all over the news.

Luna: Is she ok?

Dekker: She is.

Luna: I have a hundred questions. Where are you?

Dekker: Not far. I've got to go. We'll talk soon.

Luna: Dekker?
No answer.

A few blocks away from the St. Roch graveyards, a black truck sat parked in the garage of a dated red brick house.

Inside the truck, King watched the time, the news, and listened for sirens. It was getting quieter by the minute. And the homeowner didn't concern him at all. He was drugged and sound asleep on the floor of his kitchen. The tranquilizer would keep him out till noon.

He lowered the visor mirror. Wiping blood off his mouth, he checked his tongue. Piper had bitten him hard - but just on the edge. No big deal. It would heal quickly. He touched the fingernail scratches in his eyebrow. The sting was already fading.

Long ago he'd removed the groin cup and tossed it under the seat. He'd have been in jail without it. Grimacing at the raw edges where the cup scraped the insides of his groin, he shifted. It was tender from the force of her knee. But the package underneath was unharmed…waiting for his turn with Piper.

Smiling, he thought of tonight's easy victory. There had been no doubt the robot would throw everyone off their game. That was the point. A big cat loose in a graveyard was a shocker for anyone. And it gave him those crucial minutes with her. The test had been well worth the risk. He had no doubt now - she was the one. But they would play the game out. It would be good for them. He'd learned a lot from his time with Jessica, Katie, and Danielle.

Focusing on the next task, King opened the control panel for Vicious and hit activate.

***

Back at the graveyard, four NOPD officers working in pairs were almost finished searching the grids for evidence. It had been quiet and eerie, but they were familiar with calls to St. Roch. Though not so much with a dead FBI agent and robot.

A female officer walked by one of the Stations of the Cross along the perimeter wall and shone her flashlight inside the locked gate. Nothing. She saw the flash of light from her partner around the corner. Then she heard a sudden scraping noise on bricks behind her. She turned, and movement overhead caught her eye. She raised her flashlight and screamed as a huge alien-looking leopard snarled.

And in two jumps it was over the wall and vanished into the night.

Not far away, King raised the bed cover on his truck. Vicious jumped in.

***

Piper came out of the interrogation room and headed for the group waiting for her. She was tired of all this. She'd been manhandled. Stalked by a beast. And belly to belly with a dead co-worker. Not counting, finding the panties and map of a dead woman. She wanted Maverick and her honeymoon. That's all.

Agent Donovan said, "Take her home, Detective. I insist. All of you get some rest. I'm sending another detail out to cover you."

Maverick saluted him but watched Piper. Reading her need. He wrapped her in his arms. One hand holding her head against his chest. She closed her eyes and breathed him in. This was where she wanted to be.

Dekker met Maverick's gaze and said, "I've got one thing to say before we leave the station. No one is safe in the podcast studio anymore. Not with a robot leopard out there. And not with a serial killer on the loose who has killed maybe four people - and wants Piper.

"As her father, I've made an executive decision and leased a six-bedroom apartment on the third floor in the Garden District. It's safer. Easier for security. And hopefully too far off the ground for that beast. And it's ready for us. Food is being delivered. We need to move the team in by mid-morning at the latest. And like Agent Donovan said, I insist."

Piper hugged him. "I'm not arguing. It was crazy."

"He's a different kind of psycho, baby. And he's playing with you – not us. We need to ramp up security. We know more now."

Dakota said, "On that note, Piper, we need to meet first thing in the morning. We need your information."

She said, "No problem." Then looking at Maverick, she said, "But tonight I want you to take me to the loft. And security is fine…outside the door. And now, I insist."

Outside, Dakota and Sean took a taxi back to the podcast studio for a couple hours of sleep. Dekker took a taxi to check on the apartment he leased. And three FBI agents picked up Piper and Maverick, then headed to the loft.

***

It was almost four a.m. when Maverick and Piper unlocked their door. And finally, after sixteen hours, Maverick carried his bride over the threshold. And holding her face to his, kissed her. Hot but slow. Sensual. Piper's hands gripped his shirt, loving the taste of him.

He whispered, "Baby…" Her blue eyes met his. "It's been a wild day. I'm concerned about you. When was the last time you ate something?"

She thought. "Maybe some crackers after the podcast? But it's ok. I'm not hungry. You must be starving though."

Rubbing her bottom lip, he said, "I grabbed something at the station. Let me at least fix you something cold to drink."

"That sounds perfect."

Smiling, he sat her on top of the snack bar wearing spare gray warmups and a T-shirt from the station. Her hair was in a messy bun. She looked like a teenager coming home after a long field trip. He kissed her and said, "It'll just take a minute."

Piper watched him, thinking about their rushed wedding. Their time on the sailboat. And every minute since. He glanced at her as he mixed Sprite with strawberry Fanta and added strawberry slices and cherries. She blew him a kiss and stole two strawberry slices. She offered him a cherry as he handed her the drink.

His lips closed over her finger capturing the fruit. Piper smiled, then groaned in delight at the taste of the drink.

He laughed. "I'm jealous."

"You shouldn't be. You make me feel a million times more than that."

The look he gave her turned her insides to mush. He slid his hands up her legs, spreading them. Then pressed against her with the beautiful familiarity of love and intimacy. He said softly, "I know it's our honeymoon, but we can't overlook the elephant in the room. You should rest tonight. You've just been sexually assaulted—"

She touched his lips. "You're my hero, baby. But tonight, I need two things. A shower, and you. Both hot."

Their gazes locked, passion shoving at the door to get out. But Maverick had to be sure. This would be a tragic time for him to fail her. Piper understood. She tucked her feet behind his legs and slid her hand down his jeans and gave him a more direct answer.

The fire in his body matched his growl as his mouth covered hers. Then her shirt flew. Her pants disappeared. And her long hair covered the counter as his jeans hit the floor. Maverick groaned as Piper arched, calling his name.

***

In the Garden District, Dekker looked over the apartment he'd leased. The six bedrooms were ready. The pantry and fridge would be stocked in an hour. And the coffee pot was set for eight a.m. He was satisfied. This setup would work well as a safehouse for the team. He locked the door and called a taxi, checking the time.

Ten minutes later, Dekker texted Luna: I'd love to see you.
Luna: How long will it take you to get here?
Dekker: I'm on the porch.

Dekker heard her footsteps. The door unlocked. Luna's sleepy eyes met his as she opened the door. Dekker stepped through and shut it, groaning at the vision she made. Clouds of dark tousled hair. A short black nightgown. And matching panties.

He kissed her. Devoured her. And passion quickly picked up where they'd left off. Until reality punched him in the gut as he carried her toward the bedroom. Taking a deep breath, Dekker stopped in the hall. Grimacing at the ache he'd caused them.

Luna's breath brushed his neck. "Dekker?"

"I'm sorry," he said. "Give me just a minute, beautiful. I need to calm this fire down."

After carrying her back to the den, Luna watched him remove yet another suit jacket and gun. Sitting next to her on the sofa, he drew her on his lap. With hot silence, their eyes met.

Luna asked softly, "What happened back there? It stopped you in your tracks."

Sliding a hand up her neck in a caress, he said, "I can't have you believing this all we are. A man showing up at your door in the middle of the night, is not you. We both know that."

She nodded. It had more than crossed her mind. "So, what are we?"

He watched her for a bit, his eyes intense. "In love. And I've lived long enough to know the difference. I don't say it lightly."

"You don't do anything lightly, Dekker. And you're right. I love everything about you. Including all the secret things you carry around."

He kissed her hand. "Let's be real, Luna. You know next to nothing about me or my life."

She touched his face. "That may be true. But I think the things I do know about you are more important than the things I don't."

Love flared, and he kissed her. And Luna responded the way she always did. Like honey and wildfire. He said, "Tell me you'll marry me. Even though I'm older. Even though there are things you don't know. Simply because you love me."

She smiled, holding his face. "Of course, I will. But really, Dekker…was there ever any question?"

He pulled her lips to his. Not really.

A minute later, his phone rang. He said, "I've got to get that, I'm sorry."

She slid aside and he headed for his phone. Glancing at the caller, he walked outside.

Dekker answered, "It's not good, Sean, if you're calling me."

"No. We have a complication."

"Is Piper safe?"

"Yes. Just listen. A few minutes ago, Piper's phone received another text from King. And since we're still connected to her phone, I got it too. I'm forwarding it to you now. We'll talk later. Do what you've got to do."

The line went dead.

The text arrived and Dekker read:

The game changed, Piper.
I want more time with you at our next meeting.
It's not debatable. It will cost Jinx and Luna if you refuse.
How willing are you to keep them safe, Agent Pierce?

Dekker was in the house in an instant. Watching Luna while he made a call, he said, "I need a car with two men. Follow my tracker."

Luna stood. "What's wrong?"

He held her face. "Do you trust me?"

"Without question."

"I need you to come with me. I'll help you pack. A car will be here soon to pick us up."

"But—"

"We've got less than ten minutes. We'll talk later. Come on."

In her bedroom, he said, "Just get what you would normally need for a few days. That's it. Leave the rest. If you need anything, we'll get it."

She pointed to the suitcase in her closet. He grabbed it and packed the clothes she threw on the bed. She ran for toiletries. Then hurriedly pulled on jeans and a shirt as car lights flashed in the window.

In a minute, they were gone.

***

At the podcast studio, Sean looked through the window at Jinx and Sasha asleep on cots in the office. He refused to wake Jinx up and tell her about the threat. She'd turned over her home to the team. Let the case interfere with her podcast and self-defense classes. And tonight, she had even given them her bed. She'd insisted the team take turns and get some real rest.

Dakota and Adam were forced to take the first sleep shift. But it was iffy whether the second shift would get any sleep or not. At least at the rate it was going.

Sean heard footsteps.

Dante came downstairs with three mugs of coffee. He raised a cup and whistled for Hawk to come get one. Hawk waved.

Handing one cup to Sean, Dante said, "Here you go. I couldn't sleep so I hooked us up. What's wrong? You look like you ate too many sour gummy bears."

Despite himself, Sean chuckled. Only Dante. He said, "Thanks for the coffee." He raised his mug. "Cheers." But didn't answer Dante's question.

Hawk joined them, reaching for the other mug. He saluted Dante and took a sip, glancing at Sean. And Hawk knew Sean well enough to know that the frown on his forehead meant trouble. He asked casually, "Any news on King?"

Sean set his cup down. Pulling out his phone and scrolling, he said, "There is."

He looked at Dante and said, "And I'm afraid I'm about to mess up your day. But once you can see straight again, I'll tell you what's next."

He offered his phone.

Without a word Dante took it, and his body went rigid as he read the text. He raised eyes that flashed with fury, and fear, for the woman he loved. "I will kill—"

Sean held up his hands in clear understanding and said, "I've been there. I know. Seriously. But plans are in place. At eight o'clock we all leave for a more secure location. And we'll stay there and work this case till we catch or kill King. And he knows you too. You have got to come."

"I'm not leaving her. He'll have to go through me to get to her."

"I get that. All of us do. But for now, we let her sleep. When we have to, we'll tell her."

Dante glanced at the office where Jinx slept and nodded.

Sean handed his phone to Hawk. "Read this."

***

Dekker escorted Luna into the new safehouse. One of the men stayed downstairs until the team arrived in a few hours. The other left.

Luna watched Dekker punch three on the elevator panel. His hand returned to his right hip where the gun was. His finger tapped. She was more impressed with him than scared. At least for the moment. All she knew so far was that the podcast guy knew who she was. Which was insane. How did that even happen?

Dekker could feel Luna's eyes on him. Smell the scent of her shampoo. He forced himself to relax and hugged her. The elevator dinged and the door opened into a private foyer.

Unlocking the only door, he said, "I just leased it. I think you'll like it. Go ahead and look around and I'll run your bags to one of the bedrooms."

She said, "How many bedrooms does it have?"

He said over his shoulder, "Six plus a sleeper sofa."

"Wow. Such a small place."

His laugh echoed.

Luna glanced around. The apartment was large. And fine. Not gilded metal, chandeliers, and white carpet fine. But warm with windows, a balcony, brick walls, wood floors, with colorful rugs and furniture. The kitchen had a fabulous gas grill range and a big snack bar with quirky stools in the shape of animal legs. In a small way, the personality of the room reminded her of her place.

Dekker returned with a smile and said, "Before we talk…" and drew her lips to his. Soft and warm at first. Then hot. With a groan, he stopped and kissed her forehead.

Pointing to a stool, he said, "Make yourself comfortable. I'll start the coffee and then we can talk."

Luna settled on the zebra stool.

Hitting start on the coffee maker, Dekker said, "I'm sorry to say that your world is about to get upended with people and activity. We've had the investigation command center on Piper's case at another location. But after tonight's activity, it's moving here." He looked at the time. "In less than three hours."

Surprised, she said, "That's why this place is so big."

"Yes. Plus, security. So, why don't I give you a bulleted version of what's going on, so you can get the big picture…and we'll go from there."

"Please. It's mind boggling to me that I even fit into something this complicated. How did that happen?"

"It's simple. It started on the riverboat."

She gasped. "You're kidding."

"I wished. It turns out that the three missing women you've been hearing about on the news were kidnapped. The man who took them was on the riverboat Saturday night. Evidence leads us to believe he filmed us in the dining room where he learned who we were from our conversations. That is how it all started.

"The why is because of Piper. She is the epitome of his obsession. Which led him to call the self-defense podcast she was scheduled to be a guest on Sunday night – and where the game between them began. His name is King, and midnight was the first play of the game."

Luna remembered the news bulletin, and said, "At the graveyard."

"Yes. An FBI agent was found dead, along with evidence claiming the first missing woman was also dead."

Goosebumps covered her. "And the robot leopard? Did Piper see it?"

"It chased her to him - and kept guard while he played his game."

"That's a nightmare. Are you sure Piper is alright?"

"She's tough like you wouldn't imagine. But still, that's why I leased this place. It safer." He paused. "And the next part of the story is where you and Jinx come in."

"How? And who's Jinx?"

"Jinx is the podcaster. The petite gothic woman with our group Saturday night."

"I remember her. So, how are we involved?"

"King texted Piper a warning. He wants more time with her the next time they meet. If she refuses, he threatened you and Jinx."

That startled her. "You mean like the other women he took?"

"Possibly. But you're safe here with me. It was probably just a play to push Piper's buttons."

"So, what does Piper have to do to save us?"

"Knowing Piper…twist the tables on him."

***

In the podcast office, Jinx woke before her alarm. She got up and stretched. A cot was not the greatest, but it was better than sleeping on carpet over concrete. She stifled a yawn and glanced across the room. Sasha was already up.

Hurriedly, she freshened up and changed, then headed for a quick cup of coffee before packing. She never noticed the heads that turned her way.

Dakota and Sean looked at Dante.

With a barely perceptible nod, Dante put the boxes he was carrying down, then headed to Jinx's office. He dreaded telling her about the threat – but insisted they let him do it. Jinx was a woman always ready to take on the world. But…this threat was a whole new ball game. And their relationship was just reaching real intimacy. He wasn't sure how she would take it.

Jinx was busy unplugging wires under her desk when she heard footsteps. Smiling, she saw Dante's feet as he walked around the desk. She said, "Morning, Dante! You arrived just in time to rescue me from a tangled mess."

"Morning, baby," Dante said as he squatted close, meeting her emerald gaze. He caressed her cheek and slid fingers in her hair. "I'll just lay it out there, Jinx. I've got two things to tell you. One, good. The other, bad. But I promise the good is way more important than the bad. So, why don't we start there."

She felt the sudden wave of apprehension at bad news, and said, "Good, please."

"Marry me."

And she was shocked. Wide-eyed, mouth open surprise. Not that he'd asked. She'd always known he would - but that he'd done it with a house full of cops and investigators.

He kissed her. "I know that I skipped the love declarations but we both know we do. Don't we?"

Her lips met his. And Dante held her there…giving and taking. Feeling her. Loving her.

A few moments later, they shared a smile. She said, "Yes to both."

He said, "I could tell…and we really need to talk about when."

Her smile faded. "After you tell me what you don't want to tell me."

Anger flashed in his eyes as he said, "King texted Piper with another demand. He threatened you and Luna if she refuses to do what he wants."

Her body tensed up. What? But her mind quickly worked through the facts of the case. She frowned. "Ok. I get that we're both brunettes – I can see that angle. So, he must have seen Luna on the boat too."

"Yes. And Dekker knows about it so I'm sure he's working on that. The good thing is that we already plan to be in a safer location by eight o'clock."

"Safe enough from the metal beast he has?"

"Yes. Three floors up. And I'll be there."

"Piper's been hurt so many times, Dante. I don't want her hurt in place of me."

"They're not going to sacrifice her, Jinx. They'll outsmart him."

"Ok. I believe you. But promise me one thing."

"Name it."

"Don't leave me. Even at night. I can't wake up with King somewhere. I just can't."

Chapter 12

At Maverick's loft the next morning, the alarm went off. He stopped it and rolled back toward Piper.

She stirred, and said sleepily, "What time is it?"

"Seven…come here…" He groaned as they slid together.

Piper's eyes popped open, and she put a hand against his chest. "Wait. My alarm didn't go off. Where's my phone? What if the evidence—"

His eyes met hers. "Forget the phone."

She threw back the covers and said over her shoulder as she hurried to the edge, "I'll be right back, let me—"

Maverick caught her ankle. "You're not going anywhere." He pulled her across the sheet on her stomach.

Laughing, Piper glanced back at him. "What do you—"

But he was already behind her. His mouth moving up her back. She forgot about the phone. The investigation. Everything, as his body covered hers.

After freshening up, Piper smelled bacon cooking and music playing. She pulled her hair in a ponytail and slipped on a short, silver lace nightgown. Then added a touch of mascara and lip gloss. It was her honeymoon breakfast after all. She headed to the kitchen.

Rounding the corner, she paused to watch Maverick. He wore New Orleans Saints lounging pants that rode super low on his hips. And he danced, stacking bacon next to French toast. Then he turned off the burner and dropped down into a low hip roll.

Piper remembered the feel of that move. She said softly, "I hope that's on the menu."

Maverick laughed as he turned, then whistled. He appreciatively molded the lace to her, and said after a kiss, "Baby, we are the menu. Food is a side dish."

Her stomach growled. Then his. They laughed, and Maverick said, "Ok. Side dish it is."

They sat at the table overlooking the river.

Piper licked a drop of syrup off her finger and said, "That was delicious. If you keep feeding me like this, I won't be able to wear thongs."

Maverick said, "With the calories we are burning taking off your thongs, you should be just fine."

She laughed. "You know I'm not much of a cook, right?"

He winked. "That was never a requirement. But you can't help but pick up the cooking bug in New Orleans. Food is a huge part of the culture. I don't see us cooking at home that much anyway. Restaurants are everywhere."

"Do you have a favorite one?"

"You." And using his foot, he pulled her chair closer.

She said, "You know…we're already late if we were supposed to be at the podcast studio before eight. Oh! That reminds me of my phone…" She scooted back her chair to stand.

He took her hand. "Not yet."

Her brow creased. "You keep stopping me from getting my phone. Once, I get. Not twice." Narrowing her eyes, she said, "What's on my phone, Maverick?"

Leaning close for directness, he said, "I'm asking you to let it be. Knowing will only distract you. I messaged Sean that we'll be at the new location at ten. Until then, I'm not sharing you. I won't pull the I'm your husband alpha card often, Piper, but I am today."

"And we haven't even been married twenty-four hours."

"Which explains my reason."

"But that doesn't eliminate the fact that something important for the case is on my phone."

"And when we leave, I won't stop you from reading it. Now…come dance with me."

"I've never danced at breakfast."

He led her away from the table. Piper was surprised he didn't turn on any music but loved dancing with him. The smiles. Kisses. Hugs. And the sensual rhythm. He spun her around a few times. Dipped her. And without warning began to sing.

She stared. He never said… And she melted to the sound of his voice. A rich bass. Sexy and deep as he sang an old love song. It was crazy romantic. Especially when it ended.

***

Promptly at eight-thirty, an unmarked white van backed to the entrance of the new safehouse apartment. Three trucks followed suit. And like a well-oiled machine, everything was hauled to the third floor. Folding tables. Chairs. Dry erase boards filled with data and pictures. Video screens, computers, and podcast equipment.

Dekker and Luna stayed out of the way and watched from the kitchen.

Luna said, "I don't think there are enough bedrooms."

"It'll be crowded but the techs won't stay after the equipment is set up." He pointed toward Jinx and Dante. "I know you remember them from the riverboat."

"I do. Beautiful gothic and hungry Cajun."

Dekker laughed. "Perceptive of you. But prepare yourself. Dante says what he thinks."

"It's alright. I'm used to it. Sick people do too. It makes my heart hurt for them."

Her gentleness made his masculinity burn. He preferred to kiss her but leaned on the counter and faced her. And with one glance at his expression, her body responded.

He said, "I want you to sleep in my room, Luna. I'm your security – and your husband as soon as we can make that happen."

"I would rather be with you, but will Piper mind? That might be awkward."

"She'll see right through us and know our relationship well before bedtime."

Watching all the activity, Luna noticed the tall blonde woman looking a little out of place while everyone was busy. She said, "Who is she?"

Dekker called out, "Sasha. Come join us."

Dodging bodies, Sasha made it to the kitchen and smiled at them. "Thanks, Dekker. It's odd not being part of the action." She glanced at Luna.

Dekker said, "I wanted to introduce you to Luna, the other party to the latest threat. And Luna, this is Sasha, Maverick's twin sister."

The women greeted. Luna said, "I see the general resemblance between you and Maverick, but I haven't met him yet. I just saw him on the riverboat."

Sasha smiled. "I only met him last night. We were separated at birth."

Luna gasped. "Wow. That's got to be an extraordinary story."

"It is." Sasha said. "And I look forward to telling it once all this is over."

***

Forty thousand feet in the air, Special Agent Samantha Nash gathered her bags. The FBI plane would be landing at the New Orleans Lakefront Airport in fifteen minutes. She checked her phone to see if Sean had texted. He had. He was sending a car for her. Another text popped up. It was Gabrielle.

Gabrielle: Hey, sister-in-law. What time do you land in New Orleans?
Samantha responded: Fifteen minutes. How's it going in Lake Charles?
Gabrielle: I'm not in Lake Charles.
Samantha: Where are you?
Gabrielle: Waiting for you at the airport.
Samantha was shocked: Why would you be in New Orleans of all places? Dakota is going to be livid.
Gabrielle looked in the passenger seat: I know. And I'm not alone.
Samantha groaned: You didn't bring Raven.
Gabrielle: Raven insisted.
Samantha sighed: It's not like I can sneak y'all in.
Gabrielle: We've got a plan.
Samantha: That's what scares me. Now stay where you are. I'll come to you. Do not get out of that car.
Gabrielle snorted: Like Raven and I don't know how to use a gun.
Samantha: Dakota and Adam are going to lock you up. And Sean's going to send me back to Denver.
Gabrielle: I doubt it. You've got this.
Samantha: You owe me. Both of you.

Samantha exited the plane. Wind blew her long blonde hair as she looked out over Lake Pontchartrain. Sun sparkled on the water and there were sailboats in the distance. She smiled. This wasn't Baton Rouge, but it was close enough. Louisiana would always be home. And this was a victory lap for her - the first time she'd been home as an agent. A black SUV pulled up to meet her.

She said to the agent driving, "We need to make a quick stop in the parking lot."

After climbing in, she texted Gabrielle: I'm coming.

A few minutes later, they pulled behind a navy-blue BMW XM SUV. The hatch lifted.

Disguised in a long blonde wig and sunglasses, Gabrielle got out of the driver's seat. Raven got out of the passenger seat, red hair flying in the wind. Both dressed in pantsuits, they looked like hot agents. Ones that were about to be in big trouble with their husbands. The driver loaded their bags in the back as they climbed in.

Gabrielle looked at Samantha's frown. "Come on Samantha. You would have shown up too."

Samantha said, "Not like this."

Raven said, "It's not Gabrielle's fault. I made her do it - and don't lie, you would have already been here if it was you."

Samantha said, "I know. And I agree with why you came, but don't come crying to me if your husbands flip clean out." She imitated an explosion with her hands. "Now let's get you out of here. No one knows where King is."

***

Back at the safehouse, Sean's phone vibrated. Samantha texted: On my way there."

Security was waiting when the black SUV parked. All the doors opened. The driver headed to the rear liftgate for luggage. Samantha exited the front passenger seat. And two agents climbed out of the back wearing FBI caps. They each carried a backpack and followed Samantha inside.

Security texted Sean: They're coming up.

In the elevator, Samantha watched the floor numbers change and said, "Here we go. Three. Two. One. You're on Raven." The chime sounded and the door slid open.

When Samantha stepped into the apartment, Sean met her with a kiss. "Hey, baby, I'm glad you're here. I can't—"

And he went silent when the person behind Samantha glanced up. It was Raven. He looked at the other woman. Gabrielle.

His angry eyes met Samantha's. "Why would you bring them here?"

At the sound of his tone, everyone in the room focused on the arrivals. The two women in back removed their caps. Red hair tumbled as Raven met Adam's stormy gaze. And Gabrielle knew from Dakota's fierce frown he'd seen through the blonde wig. In a few steps, all three brothers faced their wives.

Samantha held up her hands. "Wait guys! Just listen. And if you had listened to your wives before now, they wouldn't have shown up on their own. They were waiting for me at the airport. Of course I brought them here. Now Raven, you go first."

Adam still interrupted Raven. "You are pregnant and have a son at home. What made being in the middle of this nightmare seem like a good idea to you?"

Love and wisdom made Raven's voice soft as she touched his chest. She said, "Piper was there for us a few short months ago, Adam. And she suffered a great deal because of it. How could I not come for her? But you wouldn't listen to me. Make a way for me to help without being in the way. Please."

And that truth hit him. Pulling her close, he glanced at his brothers. All of them knew what Piper had been through that day.

Still tense, Dakota pulled off Gabrielle's blonde wig. Dark hair fell down her back. He said, "Who has Skye?"

"Mom and Dad have her. You don't like me as a blonde?"

"No, though I appreciate your disguise." He lifted her chin. "Don't you dare step a foot outside of this building without me, Gabrielle."

Luna watched the three couples disappear down the hall. She glanced at Dekker. "What just happened, and who are those people?"

He smiled. "The men are Piper's cousins. Native American. Dakota is the oldest, then Sean, and Adam. Dakota and Sean as you've seen are FBI. And Adam is the owner of Quest Search & Rescue in Lake Charles – and a preacher."

Sasha said, "And the women?"

"The wives all have amazing history of their own. The brunette, Gabrielle is an artist and descendant of Pirate Jean Lafitte. And the blonde was a prosecutor in Baton Rouge, now a new FBI agent. And the redhead is Raven. A spectacular dancer, and RN with the search and rescue. She's Native American too, though she doesn't look it."

Sasha said, "Well, one thing's for sure. They sure know how to make an entrance."

Luna asked, "Who's the handsome guy that keeps watching Sasha? Is he related to the brothers? He favors them."

Dekker motioned him over and said, "That's Hawk, their cousin. He was also Sasha's hot undercover date in the graveyard last night."

Hawk heard the hot date comment as he joined them. He winked at Sasha, then smiled at the beautiful brunette with light blue eyes. "I'm Hawk. It's nice to meet you, Luna. I'm sorry to hear about your trouble. But you're in the best hands. None better."

Her telltale sign of intimacy gave them up as a couple. She leaned close to Dekker, touching his stomach. "I agree. And it's nice to meet you. But…I would like to hear more about the hot date in the graveyard. You don't hear that often – even in the emergency room."

He chuckled. "You're a nurse. I respect those skills. I've needed a few in my day."

"I'm an RN. And there is nothing like having someone when you need them. What is your profession, Hawk? I see a different kind of tough in you."

"Good eye. I'm retired military as of six months ago."

"What branch?"

"Navy. I was a Seal for fifteen years."

Luna said "Wow. I've never met a Seal. Thank you for your service. This room is full of impressive people." She turned to Sasha. "What's your profession, Sasha? If you did undercover last night, are you law enforcement?"

Sasha answered, "Detective Sasha Tate from the Tampa Police Department at your service."

Luna shook her head. "That's unbelievable. What were the odds that you and Maverick would both be detectives?"

Voices and footsteps came down the hall as all three couples returned.

Dekker said, "Hey FBI, your printer is about to blow a gasket spitting out paper. It hasn't stopped yet."

Sean glanced at the clock. "Perfect timing. We'll get it sorted. Maverick and Piper will be here in thirty."

***

Back at the loft, security escorted Maverick and Piper to the SUV. In a minute, they were headed to the new safehouse.

Piper turned to Maverick. "Where's my phone?"

He took it out of his pocket and said, "King sent you a text."

It didn't take her long to read it. And just that quick, Maverick watched her mind kick into gear. She looked out the window…battling the killer again.

In minutes they arrived. Maverick opened the door of the apartment to the sound of wedding music. And for a few minutes all was as it should be. Laughter. Cheers. And surprise hugs with Samantha, Gabrielle, and Raven.

Until Piper saw Luna cheering with everyone else. That beautiful gesture made her heart hurt. Luna was targeted simply because she had a romantic birthday dance on the riverboat with her dad. She was innocent. And in a nutshell, that was why Piper did what she did.

After a hug and kiss from her dad, she turned to Luna.

Luna smiled at the gorgeous, powerful woman in front of her and said, "I am honored to meet you, Piper. I've heard amazing things about you. And congratulations to you and Maverick – I don't think I've ever seen a more fabulous couple."

Piper smiled at the genuine warmth and gentleness that radiated from the strikingly lovely woman. "Thank you, Luna. I'm glad to meet you. I'm just sorry that it's under these circumstances." Pausing for a second, she said, "Discussion is about to get heavy in here. Please don't think you have to listen to all the unpleasant details. What's important is that you are here and safe. We'll keep you that way. Just listen to Dad."

Sean called out, "Ok, everyone, let's get started. We've got a lot of ground to cover after last night."

As the team sat at the tables, the others settled around the room. Two large video screens came on with paused video footage. One screen showed a graveyard entrance with a large stone path in the middle. It was dark and creepy like an old black and white horror movie. The other screen displayed corner views of the same graveyard.

Sean said, "I'll roll all drone footage at the same time, but don't waste your time watching the corner views. Nothing happens there till the end. I'll tell you when. Just watch the main entrance as the team arrives. It all happens fast. Here we go."

The video rolled…

There were a few chuckles in the room as four undercover drunks arrived at the zoo and headed inside. A few more laughs came as the romantically inclined couple showed up and disappeared between the tombs. Then two old men came. One slowly pushing a wheelchair.

Piper stepped out of the taxi. Hot, in her leopard suit, boots, and mask. She walked toward the gate and stopped. Basically, naked with clothes on, looking like the sexiest cat on earth.

The women in the room looked at each other. Hearing about it was one thing, seeing it another. The men knew better than to make a sound. Maverick just growled. And in the background of the video, you could hear a man's voice call out, "Here kitty, kitty…"

And they lost it. All of them. Sean had to stop the video until the screams and laughter died down. Some wiped tears. Others lost their breath. It took a while.

Maverick texted his partner Axel: I got your kitty, kitty.

Sean hit play again.

The two old men stopped at a tomb near the entrance.

Piper received the text with instructions and Sean relayed it to the team. Everything was quiet as Piper walked the shadowed path. Then a large animal shape came out of the tombs and started toward her. You couldn't really tell what it was – only that it was large and dark. Piper began to panic.

Sean sent the drone to check it out. Flying through darkness and shadows, the drone lowered to thirty feet, twenty, and ten, until it neared the image. And just as you could begin to see features, a huge mouth closed on the drone. It went black. Audio still picked up a roar and Piper's scream.

The echo of the women's startled screams filled the room.

Sean stopped the video. He said, "After this point, we didn't have eyes on Piper. And she lost her earpiece. Come on up Piper. Talk us through the rest."

Piper walked up and said, "Give me the path view in front of me before you flew in toward the robot."

The screen adjusted. She touched a large gray tomb several feet ahead to her right. "When the cat roared, I screamed, and right about here is where I darted into the tombs. I couldn't see anything but varying shades of darkness. But I could hear the cat's claws on the stones as it followed me. I was terrified as I tripped over uneven edges of concrete and ran into tombs. It was like being in a grave pinball machine.

"I was screaming when King grabbed me, covering my mouth. He was rock solid, and I couldn't budge. He shushed me softly, calling me wildcat. Telling me he'd been waiting for me."

She looked at Maverick, and said, "He pressed me against a wall and kissed me. But not savage. More like lovers. I bit his tongue and fought…until he touched the zipper."

Maverick's jaw clenched, not taking his eyes off Piper. They all knew which zipper.

"I told him he'd have to kill me to get it open. He was amused and said something about it being foreplay - that when he took me, I'd be ready." She thought for a second. "And then the clouds cleared, and moonlight hit him. He was dressed all in black with a hooded mask. His eyes were gold and his mouth bloody. I saw a few strands of brown hair. That's all I could see but I'm positive it was the guy from the riverboat."

She looked at Sean and Dakota. "I asked him about Jessica. He dismissed her and said I was too smart not to know why I was really there. He licked my palm. I grabbed at his mask, scratching him. But the mask didn't move at all."

Turning back to Maverick, she said, "He tightened his grip on my wrists and said it was too soon for me to see him…but I could feel him. He pushed my hand down his body. I kneed him in the groin – but he'd worn a cup. As we struggled, the big cat snarled.

"I dropped low for the dagger in my boot and spun to defend myself. But then…well, I froze, shocked at the robot. King took my dagger telling me Vicious wouldn't hurt me. I didn't believe him. The robotic leopard was huge. Fur head. Big teeth. Metal body painted like a leopard. Even with a long tail and razor-sharp claws. And she was very unhappy with me."

She glanced at Sean. "Can robots be jealous? That cat was mad at me."

"Artificial Intelligence is learning faster than we are. No telling what the black market is creating."

She motioned back to the video screen. "Voices were getting louder around us by this time. He grabbed me around the waist and carried me through the maze of tombs. I watched the big cat watch me – still stunned. King had no problem navigating his way in the dark."

She pointed to the big tomb where it all ended and said, "He stopped here. Kissed me abruptly and told me to enjoy my wedding gift. Then slung me in the air. I screamed for Maverick and landed on top of the tomb…on Cruze. Then screamed and fell off."

She put her hands on her hips. "These were certainly not my most impressive moments as an agent. I screamed more..." She calculated. "Eleven hours ago - than I have in years."

Maverick said, "I might have screamed faced with the big cat."

Everyone laughed and Piper said, "Only a new husband would say that."

"He would if he was smart." Maverick said. And winked.

Sean said, "Piper…everything about last night was designed to throw you off your game so he could be in control of you. Because he had to be in and out of there. Watch this…"

He enlarged a corner view of the graveyard. The drone caught King and the animal as they disappeared into darkness. But over the wall, a crowd was growing. The neighborhood was filling the streets and there was a lot of commotion. And a moment later, a man in a hoodie climbed over the wall and simply vanished in the crowd.

Sean said, "And that, ladies, and gentlemen is all we have of King. The cat, if you wondered, remained hidden until a couple of hours later, when officers were making the last sweep of the graveyard. It jumped off a tomb and then over the wall. It hasn't been seen since."

He turned off the video and said, "Let's move on."

Dakota said, "Let's start the discussion with Cruze, but it will be brief. Does anyone have any questions?"

"Do they know how and when he arrived in New Orleans?" Maverick asked.

"A private plane landed late Friday night. The pilot identified Cruze as a cash customer. He said a taxi picked him up. The taxi service confirmed they dropped him off at a gated RV park in the French Quarter. A fifth wheel was ready for him."

Piper said, "That was way too easy. He was on my tail. Paying cash. Hidden in an RV park. He could have picked me off anytime. Were they able to find out where he connected with King?"

Dakota said, "A security camera not far from the riverboat picked him up Saturday night. And he was last seen entering the RV park a short time later. A team is there now trying to gather evidence of an abduction."

Samantha said, "When do they think he was killed?"

"About five hours before the graveyard meet." Dakota said. "But marks on his wrists show he'd been chained - a prisoner for a day or two."

Dekker said, "King picked him out of hundreds of people at night. In New Orleans. A city filled with tourists and strange characters. He has an exceptional eye for things that don't fit a scene. We need to carve that in stone."

Maverick said, "Right. So, he caught Cruze watching Piper and killed the competition."

"Pretty much." Dekker agreed. "And saved Piper for himself."

Piper said, "Cruze would have known what was coming."

Sean said, "No doubt. And realized it was payback considering what he had in mind for you. But he's over, let's move on. Samantha, why don't you give us the latest information on Jessica."

Samantha flicked the laser pointer toward a large Louisiana map. It landed south of New Orleans. She said, "Jessica's remains were discovered not far from Jean Lafitte National Historical Park and Preserve - just like the map in Cruze's pocket indicated. She'd been killed two months ago. Lab results indicated a lethal dose of Xylazine in her body. That's a sedative used on huge animals. She was given enough to kill an elephant.

"And other than that, they are testing everything for evidence to lead back to King." She flicked off the laser. "And while we were able to bring closure to Jessica's family, this is not hopeful news for finding the other two women alive."

Piper said, "Do we have any DNA evidence leading to him? Were there any database hits from the DNA found on me?"

Sean answered, "No. But you gathered more than enough to match when we do catch him. His skin was under your nails. Several hairs were found on you. And blood. He's just not in the database. No familial DNA either. He's clean."

"What about on Cruze? Nothing found on him?"

"His blood was drained. He was washed. That makes finding trace evidence difficult, but they're still testing other evidence."

He pointed at Samantha. "You start."

Samantha said, "They found mud and hay at the base of the tomb. If it came off his shoes, we could get a start on his geographic location – or find out where he's been."

Dakota said, "And we should know soon what ammo and weapon killed Cruze. Then we can begin the gun search."

Maverick said, "I'll check and see if anyone in the St. Roch neighborhood reported a suspicious person or vehicle. He had to park somewhere to wait for that cat."

Piper said, "And I'm not an artist, but I can draw a rough draft of the robotic leopard. I've been searching online for animal robots and there are quite a few models – but they aren't really like the robot I saw. But what I did find was robotic big cat art. And they are not too far off the mark. It's like they combined art with a robot. This might give intel a place to start diving into dark web activity."

Sean said, "Perfect. And on that note, forensics is checking my damaged drone. If we're able to find even a single piece of cat metal in it, that would give us a huge leap on tracking a manufacturer.

"So, while we don't have what we need to identify or find King yet, we have more than what we had before the graveyard – which was a voice, a burner phone, and picture pieces of a man."

Sean met Piper's gaze. "And as of a few hours ago, we have a new text he sent to Piper." He put it on the big screen for everyone to read:

❖

The game changed, Piper.
I want more time with you at our next meeting.
It's not debatable. It will cost Jinx and Luna if you refuse.
How willing are you to keep them safe, Agent Pierce?

Piper leaned back in her chair and read the words for the dozenth time. Standing up, she looked at Jinx and Luna. "This threat was for shock value. He tipped us off. If he was after you, you would be gone. We've learned enough to know that.

"But in all honesty, I do think it means that he considered taking you. So, a touch of fear isn't bad to keep us on alert. However, rest assured that I'm playing his game. You are safe."

She glanced at the team, then focused on Maverick. "We all know that I'm the game. We're only retrieving the missing women so he can spend time with me. When we get the third woman, or before, he'll make his move to take me. I think we need to prepare for that. We can't stop the game, or he'll take more women.

Maverick sharply scooted his chair back, anger about to boil over.

Piper leaned across the table. "Listen to me. He wants me. Which means, I need to use the power I have over him and make this my game too. I've got to engage for us to find out who he is."

Maverick said, "I get the point. But no. He sets the stage and leaves us playing catch up with his mess. That's dangerous and unacceptable. At any point you could vanish."

"I know. So, I need to change the game so that it leans in our favor."

Dekker interrupted, "Explain."

Piper said, "I can insist on being involved in the game choices – location, day, time, activity. I can give him more of what he wants - but make him take more chances and level the playing field. I think he'll go for the challenge. He wants a strong woman."

Sean said, "I like it. It's a good plan, Maverick. He's made Piper the bait. We use her to catch him."

Samantha said, "Does anyone know why he chose the graveyard for Jessica and Cruze?"

Maverick remembered something and flipped through his notes. "Wait…here it is. A graveyard was one of Jessica's tourist attractions the day she went missing. Not St. Roch graveyard – but the graveyard where Voodoo Queen Marie Laveau's tomb is. It's still a graveyard."

Dakota said, "That's it. Maverick, make a list of the tourist attractions the women visited the day they went missing – at least the ones we know about. That might give us a clue where the next meeting place might be."

In a few minutes, the tourist attractions were listed in order:

Jessica, victim one: Natchez riverboat, Mardi Gras World, and the graveyard.

Katie, victim two: Natchez riverboat, the Audubon Zoo, and Café du Monde.

Danielle, victim three: Natchez riverboat, Historic Voodoo Museum, and Caesars Superdome.

Sean said, "It looks like he started at the riverboat where he could take his time deciding which woman he wanted. Then he followed them to the next place. And the next. Till he took them. They were clueless. He was simply one of a thousand faces they saw that day. The anonymous face of a killer."

Maverick said, "How do you plan to implement this, Piper? Text him back?"

She pulled out her phone. Scrolled to the text threat. Held up a hand for silence and hit call.

Chapter 13

Liam Knight shifted his BMW and hit the gas. Passing traffic, he moved to the outside lane of the Crescent City bridge near the middle of the Mississippi River. He lowered the passenger window. Wind filled the car, whipping his hair. He smiled. At 170 feet in the air, it reminded him of rock climbing in South Africa. What a rush.

He picked the burner phone off the console and with a quick glance in the rearview mirror, prepared to throw it off the bridge.

It rang. Startled, he dropped it near his feet. It kept ringing. He kicked the phone closer and snatched it. He checked caller ID and laughed.

What was Agent Pierce up to?

He raised the window heading for the next exit, and answered, "I was just thinking about you. But should I say hello to our listeners first?"

"Sure, King. We know how much you enjoy an audience."

"Did you enjoy your wedding present?"

"Not so much. Your date nights could use some improvement."

"I'm impressed you called it a date."

"Ah. You got me there. We fit more in the online stranger category. And we know what everyone says about the danger in that. Especially, since you left two dead bodies behind. Why did you kill them?"

"Come on Piper. You should thank me for killing Cruze. You wouldn't have seen him coming. You weren't even looking."

"You're right. I wasn't. And I'd be a liar if I said I wasn't glad you stopped him. But why murder?"

"He got in my way."

"What about Jessica's death?"

"That's between me and Jessica."

"What's your excuse about threatening Jinx and Luna?"

He heard the anger in her voice and said, "You're mad."

"I'm an FBI agent. I was playing your game the way you wanted. Why involve them at all?"

"It's my game. I can change it anytime."

She said, "So can I."

"What do you think you're changing, wildcat?"

"You had your turn. Now it's mine."

A frown creased his brow. "Your turn for what?"

"You set the first game in motion with Jessica and Cruze. You're not skipping my turn. You want something. You give me something. You change something. I change something. That's how this works."

He smiled at where she was going with it. Smart play. He should have expected it. He quickly thought of the pieces he had to play in the next few days. He had some flexibility. "Ok, Agent Pierce. Today is Tuesday. You pick the next meeting. Do you want Wednesday, Thursday, or Friday?"

She watched as Sean wrote the letter W and said, "Wednesday works."

"Why Wednesday?"

Irritated, she said, "Why did you give me Wednesday if you don't like it?"

He enjoyed the parley with her and smiled. "Wednesday is fine. I was just curious. Now…I give you the choice on what to wear. But I want to see skin this time, and a lot of it."

"Last time I covered every inch. Now you want skin."

"Exactly. And be creative."

"Has it occurred to you that pleasing a woman is a better way to keep one, than by force? Or is that a problem for you?"

His tone changed. Deeper now, with a spine-chilling edge of temper. "Watch your mouth, Piper. Don't push me. You forget who you're talking to. Remember…you do have to catch me before I take you."

She'd found a sensitive spot. Smiling, she said, "I take it Vicious will be there to keep me in line again?"

"You can depend on it. I notice you don't like her."

"No. And it's creepy because you do."

"I'll introduce you properly tomorrow. Things were wild last night. We will have much more time to linger on our next date."

She said, "I know a great place we can meet. How about 2901 Leon C. Simon Drive here in New Orleans? It's sweet. And not far from the lake."

He Googled it. The FBI field office. "I'll pass, but cute. Instead, why don't you choose from…let's say…the riverboat, the zoo, or Café Du Monde. Everyone likes a donut."

Piper knew the riverboat and café were out of the question. Way too many people around. She said, "And everyone likes a monkey. How about the zoo? After hours."

King paused. It was interesting how much they thought alike. Both predators, always lining their prey up. But the zoo worked for him. Perfectly. He said, "No problem. It's a go."

"What time and where do I meet you?"

"I'll tell you when it's time. I'll call tomorrow and we'll chat awhile. Maybe even a chat about the zipper I caressed on your wedding day. And just in case you wondered about that - that touch was your wedding present to me."

The line went dead.

A half hour later, Liam pulled into Estrella Steak & Lobster restaurant on Decatur Street. It wasn't far from the main hub of tourist activity in the French Quarter. He joined a group of men gathered for their monthly meeting.

The lead veterinarian saw him first and stood with a smile. "Liam! This is a surprise. We thought you had already left for your trip. Come have a seat. We haven't even ordered yet."

Liam shook hands, and said, "Then I made it just in time. And I got lucky. Something unexpected came up and I don't have to leave the States till early Saturday. So, I'm still free to give the team a hand."

"That's great news. We're swamped at the zoo. Come anytime. Seriously. Day or night. But don't forget about the Masquerade Ball this Friday night."

Liam smiled. "I wouldn't miss it."

***

At the safehouse, Gabrielle, Raven, and Luna worked in the kitchen. The wedding cake was frosted. Champagne was on ice. And a three-meat po'boy bar was laid out with sliced brisket, smoked and grilled to perfection. Jamaican grilled chicken breast. Moist and flavorful with a side of grilled pineapple. And fried shrimp. Dozens…from the Gulf of Mexico.

A platter of shredded lettuce, tomatoes, jalapeno slices, purple onion, banana peppers, cheese, and sauces sat at each end. French bread that was soft inside, but crispy outside, sat by the dinnerware and drinks. Everything was ready.

Dakota noticed Gabrielle's wave and called timeout for a long lunch. After a kiss, Maverick escorted Piper to the kitchen. Next came grace. And the wedding feast followed. There was laughter, the clinking of silverware, and groans of approval from those sampling food as they dipped their plates. And before long, all fourteen settled around a long table with legs painted like cypress trees…including Spanish moss.

After the meal and a rowdy round of conversation, Maverick glanced at his sister. "Do you like living in Florida, Sasha?"

"I did - especially the water. I love swimming. And Tampa PD has been a great job."

"What do you mean - did?"

She gave a slight shrug. "I've had some changes this last year. I handed in my six-week notice before I left."

He sensed something. "Is anything wrong?"

She wasn't going to answer that. Not truthfully anyway. It wasn't the time or the place. She waved off his concern. "Not at all. After getting a divorce and finding you, it was time to move on. That's all. A new season."

He smiled. "Does moving on mean what I think it does?"

She laughed. "If you mean, will I be closer to New Orleans. Then yes."

"How close?"

"Four hours north of here. I have a couple of job offers in Natchitoches. One at the college and one at the sheriff's department. I haven't decided which one yet."

There was a round of applause…whistles….

Maverick said, "We have some time, if you're ready to tell our story. Or would you rather it be private?"

Sasha said, "No. This is perfect." She glanced at the others and said, "Everyone is welcome to listen. It's quite a story."

No one left the table.

She said, "I'll hit the highlights to give you the big picture. Another time, we can discuss details and specifics you need to know."

Maverick settled back in his chair. "I'm all ears."

Sasha said, "I'll start with me. The state took me in after mom died. I was adopted by a military family from Boston, giving me a mother, father, and two older brothers. My father was a combat engineer for the Navy, so we traveled around the world.

"My parents told me early on that I was adopted. Not so much for emotional preparation, but more so because they believed in full disclosure for future needs like genetics, medical emergencies, history, and ancestors. That type of thing. But it would be years before searching for my birth family even occurred to me.

"When I was a senior in high school, I was offered the opportunity to go to London in the International Student Exchange program." She smiled. "And you won't believe this. The host homeowner was a detective at Scotland Yard."

Maverick said, "You're kidding."

She laughed. "No. And my first year of college in London I interned with him at Scotland Yard. That is when my passion to find out who I was began. During the next few years of college, I worked part-time at Scotland Yard and took trips to Norway doing research. But I'll get into that later.

"After college, I moved back to Boston. With a criminal justice degree, I started in patrol and moved up the ranks. Three years ago, I landed a great detective position in Tampa. It wasn't long after that, I received a package from a distant cousin in Norway. Several of mom's journals were found in an old dresser."

She paused, hit with remembered emotion. "That's when I found out she had been pregnant with twins. A boy and a girl. No one had known."

It was silent at the table. The impact of a whole new life being unrolled was intense. Maverick absorbed it, glancing away. Fathoming the unfathomable. False becoming true. Fiction becoming reality.

Sasha continued, "I don't have to tell you how shocked I was. Nor can I explain why no one in Norway knew she carried twins. All I knew was that I had a brother – and my search began. The main problem was that I didn't know your first name. And it didn't help that my birth certificate didn't say I was a twin.

"To make sure you survived birth, I searched death certificates by our last name and birthdate. But found nothing in New York. That was good news. Then came the long, cold trail of empty searches with agencies between Norway and America.

"At least until I hired an attorney. And finally, the court forced the hospital to release mom's medical records. And…there you were. After an unusual six-hour window with a Norwegian widow giving birth to two American babies, it was simply clerical errors. The word twin got left out - and my paperwork got misplaced. And no one caught the two birth certificates on the same date with the same mother. Simple mistakes ripped us apart."

Brother and sister stared at each other. Silently. And mourned the loss for what could have been.

Maverick squeezed her hand. "You've worked so hard, Sasha. Time. Money. Emotional costs. How do I ever thank you for finding me?"

"You did when you walked into the police station. You dared to believe a tale that seemed unbelievable."

They took a moment. He said, "How did you find me?"

"My attorney tracked you. Mom had information in her paperwork that she traveled to the United States to see our paternal grandparents. As it turns out, they adopted you. They didn't know I existed. And no one in Norway knew about us. We fell through the crack in every conceivable way."

"You're saying my parents were my grandparents?"

"Yes. They didn't tell you?"

"No. They said they were distant relatives. That's it. My dad wouldn't discuss Norway. Ever. Did you find out about our father?"

"Yes. He was lost at sea with mom's parents during a terrible storm. That's why Mom left Norway. She hoped to mend the estrangement with his parents."

"What happened that was so bad?"

"Dad married the enemy's daughter. It was quite a generational family feud. And for your grandfather, it was the last straw. He moved your grandmother back home to New Orleans and cut all ties."

Maverick said, "What was our father's name?"

"Captain Erik Jonas Patterson. Our family has been seafarers and shipbuilders for generations. Totally common in Norway."

Maverick walked to the window and ran his hand through his hair. He needed a minute. A mother trying to repair a rift in America. A father lost at sea halfway around the world…and grandparents turned parents.

Sasha glanced at Piper while Maverick absorbed what he'd heard so far.

Piper asked, "Were you able to find any pictures of your parents?"

Sasha said, "I have a few boxes of their personal items. It's packed in Tampa, ready for my move."

Maverick turned. "You mentioned shipbuilding. Did Dad build ships too?"

"He sure did. He'd gone into partnership with Mom's parents. After the four of them died, the shipyard passed to extended family on Mom's side. It's still alive and thriving."

"Wow. Dad would be proud that the business survived."

She smiled. "He was a good businessman. In fact, lifetime provision was made for their descendants after they married. When I showed up in Norway, I became a silent partner. When I found out about you, you became one. Welcome to Berg Patterson Shipyard."

He stared. Shocked.

She said, "And just to be clear, we are the only children of Liv Berg Patterson and Captain Erik Jonas Patterson. Seafarers and verified descendants of Erik the Red. Norse Viking. Christian. Explorer. And founder of Greenland."

Maverick scooped her up, and spun her around to sound of laughter, cheers…and tears.

Shortly, they continued with the wedding celebration. Popped the cork, toasted the bride and groom, and cut the wedding cake. Maverick licked icing off Piper's lip.

Adam whispered to Raven. In a few moments a love song filled the room. Adam said, "Bride and groom, you're up first!"

Maverick drew Piper to the middle of the room for a graceful spin and dip…and then they danced. Playful to start. Then love took over. And entwined, he kissed her and carried her for the rest of the song – motioning the others to join them.

Twelve of the fourteen danced.

***

Hawk's breath brushed Sasha's ear. "Dance with me, Detective Tate."

She met his eyes. "Do you feel the testosterone flooding this room? We need a life jacket now."

He winked and led her through the couples toward the balcony.

As the door closed behind them, Sasha said, "Hawk, last night's make out session was undercover. We are not picking up where we left off at the graveyard."

He didn't answer, just stepped close and put his hands on her hips…pulling her in. She put her hands against his chest…halting him. He smiled, and with his thighs guiding hers, backed her into a patio garden.

Sasha said, "Hawk…you are quite a man…I admit it. But the spark between us is not going to win. It's not happening. I've worked with lots of men. And just because I'm divorced, doesn't mean I'm easy."

He slid a hand under her hair. Bare skin to bare skin. He brushed his cheek against hers and said, "And I'm selective. So now that that's out of the way…kiss me."

And Sasha wanted to, despite all her denials. Strands of his long hair fluttered across her neck in the breeze. He kissed her cheek. He kissed closer to her mouth. Then his lips brushed hers, their breath mingling…

Their eyes met.

And he kissed her.

***

Dekker met Luna's gaze and pulled her tighter as they danced. After a lifetime of cloak and dagger with strangers in foreign countries, she was all he wanted. To wake up with her. Live with her. Make love to her. Luna read his expression as his lips lowered. Her eyelids fluttered closed as they kissed, her hands clutching his shirt. He picked her up and deepened the kiss.

Piper saw them. And for only a second was shocked. The love between the two of them was obvious. And beautiful. Her dad looked up and caught her gaze.

Using sign language like when she was little, he signed: I love you, baby girl.

Piper signed back: I love you more.

***

At three in the afternoon, Maverick checked the last task off his list and saluted Dakota. He was ready. A minute later, Piper sat back and nodded at Dakota. She was ready. Sean and Samantha compared final notes and waved. They were done.

Dakota said, "Ok. Let's go over all the updates. I'll go last. Maverick, you go first."

Maverick said, "Got it."

And after a few keystrokes on his laptop, he pulled up two pictures on the video screen. One was a black super cab Ford F-150 with side steps and tinted windows. The second picture was a front custom grille with fancy lights.

He said, "My partner sent me a report that was filed at the NOPD last night by a man on North Roman Street. That's just four blocks west of the St. Roch graveyards. The report indicates the man got up around three a.m. to go to the kitchen. Without turning lights on, he looked out his front window.

"Motion caught his eye. Across the street at his neighbor's house, a black truck was parked in the garage next to the homeowner's white car. A large truck bed cover was closing. Concerned, he watched. He'd never seen the truck before, and the neighbor was a recluse who never had overnight guests. Then truck lights came on. As the driver backed into the street, he was able to make out part of the Louisiana license plate. 4 I S.

"After the truck left, he went across the street. His neighbor was unconscious on the kitchen floor. He called an ambulance. Today, the homeowner is fine and back home. His story is that he heard a noise and opened the door to check in the garage. A bright light blinded him, and something stung him in the neck. He woke up in the hospital. He'd been drugged and hadn't seen a thing."

Maverick shrugged. "And that's really the only report filed that happened within walking distance of the graveyard - and fits our scenario. Hopefully this is our guy. NOPD is weeding through a few hundred black trucks of this make and model that include those license plate numbers. It'll take several hours but we could hit pay dirt."

Dakota said, "Pay dirt sounds good about now." He pointed to Samantha.

She pulled up a lab graph for everyone to see and said, "This is the results of the mud and hay found at the base of the tomb where Cruze's body was found. And, while most of the test shows typical Louisiana dirt, grass, minerals, gravel, and hay, there are a few anomalies.

"One is a small amount of oil specific to ships. Large cargo ships. And that thought provides a curious angle to the investigation. Especially since New Orleans is an international port city.

"Next, they found the hair of a Zebra and a Bengal cat. And while the Zebra could tie into the cargo ship angle, not so much the Bengal cat. But being King has a cat thing going, maybe this is his pet.

"And lastly, the green spike on the chart is an insecticide that farmers use in barns."

Samantha glanced at Piper and said, "So…a guy around animals. One that hunts. Likes safaris. Possibly around ships. Might have a black truck and a farm. And he has a sure fetish for cats and brunettes. We might need to broaden the search. It sounds like he gets around."

Sasha offered, "On the shipping angle, you might want to check with Interpol on poaching or illegal animal trafficking. Some of them make quite a name and fortune for themselves on the black market. Even some legitimate companies have a side of black-market activity."

Piper said, "Good call. Do you have any personal contacts with Interpol?"

"You could call it that. I've made a few friends during my years in Europe."

Everyone laughed.

Still chuckling, Maverick said, "Have you been personally involved in any of these cases?"

"Not me, but my friends have. Africa especially. Countries such as Mozambique, Angola, and Tanzania. And it's not always killing or maiming the animals. Some of the cases were illegally trafficked simply to avoid wildlife rules, fines, and penalties. But it's rarely best for a wild animal to be a pet out of the loop of specialists. Even zoos are a challenge for many species."

Dakota said, "Agreed. Can you give your…friend…a call?"

She pulled out her cell as she headed to the balcony. "Be back in a bit."

Dakota said, "You're next Sean."

Sean uploaded a blurry night picture of a gray SUV on the screen. It was backed up to a wall surrounding an RV park. They all knew what it was.

Sean said, "They found footprints around Cruze's camper. Blood on the ground. And deep scrapes going over the wall. A security camera a good distance away caught this on video. The investigators figure he knocked Cruze out and pulled him over the wall with something metal. An educated guess is that it was probably a pulley and cable system in the back of his car.

"This dude is prepared for spur of the moment. Drugs. Pulleys. I don't know anyone with a pulley in their car. His victims wouldn't know a thing - but simply wake up somewhere else."

Samantha said, "Chained like Cruze."

Piper said, "Or on a ship. They're both terrifying."

Sean said, "Right on that point. But he also had another tool in his arsenal. We wondered how he maneuvered through the graveyard so easily. Well, the lab located a tracker in your catsuit boots. No doubt he has one on his robotic cat too. All he had to do was lie in wait and watch all the pieces fall into place. You were always in his sight."

There was a heavy pause.

Sitting a couple of chairs down from Piper and Maverick, a thought occurred to Dekker. He asked, "Piper, did you inspect yourself when you got home? I know your body was covered in the catsuit, but your head and hands weren't. We all know how miniscule trackers can be."

Piper and Maverick looked at each other, their frown growing as they recalled their passion last night. Even in the shower. But no, they hadn't.

She said, "Not the way you mean. Which suddenly makes me feel like an idiot." She looked at Sean. "Wouldn't the shower short out most trackers?"

Sean said, "Not if it was created for land and aquatic."

Maverick's chair screeched across the floor. He pulled Piper down the hall. "We'll be back…"

***

In the bathroom, Piper stripped, then loosely clipped her hair into six sections. Maverick laid a white sheet on the floor. Standing on the sheet, she softly touched every area of her scalp as Maverick checked with the flashlight.

After a while, Piper said, "I don't feel anything."

"I don't see anything either." Maverick said. "Let's check your ears before we comb your hair."

They began again. The right ear was clear. And searching the left, Piper said, "Do you see anything where my index finger is on the top crease of the ear? Something is catching my fingernail."

Maverick checked. "Yeah. Something's there. Let me grab the tweezers."

A couple of seconds later they looked at a very small triangular piece of clear plastic. It looked like an edge of sticky tape but much stiffer.

Piper said, "It must have torn off of something bigger."

"I don't like it. Let me comb your hair."

Several minutes later, Maverick said, "No. Your hair is silky straight. There is nothing sticking out. Now we have got to check your body. It could have fallen."

"Which means it could be at the loft too."

"Let's just make sure it's not stuck on you. You work on the front. I'll start on your back."

Piper started with her shoulders. Down her arms. Under them. Across her chest. Her ribs. Maverick checked every inch of her shoulder blades. Her back. Her waist. He knelt behind her, his hands on her hips. Piper slid her hands down her abdomen.

She said, "I'm not feeling anything."

Maverick pulled her back against him, stopping her hands. He kissed her hip. "I've got the rest."

Piper watched him in the mirror. His body far outsized hers as his hands slid around her hips to the front, and he softly checked her stomach and legs. Her feet. When finished, he stood, and she turned toward him. Their eyes met. Blue on blue. Hot, getting hotter. Running his thumb over her lips he said, "It seems we have a dilemma."

She glanced at his swollen dilemma. "I see that, Detective. Explain our options."

He said, "On the one hand, we have a team of intelligent people down the hall waiting for confirmation on the findings of our search. On the other hand—"

Piper unsnapped his pants.

***

Later, Maverick and Piper came down the hall. Piper knew she was still flushed as she sat at the table. She glanced at Maverick. Her legs still quivered. Maverick winked and wrapped his hand around her leg. But thankfully everyone's eyes were on the tweezers in Piper's hand.

She said, "We found a tiny piece of plastic by my ear. But we didn't find a tracker."

Samantha brought over an evidence bag and Piper dropped in the tweezers with the evidence.

Dekker said, "So he may or may not know we are at this location."

Maverick said, "True. We should give surveillance a head's up that he might know."

Sean texted the surveillance crew. "Done."

Dakota said, "Sasha, what did you find out from Interpol?"

She said, "I called Jack Thomas. He said they'll run a report off the databases using our perimeters and send us what they have, hopefully by tomorrow. He offered to come and lend assistance."

Hawk drawled, "Imagine that."

Everyone laughed. With an amused glance at Hawk, Sasha said, "I told him we'd keep him in mind."

Maverick said, "Did he give you any tips or insight until we get the information?"

She said, "A little. He said most of the big group animal traffickers have been around for years. But they're getting older and getting out of the business. New ones are coming on board. Relatives, they think. So, they're working to gather intel on extended families to send us all generations.

"And, as far as general safari information, the largest percentile of tourists heading to Africa these days are from the United States, Canada, and the European Union. So, he said to be prepared to deal with a lot of nationalities."

Dakota nodded. "Got it. Any names they give us will provide a huge leap forward since King's a ghost."

Pausing for a minute to look at his notes Dakota said, "Moving on… We don't have anything new on the weapon used to kill Cruze. Without a crime scene, we don't have an ammo casing. And there were no bullet fragments in the body. So, no evidence. All we have is a one-inch hole that went in his back and came out his chest. Firearm specialists are leaning toward a 458 Winchester Magnum or larger. So, we can add that possibility to his growing list of weapons. A tranquilizer gun, the pulley system in his SUV, and his robot leopard."

Then he pulled up a large map of the Audubon Zoo. He said, "Piper, give us your thoughts before we get started."

She stood. "I'd rather go to the zoo. Anyone coming?"

Chapter 14

Everyone was waiting for them in the SUV.

Maverick pressed Piper against the wall. Total alpha male. With sparking eyes locked on hers, he said, "You should have given me a head's up on what you were thinking about."

Piper said, "I don't think so. You didn't want a head's up, you wanted time to talk me out of it. I do know the difference, Detective."

He kissed her. A quick, hard kiss of passion seasoned with frustration.

She touched his face. "Maverick, if we don't hurry, the zoo will close. I know King's there staking out the place. And you do too. But he won't be expecting us. Which means, if he sees us, he might get all hot and bothered and make a mistake today. Besides, I need to see the zoo for myself. A map doesn't give me the feel of the place."

His eyes slid down her body. Dressed to entice, she wore white jeans and a shirt with overflowing bosom - complete with gun and badge. And she smelled as delicious as she looked. He knew King would be more than hot and bothered.

He frowned. "I just wish you didn't enjoy being bait so much. That's alarming." He opened the door and pointed outside.

***

Dakota drove along the Mississippi River in uptown New Orleans. Turning into Audubon Park, it didn't take long to reach the 58-acre zoo. A home of more than 2,000 animals. The parking lot was still packed late in the day.

Sean confirmed the plan. "We don't have long. The zoo closes in an hour and a half. This idea of Piper's is to get the feel of the place and see if King is here. We know his voice. He has light brown hair. And gold eyes – which is rare. Five percent of the world's population last I heard. And he's strong. Six foot or taller. So, while we check out the zoo, watch for men fitting that general description. And then it's Piper's turn. She'll zero in on them looking for recognition. We'll take her lead.

"Let's go. Stay in a loose group. Casual. Friendly. Like tourists. Samantha and Sasha, no straying away from us. Period. A predator is a predator no matter what color your hair is."

In minutes, they were in the zoo headed into the large purple area on the directional map. Asia's animal habitat and special exhibits.

A tiger roared in the distance.

***

Across the zoo in the African habitat, a lioness followed the fence watching three men point out and discuss particulars of the enclosure. Behind her, lounged other members of the pride in savanna grasses or on top boulders.

The lioness growled. The men ignored her. Impatient, she jumped, putting huge front paws against the fence. She growled coaxingly. The men laughed at her persistence. A guy in sunglasses called out to her and she rubbed against the fence.

Behind the men, tourists followed the path alongside an antique train. It housed equipment for monitoring and research of the lions, as well as an observation car with clear walls.

Forty minutes later, the three men waited for the crowd to thin out. The one in sunglasses glanced at the time. The zoo would close in half an hour.

He said, "I'll take a few pictures from the top of the observation car. I'll be right back."

The oldest guy said, "Zuri's going to think you want to play up there."

The guy chuckled, taking off his jacket. Rolling up his sleeves he exposed an exotic array of tattoos and said, "I'm not complaining. My women like attention."

He headed toward the built-in ladder.

***

Maverick, Piper, Sean, and Samantha neared the Lion exhibit. Dakota, Sasha, and Hawk were close behind.

Piper said, "Not a single man fitting King's description has had gold eyes today. Zip. Nada. I mean, Gabrielle has them. Surely at least one man at the zoo would have had them."

Maverick said, "We still have the Louisiana swamp exhibit to check after we leave the Africa one. He could be lingering anywhere. Or he's already come and gone."

Samantha said, "Piper, if I remember correctly, and I'm sure I do..." The others laughed. The previous prosecutor turned agent didn't forget anything.

Piper said, "Remember what?"

Samantha said, "Didn't Kip use different colored contacts with his disguises?"

And they all thought of the home invasion in Lake Charles. Piper frowned. Maverick cussed. Dakota growled. And Sean sighed. Samantha meant that King could be wearing contacts. Maybe he didn't have gold eyes. Which meant, they didn't really know the color of his eyes.

Up ahead at the lion exhibit, Piper watched a man climb on top a train car that tourists were entering. As they drew closer, she frowned. There was something about the guy…what was it…

She stopped on the path and kept her eyes on him. Her internal profiler kicked off. He didn't look anything like she figured King would look without a disguise. She expected King to be rough and tough. Coarse.

But this guy wore tailored dress slacks. Loafers. Expensively styled light brown hair ruffled in the breeze. And she saw quite a bit of silver glinting in the sunlight. He was older. Undoubtedly wealthy. And physically fit.

The only thing that appeared wild or rough about him were all the tats on his forearms and the fact that he was climbing by the lions. You don't see that every day.

But she still couldn't see his face.

Maverick noticed Piper's concentration and looked at the man on the car. He caught the general similarities to King and glanced back at the team. But they were already watching the man as he took pictures of the fence. Till…without warning, came screams as tourists ran out of the train car. Men. Women. And children of all ages. Some fell and clambered back up, running again.

The team dodged the panicked crowd trying to find out what was wrong, hands on their weapons. And then Piper heard several new screams…including her own…as a lioness jumped on the fence in front of the man on the car. She roared at him.

Weapons drawn now…they all hoped the fence would hold.

And as the screams faded, the sound of laughter could be heard. The man on the roof laughed - a delightful husky laugh. Contagious.

Two men ran up. The older one called out, "That's what happens when a lioness has a crush on you!"

A bald guy called to the crowd, "Everything is ok, folks! Come on back. Sorry for the scare. Zuri just wanted a little extra attention."

When the lioness jumped down, the man in sunglasses turned and smiled at the crowd. But all he saw was Piper. Gorgeous and sexy in white, her blue eyes staring at him. She reminded him of Zuri. A hot female predator.

She walked closer to the train car, her hand shielding her eyes from the setting sun to get a better look at him. Liam groaned silently. And with a pure gut reaction, he jumped off the train and landed in a squat in front of her. He stood and dusted off his hands.

Piper didn't flinch. She said, "Remove your glasses, please."

Liam knew she wondered if he was King. He smiled on the inside as Maverick and the team moved closer. Guns and badges visible. He recognized the men from the marina, but he didn't know the two blonde beauties. His adrenalin rushed. This was a crazy hot scenario. Piper had just elevated the game to a new level. No problem, he thought. No problem at all.

He grinned and removed his sunglasses. Handsome and charming, his green eyes met Piper's. In a sexy Irish brogue, he held out his hands for handcuffs and said, "You can take me anywhere."

The crowd laughed but Liam watched as confusion and stubbornness battled on Piper's face. With his green eyes and Irish accent, he knew he didn't fit the profile they had. At least not near enough to pressure him with questions or take him in.

Piper persisted and stepped into his space. Close. Tempting and taunting. She looked for a flicker of something that she felt but couldn't see. She said, "What's your name?" and looked at his face for damage from the graveyard last night. But there was nothing. It couldn't be him.

He smiled. "Liam. Liam Knight. Are you going to pat me down? Please?"

Piper laughed. Genuine and beautiful. Maverick chuckled and joined her. She said, "Sorry, Liam. I'm trying to find someone."

Liam whistled. "I sure wish it was me." He glanced at Maverick and said, "Forgive me. She is quite a beauty."

Maverick offered his hand with a smile. "She's that and a whole lot more. I'm Maverick. Detective Maverick Patterson with the NOPD. This beauty is my wife, FBI Special Agent Piper Pierce." He waved at the team. "We decided to take a tour of the zoo and just happened to catch your opening act."

Laughing, Liam shook Maverick's hand and said, "Right! Sorry about the scare. I'm one of the sponsors here at the zoo."

***

A short time later, Liam looked over the top of his sunglasses as Piper headed away from the lion exhibit. His hot green gaze stripped her. Imagining what was coming in a couple of days. Heat swirled through his loins as a silent growl vibrated in his chest.

She'd been face to face with her new alpha.

***

A sensation of danger hit Piper. Hard and creepy. Nausea stirred. Alarmed, she stopped on the zoo path, looking around her.

The team stopped and Maverick said, "What's wrong?"

"King's watching me. I feel it."

No one doubted her instinct. They fanned out, checking not just the men but all the places someone could hide. Everyone knew King was here. Where?

***

Liam hid the smile as he watched the professionals scatter and hunt for him. Piper's sense of him was wild. Totally wild. Just like it was with the big cats. They knew him before they ever saw him. But he'd never had it with a woman. Till Piper. It was…arousing to say the least.

He'd have to plan something special for tomorrow night. And not be rushed like the graveyard. He intended to linger as deep…and as long, as Piper would go.

Chapter 15

Back at the safehouse, dusk was disappearing into night as Dekker and Adam sat on the balcony. They watched movement near the trees at the edge of the property. It turned out to be one of the agents on the surveillance team.

Adam looked at Dekker. "I get a strong feeling that you are about to make a major life change."

Dekker took a minute before answering. "Because of Luna?"

"Clearly. Even outside of what's happening with Piper, it doesn't appear that you are anxious to hop on a plane for another secret trip around the world."

Dekker crossed his legs and sat quietly. No response. Cool. Tough. Calm. Adam leaned back and looked up at the moon. There wasn't a cloud in the sky. Deceptively peaceful.

Not looking at Adam, Dekker said, "First available opportunity, Luna and I plan to get married. Privately. I don't want Piper to think about anything but her and Maverick."

Adam said, "I get that. Are you wanting my clandestine preacher services as well?"

"It's possible."

"I'm getting good at this."

"Yeah. I heard you were good at driving a fast boat too."

Adam laughed, thinking back to his hot boat ride with Raven to get married. "You have no idea."

***

Inside the apartment, Luna shut the bedroom door. She wanted to shower before the team returned from the zoo.

She padded barefoot into the spacious bathroom. In seconds she was out of the jeans she'd had on since way before dawn. Then she pulled off her shirt. Happily unclasping her bra, she tossed it on top the stack of clothes and rubbed her breasts. Bras were a love/hate relationship. Then her panties joined the pile.

She twisted long locks on top her head and captured them with a clasp. Brushing her teeth she watched herself in the mirror, her mind playing highlights of the last few days. Namely, Dekker. Everything about him set her off. Wild. From their meeting on the riverboat a few nights ago, to the look he gave her when he walked out on the balcony with Adam.

She rinsed her mouth and reached for a towel. When Dekker had shown up in the wee hours this morning, she hadn't known where their relationship was headed. But she'd known it was heading there fast - and she wasn't scared of the ride. She wasn't going to miss one hair blowing, dive off the cliff, spin around the bend, or flip with him. She'd known young love. But not love like this.

She stepped into the shower.

Thirty minutes later, Dekker heard music as he turned down the hall. Smiling, he stepped into the bedroom, locking the door as he glanced toward the open bathroom door.

Luna smiled at him in the mirror as she finished braiding her hair. "Hey there…great timing. I just got dressed."

He stepped behind her and kissed her neck, sliding his arms around her. "You smell good. And I disagree. Great timing would have been to catch you before you were dressed."

She laid her head back against his chest as his lips continued their journey down her shoulder. His hands slid toward the hem of her mid-thigh sundress. Black with white flowers. Not that he noticed. And then his hands were under it. Their eyes met in the mirror.

Luna groaned, her hands gripping his thighs.

He unbuttoned his pants.

Later, Luna joined Dekker in an oversized chair by the window. He drew her on his lap. He slid a finger along her jaw. "Adam's a preacher."

She smiled. "He's a little late."

Dekker chuckled. "Well…yes. However, he will marry us…privately…whenever all this is behind us. How does that sound?"

"Perfect. But why private?"

"I don't plan to tell Piper till later. I don't want her to have anything else on her mind but her husband and her future. And honestly, I just want the same thing for us. We can all celebrate together when things are settled." He paused. "Do you mind?"

"Not at all. I agree. Just us at the wedding is perfect. And we don't need anything fancy. I would like to buy a dress, but all the other trimmings aren't necessary. Seriously. There is no sense spending a lot of money. We haven't even discussed finances, combining households, or even where we would live. I need you to know that I make a decent income. My house is paid—"

"Luna…"

She said, "Wait. I'm financially stable. And while it's not a fortune, I have a few thousand in my savings and good credit. So, I can contribute to our future. What I have, is yours."

He kissed her. Could she get any more beautiful? He said, "Honey, thank you. Truly, you offer me a million times more than that but…I am wealthy. Money will never be a concern for you."

She studied him for a few seconds. "Well…that's disconcerting."

He chuckled. "That was not the response I expected."

"Why? You thought I would rather go shopping?"

He laughed.

She smiled, "Sorry. Just kidding. But on the serious side, being wealthy is not a life I'm familiar with. I've never been to a governor's ball, shopped at Gucci, or traveled much of the world. Not that it doesn't sound great."

"Our life will be what we choose, Luna. Every aspect of it. I can't wait. Literally. And on that note, I handed in my thirty-day notice. I won't be flying off without you much longer."

She slipped her arms around his neck. "I like that…but there is another thing we haven't discussed. Though it may be too late."

He knew what she meant. Kissing her softly, he said, "I'm surprised you're not already a mother."

It took her a few seconds to answer. "My husband was sterile. It was a painful issue for him, and he wouldn't consider other options. And then he died. I wasn't sure I would ever get to be a mother."

Voice husky, he said, "I'll make you one."

She whispered, "I believe you."

***

Down the hall in the makeshift podcast studio behind the kitchen, Dante and Jinx were getting ready for the podcast.

Jinx said, "Do you think King will call when I'm on air tonight?"

Dante considered it. "Now that he and Piper are communicating by phone, he doesn't need to. Unless…"

Jinx tucked silky black hair behind her ear, and said, "Unless he just wants to mess with me."

"If he did call you—"

"I would handle it. I can't teach self-defense and refuse to stand up for myself. Otherwise, what am I doing this for?"

He pulled her in his arms. "You've got plenty of fire, baby. Confidence and skill too. You've got this."

She walked her fingers up the buttons on his shirt. Her green eyes met his. He squatted, picking her up. Her legs locked around him. He said, "You hungry for me, Jinx?"

"I am…I do want you…soon, Dante."

He backed her against the wall. Pressing. He kissed her. "Jinx, define soon…or I will. I love you. You're already mine…even where I haven't been yet." He slid his hand between them. Touching her. Watching her.

Her body went hot. Breathless, she said, "Dante…you need to know…"

He whispered, "Know what?"

"I haven't..."

Still caressing through her jeans, he kissed her and said, "You haven't what?"

"I've never slept with anyone."

Dante stilled, eyes meeting hers. Desire and love swirled as the truth of her gift hit him. He kissed her. "Then we need a marriage license…and a ring. Fast. I'm not taking you without it."

***

In the kitchen, Raven and Gabrielle worked on dinner. Cajun shrimp pasta. Coleslaw. And toasted French bread.

Smoke rose above the sink as Raven strained three pounds of spicy boiled shrimp. She set them aside to cool. Smoking and fragrant. Gabrielle snatched one out of the strainer – yelping as she dropped it, then scooted it around the plate to cool it off.

Raven laughed. "You thought the smoke was a lie?"

Gabrielle said, "Funny…I'm just hungry. And I'm finished with the cheese. Here…" She pushed a bowl of chopped chunks of Velveeta, Philadelphia cream cheese, jalapeno, garlic, pepper jack, and salsa cheeses to Raven to melt.

"Thanks. Can you believe all this cheese goes into one dish? Four ingredients. Shrimp, egg noodles, cream of mushroom soup, and sixty-five pounds of cheese."

Gabrielle laughed. "At least there are vegetables in the coleslaw. Did Lexi teach you the recipe?"

Raven began to melt the cheeses. "She did. I'm taking advantage of her lessons before she graduates with her culinary degree. Besides, she's determined that I develop appropriate cooking skills. This recipe is a bit messy but well worth the trouble."

Gabrielle nodded. "Everyone will be glad. Dakota texted they were leaving the zoo in a few minutes."

"Good. It's six-thirty. Dinner should be ready a little after seven. What time does Jinx's podcast start?"

"Eight-thirty. I wonder if King will call again."

Raven frowned. "Who knows what that creep will do."

***

It was dark when Liam walked out of the staff gate at the zoo. He'd hung around and assisted the zookeepers with a large male gorilla who had been determined to rearrange his enclosure. Impressively rearrange it at that. Liam smiled. He rarely missed opportunities to see alpha nature at its best.

Almost to his car, movement caught his eye. He glanced toward the main entrance parking lot. And there she was - twice in one day. Piper and her team headed toward the only vehicle left in what he called the concrete jungle. A lone black SUV.

And just like that, the situation presented itself. Liam looked at his BMW. Should he chance it?

A taxi drove by.

***

Sean pulled out of the empty zoo parking lot. Street traffic was crazy. He said, "Dakota, watch for a tail. We only have eight miles to go, but I think every vehicle is black, white, or gray. They're all a blur."

Dakota tried. And finally said, "This isn't going to work. Take a couple of winding loops through the neighborhood. And we'll give surveillance a head's up in case we were followed."

Piper said, "I'm sorry for the trouble, but I'm glad we went. I needed the tour to prepare myself in case King sends me on a scavenger hunt tomorrow night. And even though we didn't meet up with him, I know he was there. I mean, seriously, I know he was there."

Samantha said, "Don't apologize, Piper. I would have insisted on the same thing. Besides, on the bright side, think of the men with new bragging rights. They get to say they were stopped by the FBI and questioned. They'll be pumped for days."

Everyone laughed. That was the truth.

Already figuring her answer, Maverick said, "Piper, out of all the people at the zoo, who stands out in your mind?"

She said, "Hands down, Liam. Mr. Zoo Sponsor. But…he's maybe…30 percent of who I believe King could be. And the other 70 percent is nothing like King. Liam is charming from head to toe. I bet he has a woman in every city."

Sean said, "Or a lion."

Piper said, "Exactly."

Maverick said, "There's no doubt that big feline had a thing for him. But I couldn't tell if she wanted to eat him or lick him."

Samantha said, "This conversation is getting borderline gross."

After laughter passed, Piper said, "You know, men that transport or connect with zoo animals are a completely logical direction to take in the investigation. Sasha, maybe guys in that category will be on Interpol's list."

Sasha said, "I agree. Who knows, in the long run, Liam might help identify some of them."

Maverick said, "I get that. But before we reach that point, we need to investigate Mr. Zoo Sponsor."

***

Liam sat in the back of the taxi following Piper.

About ten minutes later, the SUV turned off the main road and wound through a few residential streets. And it wasn't until Liam noticed repeat houses that he knew they were using evasive action, making sure to lose any tail they'd picked up. He chuckled. A textbook move. And one he used himself.

Two blocks later, without even a blinker signal, the SUV made a quick left turn and parked in front of a three-story building, then killed the lights. It was a typical New Orleans style structure with lots of windows and lace balconies. But private, on a large property with live oak trees. Really old ones.

Liam told the driver, "Take me back to the zoo."

As the taxi passed the building, Liam noted the address. Interesting… Luna's house was on Chestnut Street too. He knew exactly where they were.

***

Dinner turned out delicious at seven-thirty. Not a shrimp was left hiding in cheese and noodles.

Jinx's podcast went without a hitch at eight-thirty. There were no killer callers.

And the team caught up on all their urgent messages by ten. Text. E-mail. And fax.

The men planned a two-man, three-hour security team rotation so everyone could catch a decent measure of rest. Men teams only. They refused to include the women in the rotation. It had been a long three days. Or seventy-two hours. Or 4,320 minutes.

Thereabouts.

There were six-bedroom suites. One for each of the four married couples. Dekker and Luna took the fifth. The sixth one had two twin beds which left Hawk and Sasha roommates. Dante and Jinx shared the sofa bed in the podcast office.

The women went to bed at eleven.

The men hit the bed by eleven-thirty. Except Hawk and Adam. They insisted on the first security rotation.

***

At one a.m. things were dark and quiet. Hawk was on the third-floor balcony. Adam had inside patrol.

In the shadows, Hawk watched and listened. The traffic was down to a trickle compared to earlier. And hardly anyone strolled the sidewalks now. Dogs barked less and less. And it seemed the neighborhood was settling down to sleep. Except for the periodic vibrating car sharing loud music no one wanted to hear.

Adam tapped on the glass. Thumbs up. All clear.

***

Liam moved stealthily through streets, accessing yards without fences. He headed south toward Chestnut dressed in black with night goggles. He was armed with a pistol fitted with a scope and suppressor. Which meant, it was now classified as a rifle. A silent one.

The three-story building rose in the distance.

Kneeling in the neighbor's yard to the right - between the pontoon boat and RV - Liam had a clear view of three sides of the building. He slid under the boat and lay on his stomach. Propping his elbows, he leveled the pistol and looked through the scope. Enhanced with the night vision goggles it might as well have been day.

He smiled and searched the property for the security detail. And it didn't take him long to find two men. One, to his right in a cluster of trees. The other, hidden in the landscaping near the front double doors. Undoubtedly there was another agent on the other side of the building, but he wouldn't be here long enough for that to matter. He just needed one man for this mission.

Scanning the area across the street, he noticed what had to be an unmarked FBI van closer to the intersection. That would be surveillance. They would be in touch with agents on the ground and able to stir up all sorts of trouble. But he would be long gone before they even found out he'd been here.

Raising the scope, he scanned the first-floor apartment and saw kids playing video games. Not them. He scanned the second floor. An old man sat at a table on the balcony. A bottle of liquor next to him. A western movie played inside. Not them. He scanned the third floor. No lights. No movement. But it had to be them, and someone was bound to be keeping watch. He focused near a seating arrangement by the door with a lot of patio foliage. Large plants. Floral trees. Even fruit ones. After a moment, a man stepped out from behind the largest tree. He patrolled the balcony, then looked below. Then disappeared behind the branches again.

A minute later, Liam watched the security guy to his right patrol down the tree line bordering the property. He locked crosshairs as he drew closer. And pulled the trigger.

***

Hawk felt the inkling of danger and slowly walked the balcony. Nothing caught his attention, but everything was quiet. Eerily quiet. He peered three stories down into the dark. The agents were in place. Frowning, he stepped back into his hiding place. Listening.

About twenty minutes later, the commotion on the ground told Hawk something had happened. He knocked on the glass door and Adam stepped out. They watched surveillance running toward the right side of the property. Lights came on in the apartment as everyone jumped out of bed.

In a second, Dakota and Maverick headed for the elevator as an irritated Piper was forced to stay behind. She headed to the balcony.

Her dad blocked the door. "You're both victim and agent. Stay inside. You know this is all for your benefit. He could still be watching."

Piper growled in frustration. "Do we know who got shot?"

Sean hung up his phone. "Agent Lormand. He's unconscious, but alive. The bullet grazed his head."

A siren sounded in the late-night air, growing louder. Bright lights flashed off houses.

Piper said, "King didn't mean to kill him. No way he'd have missed."

Sean said, "He wanted you to know he found you."

Maverick came back inside. Adding to Sean's comment, he said, "Plus he wanted you to know he was at the zoo. He followed us home."

Frustrated, she growled.

Concern heavy in his eyes, Maverick said, "Don't take him lightly Piper. He's playing with you. I know the game of bringing the kidnapped women home gives you a semblance of safety and purpose. But truth is, it all adds up to the fact that he's baiting you. He plans on taking you in the blink of an eye. He's just showing you how easy he thinks it will be."

Chapter 16

It was barely daylight the next morning when Maverick reached for his phone. It was six. They had a little time before the alarm. He watched Piper sleep. It had taken her a good while to unwind after the ambulance sped off last night. He'd coaxed her into bed and massaged her till she finally drifted off. But he'd lain awake, holding her. Feeling her breath and staring into the darkness.

King had hidden not far from their bedroom last night and shot a man. Which clearly indicated that tonight's meeting at the zoo would be more dangerous than the meeting at the graveyard had been. And he felt sure that the second missing woman they hoped to bring home tonight was dead too. Because surely there wouldn't have been a number three - if number two was still alive.

And while Maverick understood the length and breadth of the law to save the missing and lost, he wasn't going to let Piper be a sacrifice. Whether she was willing or not.

He kissed her softly.

Piper's eyes opened. Maverick's expression was a mixture of love, passion, warrior, and worry. She snuggled. "Hey, baby."

He slid a leg over hers, drawing her even closer. "Hey, beautiful. I need to talk to you before any plans are made about the meeting with King tonight."

Not surprised at all, she said, "What's on your mind?"

"You can't be out of my sight at the zoo. King has got to see me even if the rest of the team is hidden. He's escalating. If we don't provide an obvious deterrent, he's going to take you early.

"He doesn't care if you get the other women. He's playing a game. That's true, but he's looking for an opening. And it doesn't matter how good an agent you are, you can't fight a needle. One stick and you're out."

Piper sighed. That was a terrifying thought…and probably exactly how King took the women. One brief tussle and then lights out.

She said, "Ok. I'll make a few demands. He'll agree if he wants to play the game."

"Oh, he wants to play. Just wing it wisely. Let's face it, we know number two is dead."

"I get the point."

Unrelenting, he said, "He wants to see bare skin tonight. What do you intend to wear?"

"Let's make this simple, Maverick. You pick. What would distract you?"

He smiled. "You've got a deal."

***

Down the hall, Sasha heard voices pass their room and stretched. She glanced at the other twin bed. A mere four feet away, Hawk lay on top of the covers in jeans. No shirt. Beautiful bronze skin and muscles. Long black hair on his pillow. His legs were spread, one bent at the knee, and his left hand rested where his thigh and groin met.

She mouthed, wow, and glanced at his face. His eyes were closed. Hers narrowed suspiciously. He was baiting her. There was no way Mr. Panther was still asleep. She rolled, facing his bed.

She drawled in her best Texas accent, "You have the most gorgeous skin. I am sooooo jealous."

His lips twitched as his gaze met hers. "Let's see if I rub off on you."

She laughed. "You wish."

Sitting up, he looked her over for the fifth time in thirty minutes. Sexy and feminine with long blonde waves, hot blue eyes, and long muscular legs that gave him all sorts of thoughts. He more than wished… And knew they would at some point.

Then a different reality filled the room as she sat up facing him. "It could have been you last night, Hawk."

There was no question as to what she meant. He said, "Sure. King had a chance. For a second last night, I sensed danger. Even the animals and insects were quiet. I walked the balcony staying in the shadows. But I didn't see or hear a thing. Nothing. And after those few fleeting moments something made him choose the other guy. A predator's whim."

She glanced out the window. Solemn.

He knew what it was. He said, "You've had to take a kill shot."

"Several." She glanced back at him. "But you know what that's like."

"Too much." He reached across and took her hand. "But being the good guy helps us sleep, doesn't it? Someone has got to protect the world from evil."

She looked at their hands entwined. Large and small. Bronze and fair. Caressing. And then awareness blew in like a hot blast of summer.

He moved fast, leaving her flat on her back. His body over hers…not touching…but very, very close. His hair fell on either side of her face, brushing her shoulders. His lips a tiny breath away. He said, "You know that I want this with you."

She was drenched in his sex appeal. Her mind fought her body's response. She whispered, "One kiss—"

His mouth covered hers.

***

By seven, the team discussed King over coffee while waiting on Agent Donovan to call. Dante and Jinx took a kitchen rotation and worked on breakfast. Gabrielle, Raven, and Luna weren't allowed out of bed till eight. Not that they minded.

The video call rang.

Sean answered as Agent Donovan came on the screen, "Good morning, Sir."

"Morning everyone. This will be short and sweet. I have several updates. The first is that Agent Lormand is home. He's sporting several stitches and forced to endure a week of desk duty - but he'll be fine."

After clapping faded, Dakota asked, "Did Lormand see the shooter?"

"Not anything identifiable. A cat darted across his path and ran under a boat. That's where he caught a brief glimpse of a scope. And it wasn't on a full-length rifle. We think the shooter had a pistol. And obviously a suppressor since no one heard the shot."

Sean said, "King's a mix of hit man, hunter, and predator. He wore night goggles if he had a scope."

Piper said, "Did they find the bullet?"

"It was embedded in a brick wall a half inch from the first-floor bedroom window facing the boat. Four eight-year-old boys were in that room. I don't even want to consider the what if."

No one did.

Donovan continued, "Now, for what's going on behind the scenes. Three agents scared the hell out of the CEO of the Audubon Nature Institute at six o'clock this morning. But now he is up to date on what is happening at the zoo with King tonight.

He has agreed to keep the FBI and NOPD activities confidential from any, and all staff, sponsors, volunteers, and zoo security. Some of which will be inside the zoo tonight. I repeat. Inside the zoo. Security. Zookeepers. Interns. And veterinarians. So, as events unfold, they will be told that we are conducting a terrorist drill - and just to shelter in place."

Maverick said, "We'll need pictures and a list of who is on site when we go in. Friendly fire is everyone's nightmare."

"Consider it done. You'll have it before you go in."

"Next point," Donovan said, "Additional agents and NOPD officers from other precincts will be stationed at a distance around the 58-acre perimeter of the zoo. They will not be inside.

"Sean, your drones are the eyes. You direct. Dakota, you man the ground at Sean's lead. Maverick, your sergeant will be calling you. Your partner and three other detectives are joining the team for tonight. Get them clued in.

"And Piper, stay as close as possible to Maverick and your team. Stay visible. Be prepared for surprises. King's a ghost and a killer. Besides the fact that you'll be surrounded by wild animals – even a robot one.

"So…go ahead, bait him, and show him some skin. Just get information on the missing women and get out of there. We don't need a war smack dab in the middle of New Orleans."

He looked at everyone. "Am I clear?"

An answer wasn't expected.

He said, "And lastly, no females will remain in the safehouse while this is underway. They will be brought to the FBI office until it's over. Just tell them to bring what they need to be comfortable. We don't need King to get any ideas while we are at the zoo. I'm sick of his surprises." He paused. "Now…call me with your plan as soon as you have it."

He saluted and was gone.

Dante pulled golden biscuits out of the oven and glanced at Jinx. She whispered, "Where will you be if I'm at the FBI?"

"Up a tree at the zoo. I'm going to be a watchman because I know our team. If I see anyone who isn't one of them, I let them know. That's my job. No big deal."

She frowned, ignoring the bacon she was frying, and said, "Every animal at the zoo climbs trees. I bet even the robot cat climbs."

Dante took the tongs from her when the bacon began to hiss and pop. He turned the fire off and pointed at the biscuits. He kissed her and said, "We'll talk later. Hungry people are about to swarm the kitchen."

Jinx hurriedly filled a basket with hot biscuits and pulled out a large beautifully carved board. White, about three feet long. The biscuit basket went on first. Then containers of butter, jams and preserves. Last, Dante positioned a large platter with mounds of piping hot bacon, breakfast sausage, baked egg patties, and cheese slices.

They high fived. There was enough food for a small army.

***

After breakfast, the team sat in the den discussing the video chat. First off, about Gabrielle, Raven, Luna, and Jinx's trip to the FBI office.

Dakota said, "We need to get the women to the FBI as soon as possible. We don't know what time King will call Piper. A firestorm could kick off any minute."

Dakota, Adam, Dekker, and Dante met the eyes of the women they loved. The trip clearly wasn't up for discussion. The ladies left to pack.

Sean pulled up the zoo map. Touching the main entrance, he said, "There will be fourteen of us in play at the zoo tonight. And while we don't have location specifics, we can at least project general strategies based on our visit there yesterday."

Maverick held up a finger interrupting him.

"What's on your mind, Maverick?"

"Piper and I had a discussion this morning about King. Now that she has a…let's say…negotiable rapport with him, I have a few demands of my own. She'll have to make a few things happen for tonight's meeting."

Dakota said, "And if King refuses?"

"He won't get his play date."

Piper touched his arm. "Maverick that wasn't—"

Maverick turned to face her. He challenged, "Can you, or can you not, make King do what you want, Agent Pierce?"

She snapped, "Yes."

"And can you make him do what I want?"

"Yes."

"I didn't hear you."

She grabbed his shirt. "Don't push me, Detective. I've got what he wants. He'll play."

Maverick smiled and kissed her. Hard. Everyone cheered. They were in for quite a day.

Sean continued, "So, what do you want, Maverick?"

"I want to be visible to King. Visible and armed. He's got his robot. Piper will have me. She can't be alone with him, in the dark, or out of sight – or even close to it. I insist on being close enough to intervene without affecting the point of their game.

"I shouldn't have to remind anyone that he tossed Piper around like a ragdoll at the graveyard and she's one of the toughest women I know. And then he shot a man outside our window last night. Case closed. He gets both of us."

Sean said, "Agreed. He's cocky. Bold. But he'll expect to deal with the repercussions of his actions. Anyone else have any suggestions?"

Dekker said, "Piper, do you plan to tell King about Maverick's demand when he calls today?"

Piper paused. Considering. "I think I'll wait and tell him when I'm standing at the gate giving him an eyeful of skin. That will give him more to think about than Maverick."

Samantha said, "Speaking of skin, what are you wearing tonight? Just how bare do you need to go?"

Sean drawled, "Asked the prosecutor who stripped at the courthouse to bait a killer."

Laughter filled the room.

Still smiling, Piper said, "Ask Maverick. It's his choice for what I wear. Distraction from a man's point of view."

Samantha leaned over and looked at Maverick. He said, "My plan is for her to wear blue jean cutoffs. She has a hot pair that would kill an average man." More laughter. "And a bikini top – something that can hide Sean's wire."

Sean glanced at Piper. "I can work with that. It's also time to put a tracker on you. Something unseen in case he takes you."

Piper almost argued. Then considered waking up somewhere alone with King and no one knowing where she was. One on one with him. That was a nightmare even if she had a gun. Worse than when she was sixteen.

Chapter 17

Liam had been running for an hour. Winding through the woods on the farm south of New Orleans. Along the bayou. Around the swamp. Off and on the path. Sweating. Barefoot. Wearing only khaki shorts.

Running had been his go to for endurance ever since he'd been a kid playing with the natives in Africa. He'd learned how to make his body tougher every summer in Mozambique at Uncle Jack's safari business. And he'd learned every fascinating detail about predators. All of them. But mostly the big cats. How to stalk them. Hunt like them. Think like them. Move like them. And admire them.

So much so, that he had become one.

Finishing his morning workout, he climbed the back steps and entered the kitchen. Grabbing a cold rag, he wiped his face and checked the time. Eleven o'clock. Downing a bottle of water from the fridge, he headed back outside.

Leaning against a porch column he dialed Piper.

At the safehouse, Piper's phone rang. The team knew who it was and looked at Piper. She shrugged and didn't answer the phone. Let Liam wait. The phone rang six times and stopped. Then rang again.

Piper answered curtly on speaker, "King."

King smiled. She was mad he shot the agent. He said, "Suck it up, Piper. Or do I need to come back?"

"Hardly. And you didn't need to come last night. It served no purpose."

"You surprised me at the zoo. I surprised you at the house. You are the one who insisted on tit for tat. Besides, he'll be fine. Now…thank me nicely for not killing him."

Her temper flared. She didn't answer.

"Thank me. I insist. Or my next visit won't be so friendly."

Throat tight with anger, she said, "Thank you."

And he surprised all of them when he said, "Dekker?"

Cool and direct, Dekker said, "I'm here. Come by and say hello."

"I'll see you tonight. And I'm sure we'll meet at some point face to face. How's Luna? I was surprised to find you weren't far from her house."

It was a jolt of reality for all of them. King had tracked Luna. Dekker's trigger finger twitched in anticipation of what King really needed. Killing. He said, "I get you, King. I do. But get me. You hurt them and you'll be dust in the wind over a dozen countries before I'm through with you."

King whistled, and said, "I'll take a wild guess that Piper takes after you."

"You have no idea."

King smiled. Now for the best part. "Hey Maverick."

Curt and tough, Maverick said, "What."

"I'm going to take Piper from you."

"I know you're going to try."

Ignoring the remark, King said, "I wonder what's going to run through your mind when you realize she's alone with me. I know she's tough. But we both know she can't stop what comes next."

"I'll be thinking, she better duck because I'm going to blow your head off."

King smiled. "Good luck with that. And Piper…be at the gate at seven. Behave if you want Katie tonight."

She said, "King, it's not too late to end this game. Give me the women and just vanish."

"You're wrong, wildcat. It's been too late since the first time I laid eyes on you. Don't be late."

It was silent when the call ended.

Dakota said, "We've got to get ahead of him. We're not making it hard for him at all. He's on a human safari enjoying himself. Everybody, make your calls and see what's happening with the evidence you're waiting on. Force them to rush it. We need information on King before Piper stands at that gate. We are talking less than eight hours. Now, get busy. We'll meet…" He glanced at the time. "After the women leave for the FBI. One hour."

***

Down the hall, Dekker shut the door behind him. Luna was standing at the window. A backpack sitting on the bed.

Without turning, she said, "I heard that. He knows where I live. I had wondered... But I bet he looked in the windows and watched me. I never even noticed his breath on the glass."

She sighed as Dekker's arms slid around her. Leaning back against him, she said, "It's terrifying to realize that he roams the city of New Orleans like a lion in the wild…hunting for the next victim. Silent but deadly. Hidden in shadows."

Dekker let her talk. It was never good to let those thoughts fester into fear or paranoia. He squeezed her. Kissed her head.

She turned and met his eyes. "If you hadn't come—"

He tilted her chin. "But I did. And we both knew I'd come." He kissed her. Softly.

She said, "Would you really scatter him across several countries?"

"What do you think?"

"Are you a spy?"

He kissed her. Deep. Holding her face to his, hands in her hair. He said, "This is who I am to you. That's all that matters. That's all that will ever matter."

***

Outside on the balcony, Hawk joined Sasha at the rail. He could see her tenseness. "Talk to me, Sasha."

Not looking at him, she said, "I can't get out of my mind what King said while he was taunting Maverick. I hate even the thought of Piper being somewhere alone with him. Tough but terrified. Because let's face it, if he took her, it would be an ambush. She'd be disarmed and vulnerable in seconds."

She faced him. "I refuse to accept that a woman is only as powerful as her weapon."

"Survival is a powerful weapon too, Sasha. A woman's strength is incredible in many ways - especially on the inside."

"I know. I just hate physical vulnerability. Piper learned karate because of it. And I box. But they still don't pit men against women in the ring. It would never be an even match."

Hawk said, "It's not as simple as that. It's not just women versus men. Someone loses even with a perfect match. In boxing, maybe a knockout. In war, soldiers miss their target. Guns run out of bullets. You get outnumbered. Boats sink. Someone is pushed and falls. Or one is better with a knife than another. But battles never stop being fought. Right always seeks to take out wrong."

He stepped closer. Her hair blew across the space between them. Touched him. He said, "That's the war, Sasha. Right versus wrong." He smiled. "However, if you want a little boxing practice, I'll take you on."

She smiled. "Deal."

Her phone pinged with a text. Interpol.

***

Maverick and Piper headed down the hall to their bedroom. Piper opened her luggage, refusing to let her mind dwell on King's proclamation of her inevitable vulnerability. Just because he said it, didn't make it true.

Behind her, dreading the confrontation that he was about to kick off, Maverick said, "Piper…"

Ignoring him, she tossed blue jean cutoffs on the bed. Then turning with three bikini tops in her hands, said, "I only brought a few bikinis with me. These three tops have wire in the bra. Pick one."

Across the room, Maverick watched her. "We need to talk about what King said just now."

She threw the bikini tops on the bed. Hands on her hips she said, "No. I will not allow any of you to consider me a victim. Forget it. He's playing with you. I'm not putting that in my head."

Maverick took off his gun and laid it on the bench. He took a step closer…his voice tighter. "We all know the power we wield as agents and detectives. That's a given. And the chance of him snatching you is small…but there is a chance. There is always a chance something can go wrong. Like Gabrielle, Samantha, and Raven. Human nature doesn't allow for a perfect plan."

She listened…frustrated at a truth she didn't want to face.

He held out his hands. "I know you hate this but the odds of you beating him in hand-to-hand combat is zero. You couldn't beat me now. I could take you in seconds without even hitting you. Let's test it in the improbable chance he kidnaps you—"

"Stop right there."

He ignored her and set the stage. "You are all alone with him. No gun. Barely dressed. He weighs a hundred pounds more than you. He's taller. Stronger. And wants you. His eyes devour you. His crotch swells—"

She yelled, "Stop!"

Maverick darted. She jumped across the bed. He followed. She kicked at him. He blocked it and pushed her against the wall. She screamed in rage and swung. He felt the sting on his eyebrow and yanked her up, flipping her. She landed on the bed, arms penned above her head, legs spread.

Kneeling between her legs, he lowered his face to hers. His blood dripped on her cheek. He said, "Say it, Piper."

She screamed and fought to get free. He tore her shirt open. She headbutted him. His bottom lip split. He grabbed her waistband and ripped her zipper apart. She froze, meeting his gaze, feeling the air on her stomach. Her breasts exposed. Awareness slapped her in the face.

***

Dekker heard the argument in the bedroom next to theirs. He understood Maverick's purpose. King wasn't playing around. Piper's life depended on her being ready. He flinched at the commotion and her screams. Not of pain. Of rage. Luna gasped, covering her ears. Not understanding at all.

Back in the den, the team heard raised voices…then the fight…and the screams. Gabrielle flinched and met Dakota's gaze. They both remembered their fight. Some fights had to be fought to save lives. Dakota called the surveillance team outside with a head's up that everything was fine.

Adam and Raven joined a tense Hawk and Sasha on the balcony. All four tried not to hear what they heard.

Sean stopped Dante from going down the hall. It took a little extra muscle and insistence to stop him. Samantha soothed a shocked and confused Jinx.

***

A short time later, Piper stirred in Maverick's arms. She said, "You're bleeding." And touched his eyebrow and lip.

He said, "I'm fine. But you can throw those clothes away. I don't need to remember that."

She rolled out of bed and looked in the mirror at her ripped clothes. "How long did that take? Thirty seconds?"

"If that."

She rolled her eyes.

He sat up on the edge of the bed. "It is what it is. Men were designed to be stronger. Faster. Though not smarter. You know that. Don't let his strength distract you. And you have an inner strength I'll never have. I can't even imagine the pain of childbirth."

"Well, I'm not exactly thrilled about it."

"But you know you can do it. I couldn't. But I am most willing to do my part in making them."

She laughed.

He said, "Please take those clothes off."

"You don't want to finish what you started? It shouldn't take much."

He flinched. She moaned. "I'm sorry. It seemed so much funnier before I said it. I never meant to be cruel."

He was quiet for a moment. "I was concerned that I would trigger issues with your rape."

Now she was quiet for a moment. "I can't say it didn't remind me. Of course it did. But it seems to go with the job of being a female agent. Like when I was undercover with Cruze. But at least then, I had a plan.

He said, "Right. And that's what we have got to do for you." He paused. He needed to say it. "Survival has got to be your goal if the worst happens. Even rape. Whatever he does, be ready for the next opening to escape or kill him. Or I'll kill him when I get there."

She kissed him. And loved him even more.

***

Dekker watched Piper and Maverick come down the hall. Silently. He saw awareness and peace in Piper's countenance – and not just stubborn cockiness. Good. The fight had been successful. He touched her cheek. She touched his chest. Wordless communication. All was well.

Behind her, Maverick saluted Dekker. Maverick's eyebrow was cut, and red. His lip split. Blood seeping. They shook hands. Brief. Hard. Dekker nodded. They were both aware that it had to be done.

Luna whispered after they passed, "But I had been worried about her..."

Dekker chuckled.

About that time, the rest of the team saw Maverick's wounds. The heckling began. Then it was back to work.

***

Adam and Hawk continued surveillance.

Sasha worked with Interpol.

Maverick connected with the other four detectives from NOPD.

And most of the rest of the team made phone calls. Answered calls. Reviewed faxes. Read emails. Printed documents. And updated King's profile as needed. They studied both New Orleans and zoo maps. They needed as much information in their heads for strategizing as they could.

Across the room, Sean made Piper's shorts and bikini top a technical battleground. He wove an audio and video cable along the inside seam of the top. A miniscule camera and microphone were hidden at what would be, the base of her cleavage. Almost impossible to discern considering Piper's breasts would distract King from looking closer.

He picked the top up. Checked it. The wire wasn't visible. Then he roughed it up a bit and nothing moved. This would work. He glanced at Piper. The top just had to stay on her.

Which reminded him of weapons. He picked up the blue jean cutoffs looking closely where the weapons were hidden. He couldn't see a thing. But he felt the three-inch slender metal ink pens in both back pockets. Right along the thick jean seam. Which meant, one for each hand.

Then everyone received a text at the same time. A designated tone told them who it was. Agent Donovan texted: Bring the women down. Meet you at the front door.

***

In a minute, Dakota, Adam, Dekker, and Dante had their women in the elevator.

Dakota hugged Gabrielle. She said, "My adrenalin's pumping. It reminds me of when we were on the run. But don't you dare get hurt. I mean it."

He kissed her. "Just listen to them. Don't leave for any reason. Repeat it back to me."

She thought about hitting him. Her look clearly revealed it. He winked. She was always hot.

Adam kissed Raven. He looked her over and touched her belly. "I'll be back for you. Do exactly what they tell you. If trouble finds you—"

She touched his chest. "I'll keep our baby safe and survive until you come."

"I know you've got this, Raven. Just don't dance."

"Why would you say that?"

"I imagine most of the agents will be men."
She laughed. Point taken.

Dekker saw fear in Luna's eyes as her lashes lowered. He kissed her. A little gentle. Then more possessive to distract her. But all too brief.

He said, "It might be close to midnight before this is over. You'll be safe or I wouldn't let you go."

"I know. Just don't take any chances."

He touched the frown on her forehead. "This is what we do. Save people. Like you do as a nurse."

"Perfect answer. I'll be waiting."

Jinx looked at Dante and said, "Please…no animal bites. No gunshot wounds. Don't fall out of the tree—"

He kissed her. "You just think about our honeymoon. I'm in good hands with the team."

The elevator door opened.

Donovan was at the building entrance. He said, "They'll be well guarded. I'll let you know when we arrive at the office. Now, go find out who King is."

And in a flash, their women were gone.

***

Back upstairs, it was time for the meeting. It was twelve-fifteen. Barely seven hours before Piper stood at the gate.

Sean said, "I'm going to begin with Piper's clothes." He picked up a leopard bikini top.

Dante said, "Wow. That's—"

Maverick looked at Dante and drew a line across his neck. Dante didn't finish the comment but coughed as he choked on it. Everyone but Maverick smiled. They knew better than to laugh.

Piper hit Maverick's leg. "Stop it. It's just a bathing suit."

"It's disguised as a bathing suit. It's two triangles and a string."

"You picked it out."

"So, I can kill King. I don't plan to kill the team."

Now everyone laughed.

Continuing, Sean showed them where the wire, camera, and microphone were placed. Then handed it to Piper and Maverick to look at.

Next, he held up the shorts. Faded blue jeans. Short. Frayed. Low rise and sexy. Dante covered his mouth as Hawk pulled his knife with a warning. A short round of appreciative chuckles filtered through the group.

Sean said, "The thick blue jean material provides ideal covering for a few weapons."

He pulled the silver pens from both back pockets and said, "Piper, these are tasers. They're small, but powerful at 50,000 volts. Carry one in each back pocket, tight against the seams. One for King. One for his robot.

"To turn it on, wrap your hand around it. The enclosed heat will arm them. Then all you do is aim the shiny end at the target and press the black dot."

Piper said, "I've heard of issues using tasers on robots. How well do you think it will work?"

"It's iffy depending on the robot's security programming. But if you aim for visible wires or cables for the prongs to clamp onto, it should allow the strongest volt load to reach the central computer brain.

"And since it's an animal, when she opens her mouth, wires should be clearly visible. Or, in her ears. Joints. And eyes. You get the point. It's not a guarantee, but it's a strong probability that the voltage would affect her functions long enough for you to escape. But you've got to taser King first since he directs her."

Then he opened a plastic case that held several small flat black discs the size of dimes. He said, "These are double sided magnetic trackers. If possible, stick one or more of these onto the robot. However, stay alert in case they're detected. It's impossible to know what sensors could be installed on the beast."

Piper picked one up. Tossed it in her hand like a coin. "I guess they go in my front pockets."

"Yes. But make sure to mix them with mints or change in case he's suspicious what you're reaching for."

"Can I put a tracker on King?"

Sean smiled. "We'll get to that. For now, sit on top the table and kick off your shoes."

Piper's feet dangled.

Samantha pulled up a chair and showed her three bottles of glitter nail polish. She said, "Pick one. Red. Black. Or clear."

"You're kidding. The glitter is a tracker?"

"I know. Crazy, right! Which one?"
"Red."
"Red, it is."

As Samantha painted Piper's toenails with the red tracker, Sean said, "From this moment forward, you will have two sets of trackers on you until King is in custody. Or dead. So, if the worse scenario happens and you are taken, we will follow and find you. There is no question about that. We will be minutes behind you. Not hours."

Piper met Maverick's gaze for a long second. He would find her.

Sean held up a black card with very tiny clear circles and said, "The second trackers are re-stickable. Kind of like a reusable glue dot. They will go between your toes and basically be invisible. They are super thin and feel like flesh. These are for you to use – especially on King. They will track separately from your glitter trackers. We need to know where he is and how close he is to you.

"As far as tonight goes, I really don't see King having a way to take you. He doesn't have enough time. We would be on his tail and being chased isn't what he wants. But after tonight…we won't know where he is unless he's tracked."

She said, "Got it."

He slid her clothes toward her. "Try them on. Then we'll start the investigation updates. And no messing around with Maverick. Y'all didn't fool us last time."

***

Piper put on the bikini top. Her breasts pressed tight against the small strips of leopard material, cleavage overflowing like cresting waves. Looking in the mirror, she could feel the camera better than she could see it. She sighed.

Maverick said, "What's wrong?"

"There is no way the camera will have a clear view. I might need to wear a top that's not so tight."

He sat on the edge of the bed. "Let me see." After checking the angle of the camera, he said, "I think you'll be fine. Your breasts are high and firm. And the lens is just under the bottom of them. Even if your cleavage is squeezed, the camera will still have a clear view from below."

She smiled. "I'll reward you for the high and firm compliment next time I'm not wired for audio and video."

Maverick kissed her cresting waves and said, "I dare you to take this off and reward me now. Ignore Sean."

She kissed him, then stepped back. "How about I let you dress me instead. Here..."

Holding her shorts, Maverick growled softly as she held his shoulders and stepped into them. He pulled them up, covering her G-string.

Meeting her knowing gaze, he said, "Something is wrong with this picture. The last thing I want to do it put pants on you."

She winked. "Zip me."

He licked her stomach then zipped her up. "Piper..."

She smiled. "So obviously the outfit works."

"I hate it when I'm right."

Dakota interrupted, calling down the hall, "Maverick! You have company."

***

Piper heard the commotion in the den as she changed back into her clothes. She grinned. Maverick's partner and the three other detectives must have arrived. She'd met Axel at the graveyard. He'd been quite pleased with his, "Here kitty, kitty," remark even after Maverick punched him in the chest. No telling what the other guys were like.

She hurried and joined the team, giving Sean a thumbs up. Everything was a go.

Axel winked and purred like a cat when she joined them. She laughed, already learning that he liked to keep things stirred up and interesting. Maverick introduced the three guys she hadn't met by nicknames. Rock. Bear. And Blade. The meeting began. It was one p.m.

Dakota said, "Sasha, let's start with what you found out from Interpol."

Sasha handed out papers to everyone and explained, "The people and companies on this list were compiled based on big game ship transports between the United States and Africa. Namely from the east and gulf coast ports. A hundred names are on the list.

"They're divided into three categories:

One is zoo related - legitimate enterprises and corporations.

The second is private luxury pet retail. Legitimate supposedly – but some are suspected of minor illegal trafficking.

And the third is suspected of mostly illegal activity with trafficking through black markets.

"Now, the challenge with the three categories is that people might fall into more than one. I would investigate those names first. The list provides their country of citizenship, criminal record, and suspected affiliations to the black markets.

"Oh. And Interpol suggested that we compare those names with connections to New Orleans and Baton Rouge ports within the time frame we are concerned about. Especially those connected with the Audubon Zoo.

"I also researched a little more on shipping. There are routine shipping schedules and routes for various types of cargo ships from New Orleans to Africa. Each direct trip can take up to forty plus days.

"And just in case anyone wants to know, it takes a ship seven to eight hours to reach international waters in the Gulf after leaving New Orleans."

Dakota whistled. "That's more than a start, Sasha. That's a gold mine of information. Excellent job."

"Anytime."

Dakota said, "Piper, make a note to contact the Audubon Zoo. They are already supposed to send us the list of anyone who will be working after closing today. But have them add to it all employees and affiliates of the Zoo. We need to compare them to the Interpol list."

"Will do."

"And Maverick, we need the four of you to find out which African ships have been in and out of port for the last three months. Or any other ships that have had cargo for the Audubon Zoo since the women went missing. See if anyone knows King."

"We'll take care of it."

Dakota paused and glanced at his notes. "Maverick. One more thing. How's the search on the black truck going?"

Maverick said, "All black trucks with the partial license plate number are accounted for. The last one was found an hour ago. A wrecker pulled it from Bayou Segnette - north of Jean Lafitte National Historical Park and Preserve. The owner of the truck works offshore. He returned home yesterday to find it missing from his garage. He reported it stolen. They're checking it for evidence now."

Sean frowned. "King can't be this good. No fingerprints. No vehicle. No place of residence. No identification. Just burner phones. A robot. Two dead people. Two more missing women. An injured man. And a game with Piper as the finish line trophy."

Piper said, "After tonight we'll be able to track him. Between Interpol's help and a tracker, we'll find him."

Dekker said, "We better. If he gives up Katie tonight, there's only one missing woman left before he tries to vanish with you. And that's not happening in this lifetime."

"Look." Maverick said. "The longer this game lasts, the more people he endangers. We need to go for the capture. Fake the game. Take him down. Make a deal for the last woman."

Dakota said, "And that may be the play we have to go for. But not tonight. We need more than the ghost crumbs we have in this case. We need to play the game longer. Piper? Any comments?"

She glanced at Maverick. "Let's do this, Detective. I'm ready. You'll be close and all of you will be there. I'll be armed and wired. Let's play." Pausing, she touched his hand. "I want him, Maverick."

"Then play him one last night. Get what we need."

She held his gaze. "You've got to give me wiggle room."

"Ok. But I'll let you know when I've had enough. Go for it."

She smiled. "Agreed."

Samantha said, "Sean, what about the robot manufacturer? Any hits?"

He shook his head. "Nothing specific. There are hundreds, if not thousands, of robot prototypes on the dark web. We know this one is made of titanium based on a piece found in my destroyed drone. And other than that, it's top of the line artificial intelligence. It runs. Jumps. Growls. Tracks. And looks like sci-fi art. But my concern is that it might be armed and programmed to kill. Why would he buy a black-market predator robot that isn't?"

Turning to Piper, he said, "So, be wise, but let your curiosity lead you. Check the cat out. Find a way to engage with it. And whatever you do, track the beast."

Picking up the Interpol list he said, "Now, let's get busy. We have three hours till the team needs to disappear inside the zoo. And four hours till it closes with the team in place."

***

Two hours later, a tall black man in a khaki shirt stood on the starboard side of the African cargo vessel, Orion Crest. The sister ship, Leo Crest, was docked in front of them. The ships were at the Port of New Orleans First Street terminal. He could see the Cresent City Connection bridges downriver. Not far at all from the famous French Quarter.

Jabari checked the time. King was late. He frowned. King was never late.

***

Twenty-three miles south of New Orleans, Liam zipped his jeans and grabbed a designer T-shirt. Thin. V-neck. Pale green. And tight, revealing his muscles and tattoos. He ran his hands through his hair and left his room without even looking in the mirror. His thoughts were on Piper.

He reached the kitchen and checked his phone. He grimaced at the time. He was late calling Jabari. His lifelong friend. Business associate. And confidant. Also, the one that nicknamed him King when they were kids. He dialed the number.

Jabari answered, “King. We have trouble.”

Liam said, “What?”

“There’s talk along the port that the cops and feds are asking about African ships involved in animal import and exports the last few months. They even have a list of people they’re looking for. King is on that list.”

“Does anyone here know King is my nickname?”

“No. They just know that a man named King rents a cabin or ships animals from time to time under the radar.”

Good, Liam thought. But his brow creased. Piper’s team was tying King to the animals faster than he expected. That put him in a bit of a bind. Especially since he’d met them. He had to keep them from tying King to him before Saturday. But that was difficult because he was tied to the zoo. He went through his mental checklist for a few seconds.

He asked, “Is the Orion still set to sail late Friday night?”

“Yes. After midnight.”

“When does the Leo set sail?”

“It leaves tonight at midnight. They finished loading her early. King, what’s going on? We’re legal this trip. Why are they looking for you?”

“It’s personal. Don’t worry about it. Just make sure to contact me on my business phone now. Keep us traceable and legit. And call me Liam. I’ve got to go. See you in Africa.”

“Ok—”

Liam tucked the phone in his back pocket as he took long strides down the bedroom hall. Passing his room, he stopped at the last door on the left. He unlocked the door and stepped inside. A woman spun to look at him. Long brown curls swung around her. Young. Beautiful. Almost naked.

She stared. Alarmed. Why was he back already? Did she do something wrong? Danielle whispered, “King…”

He shut the door behind him. In seconds he lifted her chin. Kissing her softly, he said, “Easy…nothing is wrong. I just wanted to check on you before I left.”

She nodded. Totally compliant. Gentle and loving even. It was safer. But she didn’t believe him. She’d never believe him. Something was up.

Liam kissed Danielle again and walked to the door. He looked back at her. He had a decision to make. Her life depended on it.

As the door shut, Danielle trembled. The look in King’s eyes had changed.

Chapter 18

Back in New Orleans, the team discussed the small list of names that fell into the three categories recommended by Interpol. Basically, the good guys. The bad guys. And the good guys that were sometimes bad.

They ended up with twenty names in total. And of the twenty names listed, only six names stood out.

Dakota said, "The name King is found with three different last names. He ships periodically with multiple countries and companies. It's not known if it's one King using different names or three actual people. Regardless, all the Kings are new on the scene and quite the shadow. No clear pictures of him either. Only a couple of fuzzy snapshots at a distance that tells us nothing."

Sean said, "And the other three names include one New Orleans native that's been arrested a few times for animal abuse, and two white African nationals that haven't been caught yet."

Piper said, "King doesn't have an African accent. Where is the New Orleans native?"

Samantha searched online. "He was reported missing six weeks ago by his wife…wow. The day after he returned from an overseas trip."

Piper said, "He might have become lunch for his illegal cargo."

Samantha said, "That's what happens. Predator versus predator. A win for the animal."

Sean gave her a disapproving look. Samantha gave him an innocent one. He pulled her ponytail.

Maverick said, "The four of us found out from the port today that the name King is known locally. Not a lot. But enough so that workers know he pays well when he ships. No one knew his last name or had met him. But word will get around that we're looking."

Piper read through the zoo's information on Liam Knight while they talked. He was forty-three years old. CEO of Lucas Corporation with a master's degree in animal husbandry. The corporation was a conglomeration of various animal related businesses, charities, and holdings in Mozambique, Africa and other locations owned by his maternal uncle, Jack Fletcher. Lucas Corporation had been affiliated with the Audubon Zoo for over twenty years.

Everyone noticed that Piper wasn't listening. She was locked onto something on her computer. Maverick leaned over and glanced at her screen. It was Liam. He said, "Why are you researching Liam? He's legit."

"I know. But he's the only face and name that we know at the zoo. And he's a big deal. I wonder why he's here in New Orleans. He's handsome. Wealthy. And I don't see a wedding ring. What's he hanging out here for? Where does he live? Who is he privately?"

Dakota and Sean looked at each other. Good questions.

Sean said, "Let's take fifteen minutes and see what we can find on Liam since he'll be at the zoo tonight. Samantha, take social media. Dekker, check his legal status here in the States. Maverick, your group can run background checks. Piper, dig around in his personal life. And Sasha, you check his family. How did his uncle end up in Africa and then get connected to New Orleans?"

***

Piper searched the internet for Liam Knight with the Lucas Corporation. Dozens of articles, pictures, and social events popped up. She scrolled and found Liam in suits at fancy dinners. On safari pointing out animals. Frowning as he carried an injured monkey into the vet. Laughing as he sat on the ground with baby lions, leopards, and tigers climbing all over him. And of course, lots of gorgeous women wherever he went.

Then she flinched at an article out of Mozambique, Africa, six months ago. It showed a distraught picture of Liam climbing off a ship in the rain. It said, "Liam's fiancé lost at sea."

She read the article. With a sigh she said, "I found my answer. Liam lost his fiancé at sea six months ago. Cara. That would make him not eager to return home to Africa anytime soon."

Maverick said, "What happened?"

"They were aboard a ship between the island of Madagascar and Africa for an animal rescue. A storm hit on the return trip to Mozambique. A large wave drug her overboard. She was never found."

Sean said, "That's terrible. Ok, team. Did anyone else find anything on Liam we need to know right now? We are running out of time."

Dakota said, "I have a few things. Liam is a citizen of three countries. The United States, Ireland, and England. And his permanent residence is in Africa."

Sean asked, "Sasha? Where's his uncle?"

Sasha said, "A little background first. Liam's mother is from England. His dad from Ireland – where Liam grew up. His parents live in England now and are both wealthy stockbrokers. The uncle moved to Africa after college and built his business – drawing Liam into the fold as a young boy every summer.

"Fifteen years ago, the uncle bought a place south of New Orleans. It's near Barataria. He was semi-retired, going back and forth between here and Africa. Then he suffered a disabling stroke five years ago. Now, he lives quietly in London. Liam runs it all. He is the sole heir."

Samantha asked, "So, does Liam live at his uncle's place?"

Maverick said, "Liam's background check shows a post office mailing address here in New Orleans. But his physical address is in Barataria. So, probably. It's about twenty-five miles from here.

"And a few other facts are: He drives a silver BMW M-2 Coupe which accounts for a few speeding and parking tickets. But he doesn't have a criminal record. He has perfect credit. And a concealed carry permit. He's never been married. No children. And has never worked for anyone except Lucas Corporation."

Sean glanced at Samantha. "Did you find any social media on him?"

She shook her head. "Not personally. Just his businesses are connected to the public. There are no personal posts."

The alarm went off.

Sean said, "It's time. While Piper gets dressed, I'll hand out your audio gear. We leave for the zoo in thirty minutes."

Piper headed to get dressed.

***

At the Audubon Zoo, Liam walked slowly by the Jaguar Jungle exhibit. He smiled as the male jaguar watched him. He was a beautiful creature. Deceptively relaxed and unconcerned from his perch. But the blink of his eyes and twitch of his tail promised otherwise. Liam knew if you entered his domain…or he entered yours...death was imminent.

It had only been a few years since he'd escaped from his enclosure one Saturday morning before the zoo opened. He'd mauled and killed several animals before two darts knocked him out.

Liam walked closer and checked the roof covering. It was critical that zoo enclosures were monitored and updated. Predatory animals were not just smart, they were determined to get out. They wanted to do what they do best. Hunt. Eat. Mate.

Liam met the big cat's gaze. They knew each other well. "I get you, Valerio. I get you."

Reaching the T in the path that overlooked the Louisiana Swamp exhibit, Liam's phone dinged. A text. He checked the time. Almost five. The zoo would be closing soon. He checked the text. One of the zookeepers needed help with a bear.

He texted: I'm by the jaguar. Coming.

He jogged down the path thinking about Piper. Seven o'clock couldn't get here fast enough. Everything was in place. Even Vicious was hidden in the zoo. All he had to do was turn her on.

***

At six forty-five, the middle-aged male supervisor in the Audubon Zoo security office performed his day end tasks. He made sure the zoo cameras were set for the night and watched the last of the day workers leave. He noted that the night workers had already checked in – at least for a while. After the animal enclosures were cleaned or repaired, many of them would go home. A few workers would stay all night. Including him. He was working double duty.

He opened the door to make a pass around the offices. A moving shadow was the last thing he remembered. He hit the ground.

Dressed in ninja-black, Liam pulled the officer back inside the office and locked the door. Pulling a syringe out of his backpack, he injected him with enough tranquilizer to keep him out till midnight - long after everything was over.

Pulling up a chair in front of the cameras, he opened his laptop, then focused on the wall of cameras. Liam knew where the zoo workers would be. But they weren't his concern. He also knew Piper's team was bound to be hidden already. No problem. And no doubt the NOPD wouldn't be far away.

He smiled. Tonight wasn't a small deal. Not only was he a killer at large, but the zoo was a major tourist attraction for New Orleans. No one wanted 2,000 wild animals roaming the streets of the city. They had enough predators already.

***

An unmarked van sat partially hidden by the large gate next to the Audubon Tea Room – not far from the main entrance to the zoo.

Manning surveillance inside the van, Sean said, "Head's up, team. Location check. Dakota, you lead."

"Dakota. Near the Zoofari Café. I can see the front gate."

"Samantha. Same."

"Dekker. Near the Asia exit. I see the gate."

"Sasha. At the primates."

"Hawk. Same."

"Axel. In the Jaguar Jungle."

"Bear. By the tiger."

"Blade. With the Sea Lions."

"Rock. In between the primates and lions."

Sean didn't hear Dante and asked, "Dante? Where are you?"

"In a tree. A lion is watching me. He looks hungry."

They laughed. It would probably be the only laugh of the night.

Sean said, "Heads up, team. It's time. I'll have eyes in the sky on Piper."

Piper followed Maverick out of the van.

Sean said, "Piper. Turn around. Let me check your audio and visual."

Turning in a slow circle, Piper said, "Do you have good visual?"

"I do. Audio check, Maverick."

"I hear you loud and clear."

"Then you're a go."

Maverick looked at Piper as they walked toward the entrance. Her gorgeous blue eyes met his. She'd taken extra care with her makeup and made cat eyes for King. Heavy eyeliner. Glitter. Long lashes. Wet red lips. And no jewelry or shoes. She just wore the leopard bikini top and low-cut jean shorts. Which meant, long bare legs and lots of skin. She was a million times hotter than in the catsuit King had sent her.

He said, "Do you have your tasers?"

"Yes, Detective."

"The trackers?"

"All thirteen of them. I couldn't hide if I tried."

"Your phone?"

She elbowed him. "Maverick…"

They walked silently the rest of the way to the gate. It was open. They waited as the drone hovered high in the air. Watching out of the view of any security cameras.

***

Inside the security office, Liam ignored Maverick and zoomed in on Piper. His eyes touched every inch of her body. Full breasts were bulging out of the leopard top. And the shorts were a hot door. That tiny zipper was about an inch long which meant he could touch her wildness with the dip of a finger.

He called her.

Piper answered the call on speaker. "I'm here."

King drawled, "I appreciate the effort you made for me, wildcat."

She shrugged. Of course he was watching her. "Yeah. Well, a girl tries."

He smiled…but saw they had a problem. Knowing Maverick was listening he said, "Get away from her, Maverick. You are not part of the party."

"Then you should have thought of that before you killed Cruze and shot our surveillance agent. Deal with it."

Piper teased, "Come on King. What's a little extra challenge for a man like you? Are you up to it?"

"Ok, Piper. I'll bite. What are you up to?"

"Vicious is your backup. Maverick's mine."

King wasn't surprised. Tit for tat and all that. "Deal. But he keeps his distance and stays silent. I'm not sharing your attention. After all, you do want Katie, don't you?"

"I'm not stupid, King. It's not like I'm going to save her life, am I?"

He smiled. Of course not. He said, "That's a conversation for later. For now, come into the zoo. Wait on the main path just past the Flamingo Café and Market. I'll call you back. Wait. Right. There."

Piper frowned. "What are you up to, King?"

No answer.

Maverick said, "He's altering his plan to fit our demands."

From the surveillance van, Sean said, "Just follow his directions for now. We'll see what he does and go from there. And head's up. The drone shows a group of zoo workers heading your way from the far side of the Asia exhibit. You see them, Dekker?"

Dekker stepped out of his spot in the trees. "In the distance. They're aiming for the Asia entrance carrying equipment."

***

Hidden in the jungle by the Zoofari cafe, Dakota heard something metallic. Samantha did too. She looked around and frowned. Then screamed. Barely two feet in front of her, the large robotic leopard rose from the tall grass and clicked together like a modern-day transformer.

Dakota and Samantha ran around the back of the building as Sean demanded an update. He'd recognized Samantha's scream.

Dakota whispered, "Easy Sean. The robot leopard is awake. And growling. She's coming your way, Piper."

Sean said, "Is Samantha—"

Samantha said, "I'm fine. That thing was lying two feet in front of me all this time."

Piper and Maverick stopped just past the Flamingo Café.

The black beast walked out of the jungle onto the main walkway a good forty yards in front of them. Its gait wasn't a smooth languid walk like real animals. But it had the slow prowl…the predator look…including the deep periodic growl to announce her presence. It worked terrifyingly well.

Moaning, Piper said, "I see the beast. Where is King?"

Maverick shook his head thinking that thing was out of a sci-fi movie. He wondered if a bullet would kill it. Or at least knock a leg off. He answered, "I have no idea."

***

Several buildings away, Liam darted into a zoo restroom. He flushed the mask and gloves. Then slid his black hoodie into the baby changing station. He ran his hands through his hair. Liam was back again.

He cracked open the door and saw Piper and Maverick. Shutting the door, he prepared for voice instructions and taped a tiny Bluetooth microphone on the inside of his shirt, then inserted the earpiece. Looping his backpack over his shoulder he cracked open the door again. Vicious neared Piper, who was backing up. Maverick pulled his weapon.

In King's voice, Liam said through a robot speaker, "Vicious. Stop."

Piper and Maverick startled at the sound of King's voice and spun…looking for him. The robot leopard simply sat. Watching them.

Piper stared at Vicious. "He spoke through the cat, Maverick. He's not here."

Speaking through the robot, King said, "Surely you knew I had my own surprise. Vicious will take care of what I want from you tonight. But first…you need to kneel."

Piper laughed. "I know you're not talking to me."

Liam was running out of time. He snapped, "Kneel! And hurry. I'm not there and you need Vicious to like you unless you prefer to be her target."

With a gritty growl, Piper glanced at Maverick and knelt in front of the beast. And Vicious looked vicious…all metal and furry with sharp teeth. Kind of like an army tank turned pet cat.

Piper said in a calm voice, "I'm going to kill you for this, King."

He ignored her and said, "Vicious…Piper is your friend. Piper, touch Vicious on the head. Now. Do it now! And say her name twice. Hurry up."

Piper heard Maverick's disapproving growl as her hand touched the massive head tentatively. Half expecting to lose her arm with a sudden snap of those jaws. And then hating the repulsive name, she repeated, "Vicious. Vicious."

And the robot purred.

Piper's mouth dropped open. And the furry metal animal rubbed her head against Piper's hand.

Maverick said, "You have got to be kidding me."

Liam smiled. Now for the next step as King.

He said, "Piper, I'm about to lose Wi-Fi. Which means…I'm leaving Vicious with you—"

Piper stood and said, "Forget it."

"Be quiet. I need to give you more instructions. Listen closely. Just say, "Vicious, come," and she will follow you wherever you go. If you touch her head, she will be affectionate. However, she will not be affectionate if you touch her anywhere else. Or, if anyone else attempts to touch her. Do I need to say that again?"

"What about Maverick?"

"She's connected him to you. He's safe – if he doesn't touch her."

Maverick said, "What if someone bumps into her?"

"Bad move. She is armed."

Maverick and Piper both said, "With what?"

"Don't mess with her and you won't have to find out."

Piper said, "That's unacceptable."

"I'm not asking your permission. And I've got to go. Now, take a walk. It's nice in the zoo jungle. I'll call you once I have better Wi-Fi signal. Our game hasn't even started yet. Oh…and don't worry. Vicious has Katie's map. You were right after all. There's absolutely no reason for you to try to save her."

Piper said, "King..."

He didn't answer.

Piper couldn't believe he had left her with his beast. Something was off. She motioned Maverick closer and whispered, "Is he playing us?"

His brow creasing, Maverick wondered the same thing and walked away. He said into the radio, "Dakota. Why don't you check with security. I'm sure they have cameras. Let's see if anyone left the zoo or if we're being played."

Dakota answered, "Samantha and I are headed there now. Dekker, come take our place by the cafe."

Dekker said, "Copy that."

***

Fifty yards to the right of the entrance, Liam walked out of the large public bathroom and waved as the zoo workers neared.

A big black man with bicep muscles the size of cantaloupes, said, "Woah, Mr. Knight! You look like you're going to have company later. Is it a blonde, brunette, or redhead?"

Liam laughed, "Why just one?"

With the group's impressed banter fading, "Jasper said, "I hear that. So, why are you here with three women waiting?"

"I won't be here long. I just need to film the big cats. There are a couple of places at the top of the jaguar and lion enclosures that look ragged. The cats might have the misguided notion of making an escape hatch. Where are you headed?"

"The gorillas. Tree limbs are getting too close to their enclosure. No sense taking chances. We're trimming around it before it gets dark."

"That's what we do. Keep everyone safe. I'll walk along with you."

***

Maverick heard male laughter as he watched Piper practice getting Vicious to follow her. He looked toward a group of men coming from the Asia area. He met the gaze of a huge surprised black man. Next to him was Liam Knight.

The group stopped. Their gazes going from the half-dressed beauty to the huge metal animal, to the big blonde man who had his hand on a gun. Jasper glanced at Liam, not sure what was happening. They both glanced at the open gate of the closed zoo.

Maverick said over his shoulder, "Piper, the zoo workers are here. Liam is with them. I'll go talk to them and be right back."

Piper turned, nodding at a frowning Liam, then glanced at the workers as Maverick joined them.

Maverick said, "Hey, Liam… Hey, guys. I'm Detective Patterson." He pointed at Piper and continued, "And that is Special Agent Piper Pierce with the FBI. We're conducting a terrorist drill. Zoo administration is on board with it. Security was supposed to send you an advisory text at seven. By the look on your faces, you didn't get it."

The workers shook their heads no. Liam looked at Piper's outfit, then the robot. Meeting Maverick's gaze, he said, "Detective, I get the need for drills. I'm just still trying to imagine the type of terrorist event you have in mind. And if you don't mind me asking, what does that thing do?"

Dakota interrupted over the radio. Maverick held up a hand to put a halt to the conversation - as he and Piper listened:

"Employee down in the security room. I repeat, employee down in the security room. Ambulance on the way. All the security cameras are out. No doubt King's been here. The fence is cut, and there's blood. It looks like he's gone. It doesn't mean he has…it just looks like it."

In the distance, sirens could be heard.

Maverick said to the zoo group, "Sorry, guys. I'm going to need all of you to hang here where I can see you. Someone's hurt and the zoo is about to get swarmed by first responders and law enforcement. If other zoo personnel call you, feel free to tell them what I said. I've got to go. I'll get back with you as soon as I know something."

The FBI surveillance van pulled near the front gate. Sean got out and radioed as he walked in, "The secret's out, team. Meet us near the entrance. We've got to get Piper and the robot out of the way and surrounded. We don't want that beast touched by anyone but Piper."

Patrol cars squealed to a stop. Lights flashed everywhere. Officers invaded the zoo as the team made a large loop around Piper and the robot, then steered them away from the main walkway.

The ambulance arrived. Paramedics ran with the stretcher to the victim.

***

Liam watched Piper. Adrenalin raging. It was thrilling to be undetected so close to her. He glanced toward the Audubon Tea Room, the zoo's event center. The lights were bright above the trees and buildings. Decorating continued for the Masquerade Ball; a fundraiser being held Friday night.

A thought crossed his mind.

***

Maverick and Piper sat on the carved bench surrounded by their team. Beautiful gardens around them. The robot sat by her…watching her without moving…without blinking…without breathing. But she did growl softly every so often. A reminder that she was alert.

Piper smoothed the fur on her head. Vicious purred.

Sasha said, "I'm impressed, Piper. You're not scared."

"I don't know if I'd go that far. But it helps to appreciate her obedience as a robot. For now, I'm the only one giving her instructions. I promise you that makes all the difference."

Hawk said, "Do you see the speaker King talks through?"

"I think it's between her eyes. It's hard to tell."

Dante said, "Do her eyes change colors? On sci-fi shows, some robot eyes change colors depending on the instruction."

Piper said, "I've only seen them gold. Like King."

Dekker left the circle and walked closer. "I bet she has a proximity alarm for anyone coming toward you Piper, except for Maverick."

Piper warned, "Daddy…"

When Dekker was ten feet away, Vicious swiveled her head and looked at him. She growled. He stopped. After a second, he took another step. She turned and growled louder. Much more menacing.

Piper said, "Stop it, Daddy."

Dekker slowly moved one foot forward. Vicious roared and prepared to leap. Dekker didn't move.

Piper jumped up and stood between them. "Vicious, come."

And that quick, the threat was over. Piper looked back at her dad. "I hope you're proud of yourself. You proved she has a proximity alarm."

He winked and went back to his spot in the circle.

Sean ended his call as the ambulance left, sirens screaming. Joining them, he said, "Hey Maverick, the Audubon CEO said to tell the group of zoo workers to go ahead with their tasks while the terrorist drill continues.

"Two security officers are on their way and will get the cameras up and running again. The NOPD has almost completed their pass through the trails and around the perimeter. We'll be back on track waiting for King to call shortly."

***

Liam watched Maverick head their way. He had enjoyed Piper's handling of the robot. Things were about to get interesting.

Maverick was friendlier this time with the zoo workers. Less tense. He said, "Sorry it took so long, guys. You probably know by now that the security office was broken into. The supervisor was injured and taken to the hospital, but they think he'll be fine.

"Your boss wanted me to tell you that two more security officers are on the way. So, go ahead and continue your work. The NOPD is finishing the sweep of the zoo as well. They won't be much longer. And at that point, our terrorist drill will continue. The most important thing for you to be aware of is do not…I repeat, do not touch the robot for any reason. Not even by accident. Avoid her at all costs."

The big guy, Jasper, said, "What if she comes after us?"

"If you don't go near Agent Pierce, the robot won't bother you at all."

"So, she's like her guard dog?"

"I wouldn't say that. Just stay in your work areas until we are done. We'll do our best not to disturb the animals any more than we already have. Deal?"

Jasper saluted him and took off with the workers.

Liam stayed behind and said, "Maverick, I'm pretty sure I've seen robots like that online now that I think about it. Can I get a closer look at her?"

Looking intently at Liam, Maverick asked, "Are you into that type of thing?"

"What thing? Any animal is interesting to me. Let's face it, with a pet like that, I wouldn't have to feed it or get hair on the furniture."

Maverick laughed. "Ok. I get that. Come with me." As they headed toward the team, he asked, "Do you remember who manufactures them?"

"Not off hand. I can check my browser at home. Do you want me to send you the link if I find it?"

"Sure."

Liam asked the obvious question. "Why don't you know where your robot came from?"

They looked at each other. Both, intelligent. But not telling the truth. Maverick said, "Quit asking questions. How's that?"

Liam laughed. It's a shame he liked Maverick.

Dakota and Samantha finished with the security office and met up with Maverick and Liam as they joined the team.

Samantha stopped by Sean and looked Liam over. Forever curious. "What's a man like you doing in the jungle this evening?"

Liam smiled as his eyes roamed her. He drawled in his Irish accent, "And what's a woman like you doing with him…" He pointed at Sean. "When there's a man like me in the jungle?"

Everyone laughed.

Maverick met Piper's gaze. "Liam wants to take a closer look at Vicious. He's seen some robots like her online. He's going to see if he has some information on manufacturers at home."

Piper said, "And does Liam wonder why we want that information?"

Liam answered her question to Maverick. "Actually, Agent Pierce, I do. But Maverick told me to shut up. So, there was that."

She laughed. "Excellent then. Come closer, but you better keep a ten-foot distance, or she'll give you a response you don't want." She pointed to Dekker. "Ask Dad. He tested her."

Liam asked Dekker, "What made you think to do that?"

Dekker smiled. "I'm good at what I do."

Liam nodded. Indeed. And he stopped about ten feet from Vicious and Piper. Piper touched her head. She purred.

"I like that." Liam said.

Piper smiled remembering the lion jumping on the fence. "Too bad she's not a real lion, right?"

He laughed. "So, what happened when your dad got too close to you?"

"She grew more threatening with each step."

"What if you come close to me instead? Does she do the same thing?"

"No, she doesn't. I presume she doesn't perceive a threat."

"How long have you trained with her?"

"Not long."

Liam smiled as he met Piper's cat eyes. He forced himself not to look at her lips. Or her overflowing breasts. He said, "Are you up to testing her again? What if I grab your arm?"

Maverick's frown was immediate.

Liam said, "Really. It's ok. I have life insurance."

And that dispelled the tension of the moment. Everyone laughed…but they didn't move their eyes off Piper and the cat. They weren't concerned about Liam at all.

Piper walked close to Liam, and he grabbed her arm. Vicious roared. Loud and furious. Piper screamed…along with Samantha and Sasha. Liam laughed and let go. Piper turned to the cat and touched her head.

As Vicious purred, Piper said, "Wow."

Irritated, Maverick said, "Get out of here, Liam. Go play with your own cats. No more games."

***

Liam smiled on his way to the African Savanna. Wrong Maverick. The real game was just beginning.

Chapter 19

Thunder rumbled in the distance as Liam sat in the dark observation room, his back to the door. He faced the glass wall that overlooked the lion's habitat and opened his laptop. Quickly working through the dark web connections, he opened the video link to Vicious. Video and sound filled his screen.

He was back in Vicious. And Piper and the team were still behind the Audubon Tea Room. He keyed instructions to Vicious and she nudged Piper's hip.

Piper was startled at the touch of the robot. She looked down. The cat's golden eyes were locked on her. Chills covered Piper. She knew.

King said, "Are you ready to play with me?"

At the sound of King's voice, the team snapped to attention…all eyes on the robot.

Piper said, "What happened to all that one-on-one time with me? You changed your mind?"

"It got a little too crowded at the zoo."

"Where are you?"

"You're wasting time asking."

"So, what's the plan?"

"We're going to take a walk. You, me, and Vicious. Maverick, you back off and give us some space."

The team vanished. Maverick followed at a distance. But everyone could still listen.

King said, "Talk to me as we walk. I'll lead."

Piper walked alongside the robot. This was not what she had expected. "What do you want to know?"

"When did you arrive in New Orleans?"

"Friday night. You saw us the next night."

"I don't want to talk about Saturday night. I want you to tell me about Friday night."

"Why?"

"You came to New Orleans for Maverick."

Knowing everyone was listening, she said, "Yes."

"Had you slept with him yet?"

Piper snapped, "If you want to talk to me, you better change the subject."

He said, "Think again. If you want Katie and Danielle, you will talk about whatever I want to talk about. Are you tough enough for that, Agent Pierce?"

Piper heard the thunder again. Maybe this torment wouldn't last long if a storm was coming. She answered truthfully. "No. I hadn't slept with him yet."

"Why not?"

"It wasn't the right time."

"So, you knew you loved him…but still didn't sleep with him?"

She tried not to think about being wired with audio and video. "Yes."

"Then you know your answer isn't good enough for me. What was holding you back, wildcat?"

"We met three months ago. And then I moved with a new job."

"That's location. That means nothing."

"I'm not talking sex with you, King."

"Of course you are. That's what our little party is all about. Now, why didn't you sleep with Maverick before you got here? Obviously, chemistry is not an issue between you. Therein lies the mystery I intend to unravel."

She evaded him. "I was injured in a case after I moved. You remember Cruze."

"Ah, that. I read the case on his computer. He deserved to die. So, why didn't Maverick come to the rescue?"

"I didn't tell him. And I'm getting tired of broadcasting my private business."

King knew. He just did. He said softly, "You have a secret, Piper. Tell me."

Maverick yelled from behind them, "Don't do it, Piper!"

King ignored Maverick. He was on the hunt. He could smell it. "Tell me, Piper."

She said, "You're wasting your time. There's nothing to say. And we're going to get wet if you don't hurry up."

Lightning flashed. "Vicious is waterproof. Now, turn and face me."

Piper stopped. They were on the far side of the African Savanna. She looked down at Vicious. Her gold eyes stared back, just like King's.

King said, "Kneel. And tell me or you can't have Katie."

Maverick screamed like the enraged Viking he was. It was killing him not to intervene.

Piper had to get Katie. She knelt in front of Vicious and stuck her hands in her pockets avoiding the gold eyes.

King said, "Look at me."

She turned to him. Eyes like daggers.

He whispered, "Katie is just inches in front of you. Tell me, wildcat."

"I was raped."

Maverick growled and clenched his fists. He would kill King if it was the last thing he ever did.

Down the trail, Dekker felt the blow to his soul. Oh, Piper… And the rest of the team winced.

King believed her. "When?"

"I was sixteen."

"Did you report him?"

"He was killed in a car accident later that night."

"That's some powerful karma that follows you, Piper. He's gone. And now Cruze is gone."

"I don't believe in karma."

"What do you believe in?"

"It's not what. It's who. Jesus. Not that I'm the best Christian on the planet by any means."

"You aren't mad because He didn't protect you?"

"No. My choice got me in trouble. He helps me save others."

King pondered her words. "You're an impressive woman, Piper. When did you tell Maverick?"

Light rain started falling as she knelt before the beast. Wet and exposed for all the world to see. She said, "When I got here. Now, that's enough. I did what you wanted. Give me Katie."

Lightning flashed across the sky. Thunder rumbled. King knew she'd earned it. He said, "Vicious will open her jaws. You'll see a plastic bag taped inside. That's Katie. I'll tell you when to reach for it."

Piper watched the massive metal jaws open. She could see the bag.

He said, "Take it."

Piper pulled her hands from her pockets and reached in the black mouth. Ripping the bag off, she heard the tiny clink of the tracker she left behind. She removed her hand, and the jaws shut. She stood and took a few steps away from the robot. Vicious made an odd buzzing sound. Piper frowned. That was a new noise.

And then the gold eyes turned red.

***

Well behind Maverick at the lion's exhibit, Liam watched the self-destruct alarm activate on the robot software. What had Piper done? Vicious would kill her. He jumped up as his screen went red. And then he heard her scream.

As Liam ran out the door, he heard Maverick scream, "Run, Piper! Run!"

***

Maverick ran toward Piper trying to understand what was happening to Vicious. The robot leopard was going through some kind of electronic metamorphosis that looked deadly. Even in the rain. She was covered in blue sparking electricity like bolts of lightning running all over her metal body. She snapped and snarled crouched on the ground like she was in pain. And then she rose and roared…and began to chase Piper.

Behind Maverick, Sean was running toward the nightmare chaos yelling at the team. To his left, the lion's observation door flew open. Liam ran out…then shot down the trail like a bat out of hell.

Sean watched. Amazed. Personally, he'd always been fast. But Liam was jaguar fast. In seconds, he shot past Maverick, yelling something. Piper was still ahead of the robot, but gradually losing ground in the rain. And the African Savanna was ending.

Liam yelled at Piper as he ran past the electrified robot, "Head to the Louisiana Swamp!"

Piper turned off the path and ran down the boardwalk, bare feet running as fast as she could. She knew everyone was following and glanced back. Maverick was passing the robot now. But Liam wasn't far behind her. And in a few more steps he snatched her up. She clung.

In no time, they reached the Cypress Knee Café, and he threw her on top of the porch. She screamed and landed hard. Scrambling to her feet, she climbed on the main roof and watched.

Maverick and Liam played a deadly game of shoving picnic tables around to prevent Vicious from climbing to jump on the roof. Liam got hit by her tail, yelled, and grabbed his smoking side. Maverick got hit on the leg and kicked her in return. She roared.

From both sides of the swamp, Piper saw the rest of the team running toward them. Then in a perfect problem-solving solution to her problem, Vicious ran toward the end of the buildings and climbed up. At which point, she began to jump from one building to the other, going back for Piper.

The team began to shoot the robot from all around the swamp. Over and over and over. Pieces of her flew. A leg fell off. Her tail. She limped with another damaged limb, her mouth spewing tiny lightning bolts.

Piper stared. Aghast, but in awe at the shear obedience of a robot to perform its mission. Maverick hollered at her to jump off the roof. He caught her. And they all watched the cat robot thing fall off the roof that Piper had just been on.

It crawled inch by broken inch toward her. But before it came anywhere close to them, Maverick ran and jumped. He landed on what was left of its head and neck. It broke off and the flickering electricity died. The beast went dark. All that was left was a trail of black metal that smelled like burnt hair.

Shocked at all of it, Piper looked at Maverick. He touched her wet face through the slowing rain, "Are you ok?" Then he turned her around to check for himself.

She mumbled something, and he looked up. Dekker was coming. Maverick groaned thinking about the rape. Piper saw her dad's pain and ran to him. Her feet left the ground as he wrapped her in his arms, turning from the others.

Face buried in his shoulder, she said, "Daddy, I didn't want to tell—"

He closed his eyes. "This is not about me."

She blurted, "I don't want to tell Mom."

He moaned and didn't let go.

She said, "Listen to me. It was a few bad hours in an otherwise fabulous life. We have got to let it go. I let it make me, not break me. And until tonight, only Maverick knew. Tell me you won't tell her."

He lowered her. "That's not going to work. The secret's out."

"No…I don't want to see the look on her face that I see on yours."

"And I don't want to imagine what that night was for you, but it is what it is. We've got this, Piper. Together."

She frowned. She didn't want to tell her.

He said softly, "You're a wife. You'll be a mother. Would you want a secret of this magnitude kept from you?"

She winced. "No."

He kissed her forehead. "The right time will come. Now, let's join Maverick. He looks ready to haul you off to Norway forever. And I don't blame him."

Joining the group, Maverick hugged her and pointed at Liam. Piper saw the ugly burn on his side. And remembered the look on his face as he fought to reach her. She walked into Liam's arms…sincerely grateful he'd reached her before Vicious.

Liam squeezed her, loving the feel of her holding him. Her smell. He knew if he hadn't been here, she'd be dead. But then again…if he hadn't been here, none of this would have ever happened. Glancing at what was left of Vicious, he knew King would have to disappear.

He'd finish this as Liam.

***

The rain stopped and lightning moved to the southern sky. The group met the Audubon CEO at the zoo entrance. Piper, Maverick, and Liam were forced to be cleared by paramedics.

As the feisty female paramedic fussed over scrapes on Piper's hands, knees, and feet, Piper said, "It's nothing. They'll be healed in a couple of days."

The paramedic said, "Hardly. You're half-dressed at the zoo with cuts. Cuts mind you! And there are animal droppings everywhere. You don't even have shoes on. You need to be dipped in antiseptic."

Maverick and Liam laughed. Liam said gratefully, "I'm glad she's your paramedic and not mine, Piper."

The male paramedic with him said, "Well, I'm not. Piper is the hottest thing I've ever seen come out of the jungle."

Everyone laughed.

Liam flinched when his paramedic made him take off his shirt. The green material had melted into the edges of the burn on his side. He still remembered the acrid smell.

Piper made a face. "That looks painful, Liam."

He winked. "It's nothing. It'll be healed in a couple of days."

She grinned at hearing her words thrown back at her, and said, "Oh, look…what a shame. Did you burn off a tat? You only have a hundred left."

He laughed. "Seriously. That is the thanks I get?"

"Quit whining. You won the race and beat the beast. What else do you need?"

Liam look at Maverick. "Her gratitude was that short lived?"

Maverick said, "You got one hug. That's pretty much as long as her tender side lasts. She's an alpha. Suck it up, Lion Man."

Dekker joined them just about the time Maverick refused to sit on a stretcher. The feisty female paramedic now after him. She put her hands on her hips and pointed at the stretcher.

Maverick propped his foot on the back of the ambulance and pulled up his pant leg. "There. Help yourself. It's nothing. It'll be healed in a couple of days."

Even she laughed.

After everyone was medically cleared, Dekker shook Liam's hand. "Where'd you learn to run like that?"

"Running for my life as a kid in Africa. I didn't have many options."

"I hear that. Piper didn't either. I owe you."

"No, you don't. Who wasn't running after them? I'm just faster and used to outrunning animals. You know, no one has told me what all this was really about. There were no fake terrorists, and her robot tried to kill her."

Sean answered, "We're on a case involving kidnapping, murder, threats, and mayhem. The killer left Piper the robot as part of a game tonight."

Liam looked at Piper and said, "Well, I'm assuming the game didn't work."

Piper said, "Actually, it did. We got what we came for. I tried to get more, but the tracker I dropped in its mouth probably set off a protective response. We knew it was possible."

Liam frowned. "You mean you don't know who the killer is?"

"Just that his name is King, and he traffics animals from Africa. And then for some reason he targeted women. Three. Right here in New Orleans. Two are dead. We still need the last one."

"Is that why you got involved?"

"Not exactly. He found me…and decided I would be number four if I didn't stop him first."

***

Less than an hour later, the FBI left with the robot. Well, more accurately, a box of pieces of the robot.

The Sheriff's Department and an FBI team were out searching for Katie near Irish Bayou east of New Orleans.

And the zoo staff moved in to clean up the Louisiana Swamp exhibit.

The zoo CEO talked with Liam and the team in the parking lot.

Piper looked over at the Audubon Tea Room still lit up and busy with people. She said, "The event center is gorgeous. I waited in the garden behind it earlier. Are they preparing for a party?"

Liam smiled as the CEO reached into his suit pocket and pulled out a handful of envelopes - beautiful with artwork reflecting the zoo.

The CEO said, "It's better than a party, Agent Pierce. It's Audubon's annual Masquerade Ball fundraiser this Friday night. And as one of the zoo sponsors, Mr. Knight has already suggested that your team be our honored guests."

Maverick frowned even as Piper smiled. He glanced at Dakota and Sean's furrowed brows and said, "Piper, I don't think—"

"Please…" The CEO said as he handed Maverick the stack of invitations. "We understand the situation. Liam will take care of everything you need. Especially security. Please let us show you how truly magnificent a night here can be."

Maverick wasn't surprised at the excitement in Piper's eyes when she turned to him. He knew it had been a long, hard few days, and she'd seen none of the real grace and beauty of New Orleans as a bride. Of course she wanted to go. And he also knew she intended to go. All the women would want to. He heard everyone laugh. They knew too.

He smiled, pulling her close. "I can't wait to see you in a ball gown."

Everyone cheered.

Including Liam. He couldn't wait to see her in a ball gown either.

Chapter 20

Back at the safehouse, Maverick turned on the waterfall faucet bathtub he'd been wanting to get in with Piper for two days. Snuggled in a large corner of the room surrounded by vibrant stained-glass windows, it was round and a deep moss green. He threw in a handful of bath salt as it filled.

Piper smiled and met Maverick's eyes in the mirror behind her. "You know a bath isn't good for that burn on your leg. Or salt."

He unclasped her bikini top. His blonde hair brushed her shoulder as he leaned down and kissed her neck. He said, "My burn is wrapped and waterproof. You need a long soak…and a massage if you're going to wear a ball gown in two days."

He slid the zipper of her still damp shorts down. Caressingly. Then scooped her up and lowered her into the tub. Piper groaned at everything. From the fabulous sensation of hot water…to the stings of her scrapes. The aroma reminded her of expensive leather and jasmine. And the spreading ache reminded her of where Maverick's hands had been.

She watched him pull off his shirt. He unzipped his jeans but sat on the side of the tub without taking them off. She said, "What's on your mind?"

"Tonight was a big deal, Piper. Your sacrifice for Katie was huge. I admire you. Though I plan to make King pay for making you do it."

"Not if I get to him first."

Nodding in agreement, he said, "It was a blow for everyone. Especially your dad. But I'm glad you didn't reveal the rest."

"King didn't realize I had more than one secret." She winced. "I just hate that Dad found out that way. And now I have got to think about telling Mom."

"Not tonight."

She nodded and brushed water over her arms. "You know, I kind of liked Vicious when King wasn't around. This wasn't her fault."

His muscles flexed as he reached under the water to slide his hand up her leg. "Machines do what humans program them to do."

"Her end was horrible, even for a machine."

"Horrible was that she was going to kill you."

"There is that. So, I guess King will go back to calling, texting, or reaching me on the podcast."

Forgetting King, Maverick slid off his jeans. His gaze met hers as he lowered into the water, sliding them together like fire and water.

***

Dekker, Adam, Dakota, and Dante watched the black SUV pull up downstairs with their women. As the flurry of beauty headed upstairs, Dakota stayed behind.

Donovan asked, "What does the team think King will do next?"

"Call Piper personally or on the podcast. The communication between them was entirely too intimate for him to call it quits. I don't see him giving up. Unless…we know more than we think we do, and he needs a new plan. Did they find Katie's remains yet?"

"Yes. I just got the call. It was bad. She had gotten loose from him and run away. An alligator attacked her. King killed it and buried what he could find of her. At least that's what the note said."

Dakota looked away without responding. A double nightmare for the family. He said, "I hope that's not Danielle's fate."

"Me too. But the odds don't favor her being alive – even though he didn't personally kill Katie."

No answer needed. Two down. One woman to go. Nothing looked good.

***

On Dakota's return upstairs, the Masquerade Ball had been an immediate hit for the women. Dekker had already hired a Hummer limousine for the shopping trip tomorrow. That's all the time they had to get ready. One day. The Ball was the day after tomorrow at eight o'clock.

A smiling Gabrielle met Dakota at the door. "I need to hear with my own ears that we are going to a Masquerade Ball. Is it true?"

He kissed her. "You can thank Piper. We couldn't tell her no. She earned it."

Gabrielle glanced at Dekker, who kept looking down the hall, heaviness in his expression. She said, "I heard Maverick and Piper were taking an early night. Was the zoo worse than expected? Everyone is avoiding any open discussion."

Leading her toward the windows overlooking the balcony, he said softly, "With King, things are always unexpected. And to make a long story short, yes, it was worse."

Concern filled her eyes. "Were Piper and Maverick hurt?"

"Minor injuries. And two others from the zoo were injured. Unfortunately, there was one death. Katie didn't survive her time with King."

She winced. That was awful. "Then what's wrong with Dekker?"

"We found out Piper was raped when she was sixteen."

Shock flashed across Gabrielle's face. "Oh, no…" Then she looked puzzled. "How did that come up at the zoo?"

"King questioned her…and caught whiff of a secret. Then he used Katie to force her to tell it." He sighed. "Piper was so brave, Gabrielle. Everyone heard it over the radio. Maverick was about to explode he was so angry.

"Then after she finished the confession, she simply completed her mission...inside the robot's mouth. Only…it wasn't over. It was just the beginning of the next nightmare."

Eyes wide, Gabrielle said, "What happened?"

"Vicious had a self-destruct feature in the event she was breached. And believe it or not, she morphed into an electrical beast and chased Piper through the zoo."

Touching both sides of her head, Gabrielle said, "This can't be real."

Dakota said, "It was like being in a sci-fi flick. And Liam, the lion man, outran the robot and saved her. The rest was a battle between man and beast until the robot was broken and dead."

Gabrielle just stared at him. He tilted her chin and whispered, "I know another superhero that fought off killers with a pet hawk and a sword to save her loved ones."

She touched his chest. "I guess we do what we have to do, don't we?"

"Indeed, we do, beautiful."

She thought of something. "Wait, where was King in all this mess?"

"Talking through the robot."

"I'm confused. I thought him being with Piper was the point of this meeting."

"He vanished. No one knows where he is."

***

As everyone headed to bed, Luna watched Dekker shut the bedroom door behind them. He paused there, not moving. Stepping out of her sandals, she kept her eyes on him. She knew Piper's rape revelation had wounded him. Deeply. And as a wife and a nurse, she'd learned that action men like him dealt with things differently. He needed to physically work it out. Engage in something. Work. Sports. Even sex.

Dekker walked to the open closet and stopped. Reaching up, he grabbed the top of the doorframe with both hands. Tight. He hung there. Head down. Legs spread. His muscles flexed under his shirt. His chest hurt and he needed to kill someone that was already dead.

He growled in pain. While he was out saving the world, Piper had needed him. She would never have told him what happened that night. Never. She was too much like him. His eyes burned.

Luna's heart broke for Dekker. She walked behind him, arms softly reaching around him. His body was rigid. She kissed his back and whispered, "Let me help you."

He let out a deep groan and turned, embracing her. Her feet left the floor as he buried his face in her neck. In her softness. Breath ragged, he said, "Not like this."

"It doesn't matter. You need me."

His eyes met hers. Struggling. Searching. She wrapped her legs around him and pulled his lips to hers. Giving comfort.

Later, Dekker kissed Luna's face as she slept. He stared into the darkness. She would be sore tomorrow. He grimaced. But the vice grip killing him had eased. He slid out of bed.

Walking around the room, he texted the office. He gave them Piper's high school information and asked for research on any young men that died in the local news the year she was sixteen. Then he waited.

It didn't take long. He had the boy's picture and knew everything about him. He knew which night it happened. And about the crash. It was all very close to the date of his and Nicole's divorce. It played a part in the horror that night.

He looked out the window at New Orleans…seeing nothing. He recalled the changes in Piper after that. The talks with her to see if it was more than teenage hormones going on. New independence. Feisty insistence on tougher self-defense training. Making Dakota increase her karate training. And her plan for criminal justice…and the FBI.

Dekker felt the first tear roll down his face. Then the next. Piper had chosen not to tell them. Pain burned him. She only shared it because of Katie. He wiped his face. He couldn't be prouder of her strength…or more devastated.

He wouldn't fail her again.

***

Close to midnight, Liam drove to a secluded area along the Mississippi River. Docks from the Port of New Orleans were lit up in the late-night sky. He pressed the window button and silently it lowered. Sounds filled the car. The water. Wind. Traffic on the river. And every so often the sound of music.

He leaned his head back and watched the port. He'd lost count of the number of times he'd traveled here through the years. Fabulous years. But after the Masquerade Ball he'd never be back to Louisiana or the States. You can't kidnap an FBI agent and think they will forget about you.

Pulling out the burner phone, he opened a new text box and hit the audio record feature. Holding it out the window, he recorded the sounds that set the stage for his last message to Piper. There would be no need for another.

Chapter 21

It was festive in the apartment the next morning. The sound of laughter. The smell of coffee. The shuffle of skillets as Adam and Hawk cooked a campfire style breakfast of bacon, fried eggs, and grilled toast. But mostly, it was because of the women's thrilled conversations about today's shopping trip for the Ball.

Across the room, Sean and Dakota went through case updates to prepare for a quick meeting after breakfast. And Piper and Maverick sat outside on the balcony enjoying a leisure cup of coffee. Alone.

***

Sitting on Maverick's lap, Piper said, "Thank you for this, Maverick. I haven't been on a balcony since my first night in New Orleans."

He kissed her. "I plan on making sure you enjoy everything you came to New Orleans for. Me."

She whispered, "Doing what?"

"Burying myself deep inside you...and watching you feel me."

Piper was gone. Melted. Everything on her responded. "Maverick…"

He kissed her neck. "I would take you right now if I could."

"And since you can't?"

"I'll talk about it."

Her phone buzzed on the table next to her quickly cooling coffee. They ignored it.

It buzzed again a little later. They ignored it again.

Dakota knocked on the window behind them.

Piper said, "Not many men chance the wrath of a husband your size."

As they came inside, the silence told them.

Piper said, "What happened?"

Sean said, "Check your text message. It's audio."

Piper hit play:

❖

The sounds of wind, waves, and a ship's horn sounded ominously through the house.

King said softly, "Morning, wildcat. By the time you hear this message I'll be long gone - riding the waves in international waters. And you won't know which ship. Which ocean. Or where I'm headed.

"The tragic ending of Vicious required a quick pause in our game. But don't worry about Danielle – you'll get another chance to find her. One day when you least expect it, I'll be back, and we'll pick up where we left off. Whether it's next month, in six months, or next year. I will be back for you."

Then there was only the sound of wind and a ship's horn.

Piper sighed and walked toward King's profile board. She touched the partial picture of him. They had just enough to see he was real but not enough to know who he was. She said, "The King I know wouldn't quit. I just don't see it."

Maverick said, "We certainly can't take him at his word. We'll have to verify passenger manifests on the ships that left New Orleans last night."

Sean said, "Agreed. I'm sure Agent Donovan will get the field office on it. There could be dozens of ship manifests to gather, then review. Which means, King will be classified as a fugitive on the run until we know otherwise.

"But for now, let's eat. We'll meet afterwards and plan. Then the day is ours. We have shopping to do. And let's face it, if King has left the States, the threat here in New Orleans is on hold…or over."

***

As everyone headed toward the kitchen, Dante met Jinx's eyes across the room. He motioned down the hall. She nodded, following him.

As he shut the door behind her, she said, "What's—"

Pulling her in his arms, he said, "I know it's sudden, but let's elope. Now. It looks like King's on the run. All we need is a marriage license and rings. And we'll find a preacher or judge wherever we go."

Jinx smiled. "Yes…"

He spun her around, kissing her, then stopped. "I'm rushing you. Do you need more time?"

"No. I just need you."

"You've always had me."

Loud laughter echoed down the hall. The clatter of dishes. Excitement about the Ball.

Jinx said, "How will you tell them?"

"Let's go eat. I'll fit it in somewhere."

***

Conversation flowed around the breakfast table. About shopping. Riding in the limousine. Where to go for lunch. And even night plans.

Sean looked at his watch and sighed. It was eight. And the meeting was next. They had this one day to get it all done. Just one. And seven women needed to pick out everything for a Ball. Samantha slid her hand across his thigh, capturing his attention. He met her eyes.

She teased, "Easy, boss man. There's time for all of it. Look at these women. Most know how to face a killer, so I know they can pick out a dress and accessories in a few hours." She slid her fingers down the inside of his leg. "I know, I can."

Sean kissed her. Both hands holding her face to his. Fingers in her hair. Not caring who watched.

Gabrielle, sitting next to Samantha said, "I don't know about any of you, but my orange juice just boiled. And I'm sweating."

Everyone, including Sean and Samantha, laughed.

A few minutes later Dekker checked his phone and announced, "Pearls Place Bridal in Metairie just confirmed our appointment for eleven. A slight tip assured dress delivery by noon tomorrow. And John's Tuxedos in Metairie assured the same delivery. So, we are set. The limo arrives at ten-fifteen."

Dakota sighed. "I have three tuxedos at home."

Gabrielle said, "Call Dad. I bet he would bring them."

"That's a great idea!" Adam said. "Add mine in there if he can make the trip. I have two at home."

Hawk said, "I'll go to Lake Charles. That way I can pick up mine. I hate getting fitted."

Sean said, "Don't we all. But I left mine in Colorado, so I have no choice."

Maverick said, "Mine won't fit. Working out took care of that."

Dekker said, "Well, I'm good. I never leave home without a few."
Dante sighed. "You are too cool for words, Dekker. I want to be you when I grow up."
After the laughter died down, Maverick said, "I know you have one, Dante. So, Sean, it's just you and me suffering a fitting."

Dante glanced at Jinx, then said, "Actually, it turns out that Jinx and I won't be at the Ball. We're eloping."
A moment of silence around the table spoke of shock, then the roar hit. Clapping. Whistles.
His arm around Jinx, Dante continued, "I'm taking Jinx away till all this is over. Maybe King will drown at sea, or better yet get eaten by sharks. Regardless, he'll still be a pile of sh—"
Jinx elbowed him and the table erupted in laughter yet again.
Maverick said, "What's your plan?"
Jinx said, "We'll pack what we have here. I'll even bring the podcast equipment. I just need to run by my apartment and grab a few things."
Dante said, "We'll need a ride. My truck's there."
Maverick said, "No problem."
Hawk said, "Why don't I bring you on my way out of town, Dante. Help you load. And escort you out of New Orleans. Which way are you headed?"
Dante and Jinx glanced at each other. Dante said, "That's still in the air."
Dakota said, "I have a log cabin on the river, jet skis, and horses. Help yourself." He pulled out his keys and wiggled them.
With a glance at a very thrilled Jinx, Dante raised his hand and caught the keys.

Dekker said, "Ok, I'm messaging the tux and dress shop. We only need two tuxedos now and six dresses."
Sasha said, "Actually, I have a dress. I won't need anything."
Piper said, "You have got to go. You might find something you like better."
Sasha smiled. "My dress is like liquid turquoise. Metallic. Backless. Cut to the waist. Up the thigh. I feel like a mermaid that walked out of the ocean."
Piper whistled. "I might take yours."
More laughter.

Hawk stood with his coffee cup. He passed Sasha and leaned close. "Come with me to Lake Charles. I dare you."

Sasha felt the tingle from where his breath brushed her ear…all the way down. Her toes curled. Knowing everyone was watching, she casually tapped her glass. "Ouch! Mine boiled too."

Through the laughter, Hawk and Sasha's eyes met. She was coming.

***

After breakfast, Gabrielle, Raven, and Luna dressed for the shopping trip. Dante and Jinx packed. And the team met for a quick meeting.

❖

Agent Donovan called via video chat. "Morning everyone. Give me an injury update before we jump into King's message. Piper?"

"I'm not even sore. Just a few scrapes."

Donovan said, "Maverick?"

"I'm good."

"What about Liam? I know he feels that burn this morning."

Maverick said, "I'll be calling him in a few minutes to discuss security for the Masquerade Ball. I'll ask him…not that he'll admit anything."

"Ok." Donovan said. "Let's move on to King's message. For you Piper, and all the other women in New Orleans, I hope he is out in the ocean. But the process of proving it is next. We've already begun. The Port of New Orleans just verified that sixteen cargo ships set sail after eleven o'clock last night.

"And while that number is not an impossible task to tackle, it is a lengthy one. Agents are already requesting passenger manifests. Three are American ships. Six African. Five South American. And two are Mexican.

"At this point, the fugitive part of the investigation will be handled here in the office. And your team will continue to handle the criminal case from the safehouse for the next few days. A smaller two-man surveillance detail has been assigned to you considering the firepower all of you wield.

"And of course, everything changes if King's location isn't on the high seas. Now…any questions…"

Piper asked, "How's the zoo security guard?"

"Embarrassed. And home with a headache and stitches. He stepped out of his office, and someone clocked him. He never saw a thing."

Sean said, "What about the blood they found on the fence?"
"It matches the DNA from the graveyard."

Dakota said, "No one saw him leaving the zoo? No video? Nothing?"
"Nothing is the right word. Audubon Park is busy even if the zoo is closed. Nothing suspicious was noticed."

Samantha asked, "Do forensics think they can get any viable evidence from the robot?"
"They're doubtful. No pun intended, but it's fried. On top of being shot to pieces. But they are still checking."

Maverick said, "Dakota told us about Katie and the alligator. Has forensics confirmed it?"
"Yes. An alligator killed her." He paused. "And I have got to admit, I find a bit of integrity in the fact that King killed it and…well, took the time to find and take care of her remains. He is a complicated man."
Maverick said, "Maybe he's not what he seems. What if one day he snapped and turned into someone he'd never been before. Unfortunately, he was a hunter that loved predator cats, and it all got twisted together."
Dekker said, "Like Jekyll and Hyde…plus brunettes."
Donovan said, "It makes as much sense as anything else. Now moving on…tell me what I don't know."

Dakota said, "Dante and Jinx are leaving New Orleans this morning. They're eloping and won't be back until this is over. They'll be at my place in Lake Charles. Hawk and Sasha will follow them there on an errand and return tonight.
"The remaining ten of us will be transported around New Orleans today in a limo preparing for the Ball. Nine of us are armed so we are fine. Other than that, we'll connect with Liam about his security plan for the Ball."
"Sounds good. Keep in touch."

Sean said, "One more question, Sir. What can you tell us about the ships? How many can the Coast Guard search in a day?"
"Depending on weather, location on the ocean, and fueling stops, they said, two, maybe three ships. We'll search all sixteen if it's necessary. The only evidence we have is a first name, a voice, and a partial picture. Which means, anyone close to fitting the profile is taking a ride back to the States. We've got

DNA and fingerprints waiting to compare. Until then, be alert and enjoy the break – and pray it's permanent. Now, I've got to go…stay in touch."

After the meeting, it was a whirlwind of activity as everyone dressed, packed bags, and made plans to leave. They had an hour.

***

Sean checked Piper's trackers before she joined the others.

He frowned. "Check between your toes Piper while I broaden the search. Two trackers are missing."

She checked… "You're right. I only have eight. Though I'm not surprised after the battle and rain last night."

Focused on a larger grid, he said, "You're right. That's where they are – at the zoo. But no problem. Eight will do."

"How long do I have to wear the removable ones? I mean, the toenail polish isn't coming off."

"Until I know he's not going to take you. Marking him and leaving a trail is your only way to talk to us as we follow you."

It was a solemn moment, at first. Terrifying, next. Even though it wasn't her first time to wait for backup. Piper said, "What's your signal?"

"My drone."

She nodded.

He closed his computer and said softly, "In the million and one chance that he takes you…if I were you, I would save all my fighting energy until you have no choice. Play him, Piper. He's intelligent. Brilliant even, but the brain between his legs—"

"I get it, Sean."

"Then slow him down. A gorgeous dose of emotion at the right time…or teasing…gives you a powerful edge. Stall him till we get there."

***

Across the room, Maverick flipped through the zoo documents. He found the cell number he needed. Walking onto the balcony, he called Liam.

Chapter 22

The Starbucks line was long as Liam turned off Magazine Street and braked behind a black convertible. A woman was behind the wheel. Blonde. Designer sunglasses. Long nails tapping on the steering wheel. He lowered his window a couple of inches and heard the music. He smiled at the unmistakable voice of Prince.

His phone rang as he slowly moved up in line. He glanced at the display. And did a double take. It was Maverick.

Liam answered, "Good morning, Detective. You're up early."

"And it's your fault, Lion Man. We've got Masquerade Ball shopping to do."

Laughing, Liam said, "My apologies."

"I'm just messing with you. We appreciate it. The women are thrilled. But I called for a couple of reasons. Do you have a minute?"

"I'm in a long line at Starbucks. I've got plenty of time. What can I do for you?"

"First, how's the burn?"

"It's nothing. I just stopped at a pharmacy for a few supplies - to protect my shirt mostly. I could care less about the burn." He chuckled. "You sure don't seem the kind of guy to ask about that."

Maverick laughed. "I'm not. Agent Donovan insisted. But I have security on my mind for the Ball. I'm staying near Chestnut and Arabella Street. Where are you?"

Liam almost laughed. This was easier than being King. "I'm on Magazine not far from Audubon Park."

"If you've got time, come by. I have two RNs here that can take care of your burn, and I'll make a fresh pot of coffee. We can talk security at the same time."

Liam didn't even hesitate. He pulled out of line and turned toward the safehouse. Acting like he didn't know where they were, he said, "Sounds great. Text me the address and I'll be there in a few minutes."

"Done. Park in the front. Security will bring you up. Are you in the BMW?"

Liam paused. Then reasoned, of course they'd run his background check. "I am. You know what I take in my coffee too?"

Maverick liked his style. "That's one way to put it. Come on over."

Liam laughed as he tossed the phone on the seat. Then considered the risk. And there was a risk that Piper would see something about him that she hadn't noticed yet. Something that exposed him. And then he was trapped right in the middle of the Task Force.

With a mental shrug he smiled. No way would he pass up this opportunity. He could almost smell Piper from here. Tomorrow, she would be his.

***

In minutes, security texted Maverick: He's on his way up.

Maverick pressed start on the coffee and headed to the door.

Liam grinned as the elevator doors opened. A large mirror in the third-floor foyer showed him looking fine. Sapphire silk slacks and matching button-up shirt with a textured weave. Styled hair. Sunglasses. Loafers. He didn't look anything like crude, rough King.

He knocked on the door.

Maverick opened it and whistled. "I feel underdressed. You didn't tell me you were meeting a woman." He motioned him in.

Liam laughed, taking off his sunglasses. "I'm always prepared to meet a woman no matter what I wear."

As he entered the room, he met Piper's gaze. She walked toward him with a fabulous smile. Long hair loose. Sexy in jeans and a crop top that matched her eyes. He wanted her on the spot. He smiled. "Hello, beautiful and brave one. It's always good to see you."

She smiled. "Morning, Liam. Don't forget bossy."

He laughed. "Never."

He waived and responded to the team's greetings from around the room. He saw the case boards for Jessica, Katie, and Danielle. Cruze. His own, as King. Video screens. And computers. This was a full-blown FBI investigation. How absolutely thrilling.

Acting surprised, he glanced at Maverick. "Do all of you stay and work here? Like a safehouse?"

"It's exactly that. And there are a few other people that you haven't met yet. They're dying to meet the hero of the hour, and the bringer of Masquerade Ball invitations."

As Liam grinned, Maverick called out, "Gabrielle, Raven, Jinx, and Luna - he's here."

Liam heard women's voices, laughter, and footsteps. Four more gorgeous women filed into the room. A new brunette. A redhead. Then Luna and Jinx. D

He held his chest in a mock heart attack and groaned. In his Irish lilt he said, "These women would give an average man a heart attack. Maverick, a little warning would have helped. I'm already wounded and weak."

As laughter faded, Maverick said, "Wounded and weak? Hardly. Introduce yourself and make their day."

The brunette with goldish eyes went first.

Bolder than the others. Tall and luscious. She said, "I'm Gabrielle, Dakota's wife. Thank you for bursting in on the scene at the zoo last night. I can't believe I had to miss all the fun."

"Ah. You're adventurous then."

"You could call it that."

"What's your weapon of choice?"

She smiled. "Knives." And she leaned down and pulled a short blade from a sheath under her pant leg. Brandished it.

Dakota warned, "Easy, Liam. She will use it."

Intrigued, Liam touched the blade. Razor sharp, it cut him. He asked, "Why, has she used it on you?"

Dakota rubbed a spot on his stomach. A tiny scar. "Once. She was near the due date of our daughter who's now three months old. She was…miserable. Anyway, I tried to commiserate with her but chose the wrong descriptive word. She drew blood."

"What word did you use?"

"Like I'm going to say that word again."

Liam laughed and glanced at Gabrielle. "I'd love to see you throw sometime."

Someone slid a wooden crate across the floor.

Gabrielle grinned. "Pick a spot."

"Really? Ok, then. Dead center."

She said, "If I hit the center, I've got some women I'd like to introduce you to."

Laughing, he said, "Maybe you should stick to knife throwing. I've got that covered."

And in the blink of an eye, her knife flew. It hit dead center.

Liam whistled. "You are exceptional."

Dakota laughed. "Her grandfather was a pirate. She should be."

The redhead was next.

Liam glanced at the woman Adam had his arm around. Shockingly beautiful with copper hair, and eyes so dark they were almost black. He said, "Hello. I'm Liam."

"I'm Raven. It's nice to meet you. Thank you for taking care of Piper. And for the Ball invitations. We are all thrilled."

He said, "I can't believe I'm asking this, but may I touch your hair? You make me homesick for Ireland."

With a husky giggle, she laid a hand on Adam's chest. Meaning, easy… "Sure. I get that request a lot."

Filling his hand with silky copper waves, Liam rubbed his fingers together. Soft fire. Fabulous.

Adam drawled, "In case you haven't noticed, Lion Man, I have a knife too and it's a lot bigger than Gabrielle's."

And with that comment, Liam remembered a news video a few months ago. A red-haired dancer running to a helicopter. Being chased. The villain got stabbed. He said, "I saw you on the news in November, didn't I? You're a dancer, Raven."

She smiled. "Yes, to both."

"Maybe you can save me a dance tomorrow night."

Raven said, "Of course I will."

Adam tapped his knife.

Liam laughed as he turned to Piper's dad. He nodded at Dekker, then smiled at the enchanting brunette by his side.

She smiled, beyond lovely. That she was kind and gentle was obvious, and instantly she reminded him of Danielle. Dessert all day long.

He said, "Hello, I'm Liam."

"Hi. I'm Luna. How's your burn?"

"What burn?" He winked. "I'll be fine. You must be from New Orleans. I hear the accent – it's beautiful."

"And I love your Irish one. New Orleans is lucky to have you here."

He figured all the agents knew his details anyway and said, "It's like a second home. My uncle has a place south of here. I've been coming for years. I have an American citizenship—"

Dante called from the stack of boxes piled near the kitchen. "Come on, Casanova. Get a move on. Come meet Jinx so we can finish packing. We are eloping today, and my patience just tanked."

Liam laughed. Hard. Everyone did. Maverick punched Dante in the arm while Liam walked over.

Dante said, "What's the deal? I'm—"

Jinx covered Dante's mouth and smiled at Liam, "I'm Jinx. It's great to meet you. I've heard so many wonderful things about you. And please forgive Dante. We are in a bit of a hurry."

Liam tried to talk…laughed again…then said, "Hello, Jinx. I understand congratulations are in order." He paused with a chuckle, and said, "One question."

Dante moaned.

Liam said, "Jinx, your voice seems familiar. Are you a reporter?"

"No. But I have a podcast here in New Orleans."

"Ah. That must be it—"

And they were gone. Dante pulled her down the hall. Liam waved at a disappearing, yet apologizing Jinx.

***

A couple of minutes later, Sasha brought Liam a cup of coffee. The team waited for Sean to upload a map of the Audubon Tea Room that Liam provided.

Liam took a sip and smiled, "Sweet with a touch of cream. Perfect. Thank you." And then he looked back and forth between Sasha and Maverick. Gorgeous facial features. Knockout blue eyes. Sculptured lips. Long blonde hair. Exceptional bodies. How had he missed the resemblance? He said, "You are brother and sister."

Sasha smiled. "Twins."

"That was unexpected. Very cool. And if I may say so, you are a beautiful woman. I'm partial to blondes if I haven't mentioned it."

She smiled. "You just like women. Own up to it."

He shrugged with a grin.

Maverick said, "What about my looks?"

Liam said, "You got the weak end of the gene pool. You'll have to live with it."

Maverick chuckled. "The shocker is that we just met this week. We were separated at birth. We're Norwegian by blood and American because we were delivered in the States a few hours after arriving."

"How extraordinary for both of you. Congratulations. And Norwegian explains a lot. You're a big guy, Maverick. I'm unashamedly jealous."

"Yeah, but size didn't help Piper yesterday. Your speed did. I owe you, Liam."

Sean interrupted. "Ok, everyone, let's talk security." He enlarged the map. "Liam, we will be a group of six couples at the ball. The men will be armed. And all but one woman will be armed. How big are the tables?"

"They seat six, but I've got two joined tables reserved for your group." He got up and touched two tables west of the stage. "Here. This is closest to the area reserved for professional guests. The private suite has a small office. Sofas. Restroom. Private parking and a security door. This will be for your group. I'll be your Audubon security."

Dakota said, "And the rest of the building?"

"Experienced security will be inside each public entrance. Four sets of double doors. Two in the front. Two that lead into the garden. Officers are armed and familiar with the building. They will know about all of you."

Maverick said, "What will be going on outside?"

Liam said, "A great deal. The patio and gardens will be decorated. Lights. Tables. Serving staff. A bar. People will roam throughout the garden. Carts will provide private rides on the zoo paths. It will be a busy night in the jungle.

"That said, every gate in the perimeter will be locked and secure. Entrance is allowed only through the Tea Room. No invitation. No entrance. And no exceptions. And expect that valet parking will be swamped."

Piper said, "Will the security cameras be manned?"

"Yes. Three officers this time."

Samantha said, "How rowdy does it get?"

"Noisy with music. Dancing. People having a good time. Speeches here and there – it is a fundraiser. There may be a few guests that drink too much, but they're escorted courteously to their vehicles with a to-go gift."

"That's classy."

"We have got to be."

Maverick said, "We may patrol from time to time. Can you give security a head's up?"
"Consider it done."

Sean said, "Is a mask required?"
"It's part of the mystique of the evening. But no. Suggested only for your entrance. It seems that women enjoy masks more than the men." He smiled. "Unless the men have had a drink or two and forget they have one on."
"Do you wear one?"
Liam smiled. "Unless it gets in the way."

***

Five minutes later, everyone was helping Dante and Jinx carry boxes, luggage, and bags downstairs. Hawk backed up Dakota's truck and lifted the bed cover.

Upstairs, Liam helped Jinx tape the lid on the last crate. Jinx ripped the tape and leaned between his arms to press it along the bulging seams.
He breathed in her perfume. Silky black hair brushed his chin. Petite, gothic-lovely, Jinx. He would have made her writhe in bed. Wild with pleasure even though she wouldn't have been willing. That was the point.
Jinx lifted her head. Her green eyes met his, and she was startled for a moment at how close they were. A weird feeling climbed into her stomach. Then Liam stepped back as Sasha and Hawk joined them.
Jinx smiled and blew it off. "Thanks, Liam! I appreciate the help."
Sasha looked around. "Anything else?"
Jinx said. "Let me make one more pass in the study. I'll be right back."

Hawk glanced at Sasha. "Are you ready?"
"Sure. My bag and purse are in the truck."
"Let's do this."

***

Jinx and Sasha climbed into the back seat. Hawk and Dante in the front. An NOPD unit waited patiently to tail them until they left New Orleans city limits.

Liam enjoyed the irony and waived along with everyone else as they pulled away. In seconds, the vehicles disappeared around the corner. A brief dagger of pain laced his heart at the wedding he almost had.

Piper watched Liam stare into the distance while the team returned upstairs. He looked heavy in thought, and she remembered the loss of his fiancé. She glanced at Maverick who was watching her. They both knew what he was thinking about.

Liam turned, not expecting to meet Piper's gaze. He recognized the look of sympathy. Obviously, she knew about Cara.

She said, "I'm sorry."

"I should have realized you'd know."

Shrugging softly, she said, "It's what we do."

He offered his arm. "How about escorting me upstairs so your nurses can fix a wound that can be healed."

Without a word, she took his arm. Maverick watched them come toward him. He couldn't even imagine Liam's pain...and didn't want to.

***

On top the snack bar, Raven laid out Liam's medical supplies. Luna grabbed scissors, a bowl of cool water, soap, and a towel.

When Liam walked in with Piper and Maverick, Raven pointed to a stool and said, "If you take off your shirt, we'll have you fixed up in no time."

He looked at the audience. "Where's the privacy curtain?"

Teasing, Piper said, "You're hilarious. I doubt you have a shy bone in your body." Then she leaned across the counter prepared to check out his burn.

Everyone laughed. Shaking his head, Liam pulled his shirt out of his pants. Unbuttoned it, then draped it over a chair. He sat on the stool.

Raven said, "Arms over your head, please."

Obedient, Liam clasped his wrists on top of his head. Muscles flexed. Tattoos too…and they were everywhere, even beyond his waistband. He smiled. "Two gorgeous nurses. God loves me."

Luna's musical giggle met his ears as she stepped close to his injured side. Her gentle fingers touched around the burn, which was about five inches long, two inches wide, and had crisp edges.

Her light eyes met his. "I'll be as gentle as I can, but I need to wash it thoroughly. Burns are easily infected. The good news is that there's only one small area that blistered. The size of a quarter."

"Ah. Lucky me."

Raven smiled and wrapped a rolled towel around his waist. Luna picked up a bowl of cool water with tiny bubbles and a pad of gauze.

Luna said, "This is the worst part. It will hurt. There is no way I can change that. I can make everyone leave if you really want privacy."

"I'm good. Besides, I have got to prove how tough I am. I'm the Lion Man."

Chuckles filled the room.

Luna continued, "After I'm done, Raven will bandage it. And if it doesn't get wet, or dirty, you won't have to change it for a week. You have plenty pre-medicated bandages."

"I can do that. I'm used to it. I've been burned, bitten, scratched, fallen, pecked, and stung. It's the nature of what I do."

She dipped the gauze. "Ok, then. Hold on…here we go…"

Liam's jaw clenched as the wet gauze hit the burn. The water felt like fire…the gauze like barbwire. His muscles tightened and it was hard to breathe. By the time Luna finished, sweat had beaded at his temples, and his stomach was in a knot. He took a deep breath, willing his body to relax.

Luna said, "I've never had a patient endure that in silence. Ever. I'm impressed, Lion Man."

He smiled, wiping the sweat. "Do I get a sucker?"

Everyone was still laughing sporadically when Raven finished the bandage.

Curious, Piper smoothed her hand across Liam's back. There were so many fabulous tattoos. She said, "They look so real. Who does your tats?"

Liam stilled at the touch of Piper's hand caressing his back. Warm. Smooth. Soft. He had so many other plans for what she would be touching tomorrow. He glanced at Maverick, then Piper, and answered, "I have a friend who does them. She's famous for her work."

Dekker's phone rang. He walked away to answer. In a second, he was back. "The limo will be here in ten minutes. It's time to shop."

***

Liam started his BMW and watched as the limo filled with excited women drive away. He laid his head back on the headrest knowing what Piper didn't.

After tomorrow, she would never see this life again. He closed his eyes as the battle raged in his mind. The man that he'd been for a lifetime insisted that he end this madness. Let Piper go. Walk away and start over. Maybe even make up for the lives he'd destroyed.

Four people had died already, but still the betrayal ate at him like a rabid hyena. Its evil laugh echoed in his mind. He ran his hand through his hair and looked in the mirror. His eyes might be green, but he saw gold.

King wasn't done yet.

Chapter 23

The limo pulled up in front of Pearls.

In minutes, five thrilled women were escorted inside. Adding to the thrill of the women already in there. They stared at the tall blonde dream. The three hot Native Americans. And the older 007 hunk. It took them a minute to even notice the women with them.

Dekker winked. "Morning ladies. It looks like all the beauties on the Gulf Coast are in Pearls today."

Everyone laughed, charmed as intended. Dekker knew a thing or two. Then following the manager, the men checked the building and stood guard at the doors. Their women began to shop. And Maverick and Sean took a limo ride to their tuxedo appointment.

***

At the podcast studio, Sasha helped Jinx pack. Or at least she tried. Jinx still hadn't decided on which dress to get married in. Would it be the white floral with a low V-neck? Or the black sheath that laced up the back.

Jinx said, "I know I should wear white. I've waited my whole life to wear it." She touched the black dress. "But this one is so me. Which one do you think Dante would like?"

Sasha smiled. "Naked would be his preference."

Jinx laughed. "That's the truth."

Sasha held up both dresses. "Why don't you choose the one you want Dante to take off of you."

"You certainly know how to cut through the chase."

"I know." Sasha said. "I wasn't always so direct…but law enforcement sharpened my soft side."

Smiling as she packed the black dress, Jinx said, "I know someone who would love rubbing your rough edges smooth again. Hawk wants all things you."

"He's not shy about it."

"And?"

"And he can wait. I need more than an orgasm."

Jinx gasped. "Wow. I can't believe you said that. You just tossed it out there like you were ordering takeout!"

Sasha groaned. "I hate it when I do that. But really, I've known Hawk only four days. Four. And that's enough on the subject. I insist."

Jinx laughed, "Insist all you want. I can't wait to tell Dante what you said."

Dante called upstairs, "I heard my name! You ready to go, Jinx?"

Both women laughed.

***

Thirty minutes later, Dante and Jinx waved, leaving Hawk and Sasha behind as they sped up on Interstate 10. A wedding was waiting for them at the courthouse in Lake Charles. And a honeymoon at a log cabin.

Hawk and Sasha smiled at the truck disappearing in the distance.

Sasha said, "They are a beautiful couple. Jinx is striking. She has the classiest gothic style I've ever seen."

"She is beautiful," Hawk agreed. "But Dante is trouble waiting to happen. Over and over."

Laughing softly, Sasha said, "He is handsome…and a handful. Their children will be gorgeous and delightful. I bet they have five."

"At least."

They rode in silence for the next few miles taking in the scenery since both were new to Louisiana. Lake Pontchartrain was to their right. A very close right. The edge of it was under the interstate. Then swamp, marsh, and wetlands were everywhere else.

Twelve miles to the left was the Mississippi River. It was nearing the end of its impressive 2,348-mile journey from where it started as a small brook in northern Minnesota. The Gulf of Mexico was its goal.

Sasha said, "Maverick has a family camp somewhere south of New Orleans. I bet the landscape looks a lot like this." She gave a short laugh. "We grew up so different, to be so alike."

Hawk glanced at her. "It is remarkable. Genes are a fascinating enigma."

She said, "Enough about me. Your turn. Tell me something about yourself, retired Navy Seal, Hawk Kingston. Where are you from?"

"I'm in the process of moving from Wyoming."

"I can see you in Wyoming. But that's a whole lot different than almost sea-level southern Louisiana. What brought on that decision?"

"Like you, life changes. I retired from the Navy and wanted to explore new land. Have new experiences."

"And new women."

He met her gaze. "You."

She didn't take the bait. "Have you bought a place in Louisiana yet?"

He said, "I have. I bought a ranch outside of Natchez."

"That's awesome. Where is Natchez?"

He smiled. "About six miles south of Natchitoches."

Sasha blinked. He'd be six miles from her. "What were the odds of that?"

"A million to one."

Her brain swirled. Long distance dating she expected. But adults spending time in a house was way too close to the bedroom. And who was she fooling? Who needs a bedroom? She had to detour those thoughts. "Well, we'll almost be neighbors. How convenient. You can mow my yard."

He laughed. She was quick…and nervous. He switched gears to find out why. "How long were you married?"

She hid her struggle with the question since this was normal conversation for singles. She just never expected to be single again. Truth is, she should have never married Luke in the first place.

Casually, she said, "Two and a half years."

"I gather you worked together. Detectives don't get much time off."

"Good guess. What about you? Have you been married?"

"No. But I got a Dear John letter after a long mission overseas. Does that count?"

"All pain counts."

He paused at the anger he picked up on. "You know, I don't mind taking a vacation trip to Florida and whipping your ex's—"

She smiled. "Sorry. As much as I like the sound of that - no. What about you? Do I need to hunt down your Dear John author for you?"

"She's easy to find. She married my cousin. Best thing she ever did. I wasn't ready to give up the Seals and I love their kids."

Sasha said softly, "You're a good man, Hawk."

"I'm a whole lot more than that, mermaid. And I can take you anywhere you want to go."

Boom. That was laying it out there. Everything about his comment was sensual. Direct. And effective. Her body responded. But not her mind. "Hawk…"

"Just let it soak in. You're not ready. But you will be."

***

An hour and a half later, Hawk exited off the eighteen-mile-long Atchafalaya Bridge into the Welcome Center.

Sasha was intrigued. The bridge itself consisted of a pair of parallel structures that carried traffic over the Atchafalaya Basin between Baton Rouge and Lafayette. After researching it, she said, "Did you know that this is just a small portion of the basin? The Atchafalaya wetlands consist of around 1,400,000 acres. Let me repeat, 1,400,000. That is larger than the Grand Canyon."

Hawk smiled. "Are you sure?"

"Google is my research assistant. Of course, I'm sure." She narrowed her eyes. "Did you already know that?"

"No." He parked and killed the engine. "But I feel better now that I do."

She laughed.

He said, "We aren't in a rush. Would you like to look at the exhibits inside? They did a great job creating it. Dakota gave me a tour. There are also vending machines and restrooms. We can explore outside too. You call it. I'm game for whatever you want."

Sasha's stomach did the rumba. He was so sexy. Way too hot. She flipped the visor down and pulled out her lip gloss as a deterrent. Wet. Pale shimmery pink. She slid it across her lips like a shield. Grown men didn't like gloss. Not that it stopped them. But sticky helped.

She glanced at him and grabbed her fringed bag, slipped on beaded flip flops, and opened her door.

They met on the sidewalk.

Sasha wore tight white jeans with more holes and embroidered flowers than denim, and a short, ruffled top. Her blonde waves were in a ponytail. She tried to hide the sexy with feminine.

Hawk wore jeans and a black short sleeve shirt that was tight on his biceps. V-neck. Laced up leather boots. And his long black hair was loose. Layered. He was a 10 on the sexy scale and knew it.

He lowered his mouth to hers. Hungry. The lip gloss didn't faze him a bit.

***

Back at Pearls Place Bridal, the women made a pact to keep their dresses a secret from the men. It was a Masquerade Ball - secrets and mystique were expected.

Piper slid her hand down the material of her dress with a sigh. Bliss on her skin, that's what it felt like. She took a quick picture of it for accessories. She still needed a mask. Heels. Jewelry. And panties. Though she hadn't decided if she would wear panties yet. That might need to be another secret for the evening. An enchantingly erotic one.

Finished with the dress, she thanked her personal stylist, and the dress was whisked away for final touches. The same thing was happening with Gabrielle, Samantha, Raven, and Luna. Smiles filled the room. Their dresses would be delivered tomorrow but shopping was just beginning.

Piper picked up her purse as she slipped on her sandals. "I'm really excited about this. I haven't been to a formal Ball in years. I've spent years in suits and jeans. That is pitiful."

"Gabrielle said, "I'm with you. We dress up sometimes, but living by the river, I'm on a horse, four-wheeler, or in a boat more than anything."

Raven said with a smile, "Well, you're missing out. There is nothing like wearing something fabulous on a horse." She held out her arms and spun. "Racing through the woods on a stallion with lace flying and a bare—"

"And is the stallion's name, Adam?" Samantha drawled.

The laughter was long and loud.

Piper said, "You know, I don't know if Maverick rides. I just assumed."

Luna said, "Well, I'm busted. I've only ridden a carousel and a carriage."

Gabrielle winked. "I've seen Dekker ride. He's an excellent horseman. I bet he'll—"

Piper covered Gabrielle's mouth, and said, "Too much information for me." Glancing at Luna, she said, "Horses are magnificent. Riding them, exciting. Romantic. Just tell Dad. He'll have you on a horse in no time. You'll never think of a carousel again."

Luna laughed as Gabrielle yanked Piper's hair in retaliation.

As if on cue, Dekker called through the door, "The limo is back."

It was a commotion as the women joined the men. Laughter. Joking. Kisses. And refusal to show their dresses.

Dekker slid his credit card to the cashier. "I've got all of it." He watched Luna. She was next to a display of wedding dresses. She touched one. Gently. Reverently almost. Spaghetti straps. Sheer lace. A little bit of nothing and totally beautiful. He handed a note to the manager.

The manager's eyes quickly found Luna and the dress. She nodded at Dekker. "I'll take care of it."

***

At the next stop, Maverick smiled at the audible delight of the women as they walked into Maskarade, his favorite mask shop in the French Quarter. The five couples spread out, each searching for the perfect mask for the secret gown. This part…the men were allowed to help pick out.

Piper pulled out a picture of Sasha's gown. "Let's find one to match Sasha's dress first."

Maverick whistled at the picture. "Hawk is going to love that dress…or the lack of one. She's brave wearing it in front of him."

"You seem pretty accepting of the direction they're headed. Or that he's headed."

"It's not my direction to choose. She found me. She left a bad marriage. She's beautiful and smart. A great detective. She's not asking my opinion. But on the other hand, as a brother, I know she would be in no safer hands than Hawk's."

They headed toward a large display of turquoise masks - perfect for a mermaid.

Dekker and Luna browsed for a while. He slid a hand around her waist as they walked toward handmade masks made by local artists. "What color do you want the mask to be?"

"Solid black, shiny, with sparkling silver accent. Worn, not carried. And I want the ribbon to disappear in my hair."

"Are you wearing it up or down?"

"Which do you prefer?"

His breath touched her ear. "On my pillow."

Her lips parted as his landed. They heard a man's cough and a woman's giggle.

Dekker turned and met Dakota's amused gaze. Dakota said, "Man, sorry about that. I didn't realize we'd wandered into the erotic—"

Dekker put his hand on his gun.

Dakota choked. Laughing hard, but silently, as he led a struggling Gabrielle to the gold section, where she dissolved into laughter.

On the back wall, Samantha stood with her arms crossed as she stared at three masks lined up on a glass counter. She sighed and looked at Sean. "Which one do you like?"

"Baby, they're all black and white."

She rolled her eyes, "You, the hotshot FBI Agent, can't determine the blindingly obvious differences between the three masks?"

He winked. "If they were panties, I could."

Not far from the entrance, Adam and Raven explored enchanting masks of royal blue. Rich in color. Regal. From bold to fragile. One color or several. Plain or jeweled. There was no limit.

Adam said, "How are you going to decide?"

"I'm not. You are. You're the one that's going to be looking at it."

"Then I want something that looks like lingerie."

She laughed and slid her finger along his waistband. "I'm good with that."

With a glance around for privacy, he pulled her tight. Both hands on her backside. He pressed. "I love you."

She smiled. "I know."

He said, "Hey, did you reschedule the sonogram?"

She touched his chest, "About that… I couldn't. The doctor was leaving for vacation."

Stunned, he said, "You went without me?"

"I knew how much—"

"I can't believe it. So, you know what we're having. Tell me."

"It's twins."

He groaned and kissed her. "Raven, my heart is going to explode. Boys or girls?"

She smiled. "One of each."

"Lance gets a brother and a sister. We need a bigger house."

"Our house is huge."

"But I'm not done yet."

Across the store, Piper looked for the second time at a rack of feminine jeweled masks. Fragile ones. Lovely, but… She said, "Maverick, I just can't find what I'm looking for. Let's go see how everyone else is doing. I might have to go somewhere else."

"Sure. We'll go wherever you want. What is it that you can't find?"

As they walked toward the counter where most of the others waited, she said, “I want it so frail I can barely feel it.”

“I understand perfectly. An invisible mask.”

She laughed as he squeezed her.

They reached the others. Luna had a store bag. Raven too. Even Samantha. Piper and Gabrielle looked at each other and shrugged.

Piper said, “I can’t find one. I don’t really care for something on my face as it turns out.”

Gabrielle said, “Me either. What other options do we have?”

A young woman at the checkout counter with cotton candy pink hair said, “A local artist just brought in some new masks. Hang on. I’ll be right back.”

Ten minutes later, Piper and Gabrielle had exactly what they wanted.

***

Thirty-five miles from the Texas border, Dante and Jinx stood outside the Calcasieu Parish Courthouse in Lake Charles, Louisiana. A lake breeze blew through the multistoried columned porch with steps that faced Ryan Street.

Jinx’s shiny black hair fluttered. Her green eyes locked on Dante as he said his vows to her. She heard his heart in every word. Felt the caress of his hands holding hers. He was so beautiful. Rich brown hair and eyes. Sun-darkened skin from being raised on the bayou. Her dream. Best friend. And about to be her husband and lover.

Dante watched Jinx’s facial responses to his verbal promises. The curve of her smile. The sultry fan of her lashes. The flush in her cheeks. But…she meant so much more than the words he said. She was his heart. Petite but powerful. Smart. And exotically gorgeous. She was almost his.

As the last word faded, he glanced at the preacher and handed him the rings. Clearly meaning, hurry up.

Gabrielle’s grandfather almost laughed. He coughed instead. There was no doubt what that look meant. Jinx bit her lip and glanced at Dante. Really? Dante’s look said something too hot to be repeated in public.

Within minutes, they’d exchanged rings bought from across the street, steamed up the porch with their kiss, signed the marriage license, and taken three pictures. Then Dante scooped Jinx up and ran down the steps.

And less than twenty minutes later they were surprised at the sudden change in landscape as they headed north out of Lake Charles. Seriously sudden. Like, the town ended at Walmart on the bank of the English Bayou, and civilization disappeared.

They crossed the bayou. Large and deep with intriguing dark water. Trees and cypress knees lined the banks. Water lines on the trees indicated the ebb and flow of the tide from the Gulf of Mexico. And then there was one intersection with a red light before they reached the Calcasieu River…English Bayou's daddy.

The bridge rose high enough for barges to still reach industries beyond town along the river. And high rises from Lake Charles stood proudly over the trees to the west. Casinos mainly. L'Auberge. Golden Nugget. Horseshoe.

After crossing the 200-mile river that wove through the area, the bridge lowered to cross a swamp that bordered the land ahead. And as trees began to line the sides of the bridge rails, the bridge ended, landing them in the suburb of Moss Bluff. The home of Sam Houston Jones State Park…and Dakota and Gabrielle.

Dante took a right and followed a long winding road through neighborhoods along the heavily wooded river and swamp. He hid a groan, preferring to floor the truck like a madman and get to the cabin. He loved Jinx. Wanted her. He kissed her hand, still amazed that this would be her first time.

He took a turn off the main road and said, "Whoever made trucks with consoles must have been a woman hater. I like the old front seats where you would be next to me."

Jinx smiled, remembering those old trucks, knowing Dante was at his limit. They'd been in the truck all day – but separated. Simmering. Sparking. And they'd already been married…she looked at the clock…thirty minutes. A thought occurred to her.

She unbuckled her seatbelt and kicked off her stilettos.

Dante said, "What—"

She pulled her dress up. Dante ran off the road. Gravel flew as Jinx laughed. He jerked the wheel and fought to drive and watch her. She slowly pulled off her panties and straddled the console next to him. Dante groaned as she kissed his neck and caressed his stomach…sliding her hand lower.

He made the last turn onto the private road. It was secluded. Nothing but trees. And steamy minutes later they crossed a small bridge, the house visible up ahead. But they didn't make it. Dante hit the brakes as Jinx slid across his lap.

Still in their clothes, he took her. Loved her. Caressed her. And devoured her. The truck rocked. The horses watched. And love had its way.

***

Hawk and Sasha followed the same route as Dante and Jinx but turned west when they got off the bridge in Moss Bluff.

Sasha said, "I certainly didn't expect all the rivers and trees. The land was so dry and flat after the Atchafalaya."

"That stretch is farmland. Now we're in Sportsman's Paradise. Water everywhere. We're close to Sam Houston Jones State Park and only thirty miles or so from the Gulf of Mexico. Lake Charles is a port city too."

"Dakota and Gabrielle's place is along the river, isn't it?"

"It is – but to the east. Adam and Raven's place is on the West Fork branch."

As they crossed a draw bridge near what looked like an intersection of rivers and bayous, he said, "We'll reach their place from the Westlake side of the river."

Before long, Hawk took a right. Sunlight flickered through the trees as they followed the river. Most houses were built off the ground. Some places looked like camps. There were wharfs. Boats. Moss hanging from Cypress trees, while Cypress knees lined the banks.

Eventually the space between homes widened until they left neighbors far behind. At the end of the long road was a Quest Search & Rescue yard sign. On top of the hill, was a large two story barndominium with a barn and multiple buildings behind it. Horses were in the corral. Next door was a two-story white Acadian style home.

Sasha said, "It's beautiful out here, Hawk. And totally private. Are Steel and Callie here?"

Driving uphill, he said, "Not today. They had a day trip planned. But Callie insisted on leaving a meal up in my apartment. And Steel gathered Dakota and Adam's tuxedos. They're waiting up there too. It's just us on the hill today."

"Where's your apartment?"

"In the barn." He parked. "It's a nice apartment, but right now it looks like a storage building with all my moving boxes."

"Wow." Sasha said as they entered the apartment. "Don't lose me in here."

Hawk chuckled as they weaved through stacks of boxes. They reached an open area in the kitchen and den with windows overlooking the hill and the river.

Sasha looked at all the boxes. "Just how big is your ranch in Wyoming?"

"A three-story house. Barn. Bunkhouse. Garage. But I'm downsizing. I just have one large load left plus the animals. That will all go straight to Natchitoches."

"How many animals?"

"A hundred plus horses. Fifty head of cattle. Six dogs."

"You're a real cowboy."

He laughed. "Nope. Indian."

"Oh gosh. I never thought of it like that."

Smiling, he said, "I'm just messing with you." He pointed at the bedroom. "If you want to freshen up, head through there. The bathroom's connected. Are you hungry?"

Yes, echoed as she disappeared.

Hawk placed two steaming plates of food on the table overlooking the river when he heard Sasha coming.

Barefoot, she rounded the corner. One hot mermaid. Hair brushed. Makeup touched up. She left her shoes and purse on the rug by the sofa. "Is that Italian? It smells delicious. Anything with cheese is my favorite."

"It's lasagna and salad with homemade Caesar dressing. French bread. And pecan praline cheesecake for dessert. What would you like to drink?"

"Water, water, or water if I'm going to fit in my dress tomorrow night."

He poured them fruit infused water over ice. Strawberry. Orange. Peach. And sat across from her. They chatted as they ate. Sasha barely dented her food. Hawk ate maybe half of his and they shared a small piece of cheesecake.

Sasha sat back. "I have got to stop. My jeans are tight, and we have a long ride back."

His eyes drifted over her waist. Hips. Stomach. Then met her gaze. He didn't have to say anything. She knew exactly what he thought.

Sasha wasn't opening that door and changed the subject. "Is your tux packed in a box?"

"Come on. They're in my closet."

"How many do you have?"

"Two. Pick one. It doesn't matter to me."

Standing in the closet, he pulled out two black tuxedos. She took one and held it in front of him. Everything was black. Shiny textured material. Skinny fit. No tie. She whistled. He would be drop dead gorgeous in it. He smiled as she swapped suits, serious about the decision.

The next tux was a sleek shiny black suit and vest. Sexy. Expensive. White, high neck shirt. No tie. She mouthed, wow. He would be one hot Dracula. Hawk chuckled.

She said, "You don't like ties."

"No."

"Well, you'll be killer in either. But I'm kind of into the black and white. You would be a smoking hot Dracula."

"Dracula. And that's a good thing?"

"It's a totally sexy thing."

"Who can argue with that? Black, and white it is."

She turned out of the closet and saw the bed. Smelled his cologne. And thought of using his bathroom earlier. She took a few quick steps across the room and glanced back at him. He laid the tux on the bed and looked at her. No words were necessary. Electricity bounced off them. Sasha swallowed at the look on his face…and stepped back once. Twice. Three times, until she was close to the doorway…and then gone.

She rolled her eyes at his laughter and straightened the kitchen.

He joined her a few minutes later and said, "I have an idea."

"I saw that."

He smiled. "That was awareness and a whole different idea. Though I prefer to go back to that."

"No. Next idea."

"I texted Maverick. Everything is calm in New Orleans. There is no news about the passenger manifests, and they are having a good time shopping. He said to take our time."

"Why? What are we doing?"

"How about a trip to Natchitoches to see where you're going to live?"

She screamed and grabbed her purse and shoes. "I'll race you to the truck!"

Chapter 24

Two hours later, the limo pulled up to the entrance of the Canal Place mall in New Orleans. Before long, five smiling couples with lots of colorful bags climbed inside. After three floors of luxury shopping, the women were ready for the Ball.

The couples discussed plans for the evening.

Maverick drew Piper on his lap. He said softly, "How about we go somewhere alone?"

She leaned against him. "We could escape to your camp. I would love to see it."

He kissed her. "I would love to take you." He knocked on the glass.

The partition slid down. The Chauffeur said, "Yes, Sir?"

"Would you stop at the nearest vehicle rental, please. A few of us will be leaving the group."

"Yes, Sir." The partition slid back in place.

The others waited for the explanation.

Maverick said, "We're going to take some time for ourselves and head out to my camp. It's about twenty-five miles south of here. The house is twelve feet off the ground. And we're armed…not counting the fact that Piper has eighteen trackers on her feet."

As laughter faded, Gabrielle, Samantha, and Raven debated their night options as the brothers listened. Should they go to an amusement park? The Natchez Riverboat? A fancy restaurant? Or Bourbon Street?

Sean said, "Scratch Bourbon Street at night, ladies."

Dakota looked at Gabrielle. No matter where they went, with all that dark hair she would be a beacon for King if he saw her. He said, "You have got to wear the blonde wig for that kind of public outing, Gabrielle."

She laughed. Delighted. "I'll make sure you enjoy the show."

"I always do…but that wasn't the point."

"Right… You say that now. Wait until you see me."

Raven continued the debate and said, "Come on guys, say yes to the Natchez. Think about it. We're in New Orleans. The riverboat has jazz. Romance. Food. The Mississippi river. And more jazz. Why would we go anywhere else?"

Adam looked at Sean and Dakota. King found the women on the riverboat. If he wasn't on the ship…

Raven turned Adam's face to her and said, "Repeat after me, King's on a ship far, far away. Or maybe shark food. He is not on the Natchez. But we will be."

Adam kissed her, and said, "The riverboat it is."

Dekker smiled at Luna. They had already told everyone they were headed for a beach. He was looking for a place with no one around and nothing but time, wind, and water. He caressed the wedding rings in his pocket. Dress on the way. Rings done. Wedding soon.

***

Maverick rented a royal blue Ram 1500. Beautiful. Shiny. Big tires. It looked like it wanted to go somewhere wild.

As she climbed in, Piper said, "Are we going off-road?"

"That's a perfect description."

She glanced down at her clothes and wished she had shorts and flip flops. "Would you stop by a store between here and the camp and let me grab a couple of things?"

"Good idea—"

His phone rang. It was the desk sergeant.

He answered, "Hey, Sergeant."

"Maverick, FedEx dropped off an envelope for you. It looks important. You might want to make plans to pick it up today."

"I'm not far from there now. I'll be there in ten or fifteen minutes."

"Pull up in back and text me. I'll have someone run it out to you."

Before long, the FedEx envelope was wedged in between Maverick's seat and the console. He ignored it as he merged onto Highway 90 and headed south toward the Mississippi River.

Piper glanced at the envelope and said, "Are you seriously going to let that envelope from a Norway attorney sit there and not open it?"

"That's exactly what I'm going to do."

"Why? We both know you want to know what's in it."

He slid his hand behind her neck in a caress. "I do. But not near as much as I want this time with you. I don't want anything distracting us. Nothing. It can wait. We'll open it later. Maybe."

She arched her neck against his hand and met his glance. She said, "I love that."

He said, "And I love what you're doing right now. Melting in those jeans. That's hot. Seriously. If the traffic wasn't nuts…"

Butterflies took flight in her stomach. She could imagine. Then a horn honked behind them. Angry toots that were most certainly cuss words in car language. They laughed and Maverick focused on traffic.

Piper closed her eyes as Maverick crossed the Crescent City Connection bridge. She tried to forget that her window faced the river. Then ignored the whoosh as they passed the massive beams holding the bridge together. The butterflies in her stomach quickly ducked for cover, terrified of the distance between the truck and the river. She tapped her finger on the seatbelt.

He noticed. "How can I help?"

"By reaching the exit ramp before we go over the side or the bridge collapses."

Maverick knew that fear wasn't always rational, but it was always terrifying. "Talk to me. Think about something else. How do you get over bridges when you're driving?"

"I stay on the inside lane. I never look over the side where boats look like toys. And I ignore thoughts of plunging over the rail."

"How in the world do you handle flying?"

"Without choice. But with stubbornness and lots of caffeine. And never by a window seat."

"And no one notices?"

"Probably. But not verbally if they want to avoid a bullet."

He smiled. "I get that. And…we're safe. We made it off the bridge."

As her eyes opened, he took the exit for the Oakwood Center mall for a super-fast shopping trip. They had somewhere to be.

***

Within a few minutes of leaving the mall with clothes and food, they left the big city behind and reached Crown Point. A small community that sat perched along the Intracoastal Waterway in the middle of national parks and nature preserves.

Maverick turned off the highway into a forest. And in no time, Piper had no idea where they were. Just trails in the place of roads. No landmarks. No signs. Only woods, swamp, and bayous. The late afternoon sun was her only hope for direction. They crossed a baby bridge.

Piper glanced at Maverick. "Are you sure you can find your way out of here tonight?"

"Are you feeling lost?"

"Totally. I bet it floods out here."

"All the time. But not today."

"How long has it been since you've been out here?"

He thought. "Six months, give or take. But that's not uncommon for a camp. Dante's cousin lives in Crown Point. He mows and keeps an eye on the place for me. In exchange, he uses the camp. It's a big win for both of us. He's a great guy. Everyone out here is."

"I don't see a soul. How close is your nearest neighbor?"

He rounded a corner, then took a sharp right. "Only half a mile. It's just slow traveling and well hidden. But…we're here."

Piper watched as Maverick drove through a patch of trees, and there it was. The three-bedroom camp was facing them mounted on top of huge pilings. An extra-wide staircase went straight up the middle to a porch. There were lots of windows with storm shutters. Rocking chairs. And it wasn't painted or fancy, but sturdy and blended perfectly into the natural setting.

"Maverick, I love it! Look at those stairs…"

When the engine died, she was out of the truck.

He called, "Watch for snakes!" as he caught up with her. Then pointed out several things. The swing hanging from an old oak tree – where a thick rope passed through holes in a wooden seat wide enough for one or two swingers. A group of picnic tables on the other side of the house. Round, concrete ones that survived floods and bugs. And had long ago ceased to be white.

Piper inhaled the aroma of nature as they walked hand in hand through the tree filtered sun. Listened to the birds. Watched squirrels scatter. Saw a few snakes. An alligator moved stealthily through the lily pads by the small wharf.

She said, "I presume you don't swim in the bayou."

"Not here where it narrows. But there's a decent clearing about a mile away with what passes for a sandbar. I've swum there more times than I can remember. And through the years, if a light hurricane season was predicted, we set up a pool for the summer. That was always a treat in the heat. And if all else failed, there was always the outdoor shower."

"This is so different from what I've known. And I never really appreciated the amount of privacy that comes with having a place like this. Like Adam and Dakota's homes in Lake Charles. Even Sean's ranch that I haven't seen yet. I've always lived in the city. Surrounded by people. No outside privacy at all. But now…"

They reached the staircase. Twelve feet tall. Six feet wide. Facing each other, Maverick said, "This gives privacy a whole new meaning, doesn't it?"

"Yes." She glanced at the road leading out of the yard. "Just how private is it here?"

He started unbuttoning his shirt in answer. She backed up the staircase one slow step at a time. Teasing. Watching him strip. Giving him a show. Her shirt dropped. Her bra. Her ponytail. Passion rose with each step they took.

Piper backed onto the porch; her jeans unzipped and barely on her hips. Maverick's hot blue gaze got taller and taller as he climbed the last few steps and looked down at her. His jeans long gone. He slipped hungry hands inside her pants and slid them down as his lips covered hers.

He took her before they ever reached the threshold.

Precious honeymoon minutes later, Piper's breathing slowed against Maverick's neck as she sat in his arms, legs around him. Her hands in his hair. His arms protecting her. He kissed her neck. Her face. His breath met hers in a gentle kiss.

He said softly, "Welcome home, Piper. It's not fancy but it's stood the test of time, and it's safe. A place for us to escape to anytime we want."

"I'm excited. I've not had a real home since I was a kid. Just leased and rented apartments as I moved around. No real meaning. No memories to savor. Nothing like this, baby. Or your boat. Or you."

He kissed her, then lowered her as they looked at their clothes littering the stairway.

Piper glanced around the porch. "Two birds are watching us from the railing. A lizard on the wall. Several spiders. And an extremely frustrated wasp nest in the corner."

Maverick laughed and gathered their clothes. He shook them to make sure nothing had crawled inside. Slipping his pants back on, he said, "Nature doesn't miss a thing. We are their entertainment."

Heading back downstairs he said, "Let me grab our bags out of the truck."

Piper watched him take every other step as he ran. Beautiful. Strong. Wild and free away from the heaviness of work. She loved her Viking.

Grabbing shopping bags, food, and the FedEx Maverick turned to head back up. He stopped as his gaze met the picture Piper made at the top of the stairs. She wore only low-rise jeans with her hair draped around her.

He said, "You could dress like that for me every day. And though we wouldn't get much else accomplished, we'd be well and truly satisfied."

She laughed. "With a houseful of children."

He grinned and jogged up. Setting the bags down, he opened a screen door with a metal grill that looked like it would survive any hurricane nature could whip up, and keyed in his security code. Then scooping Piper up, he carried her across with a smile and a kiss.

Piper explored while Maverick opened shutters and grabbed the bags off the porch.

The cabin was built with three sections. A large middle room was kitchen, dining, and seating area. And bedrooms were on each side. The floors, walls, and ceilings were made of a pale wood, rustic and cozy. She could smell it. Cypress? Cedar? Oak? She wasn't sure. Ceiling fans spun overhead.

She headed toward the kitchen. It had two back doors. One on each side of a long ceramic sink and counter. Windows above it overlooked a back porch very similar to the front.

Open-shelved cabinets were built on the left wall with colorful dishes. She tapped them with her fingernail. Painted metal. A work counter was underneath. Appliances were on the right wall. And in between the kitchen and dining area, a half dozen pots – mostly iron - hung on a ceiling rack over a snack bar with stools.

Piper heard the door and glanced at Maverick as she stepped onto a large, braided rug in the middle of the dining area. Thick. Soft. With various shades of green, brown, yellow, and splashes of lavender.

She touched a carved table that could easily seat ten. Large benches sat on each side. A chair at each end. It was amazing workmanship…except that the table had unusual feet. A mix of human and animal. What was that about?

Smiling at Maverick as he set everything he carried on the table; they began to unpack. She said, "This place is charmingly unique. But who, or rather, what's feet are on the table legs?"

"A Rougarou."

"A what?"

"A Roo-Ga-Roo. It's a bayou-dwelling werewolf based on French legend."

"Ah…so, vampires, voodoo, pirates, and alligators weren't bad enough for New Orleans?"

He laughed. "Louisiana is all about stories." He pointed at the two seating areas on each side of the front door. "That's why there's no TV or sofas. Just stories."

"Real or fiction?"

"That depends on who's telling the story."

An hour later, Maverick talked Piper into sitting with him on the edge of the back porch, their feet dangling twelve feet in the air.

Gripping the rail in front of her like a life raft, she sat in between Maverick's legs, one of his arms around her. She said, "And why was this a great idea?"

"It didn't bother you on the front porch. You never looked over the side once."

"You were stripping."

"I appreciate that. But still, it showed me that we have a little wiggle room."

"To do what?"

He pulled her on his lap. Question answered.

Inside the house, the phone rang. They ignored it.

As they took a shower, text notifications went off on both phones.

And before they dressed, Sasha called.

Maverick answered, "Hey, Sasha. I've got you on speaker. Are you enjoying your tour of Louisiana?"

Sasha said, "I am. Hey, Piper. Are you ready for the Ball?"

Piper said, "Hey there. Almost. Is Hawk steaming up the truck?"

Sasha laughed as she glanced at Hawk, who only heard her side of the conversation. "You have us sleeping in the same room and only worry about us being alone in a truck?"

Everyone laughed.

Maverick said, "Have you reached Natchitoches yet?"

"Just rolling into town. It's beautiful."

"It is. Wait until you see the Christmas Festival of Lights. It lasts for two weeks along the river in November and December. I'll have to bring Piper."

"I can't wait! I love Christmas. But…Natchitoches isn't why I called."

"What's up?"

"Did you get a FedEx package today?"

"I did. But I haven't opened it yet. Piper and I took off for the cabin. Alone. No insult intended."

"None taken. Being stalked by a killer is a bit of an annoyance on a honeymoon. I'd be running off too."

"You did. One would think you are trying to be alone with Hawk."

"One should mind his own business."

Maverick chuckled. "So, what's in the FedEx? I presume that it's either legal documents or heart ripping information from Norway. This isn't the time for that."

"Understood. But they copied me via email. Some of it needs to be returned as soon as possible. Which means, today or tomorrow."

"What's so urgent?"

"We haven't had time to discuss any of it and something came up that makes it necessary."

"Then tell me what I need to know, and I'll read it later."

"It's personal...financial issues. I figured you might prefer it to be private."

"Sasha, everyone knows everything I know about us. It's fine if Hawk hears. Put us on speaker." He laughed. "Hawk probably knows everything anyway. Sean and Dakota ran a background check on me in Lake Charles when I was panting after Piper in the fall. And now I'm honeymooning with the whole family. What privacy do I have left?"

She paused, knowing the shock he had coming.

At her hesitation, Maverick got the first inkling of a warning. He said, "Just say it…"

Sasha looked at Hawk who pulled over on the side of the road. She said, "We inherited a lot of money, Maverick. I already have mine."

Maverick's surprised gaze met Piper's as he wondered what the actual definition of a lot of money was. He said quietly, "So, what is a lot?"

"Over five million."

Maverick dropped his phone.

Piper dropped ice into two Mason jars, then glanced at Maverick sitting on the steps out front. She popped the top of a Dr. Pepper and watched fizz fill the glasses as she poured. He was processing.

Maverick heard the door and turned as Piper sat next to him. She handed him a glass. He took that, and a kiss.

After a long drink, he said, "I'm sorry to be distracted. That's exactly what I didn't want today. I'm… I'm just trying to wrap my head around that kind of money. In my head it was a dusty inheritance check that had never been cashed, and maybe a little from the silent partnership."

He took another drink and looked at her. "How do you do this, Piper? Your family? It's crazy. I can't even fathom how to be a millionaire. And I'll be honest…I'm intimidated which is embarrassing. I'm a detective. I race toward danger. Fight criminals. But this—"

Piper said, "Is simply adding things to your life. Opportunities, absolutely. Changes, some you want - and some you deal with. And for sure you'll be on a first name basis with your attorney, banker, and accountant."

"That doesn't help."

Piper figured this was as good a time as any to tell him. She said encouragingly, "You've been doing great, Maverick. Seriously."

Confused, he said, "Great at what?"

She took his drink and slid across his lap. Touching his face, she said, "You've been a millionaire since we married Monday. You received half of everything I own."

He stared. Shocked twice in the last thirty minutes. But he rallied quicker this time. "I'm not taking your money, Piper. You know that."

Pulling his lips to hers, she whispered, "Then you should have married a woman without any."

He kissed her. Hard, as shock and passion combined. Then gentled, at the sweet hot taste of her mouth. Her skin. Her desire. And sensuality took over. The rhythmic caressing of it. Maverick met her gaze as he laid back, riding the wave. She knew what he wanted…and gave it to him.

***

Dusk was falling as they sat in the double swing. They rocked softly in the breeze. Leaves rustled. Birds chirped. Love flourished.

Maverick kissed Piper's head, then asked, "Have you thought about where you want to go for a honeymoon?"

She said, "I thought maybe you would want to go to Norway and meet your family. See the shipyard. Explore where you're from."

"I do. But later. I want time with you first. Just you. No more distractions."

"Then I want to come here."

"But Piper—"

"I'm serious," she said. "We can literally go anywhere and do whatever we want. I want to spend it simply. Just you and me. No traffic. No clock. No television. No fast food. No rush. Just us, and time."

The phone rang from the porch. Again. It seemed loud and intrusive. With a sigh and a hug, they started for the cabin. They still hadn't checked messages. Which meant, an FBI helicopter could drop down any moment.

***

After pouring a cup of chicory coffee, they sat at the table and responded to messages.

First was an email from Agent Donovan:

"All sixteen passenger manifests have been received and reviewed for the ships that left the Port of New Orleans. Unfortunately, thirteen of the ships show a passenger with the first name King. Which alone is suspicious for any number of reasons. Regardless, we have got to pursue them. And they have a fourteen-hour head start.

"But the chase is on. A couple of hours ago, three agents from the Miami FBI field office left with the Coast Guard after the six ships headed to four different African ports. With rough seas tonight, it'll be morning before they reach the first one.

"Next, a few agents from the Houston FBI field office went south with the Coast Guard to catch up with five ships heading to various South American ports. We project they will board at least one of them by midnight.

"It is crucial to start crossing ships off our list. And as for your team, everything seems quiet in New Orleans, so your instructions stay the same. I'll let you know when we search the first ship."

Maverick and Piper discussed it.

"It could take a couple of days to clear all the ships." Maverick said.

Piper said, "Or more. Don't you think being couped up on a ship seems an unlikely move for a hunter?"

"Yes. But…it does buy him some time. And he could jump off at any port. Besides, he's limited from flying – unless he opts for an illegal flight. No telling what that would cost."

Insistent, she asked, "But still, would you take a slow-moving ship?"

"No. But I don't think I'm a big cat either."

***

Next…

Dante and Jinx texted two pictures. One was at the courthouse with their marriage license. Beautiful. Smiling. And excited. The other picture was a do not disturb sign on the log cabin's back door.

They laughed, totally understanding the non-subtle message.

Piper replied to her mom's voicemail by text: We're taking a honeymoon break. Do you need anything?

Nicole: I just have a question. I have an evening flight into New Orleans tomorrow. Can we meet before I fly out again?

Piper: Don't you dare get off the plane, Mom. We look just alike. We don't know yet if King is out of the country. Promise me.

Nicole: I'll promise to call when I get to New Orleans. You better answer.

Piper: I'm telling Dad you're landing in New Orleans.

Nicole: I tried to tell him myself. He didn't answer.

Piper thought of Luna and gave her mom a head's up: He's met someone. Are you ready for that?

Nicole: Of course. He's a beautiful man. He gave me you.

Piper smiled: I love you, Mom.

Nicole: I love you, baby. See you soon.

Maverick opened the FedEx package from:

Charles J. Willoughby, Esquire
C/O Jakob Nielsen, Norwegian Advokat
8221 Ocean View Drive
26th Floor
Tampa, Florida 33605

Inside was a cover letter and attached documents with bright yellow signature flags, a slim black leather checkbook, a return FedEx, and a DNA kit. He started with the cover letter:

Detective Maverick Patterson,

I do apologize for the untimely interruption of this week's meeting between you and Sasha. Unexpected legal business has arisen. I am your United States attorney of record for all matters regarding: 1) your Norwegian and American identification, 2) your birth parents, and 3) your inheritance through Berg Patterson Shipyard.

To simplify what will be explained in detail once you review the enclosures, attached is a Declaration of Ownership by Inheritance forwarded from your Norwegian attorney on request of the Executor. They need your signature on the flagged documents and on the bank signature card. They also need your DNA sample. Due to your multiple residence addresses, I overnighted this to your employer. Please complete, then drop off at any FedEx location as soon as possible.

I look forward to meeting you in the days ahead. We will have much more to deal with in getting this set into place, along with your dual citizenship and passports. It has been a pleasure to see a great resolution for both you and Sasha after all this time.

A tragedy restored is always a good day. Please let me know if you have any questions. And of course you do. It was just my weak attempt at humor.

Respectfully yours,
CJ Willoughby
Charles J. Willoughby, Esquire

cc: Detective Sasha Tate
Jakob Nielsen, Norwegian Advokat

Maverick laid the documents out on the table. The bank printout. The signature card. The check binder. The DNA kit and the Declaration from the Executor.

He flipped through years of deposits. First, death insurance deposits. Then each year an annual deposit from the company's profits. His mind boggled at the figures…and at the balance that grew. Year after year – some years more than others. He flipped pages. One million. Two. Four. Eight. And then a few years ago, the money split into two separate accounts. Exactly half. One for him. One for Sasha. And at the end of the printout, he read: Available balance: $5,342,799.00.

He looked across the room. Not seeing the cabin, but a life half a world away. Unbelievable. He signed the documents, the signature card, and completed the DNA test. It was ready to return to Norway. He glanced up as Piper walked on the porch to make a call. Watching her, he made a mental note to tell the attorney he needed a will. Immediately. Like his dad, he had a wife, and one day soon, children.

***

By ten o'clock, it was time to head back to New Orleans. Maverick closed the shutters and carried a few things down to the truck.

Piper stepped on the porch and called downstairs, "I'm going to do a quick inventory of groceries. I won't take long."

"No rush. I'll wait down here. I need to make a call."

Maverick looked around the yard and walked a little farther out, then stopped. Any walk along the bayou was not a great idea after dark. The outdoor spotlights barely reached the low deck of the wharf, and lots of eyes glowed from the water surface. Alligators...always watching for the next meal to hide in the murk below for tenderizing.

Bats fluttered across the moonlit sky. A fish jumped. Crickets chirped. Owls called. And he smelled honeysuckle flowers. Magnolia. Even the rich black dirt. Something rustled on the ground. Maybe a raccoon. An opossum. Or something larger.

A cat screamed in the distance.

He called Liam.

Chapter 25

In a kitchen a few miles away, the smell of chargrilled steak filled the air. Music too. A haunting native drumbeat with the ebb and flow of something wild. Something fitting.

Liam held up a bottle of Xylazine in one hand and inserted the needle with the other. He slowly pulled the plunger back, filling the syringe. Then he barely pushed the plunger, and a single drop of the drug slid down the needle. He laid it next to the other syringes.

Dressed in black dress slacks and nothing else, Liam reached for his margarita. A very specific margarita. Smooth taste, nothing bitter. Soft ice, nothing chunky. A layer of whipped cream with lime shavings on top. And a small ring of salt around the glass. He toasted. Licked it. And savored the taste filling his mouth.

His phone rang. Liam checked caller ID. It was Maverick.

He turned off the music and answered, "Hey, Maverick."

"Did you get a date for tomorrow night, Lion Man?"

Liam laughed. "I have a date with six gorgeous women and one of them is yours. I'm pumped."

Chuckling, Maverick said, "No doubt. And you have six men that wouldn't let anyone else near them."

"Honor received. Do you think they'll give me at least one dance tomorrow night?"

"With your accent, probably two." As Liam's chuckle faded, Maverick said, "Sorry I'm just calling you back. Piper and I snuck off for a few hours. We're at my camp not far from you."

Liam stilled at the comment. How close were they? He said, "Good for you! I didn't realize you had a camp down here. Where at?"

"We're north of Crown Point. That's what…ten or fifteen minutes from Barataria?"

Liam glanced at his gun. The syringes. This could work. He said, tone friendly, expression not, "Yeah. Why don't you and Piper drop by and have a late dinner with me? Steak and margaritas are a perfect way to end the day. I won't keep you long…not long at all."

"Thanks, man, but we can't do it tonight. We're about to leave the camp. We've got to be back before midnight. Put us down for a rain check. Did you call about the Ball?"

"I did. The zoo hired a limousine for tomorrow night. I was just trying to catch you before you made other arrangements."

"Appreciate that. What time is pickup?"

"The limo will be there to pick you up by seven-thirty. I'll meet you at the Ball."

"You're the man, Liam. You've made six women deliriously happy."

"What about the men?"

"We'll be in a tux. I'm not thanking you for that."

Liam laughed. "Understood. My apologies."

As the call ended, Liam felt the inner rush to grab his gun. A syringe. And race to ambush them along Barataria Boulevard. To take Piper right now. His jaw clenched as he fought the primal urge. Think. Focus. Bad move. He didn't know their vehicle. And his flight was tomorrow night – not tonight. Too many variables would be thrown off. He leaned over the back of a kitchen chair and gripped the wood. Tight. Muscles bulging. Just breathe.

A minute later, he downed the margarita and turned the music up. He walked on the back porch as the drumbeats spoke to him. The cool night air slid over his sweat covered chest, soothing him. Cooling him. He leaned against a post and looked across the shadowed yard.

It would be his last night everywhere he was known as Liam Knight. He'd be exposed as King tomorrow and be on the run.

But it didn't matter. He'd have Piper.

He backed the BMW up to the porch. Popped the trunk release. He sat there and stared at the raised trunk lid in the rearview mirror. It beckoned. He battled. But in the end, he went inside.

Dropping one syringe in his pocket he headed down the hall to the last door on the left. He watched Danielle through the one-way glass. She walked naked to the closet and pulled out a black sequin evening gown and unzipped it. Stepping into it she heard the door unlock.

Turning, Danielle met King's gaze. She smiled, giving him a coquettish, under the lashes promise. Then sensually posed to show appreciation for his arousal…that clearly dominated the room. She'd learned weeks ago to hide the fear that ricocheted inside her. He was so beautiful. And a fabulous lover. He made sure her screams of pleasure were real. Embarrassingly real. Shamefully real.

And a nightmare she hoped to live to regret.

Liam smiled and said, "Let me…"

She turned obediently, offering her back. But felt as danger crawled up her spine. She was running out of time. There was one last thing to try.

Liam draped her long dark hair over one shoulder and zipped the black dress like a coffin lid closing. Sequins sparkled. Perfume teased him. He kissed her shoulder as she pressed against him. He licked her neck and reached into his pocket. Flipping the cap off the needle he slowly pulled it out.

Eyes closed, Danielle whispered, "I love you, King."

Chapter 26

Back at the safehouse, it was busy as security cleared the apartment an hour before midnight. Everyone was on their way home.

The limo dropped off Dakota and Gabrielle, Sean and Samantha, and Adam and Raven from their evening on the riverboat. The women changed as the men checked messages and started coffee. The night wasn't quite over.

Hawk and Sasha arrived before the coffee had even finished. Adam ran down to help carry up the tuxedos from Lake Charles.

Dekker and Luna drove up at the same time as Maverick and Piper. Security escorted the women upstairs as Dekker and Maverick unloaded the vehicles.

Dekker noticed Maverick's smile fade as Piper left. He said, "What happened?"

Maverick said, "Nothing. But my gut pitched a fit as we left the camp tonight. There's something we're missing. Something huge that's right in front of us."

Dekker shut the car door and glanced around the shadowed neighborhood. "It is. King is not over. That doesn't mean I think he's here. But until they find him, I think we need to listen to our instinct. I'm pretty sure the others are edgy too. This was just a peaceful pause during the storm."

They got on the elevator. Dekker said, "Anything else on your mind?"

"You might say that. I found out I inherited five million dollars. I don't think I handled the surprise well."

Dekker laughed. "I'm sure Norwegian shipyards are prosperous. I'm not surprised at all."

"Well, I'm not used to savings figures out of the eleven-thousand-dollar range. But you probably knew that already."

"Then I don't need to answer."

They got off the elevator. Maverick said, "Funny thing is, Piper told me I've been a millionaire since Monday."

"That's what happens when you marry an heiress."

❖

At midnight, Agent Donovan called via video chat. His jacket was off. Tie loosened. In the busy command office, several agents worked on flickering computer screens calling information across the room. Coffee cups lined everyone's desk.

A massive screen showed the view from a United States Coast Guard ship, a 154-foot cutter with a helipad. Another screen showed an arial view from the accompanying Coast Guard helicopter. Both had search lights locked on a South American ship, the Reef Queen. Bright moonlight helped. Everyone watched as seamen scrambled around the ship about to be boarded. No doubt, terrified. Everyone knew that anything could be hidden on a ship.

Donovan explained, "The Reef Queen is about one hundred eighty nautical miles off the coast of the Yucatan Peninsula. The Coast Guard pushed to reach them before they hit port in Cancun. Three men named King are on the passenger manifest. Two are employees. One a paid passenger. Let's hope one of them is our King."

He pointed. "The boarding crew is casting off now."

They watched:

Patchy radio and speaker communications sounded between the Coast Guard and the ship. South American accents made it difficult to understand the replies. Before long, two FBI agents and eight USCG officers climbed aboard. Guns drawn in search of a federal fugitive.

FBI bodycam views split the screen.

The captain of Reef Queen was given instructions. He sent the third mate with several officers and agents to search for the three men. The two Kings in the crew were quickly located. Identification checked. The two men barely spoke English. They had black hair. Dark eyes. Small stature. They were obviously not the larger light-eyed, white fugitive at large.

The third mate then nervously explained that the paid passenger hadn't shown up for his cabin. Officers insisted on searching the cabin. King Loranger's double cabin was empty. Bed untouched. No luggage. They checked the booking paperwork. It was all in order.

Then they searched the entire ship.

Everyone else was accounted for. The video ended.

Agent Donovan said, "The missing passenger was either a legitimate no show or a decoy booking. I lean more toward decoy booking. King's a smart guy. Which means, this may not be the only no-show passenger we find. And that's not chump change. A double cabin like that would cost two-hundred bucks a day on a freighter. For example, we're talking a minimum of thirty days from New Orleans to the nearest port in Africa. That's six-thousand dollars for one ship booking. Someone would desperately need a decoy to repeatedly pay that."

Dakota said, "What about flights? Any Kings fly out of Louisiana in the last twenty-four hours?"

"Two. And they had verifiable identification, alibis, and were too old to do what our King does. So, looking ahead, this Coast Guard ship is now on the way to catch up with two Mexican freighters before they reach the Panama Canal. They are headed for Pacific Ocean port destinations.

"However, in the Atlantic Ocean, the Miami based USCG ship will intercept the first African freighter. Hopefully before dawn. But I don't think it's necessary for all of you to watch every ship boarding - unless we locate someone that resembles King. Then I'll call and patch you in. Otherwise, I'll send you updates after each ship is searched."

Dakota wrote in red marker, PASSENGER NO SHOW, next to the Reef Queen on the dry erase board.

Piper doodled on the yellow pad in front of her. $6,000 times 3 ships = $18,000. $6,000 times 6 = $36,000. $6,000 times 10 = $60,000. Where did King get that kind of money? And why would brunettes be worth that much to him?

She glanced at Danielle's picture on the victim board. So young. So beautiful. She sighed, remembering how it felt to need a hero.

Where are you, Danielle?

Maverick watched Piper sigh. He walked over and stopped behind her chair. Sliding his hands over her shoulders, he massaged. She groaned, rotating her neck with eyes closed. Her muscles had tightened like overstretched bungee cords.

Eventually all conversations in the room faded. Footsteps disappeared down the hall. Adam stepped out on the balcony for first watch, since Hawk had driven all day.

Maverick kept kneading. Spreading his fingers from her shoulders to her scalp. When she began to sway with the movement, he scooped her up and carried her to bed. She needed rest. Sweet dreams. And King in prison or dead.

Whichever came first.

***

In the low-lit bedroom, Dekker watched the neighborhood shadows through a slit in the curtain. Jeans unzipped…barely on his hips. He heard Luna turn off the water in the bathroom. Then her footsteps. Turning, his eyes roamed her body. Pink cheeks. Shoulders too. No bra. Just panties and a ponytail. She slid in his arms.

He touched her face, "I'm sorry. You're sunburnt."

She smiled. "Just a little. I'm sure it will be gone tomorrow."

"I should have considered the Ball tomorrow night. I'm sure a sunburn wasn't on your list of accessories."

"Dekker, this afternoon was perfect. I haven't been swimming in a long time. I love the feel of the water and the sound of the waves."

"It wasn't all swimming."

She met his gaze. "No. It wasn't. I'd always wanted to ride a stallion through the waves—"

His lips covered hers.

She rode again.

***

Fresh from the shower, Sasha sat with her legs crossed on a lush red rug that separated her and Hawk's twin beds. She wore baggy cotton shorts tied low on her hips and a spaghetti strap tank top. Her hair was still clipped in a messy bun.

She scrolled through pictures she'd taken in Natchitoches. The City of Lights. She couldn't wait till the Christmas festival. She smiled at the few houses for sale that had caught her eye. The river. The historic district. The plantations. Kisatchie National Forest. There was so much to see and learn.

Especially about her new job. She flipped through the pictures of Northwestern State University. Then the Natchitoches Parish Sheriff's Department. One of them would be her employer. Each, completely different from the other. And the clock was ticking. She had to choose. Was she ready to make the change?

Hawk walked out of the bathroom in a towel.

Beautiful and bare, except for terrycloth. Sasha raised her eyebrows. "That might be stretching friendship over the line a little."

He grabbed his shorts off the dresser. "I forgot to grab these."

Lippy, she said, "I wonder how many times that line has been used."

"I don't use lines. And I didn't wear the towel for my benefit."

"You could have asked me to hand you the shorts."

He dropped the towel, holding his shorts in front of him. "I'm a grown man, Sasha. A soldier. A warrior. Blunt. Bold and loyal. Being friends with me is not some casual watered-down word. I don't offer it lightly. I would die for my friends. I would die for you."

He squatted in front of her, staying covered. "You are always safe with me. Naked or clothed. Friends or lovers. Is that clear?"

Sasha knew she had pushed him. Only he was more direct than she would ever be. His wave of masculinity crashed over her. How do you respond to a vow like that? Her expression must have satisfied him. He stood and walked away. Totally naked from the back.

She swallowed. Great. Now she had to get that picture out of her head.

***

Down the hall, Maverick lay behind Piper. Her head on his left arm. His right arm holding her. She was so powerful. So beautiful. His hand spread across her stomach. Was she pregnant yet?

***

A little over a hundred miles northwest of New Orleans, an old blue pickup pulled into a long dark wooded driveway. Liam glanced at the clock. Three a.m. And through tree-shadowed moonlight he drove toward the opening ahead. He'd already researched the property and knew what he would find.

Breaking through the cover of trees, a large metal two-story house with a porch sat to the left. Quiet. No cars. No dogs. No flowers. Just empty rocking chairs. It looked vacant except for security lights inside. Which is what he figured he'd find. But the house with security wasn't his target.

Following the drive along the corral to the right, he finally stopped in front of a red wooden barn. Traditionally shaped, at least three stories tall. Large double doors. Rooster vane on top. Motion lights came on as expected. But he seriously doubted it triggered an alarm since the countryside was teeming with nocturnal wildlife. And it had been vacant for six months.

He smiled. It was the perfect spot.

Chapter 27

Excitement hit the safehouse the next morning at ten o'clock. Gown and tux deliveries arrived right on time. Black zipper bags hid the dresses, keeping with the mystery of the day. The women whisked them away, and Luna never noticed Dekker disappear with an extra one.

After that, Dekker and Hawk cooked a brunch with stuffed omelets, toast, and fresh fruit, while everyone watched the boarding videos from Agent Donovan. There had been two boardings this morning. One for an African freighter in the Atlantic and one near the Panama Canal. King wasn't on either ship. The Coast Guard added another ship to their team. Now three CG vessels hunted King.

***

And so, the day went… The Ball versus the fugitive. And the Ball won as the afternoon passed with the sound of female laughter. The smell of nail polish running the men outside. Then half-dressed women with curlers, curling irons, jeweled clips, and braids running room to room.

Men didn't understand the ritual of anticipation. The Cinderella transformation. The art of a special kind of beauty for a night. It was the feeling of magic. To become… Because to the men, their women were the magic.

And therein lay the reason the women worked so hard.

***

At five on the dot, the women were at a stopping point.

Brunette, blonde and red hair stunning. Each face, gorgeous. Masks, intriguing. Jewelry sparkling. Heels, high and sexy. Perfume lingered in the air.

Everything but the dresses. Not yet.

Now, it was the men's turn.

***

Wearing only a black sparkling thong and heels, Piper leaned against the wall watching Maverick zip his slacks. His black shirt already tucked in. He slid his hands down his thighs and met her gaze…then lowered to the rest of her.

He pressed her against the wall, arms above her head. Their cologne and perfume mingled. Lips close, he said, "You are magnificent. I want a picture of you like that when we get home."

She whispered, "You can take as many as you like with your eyes. It's not like you'll forget. But no camera. It might end up in a court case."

He ran his finger along her thong. "You are too hot for your own good."

"Says the man that wants an erotic picture of his wife."

He lifted her chin. "Let me take your picture."

She loved the look in his eyes. Wasn't that look what tonight was all about? Something on the edge. Mystery. Love. Fire. She smiled. "One. Maybe two."

He kissed her.

A minute later, Piper watched him slip the black textured jacket over his shirt. Open collar. No vest. No tie. Just him encased in black. Gun on his hip. Blonde hair falling over blue eyes. Sculptured lips. He was shockingly beautiful. A Viking model. Hers. She thought about the camera…

Maverick glanced in the mirror after he finished. He was as ready as he was going to be. He caught Piper's expression as he turned. Drawing her close, he said, "I read you loud and clear. And I don't care how many pictures you take of me when we get home. Now, hurry up and get that dress on, or you'll be late to the Ball."

She smiled as he headed out the door. The men were waiting.

***

Down the hall, Sasha stepped into her low-cut turquoise dress. She pulled it up and slid the spaghetti straps on her shoulders. And that was it. No zipper. No buttons. No belt. Turning, she glanced back in the mirror. It was backless till well below her waist. Which meant, no bra. And certainly, no panty lines. She smiled. Half the women at the Ball would be naked under their dresses.

Her phone dinged with a text. It was Jack from Interpol.

Jack to Sasha: I just got the name of one of King's associates for you. Jabari from Africa. Black man. Speaks Portuguese and a few native dialects. I don't know anything else, but my source said he's pretty sure Jabari travels on two African ships. The Orion Crest and Leo Crest.

Sasha: You rock, Jack. We needed this. I owe you.

Jack: You are welcome. And I plan to collect.

In seconds, Sasha joined the men. Dakota called Agent Donovan, who called the Coast Guard. The closest ship, Orion Crest, was only four hours away. That meant, before the clock struck midnight, they might know who King was.

Before long, the limo arrived.

***

Along with anticipation, clouds of luxurious material filled the limo. Piper was a perfect mix of elegance and mystery in silky black satin and long gloves. Luna was electric in a pale blue sequin halter gown. Sasha's turquoise dress shimmered and moved like liquid. Samantha was stunning in a white glitter and rhinestone two-piece gown. Gabrielle wore a gold strapless sequin gown the color of her eyes. And Raven's red hair was magnificent against royal blue velvet sequins.

The men sat next to them wearing black tuxedos. Different styles. Sexy. And handsome. Everyone was excited. First for the Ball. And second, for King to be locked behind bars in just a few hours.

They heard the music before they reached the Audubon Zoo.

Maverick squeezed Piper's hand, and she glanced at him. He said, "You are extraordinarily gorgeous. And mine. Warn anyone that gets out of hand."

"My gun is in my purse."

"I am your hero, Piper."

"Maverick, I'm always armed. Do you expect me to ignore my gun?"

"You could at least give me a second to protect my wife."

Everyone laughed as they turned into the busy parking lot of the Audubon Tea Room. The Masquerade Ball was already in full swing.

***

Liam gazed out the window at the quickly filling parking lot. The limo was almost here. His mind flicked through details for tonight's hidden agenda.

Car. Check.

Gun. Check.

Syringes. Check.

Everything was in place. He glanced at the time. Right at eight o'clock. Good. He planned to be long gone with Piper by ten.

What a rush.

Liam walked outside as the limo pulled up.

The valet attendant opened the door. Dakota stepped out first. He nodded at Liam and looked around. Then offered Gabrielle his hand. She took it, stepping out, gorgeous in gold. Her eyes met Liam's. She smiled as he winked and bowed. Dakota escorted her inside.

Liam watched…and waited…

Sean exited the limo. Then Samantha, a vision in a two-piece sparkling white gown and fancy ponytail.

Hawk followed next, escorting Sasha in a fabulous wave of silky turquoise and lots of skin.

Then Adam, followed by Raven, glamorous in royal blue sequins – half gown – half shorts. Perfect for a dancer.

Dekker and Luna were next. Sexy in a pale blue sequin dress, she smiled at Liam. He winked.

And finally, Maverick stepped out and reached for Piper. A long bare leg appeared as a slender gloved hand slid into Maverick's large one. Piper stepped down and stood.

Liam drank her in. She was elegant, but ravishing in black silk. Corset almost shear. Breasts shoved up. Long gloves. She was sexy and completely mysterious. Dramatic from the top of her head to the soles of her heels. She was wild. Perfect. And his…in less than two hours.

Piper smiled, "Cat got your tongue, Lion Man?"

Liam returned the smile. "Evening, sassy one. It seems so. Beauty such as yours does take the breath away." He glanced at Maverick. "I see you're going to have your hands full tonight."

Maverick chuckled. "That's every day."

Piper said, "You look handsome, Liam. Why waste that? Where's your date?"

"I've got six. You're one of them."

"Lucky me. Two men."

Both men offered their arm. Delighted, she tucked one gloved arm in each, and said, "Then come on boys. Let's get this party started."

Laughing, they entered the masked Ball.

Only Liam heard the clock ticking.

***

Inside the beautiful round shaped Audubon Tea Room, Liam led the group to their private area. Low lit hanging lights provided a golden glow. The dome ceiling was artfully draped with shear black curtains from ceiling to floor. It provided a romantic yet mysterious ambiance. The windowed walls overlooked similarly decorated gardens outside. Mystery was everywhere.

Tables for seating were set with black linen and sparkling dinnerware. Bar tables were strategically placed for those that would rather mingle than sit. A band played. Masked couples danced. And butler-style drinks and hors d'oeuvres were served. A late dinner was planned for ten-thirty. A mystery from the chef…sure to thrill.

Liam reached the special guest area where two tables were arranged as one. He pointed to a small hallway and said, "Before we sit, I'll show you the secure area."

It didn't take long. Inside, was a small fully functioning office. A seating area. Restrooms. And on the other side of the security door, was the limo. It was perfect. Private. And safe.

Sean, Dakota, and Maverick left to check the outdoor perimeter. Liam stayed with Piper, Samantha, and Gabrielle while the other three couples danced.

Liam laughed as the women grilled him with questions.

Samantha looked at Liam's tux as he talked. Black with the sheen of expensive silk. Green shirt to match his eyes. Long black tie. An extremely handsome older man. She smiled when he caught her inspecting him.

Amused, he said, "Do I pass?"

"You're a good-looking man."

A grin twitched. "Are you setting me up to get shot by Sean?"

Ignoring that, she said, "Did you know I was a prosecutor in Baton Rouge?"

"Ah. That explains the scrutiny and sharp edge."

She laughed. "Like the FBI doesn't?"

He smiled. "Beautiful and smart."

Gabrielle took a sip of wine, and said, "And she's totally sassy, like Piper. I'm the gentle one."

Piper laughed. "Said the gentlest knife thrower you'll ever meet. Luna is the gentle one in the group."

"Present company astounds me," Liam said with a chuckle. "No wonder your men are tough…and armed."

Samantha said, "It takes tough. And guns. Have you ever come up against a serial killer?"

Liam met her gaze. She had no idea. He said, "It's possible. How well do we really know anyone?"

Piper drawled, "I know them better after a background check, fingerprint, and DNA."

Laughter filled the table.

***

On the dance floor, Dekker spun Luna as the song ended. Her dark hair fluttered. Her laugh, musical. Grace and beauty filled his vision. He was lost in her. Tilting her face to avoid the mask, he kissed her, hungry for a moment of honey.

He said, "I have a surprise for you when we get home."

"Give me a hint."

"When we get home, I'll give you more than that."

***

Hawk held Sasha's bare back. He pressed her against him hard enough to intrigue with friction as the love song played. Tonight was a date. Sasha might not call it that, but it was what it was. Attraction looking for an opening to ignite a blaze.

Hawk said, "Take a walk with me later."

"Right. Just a walk?"

"To start."

"You're subtle."

"You're beautiful."

"So, you said."

Their gazes met. He said, "And your answer?"

She glanced at his lips knowing she would. But she said, "I'll think about it."

His lips brushed hers. "I'll take that as a yes."

***

Adam had learned how to follow Raven's professional leads. He might be her dance partner, but at times like this, he was more a male balance beam as her body did amazing things in high heels. Everyone watched. Who wouldn't watch fire dance?

She landed in a stunning dip. He said, "It's amazing no one can tell you're pregnant, much less carrying twins."

She smiled and kissed him. "In this dress, I'm glad. And I'm also excited to hand out gender reveal gifts. It's a perfect night. I wonder how long it will take someone to get the message."

"Not long…considering the FBI, a detective, the CIA, a Navy seal, and a hunter are at the table."

***

Maverick, Sean, and Dakota returned from checking the perimeter and quickly hit the dance floor with their wives.

With no one at the table, Liam accepted a martini from a passing waiter and headed to the office. He locked the door. Taking a case from under the desk, he removed a silencer and slipped it in his holster. At only 3.3 inches long it was easily concealable. Next, two syringes. Lifting his pants leg, he slid them in his socks and taped them on the inside of both legs. Then he checked his 9MM. Twenty rounds. More than enough.

He returned to the Ball and watched the women he was protecting.

It was eight-thirty.

Before long, he was charming them on the dance floor.

***

After half a dozen songs, everyone took a break and visited around the table. Sipping cocktails. Tasting hors d'oeuvres. Oysters Bienville. Mini fried crawfish pies. Parmesan crab dip on crispy crostini rounds. Gator bites with remoulade sauce. Shrimp corndogs and pepper jelly.

Stories abounded. Laughter. And lots of teasing.

At a pause in activity, Adam nudged Raven. Smiling, she pulled several satin gift pouches from her purse and said, "How about a gender reveal?"

Everyone clapped. All but Liam. His hands stopped mid-air. Smile frozen on his face as he battled for control.

As Adam and Raven passed bags around the table, Raven explained. "It's a game, so wait and open the bag together. The first person to guess the gender, wins."

Adam said, "Heads up. On your mark—"

Watching Samantha's anticipation, Sean said, "Wait. What do we win?"

Samantha said, "Really, Sean? No one cares! Go, Adam!"

Laughing, Adam said, "Get set… Go!"

The flurry of activity hid Liam's slower movements. He looked in the bag. A gold kaleidoscope lay in tissue. His heart slowed. That wasn't so bad. He didn't touch it, but listened as others looked through it, making comments. Evidently, the changing shapes inside were both pink and blue. Not just pink or blue. And Liam knew what it meant.

Around the table they began to get it. Samantha and Piper yelled twins at the same time.

Liam's phone rang. He excused himself to take the call.

He locked the office door and answered, "This is King."

"King, the helicopter will arrive at eleven-thirty p.m. at the coordinates you provided. Your international flight leaves the Baton Rouge Jet Center thirty minutes after midnight. Do you have any further instructions?"

"Not at all. And my guest and I won't require a flight attendant."

Ending the call, Liam checked the clock. Nine-fifteen. It was time.

Returning to the table, Liam smiled at Raven and Adam. "Congratulations on twins! Sorry I missed the cheering. Was Samantha or Piper the winner?"

Raven said, "Both. But Samantha yielded to Piper as a wedding gift."

He winked at the very competitive Samantha, then glanced at Piper. "So, what was the gift?"

She smiled. "A vacation on a secluded island in the Bahamas."

Liam whistled. "That works."

Maverick said, "Especially since they own it. Adam bought it when they got married. Then Dakota and Sean went in partnership with him."

Liam grinned. "It sounds like they could teach me a thing or two about shopping."

Everyone laughed. Liam could buy anything he wanted with his fortune. Including an island.

Several phones on the table dinged simultaneously.

The team read the text from Agent Donovan: The Coast Guard is less than an hour from the Orion Crest. Stay alert for my call.

With the increased excitement around the table, Liam knew something was up. Which was not necessarily a good thing for him.

Dakota exchanged looks with the team and met Liam's curious gaze. He said, "Something big is going down. Interpol got a tip about King. A source assured them that an associate of King's is traveling on the Orion Crest, an African cargo ship. The Coast Guard and FBI will board her in less than an hour. We hope to find out who King is. After that, he's history. Dead or alive."

Liam knew they'd found out about Jabari. But he also knew that Jabari wouldn't tell them anything. But the direct link to him would blow his identity wide open. They'd figure out that he was King. The thrill gripped him. This was the best part of the hunt.

Smiling, Liam said, "Excellent! It doesn't get better than that. Is there anything I can do?"

Dakota replied, "Yes. They'll message us once the ship is in sight. If the team could use the privacy of the office to watch by video, that would be helpful. We might be tied up for thirty or forty minutes. Other than that, just stay with the women. Hawk and Adam will be close by too. Though we don't expect trouble, you know the zoo and security like no one else."

Hawk saluted. Adam nodded. Liam said, "I'm all yours. Or rather…all theirs. I've got them."

***

Most of them were on the dance floor when the message came. They headed to the office. Sean pulled up the web link on the zoo computer while the rest discussed who would stay and watch and who would return to the Ball.

Piper looked at the computer screen with a frown.

Maverick noticed. "You don't want to watch."

"Not at night with large waves and lights flashing on bobbing ships. Boarding is a lengthy process. Call me when it's time for the interview. That's what I want to see."

Sasha said, "I'm with Piper. I'll just watch the interview."

Samantha glanced at Sean. "I'll stay with you and watch."

Dakota pulled Gabrielle close. "You're staying with me too. I can't concentrate knowing you're getting into trouble. And we both know that happens. You have a baby at home."

Raven said, "I'll go with Adam. He promised to take me on a ride through the zoo. I heard there is a lantern path. I can't wait to hear the jungle at night."

Liam said, "It is wonderful. I encourage everyone to do that at some point tonight. It's a long ride – almost forty minutes - but beautiful. And safe. Zookeepers drive the carts, and security is at every exit."

Luna looked at Dekker and Piper. She didn't want to watch the ships on a computer, but outside it was dark. She wasn't a warrior of any kind, and fear reared its head easily these days.

Dekker knew, and said, "Stay with me. We'll be done in less than an hour."

She said, "You need to work, and I've been inside most of the week. I'll stay near the others. I love the zoo."

Dekker nodded and glanced at the team. He knew they would guard her.

***

After a restroom stop, Liam, Adam, and Hawk walked the four women outside. It was gorgeous. Tables. Music. And lights. Hundreds, if not thousands, of them hung in trees around the patio and garden. Lanterns along the paths covered the landscape.

Skirts of chiffon, satin, sequins, and silk sparkled through a sea of black tuxedoes. Masks intrigued, if a trifle spooky, as guests danced to the music of old-time jazz musicians and singers like Fats Domino. Louis Armstrong. Buddy Bolden. Ella Fitzgerald. And Billie Holiday.

Adam escorted Raven. Hawk escorted Sasha. And Liam escorted Piper and Luna. They headed toward the carts.

Jasper, the big muscular zookeeper saw Liam and waved. "Hey, Liam. Are you ready to ride?"

They shook hands. "Hey, Jasper. Yes, I was hoping you'd have two free carts soon. Is that possible?"

"Sure. Two carts will be here in a few minutes. One takes the long ride through the whole zoo. And the other goes through the primates, African savanna, South America, and the swamp."

Liam smiled. "That's perfect. You are the man."

Jasper grinned with a bright white smile against his dark skin, and said, "And yet you are the one with two beauties on each arm."

Liam winked. "If only they were mine."

Everyone laughed.

A few minutes later it was decided. Adam and Raven would take the full ride. Liam, Piper, Sasha, and Luna would take the shorter ride to make it back for the ship boarding. Hawk too, but he would follow them on foot as surveillance.

As everyone waited for the carts, Liam said, "I need to run to the security office to check the cameras before we ride. Hawk, why don't you come? The more eyes, the better."

Hawk said, "Sure."

Adam said, "How long will you be?"

"Just a few minutes." Liam said.

***

Inside the security office, Liam and Hawk scrolled the cameras with the three officers. Everything was calm in the zoo. No alarms. No issues. And the gates were guarded. Liam quietly slid a blackjack off the shelf. No one noticed.

Leaving the office, they had only taken a few steps in the shadows when Liam hit Hawk on the back of the head. He dropped without a sound. Liam drug him in the bushes and knelt. Pulling one syringe out of his sock, he held it in the moonlight and flicked the needle. Then injected him in the neck.

***

Both carts were waiting when Liam returned. He said, "Hawk's borrowing a couple of things from security. Zoo flashlights and night goggles. He said for us to go ahead. He'll text me if he gets held up."

And that made perfect sense to everyone.

In moments, Adam and Raven's driver headed toward the Asia exhibits. And Liam, Piper, Luna, and Sasha's driver headed toward Africa. Piper was in the front seat with the driver. Liam was behind her in the back seat. Luna in the middle. And Sasha behind the driver, who occupied them with facts about the zoo as he maneuvered the beautifully lit trails.

Liam was easily able to put both syringes in his right jacket pocket since it faced the outside of the cart. Then he screwed the silencer on the end of his pistol as the smell of Piper's perfume caressed him. Her skirt fluttered behind her in the wind, brushing his leg. Her bare back and shoulders teased him.

His left arm rested behind Luna and Sasha on the back of the seat. He was ready.

Luna pulled her phone and read a text. Liam watched her respond to Dekker: I love you too. Wish you were here.

He glanced in the darkness. More delicious irony. Dekker was going to wish that very soon. All the men would. It wouldn't be long now.

They passed the lion enclosure, and the lioness roared and jumped on the fence. The men laughed as the women jumped.

Sasha glanced behind them. Where was Hawk? He was missing it.

Piper's phone rang.

As she answered, Maverick said, "How is it?"

"Fabulous. We just passed the lions. The female lion is still hot for Liam. She scared us. It was great."

"I should have known you would think scared is great."

"I'm an agent. Everything else is boring. How close is the ship to Orion Crest?"

"Almost there. I'll call you. You should have time to finish the ride. How long do you have left?"

"Forty minutes or so. We started late. Adam and Raven took another cart and went to Asia."

"That does sound better than looking at the butt end of a ship."

"What did I tell you? Now, let me go. I'm missing it."

❖

The cart driver turned right, heading toward the Louisiana Swamp exhibit. They passed the black bears, and he took a sharp left onto the boardwalk. It was beautiful. Fairy lights everywhere. Cypress trees. Cajun music. Draping moss. Swamps. Owls hooted. Fish jumped. And eyes from the woods glowed green.

They passed the closed Cypress Knee Café. Piper glanced at Liam. He'd thrown her on that roof to save her from the robot a few days ago. She smiled. He winked.

And as they neared the Cajun Ballroom, a smaller event center at the zoo not in use tonight, Liam pulled his gun. It lay hidden against his calf. Piper's skirt touched his fingers.

When they passed the security cameras, Liam said to the driver, "Hey, Brian. Stop in the driveway. I need to check in with the guards." He pointed to the staff road leading to the fence for the women's benefit.

The driver slowed, turned, then stopped.

Looking across the swamp, Piper said, "Do you think we'll see alliga—"

She heard the whoosh of air. The thud. And spun in time to see the second shot hit Brian in the base of the neck. Blood splattered. She dove for the ground as the driver's lifeless body slid left and fell to the deck. She reached for her purse on the floor as she spun toward the backseat.

Liam's eyes met hers. His arm was around Luna's neck, hand covering her mouth. His gun pointed at Sasha. And for a quiet, deadly second, Piper's mind couldn't believe it. He was King. Then fury hit.

Liam saw her expression change and warned her, "Easy, wildcat…and listen closely. You are their only chance for survival. This will be fast and quiet. Is that clear?"

Piper looked at Sasha's scrapes and busted lip. Messy hair. Torn dress. And at Luna's terror-filled eyes. There would be no negotiation. King…no, Liam had played her and won.

She stood, spitting Brian's blood off her lip. "What do you want?"

"You know what I want. But for now, toss your purse in the swamp, then grab the zip ties out of the dash storage compartment."

Her purse landed with a splash and disappeared. She grabbed the zip ties.

He climbed out, pulling Luna with him. He waved the gun at Sasha and said, "Kick your purse out on the ground, then slide over here. And be quick about it, Detective. Then grab the bar over your head."

Sasha paused. "Liam—"

"Don't mess with me, Sasha. Do you want to watch Luna die? Now, get over here."

Once she was in place, he said, "Zip tie her to the bar, Piper. Tight."

Piper met Sasha's gaze. They both knew Hawk wasn't coming and that Liam had all the leverage. She tied her.

Liam looked at Luna. "I'm going to remove my hand and arm. Sit on the floorboard. Don't make a sound or you'll get Sasha's blood all over your beautiful dress."

Trembling, Luna sat next to Sasha's legs before hers gave out.

Liam held his left wrist out to Piper. "Tie your right wrist to mine."

Piper did what she was told. Tucking the gun in his waistband, Liam pulled a syringe out of his pocket.

Piper grabbed his arm. "Don't hurt them, Liam. Let's go. I'll go with you. Leave them alone…please…"

He kissed her hot, hard, and fast. "I appreciate all that passion, wildcat, but I'm just going to give Sasha a nap. I need her quiet. Now, suck it up unless you want her to get the full dose. And then she can sleep forever. Either way, you're mine."

Sasha felt the needle prick her neck. The burn of the drug. Tears rolled down her cheeks. The last thing she remembered was Liam kissing her, and his words, "If only I had the time…"

Before long, Liam walked silently out the back gate with Piper tied to him. And Luna tied, drugged, and slung over his shoulder. She was insurance that Piper would obey.

Piper cringed at the sight of two dead officers crumpled by the fence. Eyes still open. More innocent victims murdered by a killer that everyone admired. She had so many questions. But most of all she wished she'd tucked a gun under her skirt.

They headed toward a remote area of the park. She saw his BMW under the trees. Why would he take a vehicle everyone would be looking for? As they got close, he clicked his key fob. The trunk opened.

Piper gasped. Danielle lay in the trunk in a black evening gown. Breathing. She looked at Liam. "You let her live."

His hot gaze met hers. "I had you on my mind."

Then kneeling, he pulled Luna off his shoulder and laid her in the grass. The ties bit into Piper's skin, forcing her to kneel with him. Then he was up again, scooping Danielle out of the trunk.

Placing the drugged brunettes, side by side, he said, "Tie them together. They'll be found soon enough."

He walked Piper to her side of the car and opened the door. After cutting the tie that bound them, he held up a syringe. "Don't make me use this or you'll wake up over the ocean. Your choice."

Piper had to get him away from the zoo. Away from the three women that needed her to choose them. She got in the car.

***

A mere five minutes away, Liam pulled into an empty warehouse. Inside was an old blue pickup. Piper knew they were switching vehicles. She casually peeled one of the trackers off a toe and stuck it on the door.

Liam stopped the car and looked at Piper. "We're changing clothes. Switching vehicles. You can't outrun me. And you don't have a gun. Need I say more?"

"What did you get me to wear?"

He laughed. "I love the way you play the game."

"I thought the game was over."

"Once I get you out of the States, Agent Pierce. That's when it's over. Meet me behind the truck."

Liam faced Piper in her gown and heels. Her masquerade mask and gloves long gone. He handed her a bag. "Here is something to wear."

And in one impatient move, he ripped his shirt open, tossing it aside. He said, "Turn around. I'll unzip you. And hurry up or I'll think you want me now."

Piper removed a pretty sundress out of the bag. Short. Red. With ruffles. Feminine and romantic. She struggled to imagine Liam shopping for it as she turned. He lowered her zipper as she stared at a wall of shadows. Air hit her body. Her dress dropped leaving her all but naked in a thong and heels. Heart pounding, she hurriedly pulled the dress over her head, her bare bottom covered again. Liam hadn't said a thing.

With her back still to him, she held the truck and lifted a leg to remove a heel – and gasped as Liam picked her up, sitting her on the open tailgate. He pressed between her legs…his arousal, bold. The acrid taste of panic filled her mouth.

Liam tilted her chin, growling, as muscles twitched in his jaw. He struggled, knowing that if he started anything, he wouldn't stop. But time was not his friend. Not yet. He took a hot ragged breath and lifted her leg, removing a heel. The other one too.

Piper was grateful. And relieved. One, because he controlled himself. Two, because he didn't know she had trackers on her feet. She swallowed. "Thank you...I'm…not ready."

He kissed her hard. "You better get ready." And taking off her wedding ring, he threw it in the dark.

***

Twenty-five minutes later, they headed north on Interstate 10. The lights of New Orleans were barely a glow behind them.

Piper was makeup free now, her hair in a ponytail. Liam had on jeans and a black pullover with a baseball cap. She had no idea where they were going. Baton Rouge? She peeled off another tracker and stuck it on the seat.

She watched the darkness flash past. Hopefully, Maverick knew by now she was missing.

Chapter 28

Maverick texted Piper the ship was about to be boarded. No response. He texted again. Nothing. He stepped out of the room and called her. No answer. Sticking his head back in the office, Maverick said, "I can't reach Piper. I'm heading to the cart station. They should be back any minute."

Dekker said, "I'm coming with you."

On the way outside, Maverick called Liam. Dekker called Luna and Hawk. Nothing from any of them. Trying not to panic, they jogged.

Jasper saw them coming. He said, "Hey, Detective."

Maverick said, "Have you seen Liam's cart?"

"Not since they left toward the African trail. They're only a little late—"

Maverick and Dekker took off running. Dekker called Adam.

❖

Adam answered, "Hey, Dekker—"

Cutting him off, Dekker said, "Have you seen Piper's cart?"

"Not yet. Are you running?"

"We can't reach them. None of them. Where are you?"

"Heading to the Jaguar Jungle. Where are you?"

"Maverick and I are in the African Savanna heading your way. Prepare for trouble and call Dakota."

The line went dead.

Adam told the driver, "Floor it and radio Jasper to call 911."

Raven said, "What happened? Tell me!"

Adam spread his jacket on the floor. He stuck his gun in his waistband. "Piper's whole group isn't answering. Lay on the floor and get your gun out. I've got to call Dakota."

***

In the office, Sean, Samantha, Dakota, and Gabrielle watched the Coast Guard and FBI board the ship. Before long, a tall black man was escorted below deck.

Dakota's phone rang. He picked up on the first ring, walking away from the computer.

Adam said, "Piper's in trouble. Maverick and Dekker are running through the African area. We're heading their way from the other side of the trail. They can't reach anyone in the cart. Not Liam. Not Hawk. Or the women. The zoo is calling 911."

Dakota and Sean ran for the door. Dakota said, "Lock the door, Samantha! Cover Gabrielle. And call us if the Coast Guard finds anything!"

***

Maverick shucked his jacket as he ran past the lions. Sirens sounded in the distance. He heard Dekker on the phone behind him. And back toward the Tea Room he heard screams. He knew Sean and Dakota were coming.

As he rounded the last bend in the African Savanna, he didn't see the cart anywhere. No voices. No people. He cut left onto the first boardwalk into the Louisiana Swamp exhibit. Then across the swamp he saw a cart race out of the other trail and stop. Adam jumped out and ran up the middle boardwalk.

Maverick ran past the dark café and event center. Pausing, he looked down the small road. The nightmare wasn't far. A dead man lay in a puddle of blood next to the cart. Sasha hung from bleeding wrists. Head back. Eyes closed. Mouth bloody. Dress torn.

But no one else.

Anguish ripped through Maverick as he lifted Sasha. She was alive. He cut her down and carried her to a picnic table. Dekker arrived. They ignored the fear in each other's eyes. Where were Piper and Luna? And where in the hell were Liam and Hawk?

Adam reached the man on the ground. He hadn't been alive since the first shot hit him. They'd both been kill shots. He hollered for Raven, then called 911 for the medical examiner and ambulances.

Sean and Dakota ran up. In a glance they took in the scene, then ran out the gate following Maverick and Dekker.

They saw two dead officers on the ground as patrol cars squealed to a stop – lights flashing. But they didn't see Piper or Luna anywhere. They fanned right toward a more secluded area not far away.

In a few minutes, Luna's sparkling gown caught their eye. They yelled for assistance. Maverick and Dekker hit their knees, checking pulses and cutting ties. Luna was alive. All four men looked at the unexpected woman in black that wasn't Piper.

Throat tight like he was being strangled with a chain, Maverick said, "King took Piper. This is Danielle. And he made sure no one would be awake to tell us who he is."

***

Back in the locked office, Samantha and Gabrielle watched the tall black man's interview on the ocean by the FBI and Coast Guard.

Jabari Igwe, an African national, insisted that he didn't know King. He had heard of him. That was all. So, they ransacked his cabin. Tore it apart looking for something. Anything that connected him to King.

They found a wallet hidden in the closet. And a passport. Not really a surprise since you probably had to hide valuables on a ship. It held American and African money, a few family pictures, a credit card, and a corporate picture ID for a shipping company. The FBI texted a picture of the corporate ID to Agent Donovan for a background check.

The other agent asked to see his phone. Jabari hesitated. The agent demanded. Jabari pointed to the drawers. It was taped underneath the bottom drawer. The screen was locked. Jabari slowly entered the code.

The agent scrolled through contacts first. No King. He went to texts. He opened any attachments. One was from Tom Rogers. He opened the attachment. Two men were in the picture. One was Jabari. One was a white man. Written across the bottom of the picture was: You and King.

Samantha zoomed in on the picture. It was Liam. She grabbed the phone.

❖

Sean answered the call, "Talk fast, Samantha. King took Piper and the women are drugged."

Samantha said, "They found a picture of King on the ship. It's Liam."

He blinked. It raced through his mind again. He said, "We'll be there in a minute. Be ready to go."

❖

The team heard his remark. Maverick said, "What?"

Sean said, "Liam is King. Let's go!"

Maverick roared, startling everyone but them. He said, "He's dead. As many times as I can kill him."

Sean said, "I'm good with that. But we've got to get my equipment to track Piper. And we haven't found Hawk."

They looked at the women being loaded in the ambulances, then glanced at Raven.

Raven said, "You go. I'll go with them."

Dakota said, "Done. I'll have Gabrielle and Samantha join you with security. Hawk—"

Adam said, "Just go. I'll find him. There's no way Liam took him. He's here somewhere. I'm not leaving without him."

Maverick grabbed the nearest officer. "We need a ride."

***

Liam glanced at the green sign in his headlights: Baton Rouge 22 miles. He looked at Piper at the other end of the old bench seat. She hadn't said a word. It had taken his adrenalin and mind a while to settle down, maybe it was the same for her.

He said, "You surprise me."

Piper said, "Like I care."

Laughing, he said, "There she is. I wondered what was up."

"I wasn't in the mood for a twelve-hour nap from one of your lullaby needles."

He said, "I didn't want to have to hurt you."

"Like kidnapping and rape doesn't fit that definition."

Smiling, he said, "You can fight it all you want, but I will please you, Piper. Make no mistake about that."

"Tell yourself that all you want. It'll never be true." She turned toward the window. Please her? Impossible. Liam would never be Maverick. And even the thought of a forced orgasm with Liam was a nightmare.

Liam watched her. She'd learn soon enough. Then flashing red lights caught his eye in the rearview mirror.

Piper startled as Liam unsnapped her seatbelt and yanked her across the seat. She landed against his thigh, one hand pushing against his shoulder, the other holding on to the dash.

He said, "Calm down and buckle up. For the rest of the trip, we are two love birds. Be convincing."

He tensed. The lights in the mirror were getting closer. He could hear the sirens now. It looked like maybe two cars. He checked his speed. Piper glanced at Liam. Smart. Old truck. Change of clothes. Smooching couple on the highway. It wouldn't be a red flag to law enforcement unless Sean had already tracked her. But he wouldn't send cops like this. No way. It would be like throwing gas on an already out of control bonfire.

Liam kept his eyes on the mirror and said, "Don't make light of the potency of your allure, Piper. I will fight for you. Now, touch me and make it good."

The cars were close. Sirens loud. And Piper didn't want any more men to die tonight. She leaned into him, running her hand across his chest. Her other hand caressed his neck. Fingers slipping into his hair. She kissed his shoulder. His cheek. His eyes met hers as the cars flew right by.

Piper watched his tension fade, and she settled back against the seat. Crisis averted.

Liam said, "That was convincing."

She shrugged. "I hope so. The FBI pays me well for undercover."

He grinned. "What would it take for that to be real?"

"If I was a zombie. Now, what did you do to Hawk?"

"He'll have a terrible headache - if he wakes up. I was rushed and injected more than I intended."

She had to believe they would all wake up. Hawk. Sasha. Luna. And Danielle. She said, "You liked Danielle."

"Obviously."

"How many accents do you have?"

He answered in King's voice, "Three. Irish. American. And French."

"That's handy."

"It turned out that way."

"Where did the name King come from?"

He didn't answer.

She looked at him. "Come on, Liam. I have questions. I'm an agent for heaven's sake. I'm curious. Give me something. You are the one that wants me with you. I thought we were becoming friends. Are we going to spend a lifetime not making intelligent conversation? How boring."

Piper could make a point like no one else. He said, "Friends in Africa gave me the nickname as a teenager. About the lions of course."

"King of the jungle."

"Exactly."

"It is a cool nickname." She paused. "So, why did you waste the name on the King I met?"

The man he used to be hid the pain of that well-aimed blow. He said, "You found out why in your research. Most of the world doesn't know me as King. Being a ghost is extremely helpful."

"To kill?"

"If need be."

"Is the killing over?"

He met her gaze. "We'll see, won't we?"

Silence fell as Liam turned back to the road. He thought about the storm that night off the coast of Madagascar. The night a killer was born.

***

Maverick frowned as he watched Sean's laptop while they sped down the road. Piper's tracker headed toward Baton Rouge while they headed the opposite direction in New Orleans. Every minute put her further away, but she'd left a tracker behind on purpose. They had to follow her trail to know what she was telling them.

Black SUVs slid to a stop outside a dark warehouse a few miles from the zoo. FBI agents lined each side of the door, then disappeared inside. Flashlights found Liam's black BMW. Empty. They'd switched vehicles. Maverick's gaze locked on Piper's ballgown on the floor. High heels. He didn't dwell on anything beyond that. Piper would do what she had to do. And Liam was a dead man walking. Execution scheduled for tonight.

Sean quickly searched through Liam's tuxedo and shoes. Dekker searched in the car. Maverick and Dakota scanned the floor for any other evidence they might need before leaving. Dakota found her necklace and earrings. Maverick found her wedding ring.

Sean yelled, "Let's go!"

***

At the zoo, officers searched the trails for Hawk.

Adam went to security to check the cameras.

The security supervisor shook his head at Adam. "There's bad medicine out here tonight. I've known Liam for years. Years, I tell you. His uncle too. I had no idea he was capable of this. He fooled me."

Adam said, "He fooled us all. Can you tell me about the equipment Hawk borrowed tonight? Liam told Jasper—"

"What equipment? They just watched the cameras—"

Adam disappeared out the door.

He began to search through the jungle style landscaping around the immediate vicinity. He found the blood spatter first. Then drag marks. Hawk was shoved under a grouping of ferns and elephant ears. He was pale and bloody from a head injury. Probably drugged. And barely alive. He called for an ambulance.

***

At the Louis Armstrong New Orleans International Airport, Captain Nicole Pierce texted Piper. No answer. She texted three more times before disobediently exiting the plane and called Dekker.

He answered on the first ring. "Nicole. Where are you?"

"At Louis Armstong heading to a taxi—"

"Stay inside. Go to security. Someone from the FBI will pick you up."

Fear radiated. Something was wrong. "Where's Piper?"

His hesitation scared her. "Dekker!"

"She was kidnapped an hour ago."

Pain shot through her. "No."

"There's no evidence she was injured. And she was fitted with trackers days ago. We are following her now."

"To where?"

"It looks like she's heading out of Baton Rouge."

"Where are you?"

"Almost to Baton Rouge."
"Was it the podcast guy?"
"Yes."
"Was anyone else hurt?"
He didn't answer.
"Silence makes it worse, Dekker."
"Hawk is missing. Three women were drugged and at the hospital. And he killed three men."
"Why is this creep still alive?"
"He won't be for much longer."

Dekker ended the call still watching Sean's computer. The monitor was a split screen now. Three views.

The left was a zoom view of Piper's toenail polish trackers. All ten were side by side, which meant her feet were together. They could tell every time she moved her feet.

The middle view showed the removable trackers. Down to seven - but one seemed further away on her left. She must have tagged the vehicle.

The third was the drone view. It was high in the night sky traveling at 210 mph. The drone would catch up with the vehicle Liam was driving in less than fifteen minutes.

And the team was traveling with three cars going 90 mph - and closing the gap. In the perfect scenario, they hoped to be close to Piper, but not seen, long before Liam stopped the vehicle.

Maverick watched the trackers leave Baton Rouge behind on a long stretch to nowhere and said, "Where the hell is he taking her? That road ends at Angola prison."

***

Piper frowned as they left Baton Rouge. Her last study of a Louisiana map showed this area mostly rural, except for St. Francisville and the prison. As civilization slipped away, her blood pressure rose. Being in the middle of the woods with Liam was not on her list of good ideas - even with Maverick coming.

She said with a touch of forced humor, "Are we going camping?"

Liam slid his hand under her dress until his finger touched the edge of her thong. He met her gaze and considered taking it further. But he couldn't afford a fight in the truck. They were almost there anyway. He said, "Have you been up here before?"

She refused to look down as her muscles tightened. Faking cool, she said, "No. But I know Angola is out here somewhere. Unfortunately, I don't figure you're heading there. What a shame."

He laughed. "You're good, Piper. But I think you're nervous."

She pushed his hand. "Don't make fun of me. When was the last time you were kidnapped? Have a little class. Maybe use the manners you were raised with instead of King's atrocious ones. Start there."

Squeezing her leg till she gasped in pain, he said, "Watch your mouth, Piper. You know nothing about King."

She couldn't let up or fear would win. "So, tell me where he came from. What does it matter? I'm going to live with him anyway."

"In time."

"Then tell me about Cara."

He backhanded her. Her head hit the glass, and she saw stars. Her lip and eyebrow split open, burning as blood dripped down her face. And the headache that started wasn't kind. She spit blood on the seat.

Liam was impressed. Piper's kind of tough, was rare. She earned her answers. He said, "Be careful on your fishing expeditions, Agent Pierce. It can be dangerous when you find what you're looking for."

He looked at her. "Cara wasn't what you imagine. And she wasn't swept off the boat. I knocked her out and threw her overboard because she killed my children."

The horror shocked Piper speechless.

He explained, "I was on top of the world before that. I had a lifelong mission for animals that meant everything. A fiancé from Ireland that I loved more than life itself. A wedding around the corner and twins on the way. My son and daughter were due in six months. We'd already named them. Decorated their adjoining rooms. And set the date for the C-section. Everything was perfect.

"So as the storm rolled in that day on the boat, I wasn't prepared to overhear Cara talking about abortion on the phone. Her abortion. Devastated, I confronted her, making sure I'd heard what I thought I did. And she admitted it. Bragged almost. Defiant and embarrassed at being caught – knowing we were done."

He tapped the steering wheel. "As it turns out, she planned to tell me she miscarried." He laughed. "And I would have believed her. Every single word." He paused as a state trooper flew past them on the bridge.

"Now, I'm not a big supporter of abortion rights. But I'm also not insensitive to the awful things that can cause people to make that decision and struggle to live with it. I know life can be hard.

"But personally, I'd spent my entire life protecting animals and children. It's who I am…it's the charities I've created. The animals I've carried for miles. The children I've carried, starving or wounded. And as broken as I was, I asked her why she did it. I mean, we planned everything. It made no sense. Why did she get pregnant just to kill them?"

His question faded.

Glancing at Piper, he said, "She simply changed her mind. She didn't want to have twins. So, I killed her as the storm hit. It seemed fitting. And I swore that the next woman that would have my children would fight to protect them. A real lioness."

Piper closed her eyes, aching at the soul death of a good man. A great one even. Now, she knew why King existed…and why he chose her. And she would bet a million dollars that Cara was a brunette with long hair. They had missed the biggest clue of all.

Liam turned on his right blinker and slowed.

***

Using the control panel twenty miles behind Liam, Sean lowered the drone to finally get a visual of the vehicle Piper was in. He zoomed in and audible relief sounded through the men. Piper sat next to Liam in a blue truck. Sean dropped the drone behind the truck to get the license plate number…and the right blinker came on.

Frowning, Sean glanced at the map and cussed. Looking at the others, he said, "He's taking her to my ranch."

And all hell broke loose in the SUV.

***

Piper ignored the panic. There was no time for that as Liam drove down a long, secluded road. No streetlights. No sidewalks. No nothing. Just thick woodlands and darkness. And a creek somewhere to the right since they'd just crossed a bridge.

He braked and turned left by a black mailbox she hadn't even seen in the dark. He stopped. The name on the box was S. NASH. She looked at Liam. How in the world did he know about Sean's ranch? He winked and headed down the leaf covered driveway.

Liam pulled out of the trees and Piper saw a two-story house and a huge barn. Vacant obviously. Liam passed the house and stopped in front of the barn. Motion lights popped on.

He said, "I've already been here. I know the layout of the barn and the land. Don't waste your time running."

Opening the door, he stepped out and threw the truck keys across the yard. They vanished in the shadows. He pulled her with him. She looked up at the open hayloft as he unlatched the barn doors and flipped the lights on.

Piper quickly scanned the inside. Some stalls were empty. Some filled with equipment. Boxes. Ranch stuff. Another set of double doors were at the far end. In between, were storage areas. Stairs to the right led to a hayloft apartment. She refused to think about a bed anywhere near them.

There were shelves with tools. More tools on the wall. Horse equipment. Wooden ladders built in – one to the hayloft – and one that went to the roof. She looked up. The ceiling was at least three stories high.

She said, "How did you know about their ranch?"

Their eyes met. He said, "Does it really matter?"

She looked away. No. Liam watched her, knowing she was fighting panic. He would just let it run its necessary course. She'd rather fight. Rather run. But really, she'd rather shoot him. But this was about what he wanted.

Turning her to face him, he touched her mouth. "Are you on birth control?"

Her shock answered him. He kissed her, and in seconds, picked her up, forcing her to straddle him as he held bare butt cheeks.

Piper pushed him. He was going way too fast. "Liam…I need the bathroom..."

His hot gaze pierced her.

She snapped, "It's been hours. Give me a second for heaven's sake."

He led her to a small bathroom. It had a toilet. Sink. Mirror. Tiny window at the top. And a few shirts and dusty towels on a shelf. He pressed her hand against his arousal and squeezed. "Make it quick, wildcat. I'm done waiting."

Bladder screaming, Piper used the bathroom, then looked around the room for a weapon. All she found were splinters and a small nail. She climbed on the sink. Through the window she could see a large hay trailer at the other end of the barn. Climbing down, she thought of the tools. Maybe…

Liam called, "Quit stalling. Get out here."

Piper leaned her head against the door. She had to do something. Surviving a rape was one thing. Getting pregnant was a different nightmare. Surely Maverick was close. She opened the door.

Liam was leaning against a stall post. He crooked his finger, calling her and said, "Why didn't you clean your face?"

"It burns. You did it. Deal with it."

He smiled. She was magnificent. He rubbed what throbbed. Piper looked away from him. The hourglass had run out. And it went against everything to submit…even to survive. And then she saw the pole. Not a rusty one. But a nice silver pole connected to the loft.

Piper said softly, "Did you know that I'm a pole dancer?"

Liam stilled. Green eyes riveted on her, he said, "Obviously not. Now, Agent Pierce, why would you offer me that information?"

Walking slow…sensual now…Piper reached the pole. She caressed it and whispered, "Maybe I can make tonight about something I'm ready for too. How about a song for a little foreplay, Lion Man? We know you're already up for a show."

Liam pulled out his phone knowing she was up to something – and didn't care. He wanted this. Music came on. Piper let her hair down, knowing Liam would never last the whole song. He might not make it long at all with the arousal he was already packing.

But it gave her a chance to use it against him.

Liam couldn't believe the transformation in Piper as she teased him. She tossed her dress without a blink and swung onto the pole wearing only a thong. Naked except for a shiny black string. He groaned and walked closer. Eyes devouring her.

She showed him her body, as she worked the pole. Up. Down. Hair swinging. Her upside-down straddle about did him in and he reached for her leg. She spun out of his reach, laughing, touching herself. He stepped closer, oblivious to anything else at all.

And with a spin, Piper kicked him on the left side of the head. A nice powerful roundhouse. He hit the ground hard, and his gun went flying. He was bleeding, growling, and struggling to get up. She hit him with a piece of lumber, and he was out – with a large gash across his head.

Grabbing her dress, she got busy…but couldn't find the drug syringes. Or the gun. And the truck keys were in the yard. Frustrated, she shoved the barn door open like she'd left and killed the lights. She'd have to climb. Halfway up a wall ladder, Liam sat up.

Ankle throbbing from the kick, Piper hurried, but in seconds the lights came on. Liam screamed her name. She turned and their eyes met. And then he was coming after her faster than she'd ever dreamed possible. Like a wild animal.

She screamed, climbing onto the loft and ran for the roof ladder. The drone buzzed her head.

Maverick was here.

***

Outside, Maverick, Dekker, and Dakota ran up the drive. Sean followed, steering the drone. Other agents came through the woods and surrounded the perimeter.

Over the radio Sean said, "He's chasing her. They're climbing for the roof. He's fast. I'll try to slow him down with the drone.

"Maverick and Dekker, find a way to get to the roof.

"Dakota, take the inside of the barn with the drone.

"Perimeter agents – do not engage. I repeat, do not engage. Piper is in the line of fire.

"Helicopters – move in! Light up that rooftop!"

***

Back inside, Piper reached the top of the ladder. Terrified. Three stories in the air. She felt the ladder shake as Liam climbed, growling. Straining, she shoved the roof hatch open.

Liam stared under Piper's dress. Nothing like watching an almost naked woman climb. This was the hottest hunt ever. He was almost to her when something burned him. Over. And over. He yelled. It was like being sliced by fire and he smelt burnt skin and hair.

It took him a second to see the laser drone, and realized the FBI was here. He kept climbing. Let it burn…

He almost had her.

***

Outside, the sound of helicopters filled the night air. Spotlights hit the roof of the barn. Maverick and Dekker shoved a hay wagon closer in case a jump was necessary. And then headed for a metal fire escape ladder from ground to roof. Maverick climbed. Dekker right behind him.

As Maverick pulled himself on the roof, the hatch opened. Piper's head and arms emerged, and she scrambled to get out. Face bloody. Terror evident.

Below her, Dakota climbed after Liam as the drone attacked him with the laser. But Dakota couldn't shoot. Piper wasn't in the clear. He pulled his knife.

Back on the roof, Piper had her right leg out of the hatch when Liam caught her left. She screamed as he bit her like an animal and clawed her from groin to knee. She fought to get away…her leg on fire.

With a roar of rage, Maverick yanked Piper away from Liam. She screamed, clutching his arms, seeing nothing but the night sky and helicopters. Balancing on the slanted roof, Maverick shoved her into Dekker's waiting arms, and yelled, "Get her out of here!"

Piper screamed, "No!" as Liam lunged through the hatch. Burned. Bloody. A large knife buried deep in his thigh. Impossibly, he stood and yanked out the knife. Maverick pulled his gun.

Six shots rang into the night.

Liam's body jerked with each like an awkward marionette. And with dead eyes still open, he tilted and took a dive off the roof. Maverick spun to Piper and Dekker.

Kneeling, Piper had the gun.

Their eyes met. They'd both killed him. She began to tremble, and her dad took the gun. Maverick had her in his arms as the first tear fell.

***

The tears didn't last long.

Piper refused to get in the basket as the helicopter hovered above the barn. She yelled over the noise, "I can walk."

Maverick yelled back, "That's debatable. But you can't climb. Especially not three stories." He pointed at his shirt wrapped around her entire left leg, not counting her quickly swelling right ankle. He said, "Every step would tear the wounds more. And there's no way you can wrap your legs around me to hold on while I climb. Get in the basket."

"No."

Dekker hid his grin and held the other end of the basket. This could take a while.

Maverick yelled to the helicopter, "Send down a double harness!"

Piper's arms were tight around Maverick's neck. Eyes closed. She was strapped to his chest as he held her, feet dangling in the air as they lowered. She sighed as her skirt blew up. Exposing way too much skin. She hadn't thought of that.

Maverick lowered his arms to block her bare bottom and watched the ambulance and medical examiner arrive. He glanced to where Liam lay. Lion Man. He'd killed eight people. Injured nine – plus, the three in the hospital. And tormented the City of New Orleans. Dying once was not enough. Hell would take care of the rest.

Maverick's feet touched the ground. He unhooked them and gave the thumbs up signal. And in a sudden flurry of dust and activity, another helicopter appeared. Maverick scooped Piper up and ran to the barn. The FBI forced a terrified rental pilot to land.

***

Thirty minutes later, the team rode back to New Orleans in a helicopter. Victorious…but somber. Only Danielle had woken up. Luna, Sasha, and Hawk were still unconscious. On top of that, they had learned that Liam hired the helicopter that showed up - and a plane. Piper had almost disappeared on a trip to an undisclosed location in the South Pacific. Only Liam knew the destination. It would have taken a miracle to find her.

Piper sat in Maverick's lap with her leg wrapped in large medical pads. She met his gaze. He kissed her cheek. Her temple. Her forehead. But she could feel the rigidity of his body. And his frown was still there with a million questions in his eyes. They'd had no privacy and no time to talk.

She said, "My wounds are painful, but minor. I might not even need stitches."

"I'll let the doctor convince me of that in New Orleans." He paused. "No secrets, Piper. Did I make it in time?"

She knew what he meant. Touching his face, she said, "Yes, Detective. I promise."

Maverick felt a huge rush of emotion as he hugged her. Three powerful words repeated in his mind. Thank you, God. Thank you, God. Thank you, God.

Chapter 29

Maverick carried Piper in the hospital since she refused a wheelchair or stretcher…or treatment until she had seen the others for herself.

In room 320, Sasha was pale on the stark white pillows, hair in a tangled ponytail. Several bruises on her face. Eyebrow and lip cut and swollen. Both her wrists were bandaged. Piper sat on the side of the bed while Maverick talked to the doctor.

The Doctor explained, "It's just the drug making her sleep. And she's beginning to react to sounds. She'll be awake in a couple of hours. We're monitoring her vitals. She is going to be fine, Detective Patterson. Even her wrists will be fine - just sore for a while.

Maverick sighed in relief.

Aware of tonight's scenario, the Doctor glanced at Piper. "She needs treatment. How is she?"

"Stubborn. And tough. But her leg's a mess. I'll bring her to ER after she sees the others. How's Danielle?"

"Fighting through a myriad of emotions and lots of tears. Her parents are on their way. And she won't tell anyone the story but Piper."

Maverick nodded…he could only imagine. "If you would, please tell her we'll be there as quick as we can."

***

On another floor, Dekker was on the bed with Luna. Holding her, attachments and all. It didn't matter that her hair was a little on the wild side, and her face had a few scrapes and a busted lip. She was still beautiful. Safe. And he was doing his best to wake her up.

He coaxed, "Luna…

Maverick stopped in the doorway, knowing what Dekker felt...again. Two women he loved had been attacked in one night. Piper choked on emotion at the picture of love before her.

Dekker noticed them. "Come in. How's Sasha?"

Maverick said, "Safe. Sleeping off the drug. Minor injuries. How is Luna?"
"The same. I'm encouraging her to wake up."
Piper smiled. "I'm glad. We'll go check on Hawk. I'll be back as soon as I can."
Dekker said, "Not till after you see the doctor."
She nodded. It wasn't a request. "I will."
"Thank you. One last thing - your mother is in New Orleans. Agent Donovan will bring her later."

***

Everyone else was with Hawk in a room near the nurse's station. Dakota and Gabrielle. Sean and Samantha. And Adam and Raven.
Maverick lowered Piper by the bed. She balanced on one leg, holding the handrail. She touched Hawk's hand. His color was off…pale compared to his usual bronze skin. And he was startlingly still. His chest barely moved as he breathed. But he was breathing on his own.
Piper glanced at the extra machines. One for his vitals. An oxygen tube in his nose. Heart wires for the EKG. A defibrillator close by. And blood on his pillow.
Piper looked at Raven. "What did the doctor say?"
"He's stable. He has a concussion and six stitches from a head blow. The cat scan was good. The problem is the amount of elephant tranquilizer he was given. It would have killed anyone smaller. His body is fighting but we won't know anything for…" She glanced at the large wall clock. "Five more hours, give or take."
"What are his chances?"
"Since he's made it this long, 60/40. That's a lot better than it was before."
Piper looked at Maverick as a wave of dizziness hit. He caught her as her knees buckled.

***

A couple of hours later she was admitted and rolled to a room. The doctor insisted she stay overnight because of a mild concussion. She had an icepack for her swollen eye. Glue in the cut on her lip and eyebrow. And ice on her ankle.
A long breathable bandage traveled inside her thigh, groin to knee. Four long claw lines had been thoroughly cleaned to prevent infection. No stitches. But the tender skin was raw and off limits for any inner thigh activity for ten

whole days. Although creativity was allowed. The good news was that any scar would eventually fade away. It wasn't deep, just angry.

The large bite on her calf ripped through the skin and had to be debrided. She ended up with five dissolvable stitches and teeth bruises. Smaller and more contained, it would be less painful than the claw marks.

The door had barely closed behind the nurse, and Piper was out of the bed – tossing the ice packs aside. Maverick went to get her a soft drink and grab the bag of clothes Adam brought from the safehouse.

Piper inspected her face in the mirror. Not pretty, but she'd seen worse. She washed around the wounds and brushed her teeth. Then tamed her hair in a ponytail.

Maverick returned. Looking through the bag, he said, "What do you want to wear with your leg?"

"Something soft and loose. Lounge shorts maybe. And any shirt will do. Did he bring flip-flops? I am not wearing those slippers."

He smiled. He wouldn't wear them either. "Yes, to both."

She had just dressed when someone knocked. They both turned as the door opened. Captain Nicole Pierce crossed the room and wrapped her daughter in her arms.

Piper hugged her mom, loving the smell of her perfume, the sounds she made, and the love that surrounded her. "Mom, I'm sorry—"

Nicole said, "I hate your job."

Everyone smiled. Piper. Maverick. Even Agent Donovan who stood in the doorway. Piper stepped back and Nicole looked her over, seeing the injuries. Hating every single one.

Piper understood. "I've been checked out, Mom. It's nothing serious. It might be ugly under the bandages, but it's nothing permanent or dangerous. I probably won't even have scars."

"Being kidnapped is serious. A concussion is serious. And bite and claw marks are atrocious. Is he dead?"

"Yes."

She nodded. "Are the others going to be alright?"

Refusing any other outcome for Hawk, Piper said, "Yes. And we need to go check on them. Can you wait here?"

"I'm not going anywhere."

Piper glanced at Maverick and her boss. Agent Donovan said, "Danielle is waiting. Dakota, Sean, and Samantha will meet us there."

Maverick pointed to the crutches. Piper said, "I'm good. My thigh is fine to walk."

"I get that. But your swollen ankle isn't. I'm not going to watch you limp around the hospital. I'll carry you. You can walk in the room on your own. That's the deal. Take it or leave it, Agent Pierce."

And for the first time in hours, Nicole smiled. She gave Maverick a hug. He knew how to handle Piper.

***

An agent stood outside room 541. NO ADMITTANCE was taped on the door. He saw them coming. "Glad to see you in one piece, Pierce. You've had a helluva week. Impressive take down."

Maverick lowered Piper. She said, "Hey Jefferson. Good description. How's Danielle?"

"Emotional. Jumpy. But trying to get herself together. She's waiting for you."

He opened the door.

Danielle spun. Eyes wide. Quickly scanning the group, she focused on the beautiful, but wounded woman. It had to be her.

Piper limped forward and said softly, "Hi, Danielle. I'm Agent Piper Pierce. Please…call me Piper. It's wonderful to see you. We've all been trying to find you."

A tear rolled down Danielle's lovely face. "King said…you saved my life. How?"

"It's a complicated story. But in the end, he traded you for me."

"You're hurt."

"I've been hurt worse." She paused. "I'm sorry he took you…for what you've been through."

Danielle looked at the men in the group, knowing they all knew the sexual nature of the crime, then back to Piper. "He didn't beat me. I'm sure he would have, but fear made surrender my wisest option. It was… It was like a sick love affair. I always felt like I was a stand-in for someone else. And I sensed other women. I wasn't the only one, was I?"

Piper recognized her perception skills. They all did. How right she had been. "No. There were two before you."

Danielle knew the answer. "They didn't make it."

"No. But you did. And that has got to be the only thing that matters. Maybe we can talk after you've had time to get this behind you. When will your parents arrive?"

"By morning. And Piper, can I ask you a question?"

"Anything."

"Did you think he was charming?"

Piper thought of the real Liam. "Totally. Everyone did. He fooled us all."

Danielle sighed. Relieved. "I was scared to trust myself anymore. I was hoping my judgement wasn't that bad."

"It wasn't you, Danielle. It was always him. Never forget that."

***

On another floor, Sasha was trying to open her eyes. She heard Raven a million miles away. She grabbed what covered her. Where was she? Her heart pounded and her head hurt as she tensed with the struggle.

Maverick closed his hand over Sasha's and leaned close. He said her name. "Sasha."

Her eyes opened. Identical eyes met. Memories flooded back. "Maverick...Liam… Where's Piper—"

Piper sat next to her. "I'm here. It's all over."

Sasha looked back at Maverick, "Luna?"

"She's in the hospital too. She'll be fine."

Sasha choked, "Hawk is missing."

Maverick said, "Adam found him. He's here."

Sasha noticed he didn't offer a status. "Is he ok?"

Maverick didn't lie. "We hope so."

***

Dekker lay next to Luna. He kissed her cheek and said, "Come on baby, it's time to wake up."

She moaned softly, moving her head on the pillow. Reaching for her eyes. Why wouldn't they open?

Dekker brushed her hair back. "Luna. Look at me."

She mumbled. Dekker was telling her something. Her eyelids flickered.

He kissed her and felt the surprise hit her. He deepened the kiss, and her arms slowly found him.

Until she remembered Piper and pushed back. "Piper—"

"She's here. Sasha and Hawk too. It's over."

Tears rolled down her cheeks. "Piper saved us, Dekker. He…he was…he killed—"

"I know. But he won't hurt anybody else."

"He took Piper, didn't he?"

"He did. But six bullets sealed his coffin for it."

She sat up. "I need to see them."

Someone knocked.

"I think they're here." He called, "Come in."

It was Maverick and Piper.

But Luna only saw Piper. Tears rolled as she saw her injuries.

Piper hugged her. Both remembering the last time they saw each other. Piper said, "I'm good. You should've seen him."

Luna wiped tears away. "You were furious. I could tell you wanted to slit his throat."

The men glanced at each other. It was unusual to hear those words from Luna.

After another knock, Sasha stepped in, a little on the wobbly side, and shut the door. Breathless, she said, "The nurses are after me."

Maverick scooped her up and sat her on the other side of the bed.

Luna winced at Sasha's injuries. "Why was he so mean to you?"

Sasha said, "Probably because I had a gun."

"He kissed you after the injection. He did the same to me." She looked at Dekker. "Why?"

Dekker said, "Because if time had allowed, he'd have taken all of you."

***

Before long, they were all in Hawk's room. Even Nicole. Most talked and watched the clock. Except Sasha and Piper. They sat on each side of the bed next to Hawk. He was beginning to move.

Sasha held his hand as they coaxed him. Teased him. Taunted him. His eyebrow twitched. His head. His leg.

Piper asked, "How is he as a roommate?"

Sasha said, "A hunk."

Piper laughed. "Right."

Rubbing her forehead, Sasha said, "My head is pounding. I can't imagine what his is going to feel like."

Piper made a face. "The doc said it'll take a few hours for all the residual effects to pass."

"I believe it."

Then Sasha slid her hand caressingly across Hawk's chest to his neck. Her fingers lingered in his hair. Piper watched her, eyebrows raised. This was unexpected. Sasha touched his lips, and he jerked.

Sasha glanced at Piper. "If this doesn't wake him up…"

"Oh, I get the picture. And so is Hawk."

His head moved. His hands. Sasha leaned down and whispered in his ear, then kissed his cheek.

Hawk heard what Sasha said. Felt her. Smelled her. His eyes opened slightly, meeting hers. Ignoring his throbbing head, he pulled her lips over his.

Everyone cheered…quietly…since it was four in the morning.

***

At four-thirty, the non-patient part of the team returned to the safehouse.

Dekker and Luna returned to her room on the second floor.

Before long, Hawk disappeared from his room and found Sasha on the third floor. He added a pillow and blanket to her bed and pulled her in his arms.

And on the fourth floor, Maverick waterproofed Piper's leg so she could shower. He waited. And waited. All he heard was water. He opened the door she'd left cracked and could see her through the clear vinyl curtain.

Piper stood under the water, leaning forward, hands against the wall tiles. Hot water washed it all away. Liam. The dirt. The blood. The memory of his touch and desire. And the case. It was finally over. But her body ached. Bruises were appearing, not that she was surprised. But for the first time, she was tired of seeing them on her body. What about when she got pregnant?

Maverick stripped and stepped in with her. He grabbed the shampoo. Washed her hair. Washed her. Silently. Tenderly.

He whispered, "Turn around, baby."

Turning, she leaned against the wall and looked at Maverick. His face reflected a powerful mixture of love, compassion…and remnants of fury. He bathed her. Dried her. Carried her to bed.

He kissed her. Whisper soft. And they were both asleep in minutes.

***

By six a.m. it was international news.

By eight, reporters found them at the hospital.

By nine, they exited the back of the hospital and headed for the safehouse.

Chapter 30

Late morning, everyone in the safehouse was silent as they watched Piper prepare to give them the rest of the story. The team. Agent Donovan. Maverick's sergeant and Axel too. And Nicole.

On the computer, Piper searched the web, then opened an image on the big screen. It was a beautiful woman. Laughing. With long dark hair and light eyes.

She walked around the table and pointed at the picture. "This is Cara. The missing link. As you can see, I missed this when I found the article about Liam's fiancé being lost at sea. The newspaper considered him the real news. Wealthy. Grieving. Famous in that part of the world. The article wasn't about Cara. Not really. It just provided a couple of small pictures of her in a hat or ponytail. I didn't research her at all. If I had – her connection to the kidnap victims would have been instant."

Agent Donovan said, "We all read that article Piper. Every single one of us missed the chance to find the link. It happens. So, was grief his motive?"

"Yes, but not in the way you mean. It was way more complicated."

She sat on the edge of the table. "We were well on our way to Baton Rouge before Liam began to talk. Till then, I left him alone. His threat with the syringe had made sure of that. So, when he finally began to talk, I dug for answers during our sharp debates.

"It turns out that King was a nickname he'd earned in Africa as a teenager. He also spoke with three accents. Irish. French. American. And then, after a particularly unpleasant conversation, I mentioned Cara."

Touching her face, she said, "He hit me, slamming my head against the back window. Which meant I'd found the motherload of what I was looking for. It turns out that Cara wasn't lost at sea during a storm. He knocked her out and threw her overboard because she killed his children."

She paused as the impact of those words hit everyone. "They had been in love. Got engaged. Made plans and were soon pregnant with twins. A boy and a girl. They named them, set the C-section date and finished the nurseries.

"That day aboard ship, he overheard a conversation that she had aborted them. He confronted her. In the end, she had just changed her mind. But she was brutal about it. And he snapped. Killed her. And vowed that the next woman he picked to bear his children would protect them like a lioness. And then I knew why he picked me.

"Right after that we got to the barn, and he had one thing on his mind. I didn't know how far behind me all of you were, but I knew I only had minutes to hold him off. And then…I simply ran out of time."

She looked at Maverick. "Coming out of the bathroom I noticed a silver pole that led to the loft. At that point, I realized I could distract him a little longer."

Maverick knew exactly what she meant. He nodded. She'd been killer brave.

Piper glanced at the puzzled faces in the room and explained, "I do pole dance workouts…along with karate. I mixed the two. A pole dance with a roundhouse kick, followed by a board upside his head, bought me time. I couldn't find his syringes or the gun. And I couldn't outrun him, so I killed the lights and started to climb. He woke up. I saw the drone. And you know the rest."

Agent Donovan looked at Dekker. "We'll show the roof video. It doesn't last long. Perhaps Luna and Nicole should step out of the room."

Dekker glanced at both women. They weren't budging.

The video showed several angles of the high rooftop.

Maverick climbed on the roof. Dekker right behind him. About twenty feet away, a hatch opened, and Piper appeared, bloody, but trying to climb out. Maverick ran for her. Dekker too. And then she began to scream and fight with hands that were grabbing her from below.

Maverick yanked her away and shoved her into Dekker's arms. Piper screamed as Liam lunged through the hatch after her, covered in blood. He pulled a knife out of his thigh. Maverick pulled his gun.

Dropping to his knees with Piper, Dekker reached for his gun, but Piper beat him to it.

Nicole and Luna jumped at each gunshot. And then Liam fell.

The video went black.

It only took 96 seconds for the scene to play out.

Everyone looked at Piper. Then at Maverick and Dekker. That life and death battle had taken place just a few hours ago. Piper made a gun with two fingers. Maverick did the same. They blew the tip. Case closed.

❖

Maverick's phone rang as the FBI removed the last of the investigation office from the safehouse. It was Dante.

Maverick answered, "I guess you saw the news."

Dante said, "I almost had a heart attack. I swear I believed he was on the ship. Why didn't you call me?"

"The dust hasn't even settled. I would have."

"I know the news gave the shorthand version. Tell me what happened."

"Dante, no one uses shorthand anymore."

"You do. I've seen your handwriting. Just say it."

"Liam took Piper. Injured and drugged Sasha and Luna. Came close to killing Hawk. And did kill a zookeeper and two policemen. But he did return Danielle. We followed them to Sean's ranch. Piper had gotten away from him and made it to the roof. Dekker and I met her there. Ninety-six seconds later, we killed him."

"We?"

"Piper and I unloaded six shots into him."

"So, he's in hell. Best news I've had all day. Is Piper hurt?"

"He hit her in the face. Gave her a concussion. And like an animal, he bit and clawed her leg while perched on a three-story ladder. And after all that, she took Dekker's gun and shot him."

"I'm just…I have no words. Wait…did you say Danielle?"

"Yes, she's alive."

"My mind is blown. We're coming home. Tell Dakota I'll leave his keys under the dog bowl."

"Dante—"

"Shut up. We're coming home."

Within an hour, Sean and Samantha left for their FBI flight back to Colorado.

Dakota and Gabrielle left for the three-hour drive back to Lake Charles.

And Adam, Raven, and Hawk brought Sasha back to Lake Charles with them. She planned to return to Natchitoches and find a place to live.

***

In the bedroom, Piper talked with her mom.

Nicole said, "I'm so proud of you, Piper. I can't fathom doing the things you do, and it scares me. Hearing bits and pieces is one thing. Seeing it play out on video is another. Are you sure you are alright? And don't you dare lie to me."

Piper looked at her mother. Here was the opening to tell her about the rape. She held her hand. "Mom…I need..."

Her mom touched her cheek. "Anything."

And Piper couldn't do it. She wouldn't. There had been enough pain in the last few days. It wouldn't help. It wouldn't change a thing. And if her mom heard about it from someone else, so be it. She wasn't going to be the one to tell her. She wasn't going to save strangers and wound her mother. Not after all these years."

She switched gears, and said, "Are you sure you are ok with Dad and Luna?"

Nicole smiled. "I love Luna! She's perfect for him. When do you think they'll get married?"

"With Mr. Secretive who knows. But soon. What about you, Mom?"

"I'm in love."

Genuinely shocked, Piper said, "Seriously?"

"Yes. You'll meet him soon enough. But for now, I've got to get to the airport. I've got a flight to Italy. My taxi will be here in a minute."

"We can bring—"

"Absolutely not. You've done enough. Enjoy being young, beautiful, and in love. Let the world take care of itself for a while. And I mean it."

***

Shortly, only four people remained in the safehouse.

Maverick, Piper, Dekker and Luna sat on the balcony drinking iced tea. Slivers of lemon floated in the glass. A nice breeze blew, leaving the smell of gardenias behind. Music played in the distance. It was peaceful and quiet after a week of war.

Dekker glanced at Piper and Maverick. He laid a set of keys on the wrought iron table. They clinked. "The apartment is yours if you want it – for as long as you want. I'll be looking for another place in New Orleans. But not today. Today, I'm taking Luna on a trip. We'll be gone for a couple of weeks."

Piper said, "I totally understand. Where are you going?"

Dekker smiled without answering. Maverick laughed.

Luna said, "He won't say. It's a surprise."

Dekker said, "And speaking of surprises, when we return, we'd like to host your wedding reception. By then your wounds will be healed. So whatever style party or location you want, you've got it. Just pick the date and we'll do the rest. Please, both of you…let me do this for you."

Piper hugged him. "Thank you, Daddy. We'll accept it as your only wedding present. We don't need anything else. I mean that." He didn't answer her. She said, "Say it."

Dekker laughed. He wasn't that easy.

***

By midafternoon Maverick and Piper were alone.

Maverick kissed her, making sure not to hurt her lip. "Let's go on a private picnic. You don't need to dress up at all."

Piper giggled. "Private because you think people will accuse you of beating me?"

He laughed. "If only they knew it would be the other way around."

She kissed him. "Where are we going?"

"Let's see if you can guess."

"Ah. A surprise. Are you competing with Dad?"

"Of course you would think that. Dress for outdoors. I'll gather everything we need."

Maverick packed bread, meat, cheese and veggies for sandwiches. Jalapeno chips. Cold fried chicken. Fruit. Chocolate. A jug of tea. Soft drinks. And a few bottles of cold coffee. They'd have to stop and get ice. Then he grabbed a blanket, sheet, and a few throw pillows off the sofa.

Piper joined him dressed in an orange and white one-piece skort. She slipped on sandals and pulled her hair in a ponytail.

Maverick whistled. "I haven't seen that sweet number."

"I've only been here eight days. You haven't seen hardly any of my clothes."

"Then I look forward to seeing the rest of them. And stay right there. I just need to grab something. I'll be right back."

***

Piper knew they were heading north when they left the apartment. Then Maverick merged onto Interstate 10 and headed northeast. When he crossed the Highrise bridge, she said, "We're going to the marina."

"You won."

"You act surprised."

Laughing, he said, "You are so much fun."

"So, what did I win?"

"What do you want?"

"A bikini."

"It's in my bag. Now guess the next surprise."

She looked in the backseat. A large duffle bag. An ice chest. All for a few hours of daylight. She smiled. "We're spending the night."

"You bet we are."

***

The boat rocked gently. The breeze was perfect. And the only sounds were birds and the lap of the water against the hull as day faded to night. Solar lamps came on. It was beautiful.

Piper felt Maverick's gaze. She leaned into him. "What's on your mind, Detective? I know that look."

He laced his fingers with hers. "The real question is what's on your mind? Talk to me."

She watched as he rubbed the place where her wedding ring had been. That was his question. She said, "He pulled it off in the warehouse and threw it." Her eyes filled with tears. "I'm so sorry, I know it was irreplaceable."

"No, baby. You're irreplaceable." He reached into his pocket. "You know how I know that?" He opened his hand, revealing the ring. "Because I found the ring…but I didn't have you. And it was hard to breathe."

Piper tried but couldn't talk. Tears spoke for her.

Maverick slid the ring on her finger. She reached for him. Wrapping her in his arms, he said, "It's not easy to surprise you, Agent Pierce."

She wiped her cheek. "It's almost like a do-over."

"Getting married again?"

"Yes."

He smiled. "Now you're twice mine."

Grinning, she said, "I like that. You know…I almost wish we could redo the night I came to New Orleans. I'll never forget seeing you heading down the hall in the middle of a crime scene. Black leather jacket and all tattooed up. Sexy to the bone." She smiled. "My biker."

He winked. "You really have a thing for bikers."

"I have a thing for you."

Passion sizzled. Maverick kissed her. Soft because of the cut, but deep – and wanting to do what he knew they couldn't. He whispered, "It's too soon, baby."

"The doctor said we could be creative."

"Piper, I want to lose myself in you every chance I get. But what you need isn't positional. And pleasure won't make what happened disappear." He touched her heart. "You need time to process. You've been attacked by two men and a robot this week. Kidnapped. Beaten and mauled. Your body may heal within ten days, but the rest of you needs to be free from this too. You don't need all that in your head. Give yourself some time to get past it and not just bury it."

Her desire to argue faded. But still she watched him. Silent. She knew what he meant.

He said, "Admit it. You know this is the right thing to do. It's wisdom – not weakness." He winked. "Besides, we can handle a few days of teasing."

"Then today is day one."

"Deal."

"And if my injuries heal fast?"

"We'll take it day by day. I'll know when you're ready for me."

She rolled her eyes. "You learned that in detective school?"

He laughed and kissed her. "I know you."

She had a nightmare at midnight.

Chapter 31

Day Two

Piper stretched out in a bikini as Maverick grabbed them a drink below deck. She winced as she shifted. The claw marks were already tightening on her inner thigh, which meant the wrong move made them crack. And her eye was still swollen with the colors of Halloween. Though her lip and ankle were a little better.

Maverick handed her a glass when he returned. "When do you want the wedding reception? We need to text your dad."

"You know they're on their honeymoon, right? He wasn't fooling anyone. Why didn't he want to tell me?"

"You're his daughter. That's the definition of awkward to me."

"Well…ok… What do you think about a private party somewhere on the lake at the end of March? Something with a wharf and gazebo. That'll give me time to want a party."

The look on his face told her he expected an explanation for the remark. He waited. She said, "I'm just not in the mood for an event right now. The Ball was party enough for me."

He nodded, touching her leg. "Is that what the nightmare was about last night?"

She took a second to answer. "It was worse. I woke up over the ocean with Liam."

"Piper—"

She held up her hand. "I need to tell you something."

"Tell me."

"After my forced vacation is over, I've decided to transfer to Intelligence. I'm going to stay out of the field for a while." She paused. "Besides, we're trying for a baby anyway."

Maverick knew there was a whole lot more she wasn't saying. That meant it was critical. He said, "Intelligence is a terrific choice. That sounds great." Now he paused. "But why don't you tell me what you're not saying."

She sighed. "At the barn, Liam asked me if I was on birth control. It shocked me. Then terrified me. Not because he wanted to get me pregnant…that was clearly understood.

"But because I wasn't on birth control. What if I had ovulated and could get pregnant for both of you?" She shook her head – horror visible. "I can't. I just can't work in the field unprotected. And certainly not once I'm pregnant. Babies don't need bruises."

He lay beside her. "I'm sorry you had to fear that for even a moment, Piper. And you are right. I agree with all of it. Especially since I plan on keeping you busy with babies for a few years. Which leads me to this… What do you think about working together?"

She sat up. "Seriously? You want to be FBI?"

"I've already talked to Agent Donovan. Let's enjoy our honeymoon and birth of baby one, and I'll complete the application process. I heard it takes about a year. Then we'll move to Quantico."

Chapter 32

Day Four

They pulled up to the camp at ten.

Maverick glanced at Piper. With a grin she slid out of the truck, excited to be here. He smiled. Her eye wasn't swollen anymore. And its once vivid colors were fading to a pastel blend of gold and pink. Her top lip was almost back to normal. She wore an elastic brace on her ankle, the limp almost gone. And her leg, while still bandaged, was better. The claw marks were healing faster than he imagined - but were still painful if stretched or bumped. And the bite looked bad because of the depth of the bruise, but the stitches were clean and healing with no infection.

He met her in front of the truck. She looked up the staircase. Maverick drew her against him and kissed her.

She said, "I see you remember the first time we went up those stairs too."

"Like I'll ever forget. Hang on." And holding her around the waist, he carried her up the stairs.

She said, "I can walk."

"But climbing still hurts you. Let the inside of your thighs heal and you won't mind the way I carry you at all."

He smiled at the passion that crossed her face. Especially since she'd only mentioned the kidnapping twice yesterday. And none yet today. It was time to ramp things up and test the waters.

Both of their phones rang as he opened the door.

Piper answered, "Hey Jinx."

"We'll be there in thirty minutes. We're stopping for bar-b-que and potato salad. Who else is coming?"

"Just Axel. Thank you for doing that."

"Sure. Did you bring dessert?"

"Yep. Fresh brownies. Ice cream. Chocolate syrup. And squirt whip-cream since Maverick reminded me it's a favorite of Dante's."

Laughing, Jinx said. "That's no lie. See you soon."

❖

On the porch Maverick answered his phone, "Do you have them?"

Axel said, "Of course I do. I promised, didn't I? I want to please kitty, kitty."

"Lose that nickname, Axel."

"Sorry. It was just one of my favorites. It slipped out."

"You'll find another one. How are they?"

"Excited. Huge. And beautiful."

Maverick smiled. "I owe you."

"No, you don't. This is for Piper. I'll be there in a bit."

Maverick joined Piper. He said, "Have you thought about what kind of changes you would like to make here at the camp?"

"A little paint. But mainly new lights. Upstairs and downstairs. The garden lights at the zoo were a dream."

Maverick hadn't expected the zoo comment. He watched her. Was there a hidden meaning?

She realized. "Wait. No, Maverick. I genuinely loved the lights. That's it. We can have our own lit garden. And did I mention I'd love a chandelier in the bedroom?"

He relaxed. "A chandelier in the bedroom."

"Yes. Can you imagine looking down at me as you—"

He backed her against the wall, arms over her head. His mouth locked on hers as his hips did his low hip roll.

Breathless, Piper said, "Wow. But I thought you said—"

"I did. But you didn't have a nightmare last night. So, you leveled up."

She blinked. "You mean like a video game?"

"You are fast."

Her smile warned him. She rotated her hips. "So, the better I do, the more I get. That's what you're telling me?"

He stopped her hips with a groan. "I wouldn't have put it that way."

She licked his neck. "Right. How would you have put it, Detective?"

"I turned up the heat. If you don't have a setback, it'll get hotter. I'm not throwing you into the fire. But we can make it a challenge. Try me, wildcat. Like I said, I'll know when you can take me."

***

Piper put the lemonade in the fridge as vehicles drove up. She heard barking. As Maverick walked toward the door, she dried her hands and said, "Who brought a dog?"

"I think Axel. Let's see."

Dante and Jinx waved, calling hello as they gathered food out of their car. Maverick waved, then laughed as two German Shepherds jumped out of Axel's truck. Maverick knelt to greet the dogs. They did their best to knock him over since they already knew him.

Piper smiled from the top of the stairs, and in seconds got delicious smelling hugs from Dante and Jinx. Maverick and Axel followed, the dogs leading the way.

Piper laughed as the dogs smelled and licked her. "Hi Axel. They are fabulous. I didn't know you had dogs."

He wiggled his eyebrows. "I have lots of secrets. But these are more than dogs. They are retired K-9s. A friend of mine has a ranch that finds the perfect family for them. These are younger than most retirees since they were injured in the line of duty."

"What are their names?"

"Mav and Goose."

Maverick snorted, laughing. She laughed. "You're kidding."

"You betcha. Meet Storm and Zorro."

Piper said, "You seem to know them, Maverick."

He nodded. "I've been out to the ranch a time or two."

She smiled, wiping her face after another lick, and said, "I think we should adopt one."

"Just one? Then I messed up."

She looked at the dogs. Then at Maverick as it dawned on her. He said, "I got you two."

Chapter 33

Day Eight

Pulling on jeans and a bra, Piper slid a hand down the inside of her thigh. Firmly. No tenderness. She pressed harder, then squatted in the jeans. No pain - just a little soreness. And she'd had a million bruises that felt like that. The same with the bite. And she never thought about the man that put them there anymore.

Maverick stopped in the bedroom doorway. "Any pain?"

She stood and glanced at him. "No. It feels like a regular bruise. The salt baths have helped. And the lotion. I don't even feel the stitches in my calf this morning. I think I'm back to being as normal as I can be until the scars fade."

He walked toward her. "Perhaps I should check. I'm a lot…harder than you."

Piper put her hands behind her head. Legs spread. "Give it your best shot, Detective."

Maverick knelt in front of her and ran his hands up the inside of her thighs with firm pressure. Pressing. Squeezing. Caressing specifically where he wanted to go. And the only look on her face was desire.

Their hot glazes collided. Maverick said, "You're so ready for me."

She groaned, "I'm dying..."

He unsnapped her jeans and growled, licking her stomach as he slid her jeans down. He said, "Let's try bare skin..."

She pulled off her bra and threw it. "Yes. Let's… And I don't care if it hurts. Don't you dare stop."

She gasped as her feet left the ground and she landed on the bed.

He wasn't stopping.

Chapter 34

The Lake House - Two Weeks Later

Dekker rented a four-bedroom lake house on piers for the party. White. Massive windows. Impressively decorated. Patio seating and dining underneath the house. And a firepit was in the front yard – already lit.

A long wharf reached out into Lake Pontchartrain with a gazebo at the end. And everything from the house to the gazebo was lit with creamy white lights. Not bright, but romantic and perfect for a night wedding reception.

Sunset would be at six.

The reception at seven.

Piper arrived before six. The photographer right behind her. The caterer was already preparing the buffet. Music played.

Dekker, Luna, Dante and Jinx were already there adding personal touches. Like pictures of Maverick and Piper from their courthouse wedding. Another with the dogs at the camp. One on the sailboat. A couple of pictures of them on the riverboat. And one of them during the case.

Dante insisted on carrying Piper's bags upstairs. She said, "Come on, Dante. What is Maverick up to?"

"I have no idea what you're talking about."

She laughed. "Like I buy that. He's been gone since ten this morning and said he wouldn't be here till seven. There's no way you don't know."

"Agent Pierce, the point is, you're not supposed to know. That's the definition of a secret."

"Give me a hint."

"And have him rip me limb from limb? I'm not ready to die. Where do you want these?"

She smiled and pointed to the first bedroom. He dropped the bags inside, and with a wink, escaped further interrogation.

Piper hung her dress. It was a whisper-thin beach wedding dress. A white lace halter with floral appliqués. Nearly shear, with a thigh high slit and a small train for bare feet. Perfect for a lake front reception.

Piper had just started her makeup when a text dinged.

Maverick texted: Hey beautiful. Leave Dante alone. You're scaring him.
Piper smiled: I doubt that. He loves knowing something I don't. Where are you, Detective?
Maverick: That was a waste of typing. You know I'm not telling you.
Piper: I might have a secret too.
Maverick: Of course you do. Mystery is the nature of all women. Not men…you can tell what we're thinking.
Piper: It's kind of hard to hide the evidence.
Maverick: Exactly. No mystery at all. Except for the position. Like the one this morning. Remember that?
Piper felt the rush of pleasure with the memory: Stop it, Maverick.
Maverick: You don't want me to stop. You want me to finish it. Again.
Piper went for payback: Then you better hurry, or I'll have to finish it myself.
Maverick felt the heat hit: I can't believe you said that.
Piper smiled: You just don't want to miss it.
Maverick groaned: You're killing me.
No answer.
Maverick: Piper?
Nothing.

Maverick took a breath trying to calm his libido. Piper's point making killed him. Especially those. Now that picture was stuck in his head. It took a few minutes before he could go back inside the tattoo parlor.

He was almost finished.

***

The Lake Charles guests arrived at six-thirty. Dakota and Gabrielle. Adam and Raven.

Sasha and Hawk weren't far behind them from Natchitoches.

Nicole had flown in from Chicago. Sean and Samantha from Denver. They were on their way from the airport.

Agent Donovan and his wife pulled up, plus a couple of agents from the FBI. Along with Sergeant Driscoll, Axel and his date, plus two other NOPD detectives.

Maverick drove up at two minutes to seven. He texted Piper: I'm here.

Ten minutes later, Piper stood at the top of the stairs. Gorgeous under the glowing lights as her lace panels fluttered. Her hair was down. Lips, rich red. And her blue eyes met Mavericks at the bottom of the stairs.

His blonde hair ruffled in the breeze as he smiled. Dressed in soft white linen slacks with a turquoise silk shirt, his body was powerful. His face sculptured, a truly beautiful man. And he only had eyes for her.

Everyone watched as they met in the middle of the staircase.

***

Gaze hot on hers, Maverick lowered his lips and said, "Let's pick up where you left me hanging on that text, Agent Pierce."

She smiled. "One would think that's been on your mind, Detective."

He kissed her, then carried her down. It was a great beginning to a fabulous party.

***

After dinner, Dekker and Luna danced in the gazebo. His hand slid down her bare back, to the curve of her hip. He pulled her closer.

Her eyes met his. "Thank you."

"You're welcome…but what are you thanking me for?"

"Asking me to dance on the riverboat a month ago. I bet most men wouldn't have listened to my friend's request."

"One look at you and they would have. It's a good thing you were watching me."

She touched his chest. "You'll always be that man to me."

He covered her hand. "Even as your morning sickness gets worse?"

She smiled. "Even then."

"When would you like to tell them?"

"Let Piper get into her new season. Maybe even get pregnant and celebrate first. I'd love that for her. We've got plenty of time before it's not our secret anymore."

***

Captain Nicole Pierce smiled at her date. The man she loved. "So, what do you think, Desmond?"

The Frenchman smiled. In a lovely accent, he said, "I think all the beautiful women in the world are here tonight. Paris is in mourning."

"I love the way you lie."

He laughed, delighted, madly in love with his fiancé. "It's hardly a lie. Look around at the beauty. "Which reminds me, when are you going to let me paint you? I must."

"No, you mustn't. I can hide a nude photograph. It's impossible to hide a huge painting. I can't even fathom Piper finding that one day."

Dramatically, he sighed. "Then I must paint it on my heart."

She slid her fingers in his hair and whispered, "What if… I let you paint on my body instead?"

Thrilled at the thought, he spun her around, "Magnifique!"

***

Maverick danced with Sasha by the firepit. "How's Natchitoches?"

"Beautiful. What's not to love about a Christmas town? I adore it."

He smiled. "Right. And it has nothing to do with Hawk."

She glanced at Hawk dancing with Piper. "He's quite a man."

Maverick laughed. "And one that could go up in smoke any minute. But he's way more patient that I figured him to be."

She smiled. "Not so patient, but he's giving me time."

"I think time is running out. You better get ready."

"Easy, brother. I've got this. Ask me about my job instead."

"It never dawned on me you would choose to be a professor at Northwestern."

"Assistant Professor. I'm still working on my doctorate."

He whistled. "I certainly got the underachiever genes."

She laughed as the song ended. "Hardly. Give me a break…you got double of all the other ones."

Hawk joined them after another song started. "Piper is off in the arms of another man. You better hurry."

Maverick stepped away with a smile. She wasn't going far.

***

Hawk slipped his arm around Sasha and pointed to the wharf. They kicked off their sandals and walked quietly on the decking.

Sasha took a deep breath and said, "I love the smell of salt water. I'll have to get used to smelling trees and the river now. It's so different – though it's probably much more what you are used to from Wyoming."

"It is. Are you missing the ocean?"

"Yes. But my saltwater pool will be installed next month. That will help. You have got to come swim."

"No doubt about that, and then you can swim in mine."

"It's a deal. I can't wait to see you do your seal team thing."

He stopped. The wind mixing his black hair with her blonde. Pulling her against him, he said, "I can do more than seal team things in the water, Sasha. I know how to catch a mermaid."

Sasha let the magical moment take her as his lips lowered. She whispered, "I just bet you can."

***

Much later, it was quiet as Piper sat on Maverick's lap at the firepit. The crackling fire was perfect for the cooling night. Those from out of town had already left for the apartment. And all but Piper's parents were gone.

Maverick said, "Have you enjoyed yourself?"

Piper snuggled. "It was perfect. I loved every minute. I can't believe it's over."

Maverick said, "Actually…it isn't. We have somewhere to be by midnight."

She sat up. "Where?"

"It's a surprise. Your bag's in the truck."

"I didn't pack anything."

"Your Mother and Luna did."

"Maverick—"

Leading her toward the house, he said, "Come on. It's time to go. Wave goodbye to your parents."

She waved at the two laughing couples upstairs, then said, "Obviously, you've gotten much better at surprising me."

Maverick laughed and carried her to the truck.

***

Piper never expected Maverick to turn toward the French Quarter. She tried to figure out where he was going. And it wasn't until he turned onto St. Louis Street, that she knew.

Glancing at him, she whispered, "You didn't."

He winked and stopped at the main entrance to the Omni Royal Orleans Hotel. He took a key card out of his wallet and said, "Room 5314. Your clothes are on the bed. Change and wait for me on the balcony. I'll be back in twenty minutes."

"Maverick—"

He kissed her. "Agent Pierce, just be on the balcony."

She watched him drive away and headed to the elevator with a smile. She knew what he was changing into.

In the room, she laughed when she saw her jeans and shirt from that first night in New Orleans on the bed. And then she saw the note: Be sure you're wet when you get dressed.

She stripped and jumped in the shower glad there was no fighting next door this time. Dripping wet, she pulled the jeans on. No underwear. She pulled the thin shirt on. No bra. And her breasts might as well have been exposed. She closed her eyes and groaned with anticipation. She glanced at the clock. He'd be here in ten minutes.

Before long she was on the balcony. Jazz filled the air. She stood there for a moment absorbing it all. Listening. Remembering. Thinking about Maverick. It was hard to believe a month had passed. So much had happened. And she froze. Then counted backwards. How long had it been? She hadn't had a period in what… She gasped. Six weeks.

She was late.

That's when she heard the deep rumble of a motorcycle.

Maverick saw her on the balcony as the chopper rounded the building. Mouth open, eyes locked on him. He pulled to a stop where they could watch each other. Dropping the kickstand, he took off the helmet and shook his hair. Killing the engine, he got off the bike and tossed the keys to the valet. He looked up at Piper and disappeared inside.

Piper screamed. There was so much going on inside her at one time she was about to explode. In seconds she was in the hall, waiting for the elevator.

A minute later the elevator chimed. She heard the doors open. Everyone got off – but no Maverick. Before long, it chimed again. A couple exited with three teenagers. And then there he was.

Tall. Sexy and powerful, dressed in a muscle shirt, tattoos, jeans, boots – and a black leather jacket. Chains jingled on his hip as he covered the distance. He smiled. She laughed and ran…then jumped. He caught her without breaking stride and kissed her.

Maverick's gaze met Piper's as he kicked the door shut behind them. She slid down, checking out her biker and stepped back as he dropped his jacket in the chair. He was hot and ready.

Taking a step toward her, he said, "I see you want a ride."

Caressing her zipper as she backed away, she smiled with a steamy look from under her lashes. "Prove it, Detective."

In a second, he picked her up and held her against the wall. Wild. And stripped her. Watching her go up in flames at his touch. He unzipped his pants and braced himself. Chest heaving, he kissed her…then took her…where only he could take her.

The End ♥

Other Romantic Suspense Books
by Patti Corbello Archer

Double Target

A modern-day western that begins at LSU and ends at a Texas cattle ranch.

Louisiana Secrets – A four book series

- FBI Thrillers -

Four heroes. Three Native American brothers.and a Viking descendant.
It's all about the women they love.

Bloodline – Book One
Gabrielle is the secret descendant of Pirate Jean Lafitte and doesn't know it. The FBI is watching her. Danger is coming to Lake Charles, Louisiana.

Obsession – Book Two
Samantha was a teenage victim. Now she's a prosecutor in Baton Rouge, Louisiana. But the villain has returned to finish what he started.

Killer Dance – Book Three
Raven is new to Louisiana, a competition dancer starting over in the land of her ancestors near Sam Houston Jones State Park. But she's still not safe. Someone's coming.

Masquerade – Book Four
Special Agent Piper Pierce arrived in New Orleans in the middle of the night with a new job and a lot of secrets. It didn't take long for trouble to find her. But then, it never did.

About the Author

Patti Corbello Archer is from a small town north of Lake Charles in southwest Louisiana. A place where nature influences everything. Especially her stories. Surrounded by lakes, rivers, and bayous, fabulous Cajun food, and intriguing history, creating a tale isn't difficult. Secrets are everywhere…and add intriguing flavor.

To date, she has published five books on Amazon in the romantic suspense genre. See her at Amazon.com/author/patticorbelloarcher.cajunlady. And she blogs at PattiArcher.com. You can also find her on most social media.

www.ingramcontent.com/pod-product-compliance
Lightning Source LLC
LaVergne TN
LVHW090552110826
845146LV00001B/106

* 9 7 9 8 9 8 6 3 3 1 9 4 2 *